www.LOTTOAPPmovie.com

Action Packed Romantic Comedy

B.Sandy 310-463-5446

The Link
A novel by b.sandy
Copyright ©2008

Second Edition

Library of Congress Cataloging-in-Publication
ISBN : 978-1-60643-020-0
Sandy, Bayardo
The Link : The Third Millennium : a novel / B.Sandy

Dr. Etcetera Media, LLC
P.O. Box 80164
Las Vegas, NV 89180
www.bsandy.com

Printed by Print Vision Pvt. Ltd, India.

The Link

This book is dedicated to you.

(Go ahead smile; it is really dedicated to you. It was about time.)

⊖⊓🐦⌐🐦●⚏⌐ ⁅⁅ ⥴⌐⟨〰〰〰⟍⟍

I
Capitulus Unus

J have been given a mission. This is the last chapter or perhaps the first, depending on how you accept my story or my history. Today my name is Sydney— it hasn't always been my name. I can start my story from anywhere, from any point in the past. But for you to understand the consequences of my actions, I'd better begin at the end of innocence, my innocence. It seemed too much to handle all at once but I had no choice. Life as I know it began to change.

Listen. Listen very carefully because perhaps we have met—then you may see or find yourself here with me, and if we have met, this is our story. To me, the paradigm shift began with my last time in the Hamptons—the last time I thought my life was normal. For many years I had a very wealthy client there. He wanted to employ me full time, as a consultant, because a position as an astrologer in a Fortune 100 company would be suspicious. In spite of his persistent and varied requests, politely, I declined. I continued providing my insight to his path, always ending sessions with the most important phrase to myself and my teacher: "Character is Destiny." To us, it remains the absolutely vital law of astrology. So I said...

"You have to believe in yourself."

"You've told me much, Sydney," said Paul. "But not that with which I should be most concerned?"

"It's funny Paul, the simplicity of nature has not changed since you were in kindergarten. Consider this: your vocabulary grew larger, your toys became more expensive, but the same rules of conduct apply. When the moment comes, you will know what to do. Character is destiny."

There was a knock at the door. "Come in," said Paul.

"I'm terribly sorry to interrupt Mr. Stein," said the butler. His white-gloved hand clutched the doorknob. "Agent Fitzpatrick informs me the pilot and the helicopter are ready."

Paul nodded. "Thank you Alfred. We're just about done."

The butler hesitated, blustered as he glanced at his billionaire boss, then about the room impeccably appointed in white. "Sir, shall I?"

"In due time, Alfred," Paul raised a hand. "In due time, neither Agent Fitzpatrick, nor the next client notwithstanding."

Sydney noticed Alfred's reflection in the mirror next to the entrance. Alfred looked consumed with worries. *He must have a big decision to make,* thought Sydney. For a fraction of a second while looking at Alfred's reflection, the butler's outfit suddenly changed into a uniform of a World War II Nazi Officer. When Sydney shifted his focus to the original, Alfred was as he had been. Sydney tried not to overanalyze the phenomena and had no doubt that this was a product of his imagination.

Alfred bowed as he backed out. Sydney settled back in his chair, recognizing Paul's need for more time, and for that room, in this way, with light glistening from his pool, sunshine beaming through high windows. It was all in his charts. Here resided his alignment. The room, the entire house, was picture perfect and primped for any home or garden magazine's feature spread, though no current magazine technology could synthesize the harmonious fragrance all about or the soothing gurgle of the pool's majestic water fountain.

Paul rose from the spare, elegant table. "We'll get you a home right here in the Hamptons. Curtail your commuting."

Sydney stood, gathering his spread of astrological charts and papers. "Well Paul, at this point in my life it would only be a waste of time. At the rate that I travel, I would likely be paying just for a housekeeper. Maybe later I'll be ready for it," he disconnected his laptop and portable printer, stowed each into a briefcase. He stopped the tiny tape recorder, extracted the tiny cassette and handed it to Paul, who put the tape on his desk.

"If you wish," said Sydney, "I can have Olive make a transcript."

Paul shook his head. "Not necessary. I have someone I trust," he motioned toward the door. "Sydney, I sold the Central American factory. I thought I'd put that cash into tech stocks."

"You should wait," Sydney said as they moved to the door in tandem. "Saturn's about to enter Taurus, which governs money. Better to keep that cash liquid for another month. After your birthday you'll have a better idea of any lurking volatility."

Paul's grasp was firm but sensitive as he touched Sydney's shoulder. "A month… Very well. Thank you for seeing me again Sydney. Here's your well-deserved consultation fee," he pulled a certified check from his breast pocket, handed it to Sydney who did a double-take.

"Are you sure?" Sydney eyed the check again, then handed it back to Paul. "I can't take this, it's too much."

"Aussie, listen to me. I have a staff of one hundred in my brokerage alone—statisticians, stockbrokers, experts. You've done for me in one year what they can't in five," he chuckled, pushing the check away. "You've earned every single cent. Enjoy it. Now you are a millionaire too, before taxes of course. Then, you settle with the feds and everything's back to normal."

"Yes," said Sydney, scanning the check, memorizing the relief and depression of each mechanically-fixed number and the multicolored stamping's gradations. Paul opened the door, peered at the military helicopter in the distance as they walked towards it.

"Are you seeing someone," he paused, "important next?"

"Going to Washington, Paul. Can't say anymore, and you would expect no less in terms of client confidentiality. Then, too, I can say in absolute terms, everyone is important, no?"

Paul Stein raised his hands. "I apologize. You see before you a businessman who will never tamper with the hen while golden eggs are being laid."

"Unless I'm mistaken, Paul, you just called me a chicken."

"Sorry, bad analogy. Have a good flight."

Sydney extended his hand. "See you later." Paul shook it brusquely then retreated to his office before Sydney could turn to Alfred, now waiting nearby.

The day was beautiful; breezy with a sparkling sky nearly more remembered than present, and carrying a hint of life on the ocean—after a storm. *This is a perfect day to see an admiral,* thought Sydney.

Alfred stood in Sydney's path. "Allow me to carry your briefcase sir."

"No thanks. This has already become an extension of my body." Sydney smiled. "I fear losing my balance without it."

They had to walk past the pool area to get to the heliport. Mrs. Stein roused from her pool chaise and set her book aside.

"Sydney! Sydney! Darling what's the hurry? Leaving already? How curt."

"Sorry, Patricia, I must."

"I have some friends, dying to meet you. Please, when can you see them?"

"Oh, have them call the office and Olive will set them up."

"But your darling, Olive's now scheduling for next year. I've one quite special friend, who needs to see you as soon as possible."

"Patricia, I'm sorry."

"Oh, please, dear man. She needs your help."

"Okay, I have to be in this neck of the woods in a month. I'll squeeze in a couple of hours but, in the meantime, have her read my new book. My version of take two aspirins," Sydney leaned to kiss her on the cheek.

"Thank you ever so. She'll be thrilled. Have a safe trip," she blew a kiss as he moved on with Alfred.

Agent Fitzpatrick signaled the pilot, then moved toward Sydney as the rush of rotors whipped the air. A cell phone was barely audible in the din.

"Sydney here."

"Sydney? It's Olive."

Sydney frowned. It wasn't like her to ask if it were him answering his cell. "What's the trouble?"

"Sydney! It's an emergency! The professor!"

He handed Alfred the briefcase, freeing a hand to shield his open ear from the chop of helicopter blades. "Tell me what's going on."

"It's the Professor. I took him to the hospital this morning. I went to his home to check on him and he was on the kitchen floor. I called the ambulance right away. They took him to Doctor's Hospital here. I thought it was a stroke or something," she gulped air, sobbed. "The doctors are asking for family members for decisions. But, oh Sydney, you have to get here. He only wants you; keeps saying 'where's Sydney, I can't die yet, get me Sydney.' Things like that."

"Olive, Olive. It's okay, calm down. I'll be there first thing tomorrow but I've got to go to Washington now."

"No Sydney, today! The doctors say he won't last that long, won't make it through the night."

"Olive, I'll be there as soon as I can. Tell everyone that I'm on my way!"

"Please hurry Sydney. Please hurry."

"I will, I will. Olive, I have to go now, ciao." He folded the phone and took his briefcase.

Agent Fitzpatrick pursed his lips, his face rigid, the tone in his voice low but forceful, breaking through the helicopter's noise. "Sir, we need to be airborne in one minute! This is a nonscheduled stop, and we have to get to the meeting on time."

"I'm very sorry," said Sydney, forcing his voice just above the noise. "I just had an emergency call. I can't go to Washington but Coral Gables instead."

Fitzpatrick looked as though he were biting his nails. "Sir, the admir...." He glanced away. "My boss is going to be very disappointed."

"I understand. I need a lift, where the nearest airport?"

"Sir, I've got orders; airborne in one minute, one flight plan, one destination. A very tight window crossing through restricted air space. My superior, the admiral will not...."

"Please, apologize to him on my behalf—it's family. I'll call him, first chance."

The special agent nodded, turned for the helicopter.

"Alfred," said Sydney, "I need to be in Miami as soon as possible."

"Stuart's available, sir. The airport's less than half an hour away."

Once moving back to the house; Sydney noticed that Paul Stein had joined his wife at the pool. Mr. Stein rose, his face questioning as he looked past Sydney to the helicopter lifting off.

"An emergency," said Sydney. "My father was taken to the hospital. It doesn't look good. The doctors are quite pessimistic. He may not last the night."

Mrs. Stein frowned. "Dear Sydney, no." She gnawed at her lip.

"I must get to the airport as soon as possible," said Sydney, "the first flight to Miami."

Paul Stein shook his head. "No, nonsense. Alfred, have Stuart take Sydney to my Lear."

"Of course, Mr. Stein. Immediately." Alfred stepped away, retrieved a small, wireless voice activated phone from his vest's pocket. "Calling Stuart."

Paul activated a second cordless. "Bob. I need birdie ready to go as soon as possible, flight plan for Miami Opa-locka." He paused, listened and exclaimed, "Good idea! And purchase some of that Cuban stationery, wooden box. I'll call when your passenger's on the way." He sat the phone on the table. "There. By the time you reach the airport the jet will be ready for takeoff."

Mrs. Stein touched Sydney's arm. "Darling, be well. Call us. Let us know how things are going."

"Thank you both," said Sydney, reentering the house. "You're so very generous. I must be going now." He crossed the lavish entertainment area with Alfred in tow, struggling to keep pace. The butler jogged ahead to open the front door. Sydney stepped out just as the white Rolls circled the entrance's garden island.

"Thanks for all your help, Alfred."

"Farewell, sir. I pray it's merely a false alarm."

Sydney nodded, hustled down the steps and opened the car's back door before Stuart could step out.

Stuart settled back into his seat. "Good noon sir. To Mr. Stein's plane?"

"Yes, Stuart, thank you. By the way, my name is Sydney."

"Very well, Sir Sydney. Please secure your belt, sir."

The car circled the driveway's crescent. While exiting the mansion's gardens, Sydney caught a glance of the Gestapo officer again. This time the vision lasted longer. The Gestapo officer extracted a device out of his breast pocket, held it in front of him like a walkie-talkie and finally motioned it to his ear. Sydney tried to focus and the officer morphed back into Alfred, the butler.

"Mr. Tobias did not leave in the helicopter to Washington. He is going back to Miami on our private jet." Alfred folded the phone and reentered the mansion as the Rolls was gaining at the front gate.

Sydney Tobias we need to talk, this time you can't deny. Sydney continued his self analysis. *Why is this happening? Let me worry about one thing at a time. Perhaps I'll tell father.*

"Bob is your uncle, Sir Sydney. We shall be at the airport very soon." said Stuart.

"Bob is not my uncle, Bob is the pilot," replied Sydney smiling, familiar with the British lexicon.

"Pardon my British expressions, Sir Sydney. Old habits die hard."

Sydney mused over Stein's penchant for British servants, their nearly-regal formality, and his preference for white. He chuckled, and considered reminding Stuart to use the right side of the road. The thought didn't last—Miami was more immediate. Sydney powered his laptop and checked on his computer program for the exact positions of the stars according to his location. He knew better than to become a slave to his chart—he only plotted for himself out of need. This was the very real practice of horoscope—the scope of the hour— and its current influences. He'd often gritted his teeth at inane, vacuous daily blurbs in newspapers. There were more than twelve possible combinations taking place with the population each day. Combine all the planets and all the astrological houses and every individual receives a unique reading or outcome. After plotting his own, Sydney checked his father's chart for afflictions.

It was not Sydney's first time on the Bombardier Lear jet. The plane did not have the luxuries of the Greyhound bus such as head room interior, Sydney laughed to himself. On the other hand, he'd rather sacrifice head room interior for two hours than two days of his life to reach in Miami. He made himself comfortable in a very short time. Sydney's head snapped to the side. He thought he heard a voice, accented, speaking his name and "Miami, not Washington." It drifted away in a haze of white.

𓊖𓏤𓃾𓏥𓈖 𓈙𓆑𓏲 𓏏𓊗 𓌢𓏤𓎛 𓄿𓏲 𓄿𓅆
𓃾𓃀𓊡 𓂋𓊪𓏲 𓂝𓏏𓈖

II
Capitulus Duo

Sydney fought a certain smugness as he approached Doctors' Hospital a mere three hours after leaving the Steins. Opa-locka to Coral Gables seemed a longer trip, time wise, than the jaunt from the Hamptons to Miami. He found Olive, pacing and fidgety, as he neared the hospital entrance. She began to break down even before he got out of the car.

"Oh, Sydney, I'm so glad you're finally here. Hurry, you've got to see him right away."

He wrapped her with both arms. "There, Olive, there. Thank you. Thank you for saving my father's life."

"I've known the Professor since you were ten. I can't believe this is happening."

He guided her toward the doorway. "It'll be okay." He draped an arm over her shoulder. "Olive, please, today or tomorrow, soon, please call the hotel in Washington. Have them ship my suitcase."

They rode the elevator in silence. She pointed weakly as they stepped off. Nearing the room, Sydney pondered Saturn and Neptune; the former ruling suffering, medical affairs the latter. And at that moment they held the fate of his father—his professor, and his best friend. He acknowledged them as he pushed open the door to the Professor's room. Now at the bed, he stood for a time, glancing back at Olive outside the room's window. Monitors hummed and flashed, charting the professor's progress by the second. Sydney held his father's hand in his. The Professor's head lolled to the side, his eyes opening.

"Oh," he said, "you're here." He freed his hand, moved it, trembling, to his oxygen mask.

"Please," said Sydney, "keep it on. You need it."

"No, Sydney. Not enough time. So much to tell, so little time."

Sydney's face scrunched. "Dad, there's nothing I don't already know."

Horace laughed, coughed. "Well, yes. But," he closed his eyes, "I'm not your real father." He grimaced, moved the mask back to his face for a few breaths. "But then, you were not my real father either."

Sydney was puzzled by what seemed to be his father's nonsense. "What? Why? Dad, what are you saying? How could I have been your father?"

"Sydney, I need a promise. Promise me that you will look for me." He took Sydney's wrist. He lowered his voice. "You must promise me you will look for me. Make the link."

Sydney nodded, humoring the old man in just the way he had so often.

"Sydney, this is serious. I'm here, and very awake." He stared at Sydney, forcing attention. "Thirty years ago, I bought you. I bought you from a family in Australia, in Sydney. You were just a year old, no more. It was, for them, difficult. But they couldn't refuse; two million was a lot to turn down, especially then."

Sydney stepped back, his breathing labored. "That is so wild. Two million, you mean dollars? Me? What? Where did you? Why?"

"Money. It's only money. Who is richer, a person who has money or one who doesn't need it?" Horace coughed, took another deep breath of oxygen. "When you become a true master in astrology, the money and the objects don't take center stage anymore. You aim for a higher purpose." His head nestled back into the pillow. He stared at the ceiling. "Oh, I could not find Him this life-time. Perhaps you will."

"What is this, Dad? Him? You've never been, you're not the religious type. Do you want that for me now?"

"Yes, and no. And I don't care. I'm not talking about that. You don't understand."

"What should I understand?"

"Sydney, I need your promise. You must look for me, teach me. Make the link!"

Sydney circled the bed, his hand to his chest. "Look for you where? Make the link to what? You're here, right here."

Horace did not know which thought to convey first. He knew he didn't have long to live. "Sydney, you got me that laptop, and I've been lazy. You stopped doing calculations by hand. You stopped using the ephemeris[i]." He glanced aside. "I must have missed something, a calculation. Damn that computer. I'm supposed to have another ten years, but look at me now. Maybe not even ten hours." He hacked again, his body seizing with the violence of his coughs. He sucked more oxygen from the mask. "Maybe not ten minutes. Sydney, please. Don't forget, keep your mind sharp. The abacus... Paper... Write, don't type. Early this year I felt my heart, erratic. Since I didn't do the calculations by hand, I didn't know if I was right or wrong, couldn't afford to, couldn't take the chance, not teaching you. I made tapes, video. Fifteen in the vault."

---

[i] Ephemeris is a table of coordinates of celestial bodies at a number of specific times for astrological charts throughout the year.

"Tapes? Teach me? What, Dad?"

"How to find me, find money, anything you…your heart desires. Great knowing, Sydney, great knowledge. Greater than the Philosopher's Stone."

Sydney stood with his hands atop his head, his fingers entwined. He had the feeling his skull would come off.

Horace raised a feeble finger. "Don't be shocked. You are Elijah. You're the one who taught me. My turn this time, but couldn't do it sooner—the planets, their alignment, finally proper." He lifted a trembling hand to his face, wiped a tear. "And, my dear boy, I had to keep you in the dark, I had to keep you safe. Sydney, this may be too much for you, all at once like this. I thought we had ten years left. Afraid not… Old Saturn is calling."

Sydney gazed at Olive standing outside the glass, her hands to her face. Did he know her? Did he know himself? He turned quickly. "What about me? My real name from birth? Is it Elijah?

"No. Elijah was my teacher long, long...." Horace looked away. "Long ago, before the birth of many countries, before America. Elijah is of a time when the Earth was flat, supported by elephants, and turtles."

"So what is your name?"

"My name, Luke Jeremiah. Your favorite pupil. What you taught me, I now leave to you. The tapes, the notes. Read them, learn, and destroy them all, please. Don't let them fall into the wrong hands, the greedy. It could upset the balance." His chin quivered. "Please, Sydney, Elijah, look for me. Promise you'll find me and make the link."

Sydney nodded. "I don't know how. I don't know, but, I will, somehow."

"That is what I needed to hear. I can go now." Horace raised his hand toward Sydney, who took it into his. Horace's voice was raspy, a weak whisper. "Until again, Elijah." He smiled softly, his gaze fixed on his son.

Sydney felt the rise of his own chest, the rush of blood behind his ears. A part of him was electric and growing, but the man before him, the man he'd known as father, seemed to be falling back, fading even as Sydney held fast to his hand. Sydney secured his grip, held tighter, but the distance increased and he knew he was helpless to stop it.

Sydney reached out to the man's face, smoothed the forehead and slowly brought his hand over the man's eyes, shutting them.

Sydney expected that the nurses and doctors would rush to his room at that moment but everything was peaceful and everything was normal, the cardiogram continued to beep at the same continuous interval as before. Maybe his father did not die; maybe he just drifted into sleep.

The doctor entered the room while checking his notes, looked at Sydney and asked, "Are you his son?"

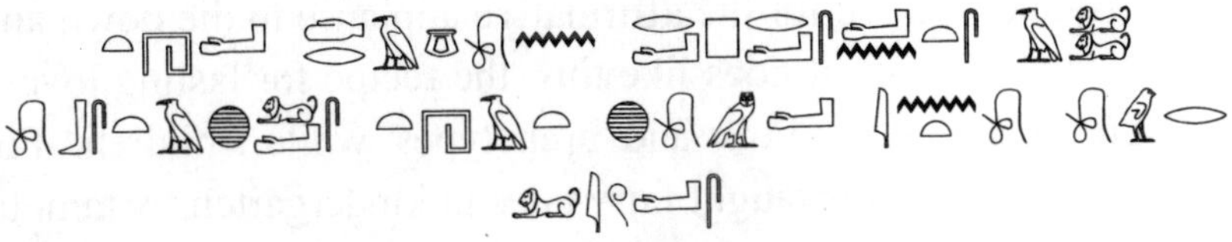

III
Capitulus Tres

New York,
A few days later

"We are back in five, four, three, two, one."

The floor director's cards came down in a single wave, as if starting a race. A woman beamed at camera three, her smile flashing even rows of shiny teeth. She clapped her hands together just as the lamp atop the camera lit red.

"Welcome back," she said. "Today, we are thrilled to bring to you professor and best-selling author Dr. Sydney Tobias, but before I bring him here I want to refresh your memory to the last time he was here. He is a famous astrologer to many celebrities. I have tried to ask him who but he never reveals them. The last time he was here he came to introduce his best seller, *Archetypes in Our Lives*. Please watch the monitors."

The live show was cut to tape; Margaret and Sydney had the interview already in progress.

"Sydney, there is a chapter here that intrigued me so much. It is called *The Recipe to Lasting Love*. I guess we all would like to know that wouldn't we?"

Sydney waited for the affirmative applause to die down and he said, "In summary it goes like this, the recipe for lasting love it is given to us in symbols and archetypes while children. For instance, everyone was taught fairy tales in kindergarten. A famous one is of a valiant knight wearing shining armor coming to save the virtuous princess locked at the tower. However, the tower is guarded by a terrible dragon. Do you know this story?"

Margaret said, "Of course I do. Audience, let me see your hands who has heard this story?

The camera scanned the audience to find all hands raised unanimously.

"Okay, Sydney everyone knows the story. Tell us more"

"Well, the mistake we make is that we hear this story when we are four or five. The boys relate to the knight and the girls relate to the princess and that is wrong."

There was a murmur coming from the audience and Margaret took the lead, "Quiet down, you will all like what comes next. Sydney, go on."

"All the elements in this story are symbols of values and archetypes in a lasting relationship. The knight in shining armor represents integrity, honesty, loyalty that both husband and wife should hold towards each other. The chase maiden at the tower represents that we should hold each other in high esteem and respect. So, the elements of integrity and respect make a relationship enduring and strong."

Margaret tried to stump Sydney, "So what is the dragon?"

"The dragon is terrible, the dragon is strong and every new day we must be a knight to fight and kill this dragon for lasting love. The dragon represents all obstacles that come into our lives and relationships. It could be the loss of a job, temptation, the bills, all the things that need to be conquered on a daily basis."

The audience erupted in applause. Margaret and Sydney exchanged glances and the monitor was back into a live feed.

"Ladies and gentlemen please help me welcome Dr. Sydney Tobias."

Sydney came from the right behind a lavish set and found the audience giving him a welcome in standing ovation. They hugged, greeted and sat down.

Sydney offered a slight smile. "Margaret, thanks for having me on your show."

"And your latest book, *Letters to Myself*, has been on the best-sellers' list for the last five weeks. That's an intriguing title for a wonderful book. Please tell our audience a little more about your book."

"Well, the book is based on the premises of improving yourself, either individually or as part of a family, and doing so in the future. It teaches you how to write letters to your offspring, even a grandson and or great-granddaughter, and show them how we survive or become who we are. Here is an example, when you are fifteen you write a letter to your future grandson or granddaughter for her to open when she is fifteen. One for each year and so on."

"You mention reincarnation. Does a person have to believe in that in order to use the book?"

"In this book I mentioned that, if there is a law of reincarnation, it's possible that we will reincarnate with the people that are familiar to us or people with whom we either have good or not so good karma."

Margaret turned to the camera briefly. "How exciting, don't you think?" she returned to Sydney. "So in that sense you could be writing yourself a letter to be read by your very self in your next reincarnation. Therefore, the name of your title *Letters to Myself*?"

"That is very good. That is exactly the reason for the name."

"So how can the book work for someone who doesn't believe in reincarnation?"

"I think the word 'believe' is too strong. Belief is often connected to religion. For example, we say the word 'love' very loosely the same way that we say the word 'believe.' Instead of using the word 'believe,' I like to say; I give it some credit. So using this premise, it doesn't hurt to give reincarnation some credit. Arguably, even if you don't give it credit, you and your family will benefit as a whole. Once you start writing down how you could have prevented your own mistakes, your grandkids or great-grandkids will gain a treasure of letters that will serve your family as a private history."

"It's funny that you said that. We tend to say 'believe' the way we say 'love.' I love chocolate, and I love my husband, and we all know it's not the same love. But tell us more."

"Margaret, that is a very good example. And, to elaborate on your example, I use 'give credit' as a way to face the belief. If you are not absolutely sure about something, you can give credit to the premise, test it, and then note your experience of it. Now the word 'believe' comes from 'to live by' and, unfortunately, 'to live by' often implies 'to die for.' People are still killing each other because they 'believe' that they are God's favorite in this entire universe. As for the private history, we should see it as a complement to our collective history. Now we are evolving as a better society because we have been keeping track, through writing, of our collective mistakes and triumphs and we call it history. For instance, if we did not keep records of all the damage caused by the atomic bombing of Japan, or the genocide from WW II, and we only knew about them from word of mouth from our parents, then we would probably relive the very same problems today. However, we have written accounts, and that helps keep those experiences with us. Now we can do the same thing privately. My book is a tool not only to keep a collective account of history but also a private history. A private history is a great way to bridge the generation gap and also to keep a private impression of the facts as they were for your family. For example, let us imagine that you found, in your attic, a diary from an ancestor that you've never met. Right there in your hands is a diary of him or her when he or she was about your age and the diary mentions the current events and their affect on your ancestral family."

"So, it's a peek into the past."

"Maybe just a peek, and maybe a chance to discern patterns. For instance, in the early 1900's we had stock market investors going into any kind of industry as long as it was a market novelty for the turn of the century. The same occurred as we entered this new millennium—money dumped into Dot-Coms without a reason, primarily for the novelty value of the offering. Of course, in both cases those were bubbles, and they burst, leaving a lot of people broke. Now, when we see the pattern repeating itself, we can guard our family from all the hype, separating the propaganda from reality. Another way of looking at it is it helps avoid the 'five-mile in the snow' nagging."

Margaret chuckled. "Yes, we've all heard it before in one form or another. Put it in another way, it's an elder saying 'you kids have it easy.' "

"Yes. And, if you read this in their diary, and you know it's contemporaneous, it's not a nagging. It's not propaganda it's reality. You're reading about your mother's difficulties or tribulations in high-school, in her own voice, at your age, it's like having a time machine."

"Fascinating… Now Sydney, you're a well-known astrologer, and so many people count on your chartings and guidance. Is there any technical information about astrology in this book?"

"When I told my publisher about this book idea, the editors asked me not to include any sort of astrological information. The thinking is most people just want to have the product and not know how the product is made. It would be similar if you ate a delicious meal in a restaurant and the chef came out and told you every single step as you enjoyed the meal. The editors also felt if I had added astrological information here, it would intimidate readers and I would lose them. It's a very easy book to read—right to the point."

"Are you touring, or do we have a singular honor on my show?"

Sydney readjusted himself in his chair. "I've been in a bit of a battle with my publisher regarding that, and I have to explain to everyone that because of family issues, I'd better spend some quality time at home. So, I've compromised with the publisher. I still have to do three more television or radio interviews."

Margaret with her quick wit said, "This is great—so we can have you next week?"

Sydney smiled unprepared for the question and said, "I guess as they say in Hollywood, 'Have your people talk to my people...' but please leave me out of this for now; I can't take the pressure."

They all started laughing for a while and promptly at the signal of her studio producer who was standing off camera, Margaret regained her warm composure and addressed the camera for another commercial break.

IV
Capitulus Quattour

ydney entered his office, breezing past Olive as she placed forms on a table.

"Hello Sydney. The interview went well yesterday."

"Thank you, Olive. I guess it's one down, three to go."

"I taped it, and I edited out the commercials."

"Good, thank you. Call them for a copy of the script version of the show. Excuse this redundancy but I would like to have that also for my files."

"I'll get on it today," she said.

"Any word on when and where for the next one?"

"Phillip didn't leave any names but it looks like a syndicated radio show, a late night TV appearance, and another afternoon show like Margaret's."

Sydney moved to Olive's desk, looked at the note scribbled with dates. "It looks like I have this week off. Have you been able to cancel my appointments for the next three months?"

"Roberto's been scheduled to fill in the consultations for you, and he'll bring to each an autographed copy of your book. I guess everything is under control. No complaints."

"Good."

"Don't forget to sign the books on your desk. Roberto needs to take them with him next week."

Sydney stepped toward his office door. "Any word from the hospital about dad's prescription?"

"I talked to Doctor Jiménez. He was very apologetic, again. The only thing they were able to tell me is that there was an intern there at the time. So bizarre. Now they can't trace him anymore."

"Yeah, blame it on the intern. Where's Dad?"

"He's in the office, waiting for you."

Sydney arched his eyebrows, offered Olive a smile as he opened his door. Horace sat in a wheelchair, thumbing through a magazine he tossed aside as he looked up.

"Hi Dad!" said Sydney. He kissed Horace on the forehead. "How are you?"

"Not so bad," said Horace, clearing his throat. "They said I'll be out of this wheel chair in another week. Mixed up meds went right to my heart. So weak. Just need to be off my feet for a while, get my strength back."

Sydney sauntered to his desk, shuffled papers as he stood. "Dad, how could they have done that?"

"First things first. When we're in private I want you to call me Luke. Secondly, I don't think this was a hospital mistake. This was a set up from an old mutual nemesis of ours."

"Well Da…" Sydney rubbed his forehead. "Uh, Luke, I feel like you'd better start telling me everything, beginning with why I have to start calling you Luke."

"As soon as you sit down. And have Olive bring us some coffee. Going to be a long story."

"Okay, I'm all ears—no appointments. The only thing that I am waiting to hear is the confirmation of the new TV interviews." Sydney pressed a button on his phone. "Olive, can you bring some coffee and cookies for us?"

"Sure thing" crackled back into the room.

Horace, now insisting on being called Luke, wheeled his chair closer to Sydney's desk. "Let me start by telling you all the things that you don't know about me. In fact, you are going to realize that you are not the first one in this situation. I was born in Germany, Bonn. A financier befriended my father and had him move his machine shop to the suburbs of Vienna. He told my father that he needed his parts to be manufactured there."

"What kind of parts?"

There was a rap at the door, then it opened; Olive with coffee and cookies on a green plastic tray. "Here we go gentlemen. Need anything else?"

Sydney shook his head. "No, thank you, Olive. Just let me know as soon as you hear about the next interview."

"Of course." She whisked out, the door closing softly behind her.

Sydney motioned to Horace's mug, and then took his own. "Please, go on."

"Where was I?"

"I asked you what kind of things your father used to make in his shop?"

"Well, back then, when a part in a machine broke you couldn't call an 800 number for a replacement over the phone." Horace eyed Sydney. "You'd take the broken part to a person like my father. He'd make a new one, or cast one. At any rate, this person who befriended my father was just keeping him busy. The German economy was in really bad shape, just recovering from the First World War, and the whole country was in pandemonium. Mr. Nielsen, that was his name, Peter Nielsen. He saw an opportunity he could manipulate, so he moved us to Vienna. I remember, once, he stood over me as I played there on the sidewalk outside my father's shop. I wore that favorite sailor's outfit, my wooden toys all strewn about. 'How old are you, now?' he asked. I told him almost eleven, and he said, 'you are becoming a big boy now. Do you have a bicycle?' I did not look up, just shook my head in that slow turn I've always had."

Sydney peered over his coffee cup. "I know that turn."

"Yes. And he said, 'How would you like to have your own bicycle?' But this time he spoke in English, no German accent. I nodded, and I looked up at him. And before I could say anything else he said, 'Now, when I see your grades are better than 90 percent, I will confirm with your father that it is all right for you to have one. And, one more thing. I am going to ask you three questions you must answer correctly for your bicycle.' And he took a small, mythology book from his coat pocket."

Horace leaned forward in his wheel chair. "Later that year I got my bicycle and I also heard that we were moving again and this time it was to England. And, with Mr. Nielsen's guidance I excelled in mathematics and history. During my first year in Oxford, Hitler invaded Poland and Mr. Nielsen disappeared for a while. The next year, because of my language and math skills, I became a code breaker for the English intelligence. I can tell you this because it is certainly declassified by now. I was assigned to a mansion in Milton Keynes, 50 miles northwest of London. The place was called Bletchley Park. My superiors knew that I was born in Germany but they told me to keep it a secret to make my work go smoothly."

Sydney frowned. "Why keep it a secret?"

"Because, although I did not have an accent, I was a German national. Some of my colleagues might think that I was undercover for the Gestapo. Remember, this was 1940."

"What did you do there?"

"I worked nonstop trying to decipher the German transmissions. My skills were pushed to the limit. The next year, trying to crack the Enigma Code, we had a lucky break. One of the

Enigma machines was recovered from a U-boat. Our work took off at an amazing pace. We began to crack code just as fast and we began to translate faster than, for the officer, it was intended. It was all that we did the whole day. Those U-boat officers had other duties but all we did was code breaking. Then, in '42, I began to work on a computer project called Colossus[i]. It was the most advanced computer at the time, though it was more like a mechanical computer than an electronic one. I made some American friends that used to work at different parts of the mansion called Hut-3."

Horace looked about the room for a moment, his eyes softening. He lowered his head, his chin meeting his chest.

Sydney searched his father's face. "What's wrong?"

"Our messages used to be called *Code Ultra*. We worked so hard to decipher those codes, only to find out later that General Montgomery ignored our reports. Our team at Bletchley Park spent sleepless nights on trying to make the war end sooner. By then our family knew Peter Nielsen very well, and we knew that he was also an astrologer, or better yet he never needed the parts that my father made for him. It was all an elaborate façade to get us out of Germany."

Sydney sat back, his chair creaking. "Why do you say that?"

"Because the parts that he had my father make, he would forget or never collect them. One day I recognized an aero-photo of our old neighborhood in Bonn, Germany flattened by carpet bombing and I began to wonder if he had foreseen that situation taking place at my first home and I began to study astrology on my own.

---

[i] The Colossus computers were early data devices used by British code breakers to read encrypted German messages during WWII. The Colossus Mark I and II were operational at Bletchley Park in 1944, ten more were built by the end of the war.

"So during my days in Bletchley Park when there was not much to do I would break codes for most of the day and study astrology by candlelight. We had mandatory black-outs because of the air raids.

"By the end of the war I was 24 and a fulltime astrologer. I had enough money from all those years as an intelligence officer and my father's shop had several employees by then. Mr. Nielsen—I took to calling him Peter because he wanted—was waiting for me in New York.

"While crossing the sea I was, eh, seduced, as they say, by Hollywood because of some actors and musicians onboard. I changed my career plans. I wanted to become a movie star or something like that."

Sydney leaned forward. "So, what happened?"

Horace sipped coffee then gently settled his mug.

Sydney tapped his desk. "Do I have to ask you again? So, what happened?"

Horace sighed. "Peter and I began to have a very similar conversation like the one we are having now; in fact, he asked me to call him by another name while in private."

"So what name was that?"

"Elijah."

"Elijah? Elijah? But, at the hospital, you called me…"

"Precisely." Horace stared at his son, waiting.

"So, now." Sydney raised a finger. "You're telling me… You're saying, I, Elijah…that I was Peter Nielsen? In a previous life?"

"Precisely."

"Don't you think that this information is a little bit too late?"

"No. In fact, I wanted to tell you all of this before the proper planet alignment because I don't think I am going to make it."

"No, I mean, *Letters to Myself*, my book. I could have used this. You should have said something."

"Sydney, I couldn't. You couldn't use it. What I'm telling you it is not to be repeated to anyone, even under torture. If this knowledge falls into the wrong hands, it can upset the balance of this planet." Horace traced a shaky hand across his eyebrow. "It already has."

"Dad, I'm not calling you Luke anymore and I think that it is too late in your life to have an identity crisis."

"In due time I can tell you more."

Sydney raised his voice. "No, Dad. I need proof. I need some evidence. I need something more than talk. I need some backing so you can have my attention. A birth mark, maybe Peter's handwriting, his picture, something to make me a believer."

"Believer? You? Is that you picking that word?"

Sydney raked his fingers through his hair. "Well, it's not everyday that I am asked to keep a secret, even under torture," he massaged the nape of his neck.

"Good," said Horace. "Let me give you a sample. Keep your feet firmly planted onto the floor, do not cross them, and give me your hands across the desk."

Sydney cleared space on the desk, brushing aside stationery, cookies, and resettling the coffee mugs. Horace wheeled closer.

"We're going to relax for a couple of minutes," said Horace, "then I'll recite some lines from *The Egyptian Book of the Dead*[i]. I want you to focus on my left eye. This experience will last as long as you keep your concentration on the eye. It'll be like a staring competition; if you lose the focus, the images will end."

---

[i] The name *The Egyptian Book of the Dead* was coined by the Egyptologist Karl Richard Lepsius in 1842. It comprises of charms and conduct for the afterlife compiled from the walls of sarcophagus. The best manuscript was smuggled to the British museum in 1888 is known as *The Papyrus of Ani*.

Sydney frowned, then nodded, closed his eyes. Both sat silently for a while, breathing slowing. Sydney's palms were face up, covered by Horace's hands. As Horace began to recite verses from the Book of the Dead, Sydney opened his eyes and gazed at Horace's left eye. Sydney felt himself lost in a thicket of foreign words, though a few stood out: Isis, Horus, Seth, Osiris. He fixed on Horace until the older man's face began to morph into someone Sydney's own age. Horace appeared to be 30. Sydney felt his breath grow raspy as he struggled to concentrate, to stay focused on Horace's left eye. Horace's face changed again, this time with the room morphing, too. It was a face Sydney didn't know; but the eyes, remained familiar. He was now confronted with a blonde young man with a mustache, in red garb. The office was gone, replaced by a Victorian Saloon. And the face evolved once more, this time pallid, Caucasian, in blue and green with a leather hat. The room resembled a scene from the French Renaissance. Through it all the faces had something in common; the age, the familiar eye. Horace fell silent, the prayer echoing in Sydney's mind as he continued to see all of images and faces. Olive's voice broke through the transformations. Sydney's speakerphone.

"Excuse me, Sydney. I just got a confirmation for a radio interview, but they're on hold. I want to know if next Friday will be okay?"

The room regained its familiar look. So did Horace. Sydney gripped Horace's hand for a moment then, his voice strained, he responded to Olive. "Friday is good. No travel, right?"

"Here in Miami. I already have the studio information."

"Thank you, Olive." Sydney watched the intercom light go off. "Okay Luke, you have my undivided attention." Sydney whirled as he spoke the words, assured he'd heard himself. He went to the window. Street traffic seemed normal. The usual delivery trucks outside, SUV's clogging the parking stalls—just a panel van seeming a bit out of the ordinary.

Across the street the same words were echoed inside a stolen van. *"You have my undivided attention."*

A woman's hands muted the radio transmission and the recording machine and dialed a cell phone and said; "It's time to execute the package." After a brief pause, the female voice continued; "Correct, no survivors."

Sydney left the window to sit back behind his desk. He massaged his forehead as he fell back into his chair.

"So," said Horace, "let's go back to our story. I was in New York City when my many lives were revealed to me, freeing me from the forgetfulness of reincarnation. There is more to this awakening that I cannot tell you now, but I was awakened to three thousand years of my personal history. Peter, or better yet, Elijah also awoke me to my true purpose.

"No need to tell you that I cancelled my fantasies of going to Hollywood. I began my inner journey. I began to understand how all my relationships with all my friends began to make sense. I delved into astrology much more than before and began to re-teach myself along with Elijah, how and when to re-awaken Elijah on his next birth. Again, Sydney, nobody should know about this. In the wrong hands it can wreak havoc on this planet."

"How is that?"

"Not only because you can see the astrological or timing patterns much better than anyone, but an awakened person can also see everything that astrology or timing has to offer. This person can manipulate others, knowing their weaknesses and virtues better than anyone. For instance, do you think Hitler could have done everything on his own, or did he possibly have help from unknown sources? How can an artist of landscape portraits from humble beginnings, rise to become chancellor of Germany and begin a megalomaniacal frenzy against the world?"

"Well," said Sydney, "I'm guessing you didn't help him, nor did Peter Nielsen. So, this means that someone else besides us already knows of this process?"

Horace bowed his head. "Yes, unfortunately. This is what it means. He is our nemesis. His name is Nicholas, the librarian. And I have no doubt he was behind this medication swap, trying to kill me."

"No doubt, but go on with the story," said Sydney.

"I had to be careful, not keep logs or diaries. As I've mentioned before, once awakened to this much history, a person is able to see and understand a pattern of timing that exists in the universe."

V
Capitulus Quinque

Horace continued, "However, it took me another decade before I could merge completely with my history. But, once I did, all my memories, gifts, languages acquired over two-thousand years, it all came back. I speak fifty-two languages without a trace of an accent. But, this knowing has not been easy. I've switched from slave to master, the repeating vicious-cycle. I built many temples in India and Mesopotamia. It was somewhat traumatizing to recall all of those lives. Sometimes I would be in control of the situation and at times the stones would crash on me.

"Many times I abused my slaves, and in my next life I would find myself being abused. So much anger, so much pain and envy. And love was so scarce that I used every fiber of my being to savor it during the recall.

"I also abused my wives, and then I became a slave eunuch in a Harem in Baghdad. I had to tend them and love them without enjoying them. I was torn inside. I loved some of them as goddesses, sisters and mothers but I had to repress all my feelings to keep myself alive.

"Next I was a merchant in Mesopotamia. I profited, I lost, I swindled my partners when I had the chance, and I later discovered we had a partnership of deceitfulness.

"Next life my family was killed when I was seventeen and I became a highwayman. This was when I met my professor for the first time. You were him, Elijah. You Sydney, you were Elijah then. Far away, deep in the desert I saw this old man approaching on a horse, a donkey in tow with a heavy load, a corpse. As you neared, I hid behind a rock, to assault you. Sydney, close your eyes, you will see, you will remember..."

On Route to Judea
2000 years earlier

Sydney reclined in his chair, and as Horace spoke, the older man's voice fell away. The room fell away. And on the open desert Sydney saw a young man leap from behind a rock.

"Old man, stop!" yelled the young man, a knife in hand. "Give up your horse!"

"No need to get excited," said the traveler from his horse. "You want the horse; I'll give it to you. It looks like a good time to stop anyway. Are you hungry? It looks like you have not eaten for a couple of days." He dismounted, brushing the young Luke who still held his knife at the ready. "Put that blade away," said the traveler, "and help me make a fire so we can eat."

The young Luke didn't move, watching the traveler take provisions from the donkey. As the older man unloaded the mule, the young Luke jumped on to the horse and kicked it to spur. The horse didn't move. He kicked it again, to no avail.

The traveler laughed, his back to the scene. "I said that I would give the horse to you, but apparently it doesn't want to be given away."

Luke kicked repeatedly, gritting his teeth as he tried to goad the animal. The horse merely stood still.

"Your attempt to rob me," said the traveler, Elijah, "has failed. I can still give you some food or I can eat by myself while you keep the back of my horse warm for me."

Luke slid slowly off the horse and ambled over to Elijah who now gathered dry brushes and branches. Luke disappeared behind a ridge, and returned with twigs and branches already bundled. He dropped them next to Elijah.

"I gathered this wood today but it wouldn't matter anyway. I don't know how to start a fire."

Elijah studied the young man. "Then today you will learn. You must be, I imagine, twenty years of age?"

"Perhaps. Likely. It is easy to lose track of time when one lives in the desert."

"One learns many things living on the road for many years, like how to make a fire, find food and water." Elijah gazed into Luke's eyes. "Are you from Judea?"

"I was born there, but I don't like to go back to my village since my family was killed."

"When was this?"

"Three years ago. Then I was taken to be with my uncle, but he put me out as a slave. I decided, better a highwayman than a slave."

"I didn't know Jews had slaves?"

"You don't know my uncle. He never liked my father. And now, with his control of the business, he retaliates against me." Luke pointed to the large figure on the mule, wrapped. "Do you carry a mummy?"

"My travel companion for the last thirteen years. He died when we were in Egypt. I paid an embalmer to prepare the body for the trip so his family can give him a proper burial in his home land of Judea."

"When did he die?"

"About two full moons, problems of the belly."

"How come the body doesn't smell bad."

"They buried the body in salt. The bad smell leaves the body with the water. The body now is very dry, fragile and light, anything could rupture the skin. That is why it's wrapped with a lot of clothes."

"What was his name?"

"His name was Saul. He was my best student. My best eyes for the sky, and my friend. I really thought that he would be the one burying me, as I did my teacher. Instead, I am taking him home."

Luke read from the ornament around the mummy's neck. "May god Horus and old souls of Egypt welcome you to the afterlife."

"Very good!" exclaimed Elijah. "Where did you learn to read hieroglyphics?"

"My father would travel to Egypt. I went with him. We would buy spices and perfume in Petra and sell them in Egypt. We brought back grains, fabrics, and gold."

"Do you know any other language?"

"My neighbor was a rabbi and he taught me to read the songs from the Torah."

Elijah stoked the fire now high, prepared the meal. He handed a copper plate with warm flat bread to Luke and they both ate in silence, dipping the bread in a vessel filled with oil and spices. The night drew on and with it, the temperature dropped. Luke reached for more wood to fuel the fire. Elijah stopped him.

"If you need warmth," said Elijah, "get the second blanket from the donkey. Fire dims the stars, and I must see them. Is the sky writ full with omens. You may read the Torah, hieroglyphics, but perhaps tonight you will learn to read the stars. Do you know the Zodiac?"

"Scorpio, that's all. My father said that when I was born Scorpio commanded the middle of the sky at midnight. He showed me the tail of the scorpion in the sky. That is all I know."

"This means then, that your sign is Taurus. When Scorpio dominates the middle of the night sky, the Sun rests in Taurus."

Elijah spent much of the night showing Luke the Zodiac. The next day Elijah awoke and began to break camp, to continue on to Judea. He soon had the mule and the horse strapped and. He turned to Luke. "Do you want to join me? I could use a pair of fresh eyes, and I can promise you that you will never have to earn your living from the end of a knife or assault travelers from behind a rock."

"Would you teach me more about the stars?"

"Just as much as you are willing to learn. And this is an auspicious time. I've been tracking the movements. Soon a Great King Prophet will join us."

"Is he the Immanuel?"

"Good, you remember your scriptures. Yes, it could be the Immanuel[i]. I fear my knowledge is deficient; however, Saul was the one who tracked the sky and aided me with the calculations." Elijah rummaged through the donkey's pack. He retrieved a pair of Roman sandals. "Put these on. They will help you in your journey. Later in the day you may mount the mule."

---

[i] Isaiah 7:14 Therefore the Lord himself shall give you a sign; Behold, a virgin shall conceive, and bear a son, and shall call his name Immanuel. Also in Matthew 1:23 The virgin will be with child and will give birth to a son, and they will call him Immanuel - which means, "God with us."

Within minutes they were both fading into the distance, their forms harder to see, and Sydney again heard the voice of Luke but now in the present as Horace.

Horace said, "Elijah grew to value my company. A person like me would also be able to keep a look-out for thieves. We left Saul's body with his family and they were our host for a short time as we rested. In the meantime, I continued to learn more about the stars and story-telling. At night I would learn the constellations and the many legends behind them. During the day I had to recite to Elijah what I had learned the night before. The story-telling was another way Elijah would earn money and food. People would gather around and he would entertain the village with one long story for three days. The first day he did not earn much money, but on the second and third day people would bring coins, animals and fabrics to hear the end of the story. It was the only entertainment that they had for months and Elijah was very dramatic. He would do all the voices and accents, and people were very entertained, like a one-man theatre production. He spoke several languages including Aramaic, Latin, and some ancient Egyptian.

"I soon, had the stories memorized. I began to participate in the dramatizations with him, and eventually began telling them myself. From village to village, for rich farmers and kings, Elijah gave counsel and service.

"We quickly became friends. I began to calculate the movement of the planets, and Elijah would interpret them. We were in Judea for a long period, and one day I woke Elijah from his afternoon nap."

"Professor wake up," said the young Luke.

"What is so important," replied Elijah.

"There are visitors in town. I was told they are wise men, as wise as you. They seem from distant lands. One I can't understand at all."

"Are they in transit or staying in town for a while?"

"They made camp right outside of town. Perhaps as many as twenty, but three different groups, traveling together. They have three masters. The others are servants and slaves."

"Help me clean up. Then I want you to go to them. Announce our visit later tonight."

There was clapping of calling outside his home. Luke stepped out to greet the caller. A young man awaited, dressed in new raiment.

"We have heard," said the young man, his speech deliberate in the unfamiliar language, "that a wise man lives in this house. He is called Elijah."

"What do you wish with him?"

"I came to invite him to visit with us tonight, before we leave your lands."

Later that evening just before sunset, Elijah and Luke approached the camp. Among the horses and donkeys they saw a strange, large animal with a hump on its back. The two were greeted warmly and shown to places to sit and rest in the large tent. Later they all dined and exchanged stories of their birth lands. The elder and taller of the trio was from Baghdad; Omar. The second man was Anaxagoras, Greece. The youngest of them was from India and was called Ramni. He had two translators. Ramni would speak first in Hindu, then in Farsi which all the others understood.

Ramni bowed, his hands clasped. "Om Namah Shivaya[i]."

The translator, already knowing the meaning without the help of the first translator, informed Elijah and Luke, "He is saluting you and God at the same time."

---

[i] Aum namah Śivāya (Aum spelled in Sanskrit but pronounced Om) the foremost Vedic mantras. Where Om is the primordial sound, Namah an offer of salutation to Shiva (which according to the Vedic texts) duels in everyone and everything. Hinduism and Christianity have the Holy Trinity in common. Father, Son and Holy Ghost have their counterparts in Brahma, Vishnu and Shiva. The Holy Ghost is known as the destroyer of ignorance and so is Shiva. God Shiva is also the destroyer (because nothing last forever and) then a new season can start anew.

Elijah covered his heart with his palm. "May peace be with you."

The message was conveyed to the second translator, then to Ramni, who bowed again, smiling.

"I see that you are not merchants," said Luke. "What brings you to this land?"

Master Omar raised a hand. "Before we speak more, we must know that you may both be entrusted."

"We are travelers," said Elijah, his hand over his heart, "and we report to no king or master."

Omar nodded. "We come to this land to welcome the prophet, known here as Immanuel. The messenger, the one who will change the world."

"When will he arrive?"

"He is already among us," said Anaxagoras. "It was our privilege to read the sign in the stars, then to visit his birthing place."

"I have been reading the sky for years and I calculated the conjunction to be close but I could not see anything else. What did you see that I was not able to?"

"We cannot know what you missed in your vision," said Omar. "The planets' calculations brought us to this land. Our accuracy, the sign that brought us to that village, to those people, to that reception of Immanuel, was a very faint planet[i] in the middle of the sky during the very middle of the time of the night, in the mid-night. This sign led us to a small village called Bethlehem."

Elijah set his cup of wine on the floor. "My long time helper, his eyes better than mine, died six months ago. Luke, my

---

[i] In Astrological terminology everything that is not a fixed star is a planet. The word planet is from Geek origin which literally means wanderer.

new companion and student, is not prepared to read all the nuances of the gods."

Luke roused. "Is there a special look to this planet?"

"It is difficult," said Omar, "very faint, blurred, and seeming at one point to have a horse's tail. I could not see it either, but my trained helper could."

Anaxagoras interrupted. "Comet. In our lands, and in our astrology, we have a name for it. We call it a comet. It means the star with long hair."

Elijah stroked his beard. "I remember seeing them when my eyes were better but, tell us more."

Ramni tapped his translator on the shoulder, and then began to speak. The translator interpreted. "When we got to Bethlehem the comet was as bright as possible, but for the untrained eye it could not be seen."

"I met Ramni in transit," said Omar, "one whole moon before the birth. As we followed the sign together we met Anaxagoras."

"That in itself," said Anaxagoras, "was most auspicious. Our entourage took all the rooms available in town and we waited for the day in which the comet would be brightest, though still faint to the untrained. We were monitoring all of the pregnancies of the village. During that comet's brightest week, two children were born, a boy and a girl. We brought gifts to both of them."

"Male and female," said Elijah. "Who were they?"

"The first," said Omar, "was of a farmer named Isaac. This was the boy child, Samuel." The second, the girl, they have called Miriam. She is the daughter of a rabbi."

"We brought gifts to both," said Anaxagoras. "To fail to do so might invoke the wrath of the gods. You must gift the Messiah, even if the Messiah happens to be a girl. We brought expensive fabrics from Persia, porcelain from Greece, and very good wine we found in Petra."

Omar's helper interrupted, "We celebrated the occasion and we had a party for the two new babies.

"However," noted Omar, "as we retired from that night of celebration one of our helpers told us in confidence that a third child was born that week. This child was born of a traveling carpenter and his young bride. They were not of the village. When we were brought to this third child we had no more gifts. We offered a few gold coins, and what we had left of our frankincense and myrrh. It was so sad—they slept with the animals, and the night was bitter cold."

"It was our shame," said Anaxagoras. "They were forced to the stable by our traveling party, because we had taken all the rooms in the village."

"And," said Luke, "what were their names?"

"John, the father, and Mary," said Omar. "And of her, the baby boy, Jesus."

"No," corrected the Greek, "the father's name was Joseph."

"So," said Elijah, "which one is He? Which one is the real Messiah?"

The old master smiled. "Oh, this is yet to be seen. I can only say that he of lowest standing seemed the noblest of bearing, and very devoted to his spiritual rites, and to his young wife. Although he assumed paternity of his wife's child, he confided in me, for I posed him no threat. I believe it true that he has not been with Mary, whom he has known since her birth. And I believe it true; she has been with no other." Omar dipped his bread into his dish of olive oil and spices. "As he conveyed this confidence, I remained skeptical—his bride is so beautiful. Then he told me the circumstances of their union, which Mary was with child, and no husband, and would be stoned to death. When John, no... Joseph, when Joseph learned of this he pleaded with her family to let him take her as a bride, he being an old widower who could take her out of town and save the family name."

The Indian stood, and then fell to his knees. "Jesus, *Saddha-guru!*"

A murmur arose among the rest of the party—a general surprise at Ramni breaking his usual silence.

"What did he say?" Luke demanded.

The translators conferred, with the second responding. "He said, 'Jesus is the Messiah, he is the true Master.' "

⌐〰〰𓃀𓏏𓎼𓂋𓏏 𓂋𓈖𓇼𓏏 𓅓𓂝𓂋 𓂋𓃀 𓂋ˮ▢⌐

VI
Capitulus Sex

T wo days later Elijah and Luke left with the Greek oracle. The rest of the caravan was going east, toward Baghdad, then diverging onto different paths. During their travel with Anaxagoras, Luke began to learn Greek, to facilitate the communication among them. Elijah studied too; going over the calculations and equations Anaxagoras used for his astrological notes. They returned to Bethlehem to look for the family of Joseph; however, as they approached the town they noted a somber mood. Anaxagoras was soon recognized, and approached by three mothers dressed in black, shouting at him. The elder spoke for the others.

"They killed our babies because of you. You are a prophet of darkness!"

More people soon joined them, all shouting, all angry. "Herod killed my baby because of you! You prophet of darkness!"

Elijah advised a hasty retreat. Even as they moved farther away they could hear the shouts, the screams, the mourning. They left puzzled, stopped at a safe distance—they had to know what had happened. Anaxagoras determined to send back a servant to approach the house of the rabbi. The servant went back with Elijah and Luke, whose accent was more local.

"Shalom," said Luke, "Shalom rabbi. We are travelers. We wish you no harm."

The rabbi stood in his doorway, his eyes cast downward. "Shalom strangers. Welcome to our village in sorrow."

"We heard many cries as we entered the city. Could you tell us what has happened?"

"The greatest tragedy. The loss of our youth. Roman soldiers entered our village. They've killed every infant too young to walk."

"Why would they do such a thing?" Luke exchanged a look with Elijah. "This is not their normal method of collecting taxes!"

"No," replied the rabbi, "they've killed our babies because of that crazy old king Herod[i]."

"Why would the king do such a thing?" asked Luke.

"Some time ago our village was visited by three oracles." The rabbi glance up at the visitors, studied them. "These oracles came to visit, to welcome the birth of a prophet. They spent time here, gave presents to my daughter Miriam, and to Isaac's boy. Later they also gave to a wayward couple."

Elijah moved forward. "Is your daughter here?"

The rabbi shut his eyes, tears rolling down his cheeks. "Herod has killed her! They've killed every baby boy, and my daughter. The villagers, to save their babies told Herod's soldiers that my baby was the one visited by the oracles. My neighbors, they were very proud. The sages had made a special trip, to visit our humble village, to welcome Immanuel as foretold in scripture. And with each telling of the visit the story grew. Finally, the fable

---

[i] Moses, Krishna and Jesus had similar circumstances during birth where the prophecy of their births is attempted to be blocked by the regional ruler or king.

became that Herod's tax collection would be supplanted, that from here would arise the new king of the Jews, born in Bethlehem."

Luke shook his head. "Herod is not old enough for such senility. How could a baby depose him? He, with the full force of the Roman guard at his back."

The rabbi shrugged.

"Please accept our deepest condolences," said Elijah. "We are also students of the stars, but were not here in time to greet your babies. We wish also to offer our sympathy to the family of Isaac and to the family of Joseph."

"I can take you to Isaac but Joseph, Mary and their baby left a month ago." said the rabbi. "Joseph and Mary were afraid of all the attention given to their son. The villagers would see their baby and mimic, mostly in mockery, a prostration to the king."

"Was Mary ready to travel?" asked Elijah.

"Mary remained weak. Still, one morning before the sunrise I heard Joseph packing his mule. He said to me, 'Rabbi, you are a link to my life's happiness, and I thank you for your hospitality.' I bade him leave after a warm meal. He declined, saying there was no time to waste."

"What of his destination?" Luke asked. "Did he say?"

"Only that he must go," said the rabbi. "His face was of bewilderment, a mixture, as if joy, panic, and resolve shared the one house of his soul. He had been visited—he knew not if in a dream or a waking vision by an angel—with the message that he must be on the road."

The travelers later visited Isaac, then returned to their encampment outside the village and told their story to Anaxagoras.

The Greek sat silently for a time. He looked up finally, studied the rest of the company. "Because we took all the rooms," said Anaxagoras, "Jesus was low-born, among the animals, cribbed in the horse feed manger." He looked at his hands. "Because of our presence, the infant boys of Bethlehem now lay dead, and the

Messiah I came to greet is forced to the road in a life-saving dash. The villagers must be right; we are the prophets of darkness."

Elijah gazed at the Greek, noted the droop of his brow, their heavy furrow. "My friend," said Elijah, "you are not responsible for the actions of others. The arrival of Immanuel, the Messiah, could have been shielded from seers like us. You are not responsible for your vision. And, there is purpose in our presence. Perhaps you were here just to fulfill the prophecy. Do not think of yourself as the center of their lives. There could be a lesson here, for this whole event to happen this way, even if we do not know its meaning."

As the main body of the company trekked toward Egypt, part of the Anaxagoras' entourage departed for Greece. They were to relate the oracle's travels, their adventures to that point. And, with Elijah and Luke now in train, the journey to Egypt required fewer of the Greek's men.

Along the way, Anaxagoras told more of his own story. Among his people he was known as Anaxagoras of Attica. He claimed a vast knowledge of mathematics and astrology, passed down by his forefathers over 400 years. He also reported that a Delphi priestess was his guide, and it was her direction that led him to the welcoming of the Christos[i].

After a sojourn of six weeks, and with many stops at different villages, the company arrived at the ruins of Per-Ra[ii], city of sun god Ra, about five miles east of the Nile Delta's headwaters. They were also six miles northeast of Cairo, so they decided to stop. This was a return to Per-Ra for Elijah, and he noted it seemed smaller. Most of the buildings were in ruins, less from

---

[i] Christ is the English translation of the Greek word Christos which literally means The Anointed One. Etymologically, Christ is a derivation of *chrism*, Greek word literally meaning "an anointing."

[ii] It is known as one of the most ancient cities in Egypt, Per-Ra became known by the Greek name with the same meaning, Heliopolis or Sun-City. Located at 30°07′46.3″N, 31°17′20″E, today it is an extension of Cairo. The Ptolemies pharaohs plundered the monuments to build their own projects.

erosion than the marauding of Alexander the Great, and the scavenging of stone brought on by the birth of the port city, Alexandria.

Elijah and Anaxagoras grew to understand each other with ease, and in the process Elijah fine-tuned his ken of astrology according to Greek calculations. Luke found his own expansion through new language, and his now-lengthening association with Elijah—a period now of more than six months. Anaxagoras made reference to the calculations and diagrams used by Ramni, a method completely different from what they knew called Vedic Astrology[i]. He'd tried to investigate but, needing two translators, and with some words defying explanation, Anaxagoras made a decision to simply appreciate that although the calculations were different, the astrology of the Hindu also led to Immanuel.

As they lounged near Per-Ra, Elijah scanned the sky and looked towards Anaxagoras standing near. "We have been together for some time. One day turns into a week and a moon phase into another. I don't want to meddle in your affairs, we have our regular clients in Cairo, but what brings you to Egypt dear Anaxagoras?"

"Knowledge brings me to Egypt," said Anaxagoras, his speech slow, words distinct. "Not Cairo, but Alexandria."

Elijah stroked his beard. "What kind of knowledge? I have been to Alexandria several times, and it made no such offer to me. What could a city so young provide a man from a land so old, so steeped in history?"

The Greek smiled. "I know what I look for; I know where to find it. Some sailor friends have been complaining. When they stop at Alexandria they must give up their books and manuscripts to be copied by the library. My friends are not alone in this tribute.

---

[i] Also known as Jyotisha it differs from Western Astrology by using a sidereal zodiac and Western uses a tropical zodiac. In sum, the essence of Vedic is to help the person in spiritual progress (sadhana) and Western in psychological progress.

As you might imagine, such crossroads must hold knowledge from distant lands."

"Masters," said Luke, interrupting, "it is late. Let us camp here for tonight. We will not make Cairo during daylight."

"Better to enter the city at daylight," agreed Elijah.

They pitched camp at the center of Per-Ra, a desolate town Elijah knew was once dominated by an obelisk. The city had been dedicated to the sun nearly three millennia earlier, and shortly thereafter, was adopted as home by thirteen thousand priests and slaves, but as the traveling company settled in for that night, Per-Ra held fewer than half-dozen inhabitants.

Elijah, Luke and Anaxagoras were facing the main square; from the wind they were protected by three still erected walls of what used to be to a temple. Although the roof was not covered; however, the walls would provide a shield from the sporadic wind gust during the night. Anaxagoras' three helpers camped together at the end of the block. Since they knew that the subject of cosmology, mythology, used to continue very late into the night, the helpers decided to buffer sound with some distance.

This gave an opportunity for Anaxagoras to speak to Elijah and Luke freely about a very delicate and private subject. The conversation among all three would encompass a blend of the local languages now that Anaxagoras had learned some Aramaic and Coptic, and Elijah and Luke had learned more Greek.

Late into the night Anaxagoras, still staring at the fire asked, "What if I were to prove to you that not only Zeus, Apollo, Aphrodite, Poseidon, and Aires are immortals? What if I were to prove to you that you and I are immortals as well, but we take different shapes and different names?"

"This is a very bold statement to make," said Elijah.

"And," added Luke, "it is against everything we know."

"A bold statement to make in Greece as well," Anaxagoras conceded. "I have been ridiculed many times, but now I am taking my chances with you. I find it unlikely, my friends, that you will visit my lands and add to my defamation. And I trust you. But I make my statement not out of faith, but experience."

"How can you live like your gods?" Luke wondered.

"We, the Greeks, believe in Olympus and the world of the underground, in Hades. Egyptians believe another Egypt awaits them in the afterlife. The oracles I traveled with to Bethlehem spoke of the same belief among other peoples. These are long-held beliefs for thousands of years. Everyone has an essence without shape, like the wind. When the body dies, the spirit takes the body of a baby nearby. The new life is given according to the goodness of the spirit."

"And what," asked Elijah, "do you call this process?"

"It is referred to as retaking the flesh, or reincarnation. Anaxagoras was not my birth name for this lifetime. It is, instead, the name of my incarnation 500 years ago. My birth name of this life is Perseus. Ah, but Anaxagoras, that was my favorite past incarnation. I was a teacher. History notes me now as a great philosopher. I taught Pericles, Euripides, and I was proud to have young Socrates as my pupil. I spent that very life trying to learn and philosophize about the meaning of life, cataloging and analyzing it. Today, this life in which I've awakened to my other lives, I cannot understand the meaning of it. It is most puzzling, why we keep coming back with different bodies, different names. I am often ridiculed when I tell people I was also Plato, student of my own previous student."

"But," interrupted Elijah, "if we, as you call it, reincarnate, why can't we remember our other lives?"

"I don't know the answer to that, so I travel to Alexandria."

"How were you awakened to your past lives? How could you have learned that?"

The Greek looked off into the darkness. "During one of my many visits to Delphi[i] I had the counsel of Pythia, the chief priestess. She preferred being called Mother Gaea. Mother Gaea knew of me from my many visits to Delphi, over the decades. She decided I should receive a gift; should I prefer, like Cassandra, eyes to see the future, or would I find more in viewing my pasts. Of course, her proffer was a riddle, but I was oblivious. I accepted my pasts, believing I would receive vivid memories of this lifetime. Instead, I see beyond, as Cassandra[ii] did. And, like her, I am dismissed. I have come to rarely speak of it now. However, Mother Gaea advised I would someday transfer this gift, to one who believed. To one whose eyes were open, to accept the expanse of this sight."

The Greek went on about his previous lives, his scientific vision, and his many philosophical approaches. He described his time with Socrates, and as Plato—the tone of the times. Luke fell deep into a reverie as he listened, one that clouded his hearing, his vision. He fell fast asleep.

When Luke awoke the next morning there was a different aura about Elijah. In a way he seemed younger, and he flashed a new, sly grin at Luke, the former highwayman, who found it all disconcerting.

The small caravan continued towards Cairo, with Elijah and Luke at the back of the procession. For a time they traveled uncloaked—the sun remained enshrouded by clouds, giving the landscape and its inhabitants a respite from the usual scorching and bleaching.

---

[i] Delphi was exalted for its oracles and temples, the name *delphus* also means *womb,* it indicated veneration for Gaia, an Earth Goddess.

[ii] Due her beauty, Apollo granted her the gift of prophecy; however, she didn't reciprocate. Then Apollo cursed Cassandra's prophecies to be unbelievable.

"Professor," said Luke, "if I might suggest, you seem different. Did something transpire last night? What did you learn from the Greek?"

Elijah didn't answer straightaway. Instead he jostled along, content to feel Luke's glances. Then, as the younger man grew restless, he answered. "I learned yesterday that this gift is not to be talked about to the uninitiated. Once talked about, this issue can only be ridiculed. Our friend Anaxagoras left Athens not only to welcome the Christos, but also in flight, to save his life. A senator, an old friend of the family, warned him that soon he would face trial for impiety and blasphemy if he continued talking about his experiences and reincarnations."

"Professor, you evade my question. Did the Greek teach you to see past lives?"

"Yes he did."

"Who were you? Cesar, Alexander... Could you remember?"

"Dear Luke, don't you see a hint of mockery in your question?"

"Professor, my apologies..." replied Luke.

"Last night, as you fell asleep, I was able to recall my two past lives and no more. Fortunately, or perhaps not so, I was no one famous or of importance. But I can say that my life today, in the clearing light of those memories, now makes more sense."

"Will you explore more of his teaching?"

"Anaxagoras informs me that more visions and memories will come to me in time, as I focus my attention through an incantation, one given to him by Mother Gaea. But the goal is not to live in the past but to understand it."

"What knowledge does he seek in Alexandria?"

"As he told us, there is a great library in Alexandria. All of the books that come ashore are copied before they are returned to their ships. He is hoping to find books from the Orient which may explain more about this reincarnation process."

"Professor, do you really believe that he was Anaxagoras, and Plato as well?"

Elijah smiled. "Why not? Anaxagoras and Plato may be big names in Greece, but I've never heard of them. Have you?" Elijah noticed Luke's shoulders shrugged. "I continue to learn about this process. Sometimes a vision comes, sometimes it is a memory. This morning I found out that I can speak Latin like the Romans. I don't remember such study, but after this morning I cannot deny it. I am happily surprised."

Luke eyed his companion. "This sounds quite amazing."

"Please keep my experience a secret; to our Greek friend it has only brought ridicule to speak about it."

"I will."

"It has been good to have his company. He has met Immanuel when I could not. He has taught us different calculations and shared his ephemeris. By the way, did you finish copying it?"

"Two days ago."

Elijah patted Luke on the back. "Very good. Yesterday, he opened a horizon I never knew existed. Maybe we should follow him to Alexandria, after our stay in Cairo. It has been years since I visited the port city."

"And I have never been there."

They entered Cairo and spent a month. Cairo was a city with a lot to offer traveling oracles. Not only had the Ptolemy nobles requested the services of men who were wise about the charm of the stars, but also people with influence. Luke noticed that Elijah began to spend more time on his own. The exercise that Anaxagoras taught him was helping him discover more memories of past lives. Elijah would do his past life recalling mostly deep in the night. On one of those occasions, Luke decided to watch Elijah practice, saw him stare at the reflection of a burning candle inside a bowl of water. This repeated the next night, and the next; Elijah cross-legged, entranced by the reflection, deep into the night. And after a while Elijah began making his astrological readings from intuition rather than calculation.

"Professor, I don't see you asking people for their natal information as often as you seem to have before. If they come with a problem, you already seem to know what is bothering them. How do you gain your insight?"

"Dear Luke, I have been reawakening myself to my other lives, and also to my forgotten knowledge of astrology from my previous lives. You should not find surprising that this is not the first time that I am an oracle, story teller and astrologer."

"So, what kind of insights have you discovered?"

"In addition to it being a natural aspect of my being, I recognize in those who approach me, familiar faces. From past lives."

"Who did you find?"

"In good time I'll tell you. You should also know that, in this last month, I have recovered about 300 years of principles, expertise and patterns. Now I can look at anyone and tell what astrological sign a person holds. As I continue to examine the person, by the way he or she is speaking, their gestures, their garments, I can build a mental map of this person's astrological chart and, consequently, make a prediction."

Luke let the subject rest thereafter, understanding he would know more as Elijah saw fit. In a matter of days the entourage moved on, northwest to Alexandria. It wasn't the intention, but they lived there for the next ten years. The city became a feast for their longings, and the ships in port always brought news and fables of battles, kingdoms and fresh politics from Rome.

Luke began to spend as much time with Anaxagoras as with Elijah. The trio became famous in town, with people lining up for fortune telling, divination and palmistry. Elijah and Anaxagoras began to take students for mathematics and calculations of charts.

Anaxagoras and Elijah spent many days at the library, paging through thousands of rolls and manuscripts, trying to find more information about Eastern knowledge of the reincarnation process now familiar to both. They were perplexed by the amount of information they'd reclaimed from their past lives—how could something so monumental go so poorly documented? Scriptures from several countries, the psalms of the Jews, mythology from the Greeks; none of it made reference to reincarnation. The only source was The Egyptian Book of the Dead.

In The Book of the Dead there was a passage in which Osiris[i], the sun god represented as having the head of a hawk, was married to his sister Isis[ii]. Isis, the goddess of fertility, had a solar disk in her head surrounded by cow's horns. Envious brother Seth[iii] killed Osiris. Isis embalmed his body with the help of Anubis, the Lord of the dead who had a head of a jackal. Later with the help of Anubis, and with Isis' powerful incantations, Osiris' soul received a new body and a new name, Horus. As Horus, god of the underworld, he was able to reclaim his throne from Seth. Elijah and Anaxagoras understood this rebirth, not as a legend but documentation of a reincarnation, though this was not the normal interpretation. They kept this knowledge to themselves to avoid charges of impiety from local priests.

After Alexander's invasion and occupation, and with that influence waning, the Nile Delta began a religious assimilation, melting and revival. Often, Egyptian gods had equivalents in

---

[i] God Osiris reincarnated with the help of his wife goddess Isis, his new name was Horus a *God of the Dead.*

[ii] Isis' name literally means throne, thus she wears a throne in her had but after bringing her husband back to life she is also depicted wearing a solar disc sustained by horns representing fertility.

[iii] Desert god considered to be gay and taking male deity Shu as his lover.

Greek mythology. Elijah pointed out to Anaxagoras that in the Psalms of Genesis from the Jewish tradition an envious brother also killed another; he related the story of Abel and Cain.

In Alexandria[i] they received news of Greece and Rome. At the end of the ten years, Anaxagoras had slowed considerably and grown homesick for his beloved Attica. He hoped the charges raised against him had expired, or at least been forgotten. He wanted most members of the senate and the regional consul gone, too. Anaxagoras invited Elijah and Luke to his homeland, and they accepted, embarking with him on the dangerous but time-saving voyage across the Mediterranean. Anaxagoras chose the method, in spite of the risk, because of his failing health and his urge to spend as many of his last days as possible with his family and friends. Elijah and Luke had both grown fluent in Greek and versed in Greek Mythology.

---

[i] Alexandria was founded by the Macedonian Alexander the Great in 334 BCE, located on the western edge of the Nile Delta.

VII
Capitulus Septem

In Greece,
One Year Later

They had been in Attica for a year when Anaxagoras sat, seemingly in meditation, with Elijah nearby. "Dear Elijah," he said, "you have been enjoying my people and land for the last year. Do you still long for that arid place where I found you?"

"I grew up there. A person with no other experience is limited to believing that the whole world is arid. Like Socrates' man in the cave, the shadows become real life. We become the animals of our habitat. Since you taught me your vision into the past, this place now seems evermore familiar to me. When the winter began I knew how cold it was going to get. I expected the depth of the rainy season. I have no other way to explain other than it is like discovering an old pair of sandals and realizing how familiar they are to your feet."

"And you, dear Luke, do our lands suit you?"

"The place is beautiful. My only worry is inadvertently stepping on Roman toes. I did not come here for a forced visit to the Coliseum."

"Do not preoccupy yourself with this idea. The Romans are no threat to you. My family has ties going back generations, and you are my guests. Speaking of guests... We've been invited to see my counselor in Delphi. She wishes to know you. I dispatched one of my servants to relate our ten years in Alexandria to her. He returned yesterday and reported she is anxious to meet you, Elijah."

"I am anxious as well. It will be an exceeding privilege to thank her in person for the gift passed on to me through you."

"We shall leave in four days. Eat well, for we have a rugged road ahead of us."

"How is that city?" asked Luke.

"Delphi has been in decay for many years. Most of the temples are in ruins. Mother Gaea lives in a farmhouse very close to the city. She does use most of the temples in secret, avoiding impiety charges from the Romans."

After a week on the road they arrived in Delphi. Luke and Elijah had grown accustomed to the luxuries of Attica; their adjustment to this new, humble place was not easy.

"Welcome, Anaxagoras," called Mother Gaea, greeting him with a smothering hug and a name neither Elijah, nor Luke, nor the servants had used in public since their arrival in Attica. He'd remained Perseus in his homeland, to avoid prosecution. "Welcome back to my home. I bade the gods to ensure your protection during your trip."

"And I offer full and undying gratitude." Anaxagoras bowed. "These are my friends, acquaintances from my sojourn."

"Finally," she said, "I get to meet the angels that I sent to save your life in Judea."

Elijah put a hand to his heart. "Your kindness flows ever abundantly, gracious lady. Thank you for the gift of vision, and for being our host." He motioned toward Luke. "This is my beloved pupil and friend, Luke."

"Great, good mother. It is my honor," bowed Luke.

"And mine," she said. "Yet, I remain deeply saddened about your family, though now you have a new."

Luke tilted his head as he gazed at the lady. *How could she know that of which he'd never spoken?*

She continued, "I had our maids prepare a bath for all. Tonight we feast, but first you must retire to your ablutions while the water is still warm."

As the others gathered their bags Elijah stood in place, seemingly hypnotized. For the first time in his life he was transfixed by a female presence. In silence he was taken by her enduring beauty. It was clear he scanned her hair, witnessing the grey but seeming awed by it. Some grey was twinkling highlights on her black hair cascading down on her back, just like the stars in a moonless night. He made preparation to join the rest, only to stop and gaze once more at her, pondering her face. It was too soon but the thought of being with her overwhelmed any other. Although for the first time he anguished with the fact that he lived a nomadic life. Romance would only bring enduring pain. He caught Luke analyzing him. *Was he this transparent?* He thought. Now he had to better conceal his thoughts. Whenever he caught a glimpse of her eyes he could see his very soul. Her look appeared to sympathize with his anguish. He knew that his fixation was far beyond attachment to physical beauty. Now he had gathered more than 500 years of his own past. *Yes, she is familiar, we must have met before.*

That night, both Anaxagoras and Elijah held private sessions with Mother Gaea, with the next day reserved for Luke.

"Dear Luke," she said, "it is quite auspicious that you have the company of Elijah's and Anaxagoras' friendship; however, as I've already told Elijah, you both need to return to Galilee. Your life is going to change, and your uncle will not appreciate your return, but return you must."

Luke began to speak, but he was cut short.

"No words from you at this point, they will interrupt the flow. Later you may ask questions. Your father, mother, and their friend were wronged by your uncle." She produced a container and handed it to Luke. "This flask contains magic for him. An occasion will come, a party, an assembly, and you will place this liquid in his drink. This is not a poison. The poison is in his own words."

Luke eyed the ampoule, and then tucked it into a pocket formed by the drape of his tunic.

"To Galilee," she said. "Events await you both and you are to meet your new destiny."

Elijah kept a musing silence during their remaining days in Attica. He and Luke finally bade farewell to their old Greek friend when the time came to join a merchant ship to Galilee. Luke boarded with great anticipation, but noticed the reluctance with which Elijah mounted and the tears in his eyes. He had not cried before leaving his home land but now he did leaving Greece.

In Galilee,
One Year Later

After a year back in Galilee Elijah finally seemed resolved to his separation from Greece, and he noted the wide berth Luke gave his uncle, who had let it be known he knew of Luke's presence, and whose advancing age hadn't curbed his mercilessness.

"You keep avoiding your uncle," Elijah said, "The best way to end this is to visit with them and live our lives."

Luke shook his head. "Mother Gaea instructed me not to trust him and only to meet him in a public party. He cannot be trusted; perhaps this is a sense that I've developed once being around you and Anaxagoras."

"We are going to have a Passover celebration next week. I think this would be a good opportunity for us to finally meet him."

Coral Gables, Florida

Sydney Tobias sitting at his desk in Coral Gables across from his old teacher said, "How did you meet your uncle?"

Horace replied, "I finally poured the magic contents of Mother's Gaea potion into my uncle's drink. His hatred towards me became even more devastating. In his hatred he was unaware that he'd confessed poisoning and killing my father and mother to take over the business. He had also confessed killing two other business competitors in the same village. I was placed in charge of raising his children and running our family business. This provided Elijah and I, a wealthy stay in Galilee but one year later we returned to our road life."

Sydney asked, "I can presume that eventually you met Jesus since you and Elijah moved to Galilee?"

"Yes we met our Dear Rabbi, young Jesus and He was quite moving. We could tell that He spoke on several levels, using parables to illustrate most points. Some of the people could understand Him and yet others could not; however, there they stayed immobile just listening to Him; nourished from His energy and voice.

"Our problem began after His death. Not all of His followers agreed. During Jesus' days, there were women and children traveling with Him, but they did not get acknowledged in the Bible because women could not be orators and rabbis. A few years later, after His death, we met one of His students stopping by and preaching to the locals. Our profession was never a problem before to Jesus Himself, but for that disciple it was. Later we met more disciples and they would not allow astrologers among them. The message spoken by Jesus was paraphrased in their many versions and understandings. Matthew[i], for instance, incorporated the idea of heaven and hell just like it was portrayed in Greek mythology, like Olympus and Hades' underground. Little statues we saw for centuries resembling Isis and Horus, later turned into Jesus and His mother Mary.

"People began to follow the followers of Christ," Horace continued, "instead of the essence of His message. The cross, for example, was supposed to be a symbol of spiritual focus but instead, it became a symbol of guilt."

Sydney reclined in his chair. "How could the cross be a symbol of spiritual focus? I thought the cross was to symbolize Jesus' death?"

"Remember just now when I said that Jesus spoke on many levels? The zodiac is represented by a circle with all the animals in it. When a person has no spiritual focus, this person becomes a very emotional individual. This person is going to start behaving like one of the animals of the zodiac. Character is destiny, which also means that this person's behavior can be predicted. What is

---

[i] Matthew was a *publican* or tax-collector for Herod Antipas. Also regarded as author of the gospels of Mark, Luke and John, these four gospels are called synoptic because of their similarities. Synoptic of the Greek words (syn = together) and (opsis = seeing).

unpredictable is when somebody strikes you on one cheek and you offer the other one."

"Just like that passage in the Bible, right?"

"Exactly. When you make a line between Aries and Libra and Cancer and Capricorn you get a cross." Horace drew a circle and wrote the symbol of the signs on the outside perimeter and connected a cross in the center, "The question every individual should ask himself is; 'Am I going to behave like an animal from the zodiac whose charms influence our heads and behavior or am I going to follow Jesus inside of my heart and not give in to anger and happiness or pleasure and pain?" he pointed to the cross inside of the circle, showing Jesus at the center of the universe and he also pointed outside of the circle, where the animal or the zodiac dwells.

"Wow!" Sydney sat forward. "So what I also get now is that astrology is not a teaching but a guide for individuals to know their zodiac weaknesses to overcome their weaknesses and to stay on path with their religious focus."

"When people open their arms," said Horace, "the heart becomes the center of the cross. For the last two thousand years the cross has been a symbol of pain, resentment and blame instead of a symbol of detachment and spiritual focus away from our animal tendencies."

"In Yoga[i]," Sydney noted, "the heart chakra is also in the middle."

"So why," Horace mused, "did we create the link? Jesus had come with a new message of hope, peace and forgiveness but

---

[i] Etymologically yoga comes from the Sanskrit which means union where as religion comes from the Latin *re-ligare* which means to re-union or even re-*link*. Therefore the goal of these very distinctive disciplines is the same to re-unite with God. Yoga has many different philosophies to comment but for instance postures is called either Hatha or Asana Yoga. Discrimination is called Jnana Yoga, Meditation is Dhyan Yoga. However most of the world tends to follow Ignorance which is called Karma *(reaction)* Yoga, the hardest yoga to breakthrough since one is lost in a vicious cycle of pain. In Karma every action leads to a reaction or consequence.

most of His followers were Jews and they were not ready to give up their Old Testament and start anew. You and I back then, could not change or show the parallel meaning that the teaching was taking place. Jesus Christ Himself, who was so outspoken about putting a price and monopoly on religion, was killed because He confronted with the money changers at the temple[i] and was creating a competition with the local rabbis. The rabbis then wanted to have a monopoly on God.

"Very soon we, the students of patterns in the sky, began to see that the patterns were taking shape again. The followers of Christ pretty soon were coining Jesus' teachings to corner God's Market. When Jesus said, 'I live a life of truth in the way that leads to my Father', but later versions got translated into 'I am the way, the truth, and the life: no man cometh unto the Father, but by Me[ii].' We were quick to discover that the followers of Christ were being caught up in the metaphor, literal meaning and not the essence of the teachings." Horace concluded, "How could we find Christ again to guide the people in the proper way? His message was being corrupted to form a monopoly on God."

Across the table the images began to form in Sydney's head, taking him back to the past...

Alexandria, Egypt,
Year 36 C.E.

In Alexandria the aging Luke, now in his early fifties, said to his old teacher Elijah, "Professor, we need to do something with the powers that we have. We both have seen the connections to our

---

[i] Matthew 21:13 And (He) said unto them, It is written, My house shall be called the house of prayer; but ye have made it a den of thieves.
[ii] John 14:6

previous lives which we keep secret among ourselves. But, how can we keep this link of understanding open?"

"Do you think that we can meet Jesus again?"

"Not with the same name, but it is evident if we have the power to dive into our past, Jesus must also have the same knowledge we do."

Using equipoise in his words Elijah spoke, "My father named me after the prophet Elijah. I remember that Jesus spoke so much about Elijah that he was asked how he was so familiar with the prophet, since Elijah had died before He was born. To that He said, *Elijah truly shall first come and restore all things. But I say unto you, that Elijah is come already, and they knew him not, but have done unto him whatsoever they listed[i]*."

Luke gazed at the older man, his face brightening. "Prophet Elijah must have been that John who baptizes; he was Jesus' cousin. This means that he was part of Jesus' spiritual family as you are part of mine, even though we are not blood relatives this lifetime."

"All the new called Christians claimed that Jesus will return. What if I were to calculate his return the same way I calculated his coming?"

"Now we have more experience," said Luke, "and we both can recalculate the results."

After giving their apprentices the task of preparing the ephemeris or orbit calculations of each planet and orbit for the next fifty years, Luke and Elijah began their calculations. During the process Luke felt a presence—he peered out the window of their studio in Alexandria. Down below sat an ever-present transient; unshaven, unkempt, always to himself: a drunken wanderer called Theophilus. Luke had sometimes offered the man the abundance

---

[i] Matthew 17:12, 13 Clear mention of reincarnation mentioned on the Bible by Jesus Himself and quoted by Matthew. — *Then the disciples understood the he spake unto them of John the Baptist.*

from feasts, and so had Elijah. The alcoholic vagabond's presence was ignored.

A month later the calculation results for the return of Jesus within the next 30 years did not return the omens they sought. Luke studied the findings, shook his head, and looked them over again. He returned to them for several days, without satisfaction. In fact, even the calculations for the next one hundred years did not generate the omens that they were looking for. It was six months later that they had ephemeris calculations for the next three hundred years.

They were deep into the ciphering when Elijah saw a point. "Luke," he said. "Take a look at this chart, on the conjunction of the Julian Day of 101,000 from now. This is close to two hundred and seventy six years."

"The pattern is very close to 36 years ago, when we first met."

"Note Saturn and Jupiter," said Elijah. "They have made enough revolutions to be precisely at the same point from each other. What we cannot calculate is; if the sky is going to grace us with the same comet."

"Professor, we have a bigger problem than that."

Elijah continued to gaze at his scribbles. "So, what is the problem?"

"Even the sons of our sons will not be alive at this time."

"Then there is just one way to proceed," said Elijah. "We must find a way to reawaken ourselves to our past in our next life. Since I am older than you, it is natural that I will be the first to reincarnate."

Luke felt his heart race. "When and where will I find you? We saw our past lives. There is no guarantee that we would be willing to learn our science in our next life. There is something missing in this riddle."

Elijah sat pondering. After a while he tilted his head, his eyebrows arched. "The answer to this riddle is here in Egypt. There must be something in the Book of the Dead that we must look for."

"Perhaps," said Luke, "Mother Gaea could help us."

Elijah shook his head. "It was very difficult for me to say goodbye to her. I don't think I could do it again. Besides, who knows if she's still alive, and in the same place?"

𓀁 𓂝𓏏 𓂧𓏤 𓂝𓏏𓏤 𓂝𓏏𓊪 𓂝𓏏𓊪𓆑𓏏𓏤

VIII
Capitulus Octo

Coral Gables, Florida

live's voice crackled over the intercom, shaking Sydney from the familiar, arid landscape of Egypt.

"I'm going to get some lunch. Do you want something?"

Sydney took a moment to gather himself. "Yes, Olive. The usual from Mario's. Two of them and yours is on me. Also, could you take my car and gas it up? Use the corporate card." He depressed the intercom's bottom.

Horace held up a hand to silence Sydney. "Why tell you this story? You would feel it, see it if I reawakened you."

The floor of the office quaked violently. The men heard glass shatter, structure crumble. An explosion.

Sydney was up quickly, rushed to the window. "Oh my God! Where is Olive?" he saw his car below, but ripped apart, shredded. "The roof and the hood are blown away!"

Horace sat in his wheelchair, still on the other side of the desk. "Oh my God!" he exclaimed. "That was meant for you. The Librarian! He must be near! He's here to stop *the link*. We don't have any time!"

Sydney turned. "What? What's this?"

"No time to explain. We must leave at once!"

Sydney grabbed the phone. The line was dead, apparently severed by the blast. He reached into his breast pocket but his cell phone was missing.

"Sydney, if I could I would get up and run. We need to get out of here at once. We could call 911 but our lives are in danger. If we're both killed *the link* is severed."

Bullets shattered the windows, splintering mahogany woodwork throughout the office. Ducking away from the window, Sydney raced to Horace and wheeled his chair away. "Hold on old friend! Gonna be a rough ride! Keep your head low!"

As he pushed Horace along, Sydney discerned the bullets were coming from across the street, and a little south. Their escape would have to take the emergency exit on the other side of the house-turned-office. But their charge through the door set off a piercing alarm. Inadvertently, they'd signaled their assailants—or as many goons as they could—of their exit behind the building.

Sydney ran on, trying to create as large a gap as he could between themselves and their attackers. As he hustled on he was bothered by a niggling hiss, a whispering call, as if from the shadows—someone lurking, trying to get his attention. He ignored it, as best as he could, focusing instead on their escape, unaware that the hissing was the ricochet of bullets apparently fired through a silencer. Ahead of them a car window shattered; the sound put him in mind of water being dropped from a five gallon utility bucket. He yearned for the luck of all those movie action heroes—the grace to have two hours where bullets did their best to avoid the secret agent and his gadgets. Sydney was no secret agent; bullets treated people very differently in reality. Sydney turned the first corner that he could find, and paused briefly. For a moment he was fully erect, catching his breath, and realizing that the nudge at his foot, moments before, had been a bullet candidly extirpating the heel of his left shoe.

"Luke are you okay?"

"Nothing hurts," said Horace. "We must find a place to hide."

"Are you overdue with a book? Library fines? This is ridiculous!"

"Sydney, this is the work of our old nemesis Nicholas, a Vatican librarian. I was very close to finding him twenty years ago. He must have been your age back then. I was certain that I found him but he eluded me."

"He's a Vatican librarian? Holy Moses, how can this be?"

Sydney pushed off again and soon entered an office from the back through the parking lot. Like his, it had gone from residence to business—a common conversion in Coral Gables—and its front windows faced the busy, lunch-time traffic of Ponce de Leon Boulevard. Because it was lunch, the office sat deserted, the occupants apparently out for a quick pick up. In the meantime, the overconfident shout of police and fire sirens pierced the rumble of street noise.

"Elijah, pay attention," murmured Horace, signaling Sydney to kneel. "I may not have another chance so I must do this now."

Sydney knelt slowly, still a bit put off by this other name. "Here I am," he said, though his focus was on the scene outside.

"Forget about that," Horace commanded. He raised his hand. "Focus here. Remember our exercise in the office?"

Sydney nodded.

"This is very similar. I need to give you a charge. This is not the way we've done it before but I think our time has run out." Luke, the man known for so long as Horace, placed both hands around Sydney's head, with Horace's thumbs and index fingers enveloping Sydney's ear lobes. "Keep your eyes locked on mine."

Sydney began to hear the earlier prayer, but this time Horace's eyes had a different purpose, charged with a look that to

Sydney felt like an X-ray hitting the back of his skull. For the second time that day the room began to morph. The strange office corridor soon filled with shadows and lights in cluttered movements. Hundreds of images suddenly began to show in his mind, and they moved faster by the second. He lost track of time, not knowing if it was a second gone by or many minutes, as with dream time. The last image of himself as Elijah, Luke, and their first meeting, two millennia ago, was steadily taking shape, only to be interrupted by a scream. A Latino middle aged woman stood nearby, back from the streets bringing her lunch. Her eyes wide, as she stared at the puddle of blood from Horace's left leg.

Sydney struggled to regain his senses, to come out of that other realm. Before him, outside of the office's windowpane, was a Caucasian man with sunglasses, wearing a coat too hot for South Florida at any time of year. Inside the office, partially blocking his view was a female clerk returning from her lunch break. In a matter of moments the man pulled a gun from inside the jacket and, before Sydney could think to protect Horace, the man was firing—"thup-thup" rang from the weapon as its barrel blazed. As he fell back, Sydney watched Horace ejected from his chair, falling on top and towards him. Two bullets had struck him from behind and lifted him up. The assailant had shattered the front glass with his automatic double burst which made the office view temporarily blocked.

Maria Conchita had walked in the wrong place at the wrong time, in the line of fire. She found herself with her back towards the assailant and facing the target, two men on the corridor in a pool of blood. The elder was on the wheelchair with his back to her and the second on his knees facing the first. Her screams continued when the bullets pulverized her sandwich in sync with the noise of shattered glass behind her.

Amidst the woman's screams, the attacker continued to pump his weapon, until his chamber was empty. With the police nearby, and the magazine spent, it was time to fall back and regroup. He was a professional, not a gambler.

"Elijah my old buddy," said Horace as he lay next to Sydney, "I must be losing a lot of blood. Everything is turning dark... Before I go, take this notebook from my vest pocket. This should help you immensely. This is a scribble in my pocket with special reference to find the return of Jesus. I also have a special ephemeris in the house. Look for your old friend Lucia if you need help."

"Who is Lucia?"

"Everything is dark now... Please find me in my next reinc...."

Horace didn't finish his sentence, his head drooping to the side.

"Call 911, now!" Sydney shouted.

Maria Conchita, staggered to her desk, her legs wobbly, she dropped the second half of her sub. As she spoke into the receiver she scanned the office, apparently still trying to understand the circumstances.

Sydney still bonded to Horace watched as she morphed through personae, going from a grey, modern suit to a very Victorian red dress and hat. As Sydney tried to make sense of his vision, the image went back to normal; a woman in grey, Conchita was coming to terms with her office being turned into what resembled nothing less than a combat zone.

"Yes," she repeated, "this is an emergency. One person has been shot." She paused, "Northeast corner, Ponce de Leon and Segovia."

Sydney soon realized his clothes were drenched with Horace's blood. Perhaps the same burst of bullets that had destroyed his shoe must have grazed Horace's leg's vein. Horace's blood flowed into a groove an inch wide, a particular thick grout line which is necessary to lay the uneven *Saltillo* clay tiles. Sydney gently rolled Horace's body over, and noticed a medallion that he had never seen before.

Sydney gently removed the chain and studied the object. The Medallion and silver chain had an asymmetrical random line in the front. The back was adorned with a relief of a cross that separated the four elements; air, fire on top and water, earth on the bottom. As he studied the medallion he was taken by another flashback. An older man was handing the medallion to a young man. This old man he recognized as himself, Peter Nielsen. Sydney was aware that the younger man was Horace.

Peter Nielsen said, "It's time to leave now… This belongs to you. The librarian is dead, but you need to find him before he awakens himself. We need to stop this disruptor. In this world war alone, he was able to kill millions and millions of Jews, Gypsies and Astrologers. He burned all the books that he could. You must find him! I don't want to see him creating another monster like Hitler. We need to stop his disruption for good. Defend yourself, and don't forget to look for me in 1972, in seventeen years." The image was fading away with Peter Nielsen's last words.

Sydney's attention to his vision was so complete he was at first unaware of the three Coral Gables Police officers already at the premises. One male officer held Conchita's hand as a display of support. Another stood at the door, keeping it unobstructed for the paramedics. The third, a female, took Sydney's hand and helped him up. As he rose, Sydney noticed the paramedics entering the office, gallantry and conviction in their eyes, resoluteness in their ability to make a difference and bring Horace back to life.

Sydney, to prevent the desecration of his teacher's garments and solemn look, said to the paramedics as they were about to begin, "He had lost a lot of blood before he was shot twice in the back."

One medic looked and noticed that the body was very cold and the loss of blood was prevailing. They exchanged a look in consensus of their next move: Estimate the time of death and proceed with the paper work.

The female officer, tall and blonde, turned to Sydney. "Do you know why this has happened?"

"No, but I think I was the main target... My secretary was taking my car, going to get lunch for us."

"Was she shot?"

"No. The car exploded when she started it. The shooting began seconds later. My dad and I were trying to escape."

"Hold on here," the officer said, pointing to a chair. "Gotta call my dispatcher." She keyed the mike attached to her epaulet.. "Officer Larson to dispatch." The squelch of a response was short and undecipherable. "I have a 10-47 connected to that 10-31 within the hour, two fatalities. A third is being pursued by a contract or a professional. Can you send Chavez or Burke here?"

The view from the hotel room was uncalled for, it was a cheery and sunny North Miami Beach; ocean waves rolling ashore, lapping up to beach-goers. Sydney wasn't enjoying the view. He stared through the window from his bed, waiting for the staccato knocks to end after the now-familiar pattern. Before he could speak a police officer entered the room.

"Hello Sydney," said Lieutenant Jason Burke, strolling toward the bed. "How do you like your accommodations here?"

"Hello Jason. Not bad, but I would like to go home before the funeral tomorrow."

"Sydney, things are not getting any easier. I don't know how to break this to you, or even where to start."

Sydney pinched the bridge of his nose. "Oh no, what happened now?" he swept his hands over his face. "I had a teacher who once told me, in Texas they have a saying; 'When you have to eat three frogs, start with the biggest one first." The lieutenant frowned. Sydney went on. "In other words, bite off the biggest one first, and the others will be easier to swallow."

"Roberto was found dead in New York City."

Sydney put his feet on the floor and slumped forward as he sat on the side of the bed. "How did it happen?"

"It looks like he resisted a robbery and was shot."

"Do you believe that?"

"No I don't. The timing." Lieutenant Burke moved a chair closer to Sydney. "What kind of astrology are you all doing that's getting you all killed?"

Sydney gazed at the lieutenant, his expression flat.

"And," Burke went on, "there is one more thing. Have you made any enemies in Russia?"

"Russia?"

"Well, your car, your house, they both had…." Lieutenant Burke was interrupted.

"You said, my house?"

"Well, I'm sorry. I Should have mentioned that too. Your house was burned to the ground two days ago. The lab tested the signature of the compound used to break open your safe. It matched the explosives that ripped your car apart."

"Wait. Not only was my house torched, but you're saying my safe was opened, too?" Sydney massaged his forehead. "Oh man!"

"Any idea what was stolen?"

"Could only be one thing, a gift from my father. I didn't have a chance to see it yet but it was something that would probably keep me alive."

"Like what?"

"Lessons that he recorded on some tapes. But, I never saw them."

"I don't think that there was much left of them. The plastic explosive used on the safe destroyed everything inside."

"Any more bad news, lieutenant?"

"Unfortunately, one bit more. With the amount of explosives involved, jurisdiction goes to A.T.F.[i] And, if Roberto's death is linked, you've got F.B.I.[ii], too. I've gone through channels but, no contact from either yet. All that's to say we're not going to be able to cover you, or provide surveillance and protection. I hope you have some other way to feel secure for a while."

"A friend has a house in Coconut Grove. I should be safe there, for a while. He's a big roller, likes to have security around the clock."

Another knock at the door. Officer Delgado leaned in, a cell phone in hand. "It's for you sir. It's better if you take it over here."

"Please excuse me, Sydney."

"Take your time. I'll start packing."

The lieutenant bounded into the room a few minutes later. "I have some good news." Sydney continued packing as the lieutenant went on. "The F.B.I. is in. You hadn't mentioned that another of Horace's students had been killed in the same way.

"Lieutenant, I realized that just this moment, as you brought it up. Marcelo, he was gunned down last year, only, he

---

[i] Bureau of Alcohol, Tobacco, Firearms and Explosives.

[ii] Federal Bureau of Investigations; the FBI is in assigned domestic or national surveillance.

wasn't so close to us. He was with us for two years taking lessons. He seemed to be drawn to Dad, but then he decided to move to Hollywood, work with celebrities. He was robbed, too. Shot at point-blank range at an ATM next to the supermarket. Since Roberto was killed the same way I can see a connection as well."

"Was there anything interesting about the three of you?"

"We were all the same age. Marcelo was two months older and Roberto was one and a half months younger than me."

"There must be a correlation. The Bureau has profilers. They're better at putting a motive together than our department."

Sydney's mind raced forward, doing its own profiling. And it occurred to him the 'pseudo-librarian' must also know how to calculate reincarnation. That was why Horace's students of Sydney's age were being killed.

Jason raised a finger, as if to ask a question. He hesitated, stuttered. "Sorry if this question offends you," he said finally, "but, couldn't Marcelo and Roberto tell that they were going to be killed? Well, they both knew astrology."

"They couldn't command the influence of the stars. I guess you could say where do we find the influence of the stars when an airplane falls down?"

"I don't know, where?" asked Jason.

"You check the chart on the pilot."

"Interesting," Jason said jokingly. "Next time I get on a plane I'll ask the pilot if he checked his horoscope."

"I should be ready in another five minutes," Sydney said, packing his larger suit case. He retrieved paperwork, his computer, other items from the table.

"Take your time. You should wait. Couple of agents will be along soon, to work with you."

"Do you mean guarding me?"

"You could say that, but I guess they think that your assailant is going to strike again. They'd like to be there before the fact, since your guy came so close to succeeding this last time."

Three hours later there was another knock at the hotel door. Not waiting for an answer, a man barged in, followed by a second. Both flipped open wallets, flashing FBI credentials.

"Inspector Torres," the first agent barked, his tone intimidating and authoritative, "FBI Miami."

"I'm agent Swanson," said the second, just as business-like but in a milder tone. "Please call me Dennis."

"My name is Sydney. I thought you guys would only come out dressed in suits."

Torres arched an eyebrow. "If we wanted to stick out like sore thumbs we would do just that. This is Miami, 92 degrees in the shade and humidity so we have to rethink our dress code."

"We're going to be your detail," said Swanson, "Your guardian angels, your shadow if you prefer, for the next week. Our schedules are going to overlap. At least one of us will be with you around the clock. Tomorrow another agent flies in, he lives here but he had a meeting in Washington, putting together all the information of your case."

Torres cocked his head to the side. "Jason tells me you have a place to stay in Coconut Grove. Is that true?"

Sydney nodded. "That's right. It has a security system, staff. It's right next to the Coconut Grove Playhouse off the Main highway."

"Not bad," said Swanson. "I like jobs like these. At least I'm not crouching all night at the docks, fighting mosquitoes while I case smugglers and traffickers."

Sydney was saddened by the comment. His dilemma was a "job" to these men. He gave Swanson a hangdog look as he picked up his bags.

Swanson grimaced. "Sorry," he said, "didn't mean to say that this was a good thing."

"Zip it," grunted Torres, "You talk too much. Let's go."

Sydney was sitting on the right rear seat of an unmarked police car. As they were caught in a car procession and the many traffic lights in the city life of Coconut Grove, Sydney noticed a local cab company. He programmed the number displayed on the cab's door. Shortly after, they were crossing a gate in front of the mansion on Main Highway. The mansion was sheltered by banyan and giant fichus trees.

"Hello, Mr. Tobias." The maid reached for Sydney's bags. "Mrs. Stein said you'd be staying over for a while. Let me show you to your room."

"Thank you Carmen. This is Agent Torres and Agent Swanson. They'll be coming and going for a while."

Swanson extended his hand to the maid. "Mucho gusto."

"*Que bueno. ¿Hablas Español?*"

"Still learning," he said. "I need to practice."

"How about you, Agent Torres?" asked Carmen.

Swanson broke in. "You can call him Bill."

Torres remained silent, seemingly oblivious to the question as he scanned the grounds.

"Lock him up for three days without food and water," said Swanson, "then he'll say something in Spanish."

At this point Carmen looked at inspector William Torres with incredulity, wondering why the need of indistinctness towards his own ethnicity.

"But I've heard from reliable sources, if he has a Spanish paella[i] dish for lunch he might speak Spanish and even reveal safe codes."

"You talk too much," Torres uttered in monotone. "I am going to walk around the grounds and check for entries."

They approached the stairs in a single file, suitcases in hand.

"Here is your room," Carmen pointed as they reached the top of the stairs. "There on the right is the black-board you wanted. This was the biggest one they had, five by three at the office supply store. From what I understood they don't come in black anymore. It did come with some markers."

"Thank you very much Carmen. Is Luis around?"

"He is. He's just out getting some things for the garden." She began to walk away, and then turned back to Sydney. "I don't know how to bring this up but, all I can say is, I am very sorry for your dad and the stuff that you are going through."

"Thank you Carmen."

"Nice place," said Swanson. "This must be the guest room. Even better than my apartment."

The corner of Sydney's mouth creased in a smirk. "Well, are you a Gemini?"

"No way! That is spooky. How can you tell?"

"Let me make another guess. You were born at about three or four PM?"

"Actually 3:35 PM. This is unbelievable! I mean, when you first told me my sign I thought it was a lucky guess. But then…how did you do it?"

Sydney opened a suitcase on the bed and began filling drawers and bathroom cabinets. "Astrology is about reading the signs. You gave yourself away by your manner of speech. Gemini and Sagittarius love to tell jokes but Gemini loves to communicate and express."

"Interesting. What about the time?"

Sydney ignored a small battery that fell from his bag, hit his foot, then rolled under the bed. "Secret stuff like detective work and investigation is ruled by Scorpio and the eighth house on the chart. This means if you are born at three or four PM you will have the need to investigate. A Scorpio rising also has to probe. All I do is use the archetypes known in the zodiac and clock it accordingly for a reading. Backwards in your case."

Agent Torres walked in. "The place looks good. Lots of high walls. Motion detection everywhere. Very professional work."

"Hey Bill, this is far out. He guessed my astrological sign and the time I was born."

"You probably gave it away because you talk too much. Go down to the car and wait for me."

"Good night, Sydney. If you have time could you... Never mind, don't worry about it."

Torres watched Swanson leave, then turned to Sydney. "Let me know if he begins to bother you."

"No. He's fine."

"Funeral tomorrow as scheduled?" asked Torres.

"As far as I know, all the wheels are in motion," answered Sydney.

"We'll have some extra help in and out of the funeral home. If there are any surprises we'll be there."

---

[i] Paella is a traditional Valencia and Cuban Sunday dish. The main ingredients are rice, saffron and olive oil, but usually garnished with vegetables and meat or seafood.

Sydney's brow furrowed. "There's going to be a lot of important people there, even a few TV cameras as far as I know. I don't think we'll have any problems."

"I don't make predictions; I make sure we are not going to have any problems."

Sydney nodded. "Thank you for taking care of that then."

"Good night. Should I close the door?"

"No, that's all right. Good night."

ᐁᑊᐁ ᑲᐧᐱᑌ ᓭᐱᐊ ᐧᐩᐁᑫ ᑫᐁ ᐩᑫᐧ
ᐧᐧᐁᐧᐁᓭᐱᐧᐁᑉ ᐃᐧᐧᐧᐧᐃᐧᑕᐧᐧᐱᐁ

IX
Capitulus Novem

S ydney was nearly finished unpacking when he found himself at the bathroom mirror. He'd started the hot water, priming the cold from the pipes so he could get a warm shave. He stood in a reverie, remembering his last hours with Horace, staring into his eyes, realizing now that he had only his own. He wondered if he could do the very exercise from a few days ago on his own. He didn't have the benefit of the incantation, only his reflection in the mirror. He concentrated on his left eye without skepticism yet with ambivalence; an unknown energy began to move him. The image around the eye began to morph. A sudden fear seized him and he wanted to break the concentration. He couldn't. The face staring back at him was of an old man in grey garb and a cloak.

Constantinople, Turkey,
1091 C.E.

Sydney did not know his name, but he knew that he was this old man. He was now filled with panic and stared at his image reflected on the water fountain. He could not bring his arms about. They were tied to a beam, spreading his arms open behind his back. The image of his face remained reflected in the water. He tried to raise his head but couldn't and was left with a view of himself and parts of buildings to his left: the towers and dome of Hagia Sophia in Constantinople. And he was not alone—there were figures behind him. A gloomy day, no sun in the sky, no sense of direction. He knew to plead with his captors, but before he could, his head was immersed in the fountain's pool, held there, and he could feel the asphyxiation begin just as his head was pulled back by its hair.

"Heresy!" shouted a voice, "profanation, sacrilege and blasphemy! How dare you go about changing facts of the Holy Book? How dare you speak about those times, old Salin?"

It all came back to him in a rush. He was Salin, and in mortal danger. He struggled for enough air in his lungs to argue a defense, but before he could his head was again shoved under water. He could taste the body's refuse gases filling his nasal passages, the sensation of ever-limited consciousness. Again, his head was jerked out of the water. He began to cough. The voice intoned once more.

"You dare this affront to Pope Urban II[i]. He knows how to deal with devils like you! You should have left with your kind when the city was retaken. We could make an example of you, only there's a special demand from Rome. His Holiness will deal with you himself. That's your reward for muddying the New Testament, for trying to overturn one thousand years of God's Truth."

"He is a heretic!" shouted a second voice, "a sorcerer. He reads fortune!"

---

[i] Born in France 1042 as Otho of Lagery, was Pope from 1088 to end of July 1099. He launched the first crusade to retake Jerusalem, he died 14 days after the first crusade was in control of Jerusalem.

A female joined in. "The Pontiff will make a Christian of you or you'll go to hell!"

"Indeed," assured the first male. "Beg Jesus to save your soul, heretic!" Salin coughed and sputtered as the man continued. "Array him with irons and then to the docks. He's bound for Rome, and no sorcerer's tricks as he goes."

Cocunut Grove, Florida

Sydney's head cleared with him back in Coconut Grove, in his protected surroundings. He felt his heart pound, awoke to the steam now fogging the mirror. He closed the faucet and wiped the glass clear. He gasped at his reflection; at blood coming from a nostril. He lifted a forearm, avoiding his own eyes as he reached for a tissue to clean the blood. A moment later he was at the edge of his new bed, trying to still his heart.

As he sat the wooden floors creaked—someone was approaching. Sydney scrambled under the bed, not sure why but feeling the need for stealth. His door opened to unknown feet. Sydney felt himself struggling with something familiar—old ghosts claiming his memory.

Vatican Underground Prison
1093 C.E.

A nearly-spent candle broke the dungeon's darkness. Salin crouched under a different bed as yet another door squeaked open on rusted hinges, announcing the arrival of his host. A brighter candle lit the room.

A voice huffed. "The sorcerer. He's gone."

"He must have vanished from us to his false gods," said a second man.

The first man laughed. "Get out from under the bed Salin. Your kind of sorcery is no good here in the Vatican."

Coconut Grove, Florida

"Sydney, what are you *doin'* down there? Are you playing hide and seek? I brought some fresh towels."

Sydney regained his senses, recognizing Luis' Cuban accent. The dungeon fell away, leaving only his new dwelling.

"Hello Luis. Just looking for my battery here. I dropped it earlier while unpacking. Let me get out of here."

"*Me and Carmen* can't go to the funeral, but *we very sorry.*"

"Don't concern yourself, please. I thank you and Carmen for making me feel at home."

"If you need *somesing* just let me know."

"Yeah, maybe you could help me. I need a bowl."

"*I go* to kitchen and *bring you bowl.*"

"It would be better if it was a big bowl."

"How big is the bowl?"

"Just large enough to give a dog a bath."

"How big is the dog? I didn't see any dogs with you."

"Don't worry about it. I'll look around and I'll find something."

"Okay then. Dinner will be ready soon."

"Thank you Luis."

Sydney went right back to his room after dinner, using his black board to summarize what he could. With the aid of his laptop he began to create a timeline for all the events that had occurred so far. On the left, according to the previous conversation with his dad he began a line from left to right. At the end of that line and under it he wrote "Today April 2nd, 2001 USA" and at the beginning and again under the line he wrote "Six month B.C. JUDEA" In the middle he wrote year "1088/1099 P. Urban II, Constantinople/Rome," dates which Sydney retrieved from the Encyclopedia from Paul Stein's Library downstairs. Above the lines he wrote the names of Elijah and Luke Jeremiah at the beginning, over the Pope's timeline and name he wrote Salin. Respectively, he wrote "Early 1900's England/Vienna/England" and above he wrote "Peter Nielsen." Another nugget to the right he wrote "1920/2001 Bonn-GER/USA" and above he crested an "H." for his late teacher. The next entry was "72 Sydney-AU/USA" and above he wrote "S.T." as an abbreviation to his own name.

Sydney stepped back, stared at his timeline in hopes of making sense of the stories that he'd heard and the visions that he'd had so far. "There must be a pattern, a connection," he thought. He dimmed the ceiling light then gazed again at the black board, this time lit only by the bathroom light. Fatigue and Carmen's cooking were overpowering his rationale. It seemed a good idea to think about it while resting his head on the pillow.

Vatican Underground Prison
1093 C.E.

"Salin, relax. I am your only friend here," said yet another voice. "It is me, old friend, Nicholas. You know me so well. Father Nicholas, the Vatican librarian to the pontiff himself. Men of our stage in life should have no barriers. You have passed your fifty years and five, as have I, and you know of this life as I do. We are brothers. Relax."

Salin remained silent.

"We don't need to use torture anymore..." concluded Nicholas.

Salin interrupted and said, "What else do you want to know? I've told you everything."

"As I said, torture is for the low-minded. We are both scholars. I am going to let you in a little secret. I know as much astrology as you do, if not more. I have in my charge and keep the best and largest library in the world. Yes, there was that quite unfortunate, tragic accident in Alexandria's Museum, but that was so many years ago, was it not? Only two centuries after our Messiah. And so much lost...500,000 scrolls. By this twist of fate the Holy City boasts the best source of man's knowledge. I am working on a private edition right now. This one I call "The Millennium Life of Salin" I could no longer let Father Sergious, my assistant, join me. In fact, he had the most untimely, mortal accident the other day. He began to speak of our interviews, his tongue unguided. Then the sudden illness, a hastened demise and death. Poor Sergious."

Salin remained silent, sitting in a chair, his hands bound in the arm rest.

"You see, Salin, what keeps you alive is my need to finish my private book."

"You should have killed me already. I've told you everything by now."

"You are going to tell me your story again and if you miss one detail, then we are going to take you back to your least favorite room. Your purgatory, to relieve you of your sins. Now, what of Judas Iscariot, his life?"

"Like I've said, Judas saw himself as the only intellectual amongst them, the disciples. When I met him he'd always set himself apart from them, and even years later, after the death of Jesus. He spun into a melancholy, his heart heavy because the others did not want him to preach. Judas hailed himself an erudite and the only student of the Torah, other than Jesus. The rest were fishermen, laborers, commoners and one ex-tax collector. He told us, Luke and I, that everyone else had a wrong understanding for starters. The entire group felt impelled to attach the Jewish tradition to the Bible. Judas mentioned that the teachings of Jesus stood alone even though Matthew began to preach about heaven and hell since these were the values that were familiar to most, from Greece, Zeus' Olympus and Hades' underground."

"Do not stop." Said Nicholas, "Do not preoccupy yourself with me taking notes."

Salin continued, "Judas had many complaints. Utmost was his worry that a new sect was being formed from all the influences of the area and times. For instance, very soon the image of Madonna and baby Jesus were being cast from the same famous forms that were made for goddess Isis and baby Horus in her lap, from the Delta, in Egypt. Then the idea of heaven and hell that Matthew propounded. And there was more. Jewish holidays were weaved into Jesus' Message instead of having Christianity stand alone." Salin sighed, letting his head roll back as he closed his eyes. "Judas also told me that he was not a man of need, he never needed the money for Jesus. He was betrayed himself, by the people who told him that they wanted to debate Jesus. When the Sanhedrin[i] persuaded him to inform where Jesus was, he was convinced that Jesus was going to be able to overcome them all in a debate. When Jesus looked in his eyes and said *That thou doest, do quickly*[ii]. Judas believed Caiaphus and Annas would be defeated, by the Christ's truth.

---

[i] The Sanhedrin in Hebrew meaning is sitting together or assembly is the council of Jewish sages who constituted the supreme court and legislative body of Ancient Israel.

[ii] John 13:27

"Jesus had very powerful command in his words. For instance, when he told Peter to deny Him three times, it's mentioned in the book of Matthew *That this night, before the cock crow, thou shalt deny me thrice[i]*, Peter was not afraid of dying. There is an inference of guilt that Peter was afraid. Peter understood if he was to get caught, then he could not spread the gospel and his experience with Jesus." Salin paused and asked a question, "Why has the Bible been changed throughout the centuries?"

"You do not ask the questions here but since we are both scholars I am going to let you in a secret." Nicholas got up and walked to the door. When he heard the guards talking outside he came back and sat down. "We do it for the good of the church. People are simple. They don't need complicated laws for the spiritual world. We keep God simple for them so they can go about their lives and worry about something else. We, the clergy are equipped to analyze God. To theosophy if you will. We make the decisions. We know what is good. Dogma simplifies all of the answers."

"Couldn't you let people find their own answers? Why do you have to control everything?"

"Kings and generals think that the power lies at the end of the sword. They think the power lies at the strength of the army. The merchants think that the power lies on being the only provider of a certain good, on the monopoly of the good. But I tell you this; the power rests with he, who controls knowledge, with the writer and keeper of books... The power to control kings, generals and merchants alike, the power to control the world lies in the keeper of the library. For the good of the Church, I your humble servant Nicholas, am polishing and simplifying the message of Jesus."

---

[i] Matthew 26:34

"For the good cause of the Church?" asked Salin distrustfully.

"Yes brother Salin, for the good cause of the Church," repeated father Nicholas, "You see? Weapons and soldiers can only hold a region or a parcel of land for a while; and it is very uneconomical. Yet rephrasing the Bible, *we* can control a continent forever."

"Don't you feel like you are monopolizing God just like a merchant monopolizing his goods?"

"Let me ponder that. The thought had not occurred to me." Nicholas picked up his quill and inked it. "Salin, now we discuss your future. How, where, when will you be found in your next life? Does Mahud know where you are going to be?"

"We were working on the calculation of my next birth when I was taken from Constantinople."

"Why do you want to be found?" asked Nicholas, very academically.

"We want to be able to meet Jesus again."

"But, for the good cause of the Church, of course, I don't think you should. Besides, don't you think if Jesus came back He would descend from the sky, right into our realm? He would return to the people who understand Him, the people who prepare the world for his message."

Salin remained silent.

"It's wrong," said Nicholas, "to try denying our power. We are doing the work for Jesus and, as far as the Jews are concerned, I will take care of them. They will pay for what they did to Jesus."

A sudden thumping at the door interrupted them. Salin and Nicholas both turned to the dungeon's door.

Coconut Grove, Florida

A sudden thumping at the door roused Sydney. He sat up, aware at that moment he'd fallen asleep, fully clothed, while staring at the blackboard.

"One second, I'm coming. Who's there?"

"It's Carmen."

Sydney opened the door. Carmen glanced at him, frowned at his clothing, and then looked past him to the bed already made. "Have you been up long?"

Sydney brushed on his shirt absently. "No. I just woke up. Maybe I was too tired; fell asleep with my clothes on." He wiped his eyes. "What did you put in that food?"

"Nothing special, but I guess you never had a good Cuban dish made for you. Next time go easy on the seconds."

"Thanks for the tip. Is breakfast Cuban, too?"

"Why spoil the surprise, and the appetite? Freshen up and come down."

"I will be there in a few minutes."

As Sydney entered the kitchen, Lieutenant Jason of the Miami Dade Police sat having breakfast with Luis. Carmen attended her pots and pans.

"Good Morning Jason," said Sydney as he sat. "I thought my case was out of your hands now?"

The lieutenant sipped his coffee. "Technically it is, only, I'm here organizing the details for the funeral. We do the ground work, the Feds take the credit. Today, for example, there'll be so many celebrities around, that the mayor himself has put me on the case. Our presence here will mainly be in uniform but we will have a few plainclothes as well, maybe as many as ten."

Sydney felt his surroundings shift. Jason now sat in Roman garb, a gladiator's sword in hand. Before Sydney could rationalize the sudden change, Jason morphed back into his MDPD[i] uniform. Sydney lost his sense of balance and gagged on the coffee.

Jason stood quickly, extending a hand to Sydney. "You okay?"

Sydney cleared his throat and noticed Carmen staring at him. "I'm better now… Burke, your last name is English, right?

"Yeah."

"Do you have any Italian in you?"

"Actually, my mother's side is from Italy. I also speak Italian because I was part of the student exchange program while in high-school. What makes you say that?"

"Your profile. Must be it… I bet in Italy they took you for a local." Sydney lied to avoid explaining his visions.

"As a matter of fact they did."

---

[i] Miami Dade Police Department.

𓀮𓈖𓏤𓆑𓈖~~~𓆓𓈖𓊪𓏏 𓂝𓆑 ~~~𓆑𓂝 𓉐𓈖𓊪
𓆓𓏏𓂻𓆑𓂿𓆑𓋴𓊪𓏏 𓂺𓂝 𓏭𓈖𓇓𓆑𓈖~~~𓆓𓈖𓊪𓏏 𓂝𓆑

X
Capitulus Decem

*M*iami, the business capital of Latin America, favorite spot to low budget movie producers and political scandals, and an unorthodox climate. Hot and humid, gloomy, stormy, clear and sunny — a weather prediction for just one day. This April afternoon brought the usual tropical storm for the day, then turned sunny and clear again. The church at Devon Road near the Main Highway was a walking distance from Sydney's temporary home. The church was a combination of traditional architecture and the use of the natural, coral rock of Florida. Part of the entrance and most of the walls were draped with vines and bougainvilleas. There were garden grounds adjacent to both sides. The abnormal influx of cars flooded the lots and the adjacent streets. That section of Coconut Grove had a continued canopy provided by the large fichus and banyan trees.

Inside the Church, at the altar, a large picture of Horace was mounted on a stand. In it, Horace smiled at those coming to honor him one last time. The mass was Christian but non-denominational—an attempt to accommodate friends, clients and guests of all faith. During the sharing, guests took turns to speak of their experience and friendship.

Finally, a deacon nodded to Sydney. Sydney reached for index cards, scribed with reminders of his main points.

"My teacher, brother, father and best friend is no longer among us. He touched us all with his teachings, his advice, and most of all, his friendship. Now he lives through us in our memories, and in the way that he touched our lives. Years and years ago, before I became an astrologer myself, he would allow me in, during the reading consultations so I could understand the purpose of his work. One of the times that he touched me with his talk was when he was giving advice to a person recently separated. It was beyond this person's ability to do anything about it, and he said, 'We all come here to form a spiritual family through which we can learn and teach. When the lesson is over, we move on to create a new family.' His words are with me more than ever today, with my feeling that he has left us to be part of a new spiritual family. I don't think I have learned nearly all he had to offer. If I was one occupied by belief in 'perpetual death' today would have been a day of extreme sorrow. Today, for most of us, especially for myself, we are experiencing a celebration of the life of a friend who has left on vacation until he comes back again with a new name and a new look. I am going to meet him again and so will all of you, either before or after we take our own vacation breaks. Once again, thanks to all of you for coming to Roberto and Olive's wake a couple of days ago. Our sorrows and sympathy will be with them as well. They were special friends and part of our spiritual family. Thank you, from the bottom of my heart for being here today."

As Sydney left the podium, the deacon made an announcement. "Thank you for coming. We have refreshments in our garden. Please join us if you want to continue to celebrate the lives of Horace, Olive and Roberto. May God bless."

Sydney's reminiscences with his many friends and clients evoked a certain sadness for him, but he also knew it to be a part of life though it wasn't an everyday occurrence. As he visited he noticed a young woman, seemingly in her early twenties, regularly glancing at him from a distance. As the reception ebbed she approached him with her right hand extended.

"Mr. Tobias, my name is Stephanie."

"Call me Sydney, please."

"I never met your professor. I came for my Aunt Lilith, an old friend of your father's. She couldn't make the trip." Stephanie handed Sydney a business card. "She says she's available to you in case you need some hard-to-find help."

Sydney read the business card *Lilith R. Black, psychic and advisor, Encinitas, CA.* He read the phone number and a P.O. Box.

"I think this has come at a very good time. Can I see her next week?" asked Sydney.

"Drop in any time you want." Stephanie pointed to the card. "She'll know you're coming."

Sydney smiled.

North Bay Village, Florida
One Week Later

"If you're just tuning in, welcome to our radio show, *Shawn Hennessey Live* coast to coast. Thanks to our sponsors, and folks please support your local sponsors. Now, before I cover some of the topics of the second part of our show today, you regular listeners already know that I," he said, dragging out the "I" as if it was a word that had three syllables, "am a stickler for the truth. I'm sorry if this topic offends some of our listeners, but today we have an astrologer with us. I know that many of you, the 'agree-heads' as you like to call yourselves, are already rushing to your phones. But just hold on. Not yet. We'll be right back after these announcements.

"We are back, and I am welcoming our guest "Sydney Tobias, author of many books including the one I have in my hands called '*Letters to Myself.*' Mr. Tobias joins us live from our studio in Miami Beach, Florida. Hello Sydney and welcome to our show."

"Thank you Shawn for having me."

"You are certainly a very courageous person because our listeners know that we have a hog-wash detector."

"I've heard your show a few times and I am certain that you are familiar with hog-wash."

A little dead silence was heard over the air and the announcer continued, "So Sydney tell us about your book."

"First, I want to thank you Shawn for being open-minded and having me on your show." Sydney was interrupted.

"Here at Shawn Hennessey Live, we see ourselves as the most open-minded people."

"At first, at the insistence of my publishers, I did not think that my book was channeled to your audience but perhaps I was wrong and it can help your listeners as well. The book teaches how to create a guideline for a letter to yourself or someone other than you."

"But the book is named *Letters to Myself.*"

"The book is named *Letters to Myself* because following these exercises one could eventually leave himself or herself notes from a previous life and benefit from it. Usually..."

Sydney was interrupted by sounds of pigs feeding at a trough from a recorded tape.

"I'm sorry Sydney, the hog-wash detector was activated so we have to have Amazing Dr. John, former magician and skeptic at heart join our conversation."

"Thank you Shawn, and I'm glad to be back."

"Doctor John, the hog-wash detector was activated, so what do you have to say?"

"A lot of voodoo doctors come around and start forming new religions and new rules for Heaven and Earth. Beware of false gods. There has never been any proof that astrology has a basis in reality and most of the time astrologers are more post-dictors than predictors. How can the stars, millions of millions of miles away, have any influence on people?"

As Dr. John debated, Sydney started scribbling four responses in a note pad.

"It's your turn Sydney;" Shawn said.

"I have three points to cover. First, I would like to ask. In what subject does Doctor John holds a Ph.D.?"

"People call me doctor. I don't call myself doctor. They call me doctor because I am meticulous and the stuff I say makes sense."

"Very well, in that case I will address you as John and you will address me as Doctor Tobias because unlike you I hold a Ph.D. in psychology and a minor in philosophy. My next point is that I agree with John. There has never been any proof that astrology works and it is easier to make post-diction than prediction."

"Ladies and gentlemen, this is too much! I want to hear more of what Dr. Tobias has to say."

"I am one of the few astrologers who'll tell you the daily horoscopes give astrology a bad name. There are more than twelve possibilities to anyone's affairs on any given day. But, for many of my colleagues, the money is good and hard to turn down. Astrology to me is not a science of prediction. Astrology is a science through which one can learn about his own nature. I am also one of the few astrologers that I know who love the fact that astrology is not mainstream one hundred percent, because if it were then it would also become a very powerful institution. Can you imagine a person being taken to jail for his astrological tendencies of committing crimes in the future or home loans denied because, with some people's charts there is a tendency to be extravagant with money, like Jupiter in the Second House? The astrological chart could be tied to everyone's credit report. It's a beautiful thing that astrology is not a powerful institution. I've never heard of two different schools of astrology engaged in a full-pledged war dragging with them thousands of lives.

"My last point is that astrology could have nothing to do with the stars. In ancient times, the oracles and wise men observed the animal behavior of people and from that observation it gave birth to the constellations in the sky. Think about it. Could the constellations in the sky give shape to anything other than Greek gods?"

"Of course it could. It could give shape to anything," said John.

"If you have a Ph.D. in psychology, what makes you follow astrology?" Shawn asked.

"The archetypes of astrology and psychology came from the same place, Greek Mythology. In ancient times they did not have Freud or Jung, they had the Greek gods through which they tried to understand their own nature. The ancients knew of the Oedipus complex[i] to create a myth and today it is in our psychology. But astrology is absorbed into your language too."

"Give one example," asked Shawn.

"I'll give you more than one. Lunatic, the bull market, I got the flu."

Shawn interrupted. "The bull market is not an ancient phenomenon. How can you say it is astrological?"

---

[i] The Oedipus complex is a term coined by Sigmund Freud to clarify the basis of certain neuroses in childhood. It's based on the Greek myth of Oedipus, who accidentally killed his father Laius and married his mother Jocasta.

"I agree the market as we know it is a recent phenomena, traceable only to Adam Smith's guidelines for our economy published in 1776, *The Wealth of the Nations*. But, by coincidence, Taurus the bull rules finances in our lives and money and wealth."

"Amazing!" said John. "I'm a Taurus. How come I'm not rich? How do you explain that?"

"Usually, I'd get a fee to answer that. But another aspect of bull, what's sometimes referred to as tenacity, is also known as stubbornness. This means that I will never change your mind and I would not even try."

"You are darn right."

"When it comes to mounting, let me mount a horse instead of a bull. One is up for a rough ride when arguing with a Taurus. See, these animalistic archetypes are called the zoo or zodiac."

"Speaking of fees, I heard that you have some very wealthy clients. What can you tell us about that?" Shawn asked Sydney.

"Nothing."

"If he has very wealthy clients," said John, "how come he's not playing the lotto and becoming a billionaire himself playing the market?"

"Your answer, Dr. Tobias."

"My answer is that with this premise of thinking, a doctor should never get sick, a mechanic would never have car problems and a surgeon should diagnose and operate himself. I will protect my client's confidentiality even when they are doctors in psychiatry or psychology. A doctor friend of mine practicing psychology sometimes can't find answers to his mood, and he calls me to check and see if he is going through a planetary transit, to see if he can ride it out or needs to take medication. There is an old saying in astrology that goes like this. 'Millionaires don't hire astrologers but billionaires do.' I saw on a documentary that JP

Morgan and Vanderbilt used to have astrologers on their staff. The calling of a teacher is to teach. The calling of a doctor is to heal. A mechanic has to fix, and an astrologer is not to play the lotto or the stock market. The calling of an astrologer is to guide oneself or the people around him to the influences and timing of the Universe."

Shawn coughed. "It was really interesting what you said sometime ago, that astrology is not mainstream. Do you get a lot of heat from other astrologers for saying things like that?"

"Astrology in ancient times used to be taught only to the initiated, and it was passed on and kept alive through the teacher and apprentice's relationship. Today, one can go to any supermarket and book store and read up on what their influences are. Astrology is not an organized religion. I don't answer to headquarters in the Vatican, Salt Lake City or Mecca. It is time and history that filters out the bad astrologers, because people realize that the substance that one astrologer is teaching, either makes or does not make sense in their own experience."

"There you have it folks," said Shawn. "This was astrologer, author and as we just learned today, doctor, Sydney Tobias, telling us about his new book, '*Letters to Myself*' and he was able to pass the hog-wash detector; a rare occurrence on our show."

"Thanks for having me on your show. I hope to hear your hog-wash detector whenever someone calls our friend John a doctor."

Sydney was listening to what was supposed to be a live broadcast. Instead, he was actually listening to his own show recorded a day earlier. From inside the van parked across the street in stealth mode he heard the show unedited for most of the recording except for his last phrase. Nationwide, the listeners heard the ending like this:

"Thanks for having me on your show."

"You are listening to 'Shawn Hennessey Live' coast to coast radio show and we are going to be right back after we pay some bills. Stay tuned."

The radio show went into a commercial mode. Agent Torres, sitting behind the wheel, shut it off. The other front seat was occupied by his superior, Rick Sarturo, an agent as yet unfamiliar to Sydney. Sydney was sitting in the back seat of the van, monitoring all the people in and out of the studio. A few minutes later, agent Swanson disguised as Sydney, getting into Horace's old Lincoln, currently being used by Sydney.

"Dennis the Maniacal is now leaving the studio and heading east on the causeway to Miami Beach in a white Lincoln." The two-way transmission was interrupted by a soft squelch.

"Stay put," Torres grumbled into his mike. "See if he picks up a tail."

"Already has. Grey Sunfire coupe."

"Proceed with caution. We'll follow you and switch later."

The unknown caravan proceeded east. The causeway suspended over the water crossed North Bay Village and eventually died at Collins Avenue. Dennis had made a right turn that was also a short cut to South beach; he took Indian Creek Road. It was a nice drive with sporadic views of the water channels and the intercoastal waterways. Sydney noticed that they had followed most of Collins Avenue, and he wondered if Dennis was going to take the MacArthur Causeway back to the mainland.

The two-way crackled again. "Dennis has stopped by the Crabs' restaurant. The Sunfire coupe is illegally in the fire lane across the street. I am going to continue to drive by and get a description of the driver… Stand by…" A squelch was heard. "Caucasian brunette female, petite, must be about thirty."

"Do you have fans?" asked agent Torres as he found a place to park and monitor the stalker's movement.

Sydney shook his head. "Not that I know of."

"Bob, the Sunfire is moving. Stay with Dennis. Check for a second tail."

The trio in the van resumed their stealth chase. The Sunfire took MacArthur causeway and moved west towards downtown.

"We don't have probable cause to stop this car anymore," said Torres. "What should we do?"

"Check to see if we can get a black and white on the radio," said Sarturo. "Stop her for routine traffic. See if we could get something out of her."

A few minutes later a Miami Dade Police Department green and white Chevy Caprice was gaining speed on the Sunfire; pulled it over using its red and blue lights. The van slowed as it passed, with all three men trying to case the girl. Even behind her sunglasses she showed annoyance.

"We will get a report from the police officer in half an hour if he doesn't book her." Bill looked at Rick and glanced at Sydney.

"Maybe she'll get a ticket," Sarturo chuckled. He glanced back at Sydney. "A little souvenir from Miami."

"What makes you think," Sydney asked, "that she's from out of town?"

"Sunfires are usually economy cars, used by major rentals. That car's not even a year old, and she's got Florida plates but no county…just 'Sunshine State.' Rental written all over it."

One hour later Bill and Rick caught up with Dennis at their office. Sydney was there but anxious to go back to his calculations and writing.

"So how much did you charge the account?" Torres asked Swanson.

"I just had a few snow crabs. I did not want to look suspicious and leave immediately."

"You could have used the bathroom and had a soda," said Torres.

Police officer, Delgado, came in and joined the group. He saluted everyone then began talking to Torres. They were old acquaintances. The others listened in.

"The subject's name is Lourdes Cler Clement. Naturalized, born in Canada. Her first time in Miami. Says she's here on vacation from her job in Chicago."

Torres narrowed his brow at the officer. "That can't be it now, Delgado. Anything else?"

"I also asked how her vacation was so far, and she told me that she thought that she'd seen saw an actor from that movie with the Dinosaurs. Can't remember the name. Anyway, said since she had no particular place to go, she followed him for a while."

Sarturo broke in. "How did you find out that she was following someone?"

Delgado smiled. "People are more afraid of my pen than my gun. When they see me with my ticket pad, they start telling me their life history as much as they can to get out of a ticket. Usually the way they think is like this; now that you know me that much, you are my friend and you shouldn't give me a ticket."

"Single? Profession? Kids?" asked Dennis.

"Single, no kids, and a librarian."

Sydney felt a cold chill descend his spine, followed by a squirt of adrenaline in his stomach giving him a sensation of discomfort. Could he tell these agents? Would he be ridiculed for trying to be killed by a librarian or a member of the PTA? Could this be a coincidence or a person with a mission after him? He was ready to face his first assailant, but things now had become mysterious. He needed to protect himself.

"Thank you Chris," said Rick Sarturo.

"Don't mention it." Christopher Delgado shook Torres' hand and left the room unceremoniously.

"So what do we have here? No attempt on your life during the funeral, and this time you are being followed by a lonely girl from Chicago that thought you were someone else," said Torres.

"I don't know what to say for Marcelo, Roberto, Olive and my dad; they are dead in less than one year," said Sydney, "Why do we all have to be killed right now?"

"What kind of enemies do you have?"

"I wish I knew the answer to that."

"How about your father? Did he have any enemies?" asked Rick Sarturo.

Keeping most of his data secret Sydney said, "He mentioned that there used to be a nemesis of his but no names or location. The only thing I know is that the guy used to be a librarian."

"In our job there is no such thing as coincidences. Dennis, see if you can reach Chris and ask him to get a report of everything that we can find on that girl. Then follow up and see what you find," ordered Agent Rick.

"Right on." Dennis hopped off the desktop and left the room.

"It's time to go home," said Sarturo. "Give me a few minutes I'll be right back."

Sydney found himself alone in the room. He could hear some of the muted conversation down the hall.

"Man, not today. Can't I have today off? The Heat's playing the Wizards, guy, playoffs on the line. And you want me to dog-sit this voodoo doctor." It sounded like Torres.

"Your turn. You should do it like me—the VCR's always ready to go. When I get home I can see what happened. I kind of like it. I don't know who won, and I can fast forward the commercials." It sounded like Dennis.

Sydney thought, *Voodoo doctor, followed by a librarian in Miami, Pope Urban II, torture chambers, Russian plastic explosives. What is the commonality?* He needed his charts, his laptop and a place to hide for a while. Hopefully he had it.

Rick Sarturo came back and said holding a padded large envelope, "Sydney, most of the stuff in your house has been burned down. What wasn't destroyed was damaged by water, but, miraculously the contents of this box made it. We put them in this envelope for safe keeping. All yours now."

Sydney examined the envelope—it wasn't much. Only three items: a picture of himself and Horace and another one of Horace, Olive and her dog. The wooden frames had signs of the scorch. In the bottom of the envelope was an old notepad, very old, protected by leather padded covers. Sydney examined the pages. Most were written with fountain pen, mainly numbers. Sydney noticed that instead of years and month and date, the notebook had the Julian calendars counted in days. Unlike the first book, this one had references to the previous two millenniums.

"How did this notebook survive the explosion, the fire and the water damage?" asked Sydney.

"I was there when the demolition crew was cleaning up the place. The book wasn't inside the safe but under it. When it was blown open, the bottom stayed intact. In fact, I think the blast pushed the safe into the slab protecting the book from the fire on the sides. Is this book a good thing for you?"

"It is yet to be seen. I could compare it to my notes and check to see if these calculations and data are still good for something."

Sydney stared briefly at the photos then placed them back into the envelope and left the room with Rick. Dennis and Bill were outside the room, comparing notes.

"What do you guys have there?"

"This could be interesting or it could be a mistake," Torres said, taking the page away from Dennis and handing it to Rick.

"What do we have here?" Rick started to scan the page. "So this looks good. She is a librarian, lives in Chicago."

"The problem sir, is her age." Dennis pointed to the part of the page where it showed the place of birth. "Officer Delgado said that she was in her late twenties, but according to this sheet she's 97."

"Did you double check this information?" asked Rick.

"Yes," Dennis nodded. "I pulled her social out of the driving records. Confirms she's 97. Either we all would like her plastic surgeon, or she stole someone else's identity."

Rick turned to Torres. "You stay with Dennis tonight. I'll double this watch until we can solve the problem on this chick." He shook the data sheet. "Can I keep this?"

"I'll print another one from my computer," said Dennis, "and include it in my report."

Torres grimaced. "I had plans for the game tonight."

"Here is the run-down. Four people are killed in less than one year. Sydney said that the only enemy his father had was a librarian. The girl tracking Dennis down happens to be a librarian, and now she is also three years shy of being a centenarian," a brief pause, "You have a VCR, don't you?"

"Yes," Torres said giving a glance to Dennis.

Sydney was back at one of Paul Stein's winter homes, in Coconut Grove, and happy to note that the sunsets were getting later. Spring brought the ever vital force back to everyone's lives, but in Miami it's really hard to read the seasons since everything is green all year round.

Bill Torres licked his lips. "Carmen, this was divine! I never ate a paella this good."

"Luis, now I know why you carry an old spare tire. Carmen is a real terrific cook. Don't believe everything that Bill says. His last paella is his best paella," Dennis said.

Sydney smiled, pleased that Dennis and Bill had found a better mood, even though they'd been taken away from their basketball game. "Carmen, I agree with Bill. This is divine. You have given me a new respect for Cuban cooking." Sydney pushed away from the table.

"Of course it's good food," Carmen said, arranging her pots and pans, "did you ever see a skinny Cuban? I don't *sink* so," she chimed, affecting a thicker Cuban accent. She turned suddenly, noticing Sydney leaving. "Not so fast. Sit back down. You haven't eaten dessert."

"What's for dessert Carmen?" asked Luis.

"Flan."

"Sydney. You better sit down. The flan is very good."

Carmen later followed the flan with espresso.

"This is very good, thank you Carmen. I'll be in my room." Sydney left the table and noticed a smile on Bill's face for the first time. *Yes, Dennis was right; Bill was a different person with paella on the plate.*

Sydney was back in his room, enjoying a cool breeze caressing the evening. He left his upstairs windows open, giving him command of the house's front yard and drive circle. As he stood looking out, he heard the murmur of voices below.

"Our evening was spoiled because of this voodoo guy and a librarian," said Torres caressing his stomach, as if he was a king after the feast.

"Can you keep a secret?" asked Dennis.

"What is it?" Torres noticed that Dennis was pulling out a small flat portable TV set from his breast pocket and showing it to him. "Secret? What secret? I don't see anything."

"Let me patrol the grounds here, and I'll be right back in time for the game."

"Hurry up, starts at 7 PM," said Torres.

XI
Capitulus Undecim

Sydney was content that things fell into place and he was not the antagonist of a fun evening. He retired to his room. He opened the book and, using his calculator, started to make more notes to correlate with his data and bring all this information up to date. In one of the notes he found the name Lucia and more dates and numbers. Sydney murmured the name Lucia; he needed to know more about her. He leafed through the pages, found more numbers with her name next to them. Some of the entries were separated by forty thousand days. He made a conversion using his calculator and realized the length of time.

"Man… This is more than, wait… this is close to one hundred and nine years." Sydney put his calculator down on top of his bed and wondered if he could try an experiment.

Back to his book, he continued to look for the names and numbers. He recognized the astrological symbols and three other sets of names. Some of the names had the initial "E" hyphenated to them, some had "L", and some numbers had "JC+?" (cross) initials, no name, and question marks. There were three distinct columns: the first, he realized, was for Julian or precise dates, the second for latitude and longitude, and the third column had the planets' symbols, the main conjunction and inference to each other.

He walked into his bathroom and decided to try something with more control. He opened the cold tap and let it run—not too much this time but audible enough. The light of the bathroom was dimmed, but he could still see his face. He looked at his left eye with concentration and started saying and repeating the name, "Lucia, Lucia, Lucia…"

Vatican Underground Prison
1093 C.E.

Sydney felt a mixed thrill of excitement and fear in this new experience taking place again. The room darkened. He recognized his surroundings; he was Salin again. He felt he was older than his last vision. He had a sense that he was ready to welcome death, but a sense of righteousness couldn't allow him to take his own life. To succumb to this act of desperation, to take one's own life, would disrupt nature, the stars and, consequently, the link. The dungeon door opened, but he didn't move away from his spot near his bed. There he stood. A nun had entered his room; a woman a few years his junior, yet a mature lady. She had a lot of vitality in her.

"Here is your food Salin. May Lord Jesus be with you."

"Thanks for the food sister. Are you ordained? I've never seen you before."

"No, I am not ordained. I am just doing my part to help the sisters. They let me wear the habit to insure protection in this area of the Vatican."

"This is a nice meal, better than the ones I had before. I had meals like this taken from me. Perhaps this one too, will be stolen by the guards."

"Start eating. Once you touch the whole plate they will let you have it. That's why I am still standing here." She noticed her privacy compromised by a guard looking through the door's windows.

Salin began to gobble up the food from his plate with a wooden spoon. "This is good." As he continued to eat he noticed that she held a small leathered pouch, no bigger than her thumb. She handed it to him.

"Hide this in your mouth when they take you away from here tomorrow."

"What is this for?"

"It is to take away the pain, when they take you to the pyre. The church is going to burn you at the public square, as an example to others who want to follow sorcery like yours."

"Finally! I'll be free from this dungeon..." Salin put down the spoon. "What is your name?"

"It's better for me if you don't know it. But, I know that your name is Elijah, and Mahud, and your old friend Luke is alive and well and outside the grasp of Nicholas. It's time to go now."

She rapped on the door with the guard responding.

"Blasphemer," she said with a hiss though, with her back to the guard. Her face hidden from him, she smiled at Salin. "Change your ways. Let Jesus into your heart or burn in hell!"

Salin continued to eat, but he couldn't stop a tear trickling down his cheek. Luke had escaped, and his own persecution would soon come to an end.

A guard roused him the next morning, ordering him to get up to leave the cell. His old vision betrayed him—he couldn't find the pouch. He ran his hands frantically over the bed, to no avail. The guard then stooped, picked up the pouch off the floor.

"Do you search for this, old man?"

"Yes, thank you. Can I have it?"

"Not so fast," snapped a second guard, standing at the door. He inspected the pouch. "Who brought him food last night?"

"Who brought you food last night, blasphemer?"

"I don't know. She didn't tell me her name."

"We can find out," the second guard grinned. "Take him away. Today the rabble will witness what happens to people like you."

With old Salin too weak for shackles, they used a rope to bind him to the linked procession exiting the prison. As they neared Rome's outskirts, he saw the pole and small platform and it impressed him—his life would end soon. He was lifted to the platform by the very rope that held him bound. His arms were now raised above his head, holding him in place. Wood and old ragged clothes were being gathered around the base.

A voice shouted out. "Not yet! One more blasphemer is joining him."

As a small band approached the neighboring platform, Salin recognized the woman who'd served him the night before. Her habit was gone. She had long hair streaked black and gray, and wore the garments of a gypsy and fortune teller. People gathered around the square. In the distance he made out the form of Nicholas, but now in a more modest, clerical attire.

Salin's brow furrowed. "Why do they bring you here?"

The woman remained silent, waiting for her executioners to move away.

"I'm sorry to say I lost your gift from last night. Perhaps now you can tell me your name."

"My name is Lucia."

"How do you know of Luke and I?"

"I have my ways, my visions, and my gifts."

115

Salin tried to re-position his hands, hoping to loosen the taut ropes for more circulation. "Why did you come to see me yesternight?"

"It is because of a promise I made to you more than one-thousand years ago while in Delphi. I would be back in your life during your time of need."

"If you have visions, didn't you see that you would end up here with me?"

"I think I did, because I knew I would."

"The fire is getting high. I think it has burned off the rope around my waist."

"Then come over here."

Salin moved his torso. He was now face to face with Lucia. The nearness shook his memory, reacquainted him with her eyes. "It's you!"

She pursued his lips, offering Salin a kiss. He responded, and was surprised to feel a liquid flowing from her mouth to his, its taste bitter, and yet sweet. Within seconds he felt numbness and the heat of the fire falling away. But he couldn't be sure if he was responding to the potion; perhaps her kiss, or her love, giving up her life to numb his pain. In spite of his predicament, he felt his heart growing in ecstasy, recalling a love of a thousand years ago and a promise coming to fruition.

Coconyut Grove, Florida

Awakening from his vision, Sydney found himself sitting on the floor of the bathroom, the water still running in the sink. He struggled up, moved to the window. The agents' car sat parked in the same place, the small TV glowing in the car's darkness. Beyond them the gate was closed. Sydney went back to the bathroom, turned on all the lights. Sydney came to the conclusion that it was better to accumulate as much as he could from all Horace's stories. Better yet, the description given to him by young Luke, two thousand years ago, would be enough to bring him back to his old memories. Perhaps he would remember more of it in the process and adapt. He knew it was neither the running water nor the mirror, yet there was some essence of a kind of energy responsible for the deed.

Lost in thought, and reminiscing on his first encounter with Lucia, Sydney realized it was time to act. He set his alarm for 4:30 AM; an early start to find the bowl, candles, incense, all to create a mood for meditation as described by Horace. Sydney scanned the radio dial for a suitable wake-up station. As he did so, he came across audio feedback, as if a microphone were held next to speakers. Much of the dial carried the screech.

"What is going on here?" he said, only to hear his voice echoed by the radio. Only one conclusion; his room was bugged. His first thought was to ask the agents if they'd planted it, but he was soon distracted by a splash. It was as if a large bucket of water were dashed against the front door. But at this hour of the night? Sydney went to the front window. The agents' car sat in place, but its rear window was gone. The watery sound had been shattering glass. Sydney startled at the realization, hustled to slip under his bed. There was the bug with its low-light LED blinking. He raced to his bedroom door and locked it.

Then it occurred to him that a bullet could blow the lock away. A chair wedged against it would deliver a few more precious seconds. His cell phone had the number for the dispatcher of the taxis in line on the side of the Coconut Grove playhouse, almost walking distance. Ordinarily, he would run to it but that was not the time. Sydney just had enough time to find his laptop and open the window looking out to the side of the house, but he was too high to jump.

The night vision scope gave a full view of the two FBI agents sitting inside their car. Through the scope, the sniper saw that they were distracted—their silhouettes enhanced by the glow of their TV. The shots had to be fired through the closed gate so as not to arouse the officers' suspicion. The preparation was interrupted by a voice over the sniper's receiver.

"Lucia... Lucia... Lucia... Lucia... Lucia..." The space between the repetition of the name was increasing with each succession. A new sound was introduced to the transmission. Static? Running water? "Lucia... Lucia..."

The first target should be the one less entertained by the game. The second target, the one more engrossed, might not immediately realize that his partner has been shot. The scope kept panning from the first officer to the second and back again as the sniper practiced his double-kill move. The sniper looked at his chronometer and saw a lapse of a whole second. He needed to shorten the time, more practice was needed for those shots. He needed to time his breathing with each sweep. One bullet... One target...

The last three sweeps took him less than a third of a second. Diffraction from the windshield was accounted for. He was ready; it was time. The silencer made his job more tolerable—the rifle's recoil onto his shoulder was a reminder of deposits into his bank account. First kick, sweep, second kick. The second 7.62 mm bullet left its Dragunov's chamber, avoided the bars from the gate. It pierced the frontal double pane windshield and it was not content with Swanson's cranial box, it exited and shattered the patrol car's rear window. Now the clock was ticking. No sounds in his receiver—his final target was probably sleeping.

He collapsed his tripod, rested his SV-98 Dragunov,[i] adapted with night vision scope and silencer, on the floor of his SUV. For a professional, different tools are essential for different parts of a job. Now he took a semi-automatic pistol with a silencer, ready to execute the essence of his contract.

He triggered his radio transmitter, but it did not open the gate from outside. The second option was to set the device into maximum transmission mode and throw it behind the gates. It worked as specified in the mercenary underground publication. The gate triggering devices gave the illusion that a car was advancing towards it and continued to emit the same powerful code in a wide range of signals until the battery died. The house routine had been studied. The maid and her gardener husband had retired for the evening to a separate house in the back of the mansion. Luis loved to blast the volume of his TV movies, and the assailant noticed the faint sound coming from behind the house. Another lucky break: the front door was unlocked. He knew where Sydney's bedroom was but he still needed to approach with timely caution. Thanks to the earlier bugging, and the monitoring of the target's movements, everything was familiar. He reached the second floor, went to the bedroom door and gently turned the doorknob. It didn't give to the pressure, apparently locked from the inside. He fished for a coin in his pocket, found a dime and inserted it into the door's lock-slot. He searched for his Swiss Army to use the screwdriver's option, but it was left with the rest of the arsenal. The killer needed to improvise and yet ruin the element of surprise. He scanned the corridor for a tool, the adjacent bathroom offered options. He returned with the nail clipper flap. It fitted the door knob like a screw driver into the door's lock slot. The lock's outside groove changed position. Show time!

---

[i] SV-98: *Snaiperskaya Vintovka* sniper rifle, model 1998.

But, the door wouldn't budge. It was time to use the tools of the trade. He stood back, fired two bullets and shot the double door. The door remained mostly in place. With another nudge from outside the chair propping the door fell. No sign of Sydney in bed—time to play the deadly game of hide and seek. The killer stood back from every door that he opened, sliding mirrored closet doors, bathroom and found nobody. It was time to look under the bed. He found his own bug blinking and took it back. From the other side of the bed he noticed a make-shift rope, curtain trimming, tied to its leg. He advanced to the other side of the room.

There was a noise downstairs. A car door slammed shut. The contracted killer rushed to the front window in time to see a yellow sedan, a taxi, speeding away from the house. It was time to regroup, to leave. His contract had escaped, but with luck he would be able to catch up. The touristy Coconut Grove traffic was less forgiving at night.

Maurice Bernard, a black Haitian immigrant, was glad to finally move to the front of the Playhouse taxi line. The event for the evening was not finished yet but he got a call from his dispatcher. It was his lucky night—the pick-up was close. As he approached the house he saw a dark-colored SUV parked near the entrance and the front gates open. This meant that his passengers were ready to go and no intercoms. A Chevrolet Caprice was parked at the entrance, but Maurice scanned for someone with bags or suit case ready to come out of the front door. He got out to help his fare with bags, if there were any. As he did he noticed that the rear window of the Caprice was shattered. He approached the car and noticed the bodies at the front seat.

"Ave Marie!" he couldn't swallow, "*Merde!*" an adrenal chill washed over him.

He ran to his car, was driving away even as he slammed the door shut, and left tire tread marks while burning rubber in his panic.

Sydney scanned the room for an exit. One window led to a very steep roof, another to the side of the house. He grabbed the drapery's accent rope and yanked it from the window frame; then another, and another. He tied them end to end, then to the leg of the bed. He tossed the rope out the open window and peered down after it—it would still be a substantial fall. His other option was to walk around the roof and find a way down. He scrambled out the window only to find the pitched roof steeper than he'd expected; about fifty degrees. And it was treacherous, being at least forty feet off the ground, his stability dependent on the mercy of an old gutter, rotten with the accumulation of wet, dead leaves and south Florida's constant rain. After advancing about fifteen feet he discovered that the rusted gutter allowed his foot to sink in ever so slowly. He came to the end of the line. He could remain immobilized; end his life by sudden impact with the pavement below, or get shot. He still had his cell phone in his hand and managed to click the talk button.

"Dispatch, good evening."

"I am very close to the Playhouse at the Coconut Grove on Main Highway. Could you send a car as soon as possible? I'm late for the airport and there's an extra twenty dollars if the driver can be here in less than five minutes."

"I'll see what I can do. Give me the address."

After giving the particulars Sydney hung up, then dialed Rick Sarturo's number—also programmed into his cell from earlier in the day. It rang twice, with Sarturo apparently noting the caller ID.

"Sydney, what's the problem."

"I think Bill and Dennis have been shot dead in the car. I'm at the edge of the roof outside my room." He noted a double thud; bullets against the front door, the impact heard in spite of the silencer and felt through the house because of their impact as strong as a carpenter's hammer.

Sydney froze. There was the shadow of his own angel of death, looking for him. His adrenaline rush seemed wasted—he was locked in place.

"Sydney, are you there? Can you hear me?" Rick paused, "If you can hear me help is on the way. Hang tight." Rick hung up.

A few seconds later Sydney got a good look at his goon. It was the same attacker that he'd seen through the window at Coral Gables office when Horace was killed. The man leaned forward, followed the rope that led to the window. Sydney began to see the gunman morphing into a French soldier. A black three-cornered hat with gold edging crowned his head. His shirt now had frilled collar points, set off with a muslin cravat, his sleeves floppy in the style of the Renaissance. The attacker stuck his head out the window and peered down the rope. Sydney closed his eyes, trying to erase the historical image. As Sydney opened his eyes, he saw his assailant jerk his head at a noise downstairs. The killer moved toward the noise, leaving the window. Sydney's body, sprawled against the roof, felt and heard the rushed steps of his attacker as he left the house. He could finally move again, but with each step the gutter became less forgiving. He had to take his chances; no time to wait for help. He slithered across the roof, careful to distribute his weight the way a snail does. It would take him a whole ten minutes to travel back the distance he'd earlier covered in a few seconds.   As Sydney reentered the room he heard the sirens approach the house. A white patrol car entered first, bearing the blue highlights of the City of Miami, on its heels, a green, beige and white from Dade County followed.

Sydney heard rushed steps coming upstairs.

"Keep your hands up!" shouted the first officer.

The second officer aimed his gun at Sydney.

"This is an FBI crime scene. Rick Sarturo is in charge of this investigation."

"Rick, this is Sydney! I'm upstairs!"

"Be right there, kid. Hold tight."

The first officer stopped his advance to handcuff Sydney. Sarturo entered a moment later, noting Sydney's face and shirt dirty with mildew from sliding on the roof tiles.

"How are Bill and Swanson?" asked Sydney.

"Both of their heads were blown away," answered Rick. "It's not gonna be fun making that phone call to his wife tonight. How did you escape?"

"The goon must have thought I left in the taxi that came to the front of the house. They are right across the street and they were here in two minutes. I first thought I could circumvent the killer. That is why I called them. The killer was in my room, from where he heard the cab driver haul ass out of here."

"Did you get a good look at him?"

"Sure. Same person that killed Dad a week ago."

"How about the house caretakers?"

"I don't think they heard or saw anything."

"Sydney, what is this? Pope Urban II and all of these calculations on the blackboard?"

"It's nothing important. I was doing some research for my next book. You can erase it if you want." Sydney motioned to the blackboard to erase it.

"Not so fast. This is now a crime scene. After we take photographs you or the maid can clean it," said agent Sarturo.

"No problem," Sydney said. "I think it is better if I leave town for a while. I mean, if I can leave town? May I?"

"I'll let you know tomorrow morning." Rick looked around. "Why don't you pack and go to a hotel tonight." Rick pulled a card out of his wallet. "This place is in downtown. You won't need plastic or cash. Your check-in name is Rick Sarturo and on the back of the card there's an account number and check-in code. Don't worry about ID…they won't ask."

Inside a hotel room in Miami Beach's Art Deco district the walls echoed with the sound of a female voice screaming.

"You lost him! Vladimir, I thought you were the best!"

"He had a lucky break." The Russian answered without an accent.

"No Vladimir, he had two lucky breaks! Do you remember running in a shooting spree in Coral Gables? He is in good shape but, he does not know martial arts or how to evade bullets."

The Russian was silent, waiting for his next orders.

"This should have been just as easy as Roberto and Marcelo. Here is your money, and I never told you to kill the cops."

He picked up the money tossed onto the bed. "You don't get a discounted rate," he said. "The deal is half of the money now and the other half if the job is finished or cancelled."

As he finished his sentence he reached into his inner coat pocket. There was a thud at the wall right behind him. Vladimir turned, noticed a palmetto bug, more commonly known as a Cuban roach, pierced with a dagger in the middle of it. As he turned around, he found that his boss, the female host, had another knife ready to be launched at will.

"Lucky for you," she said, "you were not reaching for a gun. Otherwise, I would have killed the bigger roach. In fact, my only indecision would be whether to put it through your nasal cavity or through your eye socket. But we've known each other for a while now. Let me put it in terms that you will understand. If I still see your face here in the next five seconds, it is going to be your choice to be either just fired or terminated."

"This was not part of my duties, but perhaps it is valuable to you." Vladimir raised his right hand and said, "May I reach into my coat pocket?"

The female nodded for him to proceed.

Vladimir pulled out one antique leather bound book and tossed it to her side of the bed across the room. "If it's not valuable to you I can always keep it as a souvenir. Otherwise, I want the difference of my fee for it."

The female opened the book with the knife still in her hands. She scanned the many notes, calculations, and astrological markings.

She changed her tone to pleasantries, "Vladimir, I was so quick to judge you. This is a very interesting book. What made you take this from him?"

"Ms. Orman once said that she likes antiques books. It's good business to keep the eyes and ears open." Vladimir reached for his duffle bag in which he had some of his plastic explosives.

The female reached for a bundle behind her on top of the table and tossed it to him. "You may leave this bag where it is. I'll have use for it. One more thing Vladimir, you have worked alone, let's do one last run together, perhaps Sydney's lucky streak will end. I'll double the contract price."

"Sure," answered Vladimir.

"It is nice doing business with you, Judy," he said. "Take care, I'll keep in touch." He backed away from her, fumbling blindly for the door knob to make his exit.

"My regards to Inna," she said, "and the kids."

Vladimir stood stunned for a moment, the door ajar behind him. "How do you know my wife's name? And that I have kids?"

Judy spoke in Russian, "It's good business to keep the eyes and ears open, comrade Vladimir."

Judy Orman, also known to the FBI as Lourdes Cler Clement, was finally alone in her room. She spoke softly as she paged through the book. "You did very well comrade Vladimir Petrov. I have been looking for this book for a long, long time. Still, if you want a job to be done right, you must do it yourself."

Judy Orman opened her laptop, offering thanks to her cable modem connection. She logged onto the Internet, a luxury few hotels offered. She was soon into the FBI's secure site. "Where are you Sydney?" she murmured. "Would you be courageous enough to sleep in the same place? Perhaps you're in an FBI safe-house tonight. Oh, that's quite rich. Rick Sarturo has checked in downtown, even though he and his family live in Coral Gables. For two days. Very good! So we can take a break tonight."

XII
Capitulus Duodecim

Sydney awoke the next morning glad for his experience. His surroundings, now seen in daylight, were even more unfamiliar than the night before. He scanned the hotel room, found his belongings, reached for his wallet. *How much money do I have?* He thought, *Not enough for a quick getaway.* Among federal notes was a card handed to him at the funeral. He recalled the invitation. *Just come anytime you want. As you can see she's a psychic. She'll know when you are stopping by.* "Good." He said it aloud, placed the card back in the wallet and popped up from bed. "Let's see if you know that I am coming."

Judy Orman looked no more than 32, known to the Miami Police Department as Lourdes Cler Clement, a 97 year old librarian. She kept her hair very short like a Spartan young soldier to conceal her beauty and formidable body. Her cell phone rang for the first time. She noticed the caller ID's number and before answering she patched her head set through a voice distorter. The caller on the receiving end would be convinced to be talking to a man. Everything was ready to go and she pressed the answering bottom.

"*Mar'Haba habibi...assa'lam aa'laykum.*" Judy greeted in a flawless Arabic, maybe a bit archaic to the new millennium. After a pause she continued, "Everything is moving according to schedule. Have the funds been transferred?" short pause, "Good... I have to be in Florida for business, I should finish it in a couple of days... Good that you called... Ma-a ssa'la:ma." Unceremoniously she severed the connection on her cell phone.

Judy looked at the piece of paper on which she had transferred the hotel address to find Sydney. She wore a business suit that would blend her in well as an office person in downtown Miami. She entered Sydney's hotel.

"Good Morning and Welcome... How may I help you?"

"My bags are coming from the airport. I've never been to this hotel before. Is it possible to check one of your rooms first before I check in?"

"Naturally, I'll need a credit card or driver's license."

Judy took the elevator to a different floor than her key card was assigned to. No cameras were visible on the elevator walls. She felt comfortable to put her gloves on and assemble her semi-automatic with a silencer. She tucked it into her vest before the elevator's doors opened.

A door was opened at the end of the corridor and she hastened her pace. Once she was in front of it she noticed that the door was being kept from shutting with a door latch. It was a delightful opportunity, especially because it corresponded with the number in her notes. *Sydney is on the other side of this door.* She thought that nine bullets in the magazine cartridge were enough to take care of four targets, if that came to be.

As silent and cautious as a predator, she opened the door. The bed was undone and the TV was blaring cheery morning show hosts. She reached for the hardware nestled on her side holster as she noticed a movement coming from the bathroom.

"Hello there. Did they give you this room? I have not finished and turned it in yet," said the maid.

"No, don't worry I came looking for a friend but apparently... I must be late!"

"He checked out about an hour ago."

"Silly me, could I make a phone call?"

"Dial nine first and wait for the tone."

Judy advanced to the night stand as the maid retracted to the bathroom. The hotel printed note pad was standing on to it. Two pencils were resting next to the notepad. She took the note pad and the pencils and pocketed them.

Next door Judy entered a restaurant and ordered coffee. At the table she broke one pencil and snatched out the graphite stem. The Swiss army knife provided the nail filer and she began to pulverize the graphite onto a napkin. With gentle strokes the graphite from the napkin was revealing the negative of the of the notepad's previous page. "Flight 1309 Gate C47." She packed and left before the coffee arrived.

No lines at the Miami International Airport counter—a good sign.

"I need a ticket to San Diego. Your next flight."

"We have a flight, nonstop, leaving in 45 minutes." The round-faced attendant's voice was cordial.

Sydney turned to take his bags from the porter. Instead, he saw a Caucasian king, fully-decked in a regal red garb with gold crown, handing over the luggage. The king quickly morphed back to the Black Jamaican who'd taken Sydney's bags at the curb a few minutes earlier.

"Have a good flight, *mon.*" The porter's thick accent rang out as Sydney tipped him.

"I need to find a way to control these things," Sydney muttered, turning back to the counter.

"I beg your pardon;" said the ticket agent, now arrayed in an English white lawn fichu dress. White feathers adorned her oversized, light-purple velvet hat which was laced under her chin. The dress was traditional for the affluent French and English of the late 1700s.

Sydney raised a hand. "No, nothing to worry about. Just, the porter looked like somebody I know... I knew." He handed the clerk his frequent flier card as she transformed back into her airliner uniform.

The airport security offered no resistance. The underpaid x-ray technicians were chosen at the discretion of the lowest bidder for MIA Authority. Now nestled in his seat, Sydney wondered if he had enough cash. *Would twenty-thousand dollars cover my expenses? It should.* The flight was on its way and, so far, uneventful. Sydney reflected on his last conversation with Rick Sarturo, from the hotel room.

"I need to see someone out of town. Is it okay to leave, or am I a suspect?"

"Sydney, I need to tell you something. It would be better if you came in."

Sydney sat straighter. "Let's cut to the chase. You have something to say, say it."

"Sydney, you need to be careful. I just got the ballistic results and the bullet is from a Russian sniper rifle. I don't know why someone would go through the trouble. We have better guns."

"I once met a violin player who refused to touch any instrument other than his own. I am not a profiler, but I was called in a few times to help the FBI and the CIA. I think we're dealing with either someone that has no local connections or a professional that likes and knows his hardware very well."

"The thought did occur to me…"

"I am very sorry about Dennis and Bill."

"I feel guilty because the way the shooting was conducted it wouldn't have mattered if it was just one of them."

"I have a few deaths in my mind too. But once you're running for your life you don't have time to look behind."

"Where are you going?"

"San Diego." Sydney paused, "California, not Texas."

"Thank you. Keep me posted. Don't let people drop dead around you."

"I'll certainly try not to."

Was there more after this? I'll certainly try not to. I'll certainly try not to. The sponged sound blocker he had put in his ears brought the jet's engine noise down to a softer, tolerable hum. *…certainly try not to.*

And Sydney dozed off.

Vatican Underground
Castigation and Truth Extraction Chamber
1093 C.E.

"Salin, you don't have an escape from here. None of your friends are around. Only the truth will liberate you. You will have to tell us everything. We have all your notes. Can you tell us where to find your friend Mahud?"

"I'll certainly try," said Salin looking back at his red-hooded inquisitor.

Salin raised his head and found himself suspended with his hands cuffed to chains, stretching up to the contraption where he was locked in. The room looked familiar. A violent pain coursed up from his back and made him remember—this was not his first torture here. A burning, shocking sensation was lashed on his back just as the crack of a whip pierced the room.

San Diego, California

Sydney jerked his head forward. *Was this a nightmare? It couldn't be—the room looked familiar.* Pondered Sydney

The cabin's speakers crackled. "This is your captain. We'll be landing at Lindberg Field in San Diego in a few minutes. The local time is 2:00 PM and the local temperature is 72 degrees. Flight attendants please prepare for landing."

A flight attendant's voice followed, giving routine landing instructions.

Sydney's rental car sped north to Encinitas, which the rental agent told him would be easy to find. San Diego's Spring was set in full, with a lush, green tapestry covering the hills on both sides of I-5 Freeway. Purple and yellow wild flowers dotted the landscape, creating a stark contrast against the cloudless, sharp-blue sky.

The Encinitas Blvd exit was easily found. A big arched green sign crowned the 101 highway. The sign also read "Encinitas" in white and neon type against a green background. Half an hour later, Sydney stood in line at an Encinitas' bistro.

The woman ahead was much his senior — by two decades he figured. White highlights streaked her dark blonde hair, the telltale strands hidden more by attitude than hair coloring. She seemed familiar. They exchanged a brief acknowledgment as he looked for a table. Sydney took the little table flag denoting his order and chose to sit outside, near the sidewalk.

While nursing his coffee and enjoying the view, he noticed the lady he'd just greeted had taken a seat two tables away. The sinking sun was blocked by the restaurant building. Sydney discovered, as soon as his food arrived, that the restaurant harbored bold beggars: tiny, fearless sparrows. Two stood on his table, waiting for crumbs. Their bravado shocked Sydney, who'd never seen tiny birds venture so close.

He laughed out loud, "I don't believe this!" Sydney muttered to himself.

"Are the birds bothering you?" the mature blonde asked.

"They are more startling me than bothering. I've seen pigeons do this before but never sparrows."

"You must be from out of town."

"Yes I am. I just arrived a couple hours ago from Miami. Are you a detective or a psychic?"

"The partial view of your airplane boarding pass in your shirt pocket gave you away."

Sydney pulled it out, crumpled it and left it at the table with what soon would be leftovers.

"So how do you like our little town so far? What brings you here, business or pleasure?"

"It's hard to say. At this point I would say business, but it could be an old friend."

"What business is your friend in?" asked the lady.

"She is a psychic and..." Sydney's voice was interrupted by the blaring passage of a commuter train just a block away.

"Is her name Lilith Black?"

"Yes, do you know where she lives?"

"Yes I do, she lives in my house." She waited a little bit for a reaction and said, "I am Lilith."

"Stephanie was right. You came here to greet me!" Sydney got up from the table and walked towards her.

Lilith did not respond.

Sydney knew that his guess was right, "You also must know what's afflicting me right now, right?"

She got up from the chair and gave him a hug in understanding as he approached. "Let's go to my house. There's not much time left. The conjunction according to Horace is just in time."

Sydney joined her table and gobbled his lunch. As they turned around the corner going towards her house he noticed his rental car and said, "Should I take my car?"

"Leave your car here; it is just two blocks away. We can walk to my place, it is right by the water.

Lilith's house was decorated with motifs from different places around the world. It was an eclectic mixture but not too busy—the walls held their share of space. The house, built on a cliff, was graced with two floors, with an ocean view and accompaniment from each room. The constancy of the waves was like a soothing, calming chant.

"It's a lovely place," he said. "You must have awesome sunsets here."

"I am really blessed. I moved into this house twenty years ago. Stephanie, my daughter, was five when we moved in." Lilith filled one kettle with filtered water.

"I thought she said she was your niece."

"She always does that. I guess it makes it easier for people to relate to me if we have tenuous bonds; or perhaps she's embarrassed of her mom." She placed the kettle on the range, turned on the heat.

"You're the psychic. Is she?" Sydney asked.

"Embarrassed? A little… I guess I was not a normal mom like those of her classmates. Still, she's proud."

"What is on the stove?"

"A little tea for your jet lag. In fact, I think it would be better if you took a nap. We're going to get started pretty early tomorrow morning. About three."

"Why so early?

"Because of noise."

"But I can hear the ocean from here, I'm sure we will be able to hear it in the morning as well," said Sydney.

"I am not talking about aural noise. Mental noise. During that time of the morning the mind is more conducive to travel. I mean, transcendental movements of the mind. The meditative state if you wish."

"This is a first for me. I've never been to a psychic," said Sydney.

"And I've never had my chart done. At least, not in this lifetime," she chuckled.

"Do you know what we're going to be doing?"

"Horace gave me a guideline. I suggested to him that this meeting could occur, and he didn't want to take chances."

"Did he awaken you?" Sydney asked.

"No, but he offered it to me and said it would make it easier for me to do it to you. However, he told me that the shock and the pain would have to be relived and besides, you both had an understanding not to take any more travelers." The whistling kettle took her away.

"I find it hard to believe," said Sydney as Lilith returned with two mugs, "that you would turn down an offer like that. My book was just released and while I was researching it and talking to people, most of them were very keen to find out who they were."

She sat for a while, pensive, then said finally, "Please don't take this as disapproval, but I think if we were meant to know who we were, then God would let us know without any challenges."

"I am just doing this today because someone is trying to kill me. Perhaps with your help I'll finally know what is going on."

"Horace told me about your first days and first awakenings…"

"I find it fascinating," Sydney interrupted, "that you chose not to do it."

"My psychic energy lets me know everything I need to know from my past, and my future, on a need-to-know basis." She put her mug down. "Odysseus or Ulysses, was offered immortality, but he was never tempted because he knew it was grander remaining present-centered."

"But Odysseus was a mythological character."

"Whether or not he was, he made a choice. I made a choice."

"So did we meet in our past lives?"

"Of course we did. We all did, otherwise reincarnation would not work."

"I have been having a lot of visions lately. They began a week before Dad died."

"What are your visions like?"

"Usually, out of nowhere, people that I don't know begin to morph into someone of a different era, different race and clothing. I can't control it. It always takes me by surprise."

"Horace spoke to me about this. He told me that it would be a sign that the time was right, but first, I've prepared your bed. Go take a nap and you will be ready for tonight."
The room was utterly black.

Lying in bed to take a nap was not an easy task for Sydney, especially in the afternoon and particularly when he knew that he was the ultimate target. All his attempts to relax were in vain, so there was no other option but to concentrate. Perhaps concentration would bring him to sleep while relaxation couldn't. In a pitch back room there was nothing to concentrate on. He had other four senses to find the object of his concentration, visual was not available. *Touch?* Sydney thought followed by a *No, Olfactory? No...* *Taste? No... Hearing? Yes!* Hearing would be the object of his concentration. Besides the occasional wood creaking coming from Lilith's steps, the ocean sound grew on its glory every second and Sydney focused his attention. As he waited for the sound of the next crashing wave, his mind was forming a new but familiar image.

Sydney found himself in another place and time, a renaissance garden, and someone called his name but in French.

Château de Versailles
1751 C.E.

"François, wait! I cannot haste in this dress."

Sydney now, François, turned and smiled seeing the face of his beautiful fiancée Lucia. In a few seconds she caught up with him and they were together. He bowed at her approach and offered his arm as support for a walk. She accepted and they commenced to walk and enjoy the garden. The grass twinkled with sunshine bouncing from an earlier rain. A bird chirped at the distance heralding the rebirth of Spring.

"François, we will be married in three days! Are you excited?"

"Lucia, I have been walking on the clouds, and my every thought is how to begin our life together."

"So are you going to accept father's offer and run the factory?"

"I could help him with the books, but I am not a business man like him. I also cannot abandon the city for the country. I cannot abandon Paris. She needs me."

"I am getting jealous, Paris comes first and your loving wife second?"

"That is not what I meant and you know that. I cannot stay away from my books and my students."

"Paris, books and students, perhaps if I become your student again you will look at me with kinder eyes?"

"What has possessed you to be so jealous today?" asked François.

"I don't know… I don't want anything to change… It feels like if everyday I woke up was three days from getting married I would be happy forever." Lucia pressed her arm strongly onto his in a cuddle as they walked.

"So, the expectation of waiting for dessert tastes better than the dessert itself?"

"I guess so..." She smiled, "are you prepared to promise to be my husband until death takes us apart?"

François turned to face her and paused, "Yes, but I am also prepared to promise a lot longer than that if you want me to."

Encinitas, California

Sydney woke up to a pleasant incense scent. Then he walked to the adjacent room and found Lilith seated cross-legged waiting for him. She extended her hand showing him a place to sit, "I had a terrible vision the last time Horace was with me… A little boy was killed. Ten years were taken away. He would have lived ten more years and ten years had to be paid. I had also told him that his task would not be finished. Then he told me about *The Link*. He was afraid that for this exclusive time he could not finish his task. Then he taught me.

"He said that if he died I would hear from one of his pupils or partners. So I kept tabs on you, Marcelo and Roberto. After Roberto, Marcelo, Olive and Horace died; it was my time to act so I sent Stephanie to bring you to me.

"If it were up to me, I would leave things to progress the way they are meant to, naturally. However, it's not a decision that is up to me."

"You said, you would leave things to progress... What do you mean by it?"

"I would let *The Link* be severed, but it's not my decision. You are the one to decide it."

"Are you going to try to change my mind?"

"People can decide to change their minds on their own. Have you ever heard the term cryptoamnesia?"

"Of course I have, forgetfulness of our past lives..."

"Don't you think if God wanted us to know about our past lives, God would have given all of us the ability to make the Link?"

"We don't have wings, but now we even fly to other planets. Do you think it would give us problems if all of a sudden everyone could make their own Link?"

"It's all about Divine Justice. There is a part in the Torah and the Bible that preaches *an eye for an eye and a tooth for a tooth*. Us, mankind took this divine law of karma that was supposed to be honored on the next reincarnation under the similar circumstances in their own accord. For instance, to hang John

139

Wilkes Booth[i], it is not the same punishment that he inflicted on Abe Lincoln. Booth had to become president to be shot in the head. So now if I go on the public square and say that JFK was the reincarnation of Booth, they will crucify me. But to me, this is how an eye for an eye works. Even if takes more than one lifetime."

Sydney said, "In the meantime, we kill people that kill people, so our governments become legalized avengers... Now, we were supposed to take them away to penitence, to repent their crimes, in places that are known as penitentiaries. Instead, we kill them, taking away the time for penitence from many killers. They are soon to be reincarnated to be killed by their previous victims. There is no time for healing and we just create a vicious cycle."

Lilith said, "I don't like the death penalty either. Once a person asked me, 'So as a taxpayer; am I supposed to feed this person three meals a day, room and exercise while I have to find work and feed my family?"

Sydney contested, "To allow their time for penitence[ii] is a greater call as a Christian than trying to save a few cents from their tax return. I am afraid if cryptoamnesia is conquered, we are going to kill Timothy McVeigh[iii] 168 times as soon as he is to be reincarnated."

Lilith commented, "I am also afraid that people will still be lost in their past life, longing for squandered wealth and unfinished revenge. Changing the paradigm of our lives and karma completely."

Sydney said, "I have a more optimistic view than you. I think if people find out who they used to be, it is going to be the

---

[i] Booth (1838 - 1865) died from a bullet wound on the neck after dragged from a burning farmhouse.

[ii] In the 17th century the Quakers promoted education and the humane treatment of prisoners and the mentally ill. This concern continued in the 19th century when Elizabeth Fry and Joseph John Gurney fought for compassionate treatment of prisoners and for the abolition of the death penalty. Later when prisons were built in the USA, they had a more humane approach; prisons would become a place for penitence and not only punishment thus the name Penitentiary.

[iii] The Oklahoma City Bomber whose actions claimed 169 lives including his own by execution.

end of racism, the end of bigotry and the end of all religions because then, we will find out that the Muslim or the Nazi in this lifetime was the Jew in the last. The white was black and vice-versa. The boy was a girl and so on. It could be the equalizer that we are waiting for."

"Do you really believe that?" Lilith continued with incredulity "Do you think we are ready to handle this knowledge?"

"As humanity, I don't think we are ready to handle fire. I don't think we are ready to discover extraterrestrials. After the novelty of discovery, we are going to try to save their souls by trying to convert them to one of our religions, or they could say that they discovered us and now they will try to convert us to their 'Sacred Space Monkey' or something like that. Our lives are going to change from Holy Crusades to Galactic Wars."

"There is a sense of hope and a blank slate if things are kept the way they are," said Lilith.

"Right now there is no sense of hope for me. There is only one thing, death and very soon. Your help is the only thing that may save me. At least, I need to know who is trying to kill me. I even feel that your life may be in danger since I am here."

"I had to have this conversation with you because I don't know if I'll be getting it right. But one thing I'm sure of, there's no turning back. Don't worry about my life; I am in good company." Lilith pointed to a wall covered with masks from different parts of the world. "If I am in good company so are you. You are safe now... It's time."

Sydney felt safe now. Whoever his distracters were, they were far away and it would take them at least a couple of days to track him down or to extract the information from Rick Sarturo, which was very unlikely.

XIII
Capitulus Tredecim

$\mathcal{T}$he room was illuminated with candles. They were both seated cross-legged on opposite sides of a silver bowl, large enough to immerse an infant. On Lilith's right and left, she had decanters full of water at her reach. At this point Sydney was trying not to overanalyze the situation.

"Please relax and try to focus on my voice and on my prayers. You are going to hear the same incantation taught by a Delphi priestess and passed down for the last two thousand years. Horace made me memorize these words, he corrected my pronunciation. These words are meaningless to me, but he told me that these words are what it is going to bring you back to your *Link*. These words are sealed into your subconscious much like the visions from your past lives. Concentrate on the sound of my voice and relax." Lilith began to dispense the first carafe with a humming sound that blended with the sound of the water.

Sydney was very alert, concentrating on her voice. When her voice turned into a prayer he recognized some of it from the earlier session with Horace in his office. Coptic? Greek? He couldn't remember. Sydney lowered his eyes to the water while the third carafe was being poured into the bowl, and the prayer and the water became one. Consciousness and unconsciousness became one. Light and darkness were emanating from the water in the bowl and they became one. Past and present images were rising from the water as well. Sydney was contemplating the images, the speed that they took over his understanding and overwhelmed him and logic. The speed of multiple images, sounds, scents and pain were giving him a sensation of falling into a well, and he did.

Something began to defy reason, Lilith's movements seemed strange and soon Sydney realized that his conscious time moved backwards.

Sydney began to relive the moments backwards. The water was defying gravity and jumping back into the carafes. Their recent conversation was relived in a fast rewind. The airplane took off and flew backwards to Miami. He found himself hanging on the roof shingles trying to save his life. He was talking to Horace a few minutes before his death. He was talking to Mr. Paul Stein at the Hamptons. He was twenty, he was twelve and he was a baby and now he recognized the words, from his real parents, "We don't care about the money! Mr. Horace Strauss we believe that Noah, our baby, came for a mission but we don't understand why we cannot be a part of his life," said the lady. "It is the only way I can educate him," responded Horace. "No worries mate, let's go before we regret," said the husband. *Noah is my birth name this lifetime*, Sydney had a quick revelation of his legal name.

Sydney felt that now he was inside of a bag. That was no bag it was a womb. That was followed by a bright and intense light. The images didn't stop and in rapid succession they continued. He then, recognized himself as another man in World War II London under attack by the Nazis' bomber raid. The scenes became faster and faster as time moved backwards. Everything was becoming more familiar to him. Unlike human memory, in this spiritual memory he could recall each single scene, taste, euphoria, and pain. There were things that he wanted to forget, but they came back. Although he was in this reverie, he remembered Lilith's words, "There's no way back." He had to enjoy his linkage rollercoaster ride and he did.

After all the revelations he opened his eyes to find that Lilith had fallen asleep and some of the candles had expired. There was something different about Lilith. He realized that he could see beyond her shape and age. She had been many other historical figures and Lucia as well.

There she was, Lucia, *lux*, light, his friend and beloved from many lifetimes, and here lying in front of him and again protecting his mission, the reluctant traveler in *the Link*. There would be no story to be told if it weren't for her first gift of sight beyond birth and time.

Sydney was about to call her name, "Luc..." He corrected himself, "Lilith, are you awake?"

"No, just snoozing. I couldn't sleep during your trance. You cried and laughed; and spoke several languages I couldn't understand. So I ask you the same question? Have you awoken?"

Sydney was debating himself how to answer her, and during this small interval they both heard a thump coming from upstairs.

Lilith looked at Sydney and his renewed posture and demeanor, no longer slouching but erect, no longer afraid but intrepid. Lilith observed him as he rose from his cross-legged posture to standing as if he was hoisted by invisible cables. Sydney moved towards the door silently and with the poise of a Samurai. "I'll take that as a yes," she murmured to herself.

Sydney turned and gestured to her, asking for silence and whispered, "Don't come up, I'll come back."

He closed the door behind him and advanced to the first step. He took the steps two at a time with the grace of a feline. Once upstairs, the room was not as dark, the kitchen light flooded part of the living room. The first sign of sunrise was filtering towards the west side of the horizon. Sydney moved about and gave his back to the windows and ocean view as he scanned the kitchen methodically. Sydney did not find anything unusual; however, he heard three faint whisperers and he ducked to the right. On the cabinet door he found three shuriken blades[i], commonly known as throwing star knives.

Still with his back to the shooter he said in flawless Mandarin, "I reckon these knives are at least 300 year old. They belong in a museum."

Sydney heard a fourth noise and he grabbed a wooden mask from the wall, turned and placed it in front of his heart. At this point the totem was pierced by a fourth shuriken. *Luke,* thought Sydney, *I know I've reincarnated as a reluctant warrior this lifetime but your forceful insistence on Tai Chi made all of my muscles ready to adapt to my Kung Fu knowledge from past links, thank you.*

Sydney looked at his assailant and said in English, "Hello Nicholas, I always thought you threw like a girl." Sydney paused to study Judy's reaction and continued, "Very clever. No wonder Luke couldn't find you, he was looking for a boy and not a girl."

Judy said, "I knew that you had the time of my death and it would give you both more accuracy to find me this lifetime, but how did you find me after World War II?"

"You first, how do you *link* yourself by yourself?"

Judy sprinted from across the living room towards the kitchen and said, "*Acta non verba.*"

Sydney understood this was no longer time to talk but time to fight. He noticed that Judy used the sofa as a springboard to deliver a kick to his head. Sydney simply moved out of the way

---

[i] *Shuriken* literally means in Japanese *hand released blade* commonly known as throw-knives or star knives.

and repositioned himself. Judy's Shaolin Kung Fu moves were blocked by Sydney's defense. The allegorical fly on the wall would appreciate the beauty in their movements, but with uniform precision and grace.

After five minutes fighting and dwelling in a living room unreservedly destroyed Sydney said, "I can use the exercise, but this is getting boring. Why didn't you borrow the Dragunov from Rusky?"

"It's in the car outside."

"Good, the FBI and the ATF might like to match the bullets."

"No use fighting you now." Judy looked at her wrist watch. "It's time to go." She turned around and ran towards the balcony and cliff. In a move that looked like either Tarzan or Spider-man, she swung towards the roof.

Sydney heard her hurried steps passing by, he turned around and saw Lilith coming upstairs.

"Are we safe?" she asked.

Before answering, Sydney recollected his thoughts. He remembered that Judy has looked at her precision watch no less than three times during their encounter and again later, before she left. So he asked, "Do you have your car keys?"

"They are in the ignition."

"Run to it." He grabbed her by the arm creating urgency. "I'll drive if you don't mind." They both sat down in the car. "More than ever, seat belts!" he screamed.

He turned the car on, revved up the engine.

Lilith reached for the driver's sun-visor and said, "This triggers the garage door to open." She depressed the button.

"Sorry, no time!" Sydney threw the 300ZX in reverse, blowing the double garage door out of its frame and dragging the door to the street. He turned the car facing north and looked at the house without a garage door standing alone and venerable in the glow of the sunrise.

"Look what you did!" exclaimed Lilith, looking at her prized homestead.

The house exploded before their eyes and tumbled down the bluff fifty feet towards the waves below.

"Oh my G...!" she didn't finish.

"I saw what I did, I saved our lives!" Sydney exclaimed.

The sound of guns being fired, triggered Sydney to accelerate and shed his dangling garage door from top of the car. They sped north but not fast enough to outrun the bullets, one of them had just pierced the rear window, fragmented the glass and scrapped his rear view.

"Right on the next block, to take us out of here." said Lilith.

Before Sydney turned right he saw in his rearview mirror a red mustang that took upon chasing them. "We have company."

"Turn left here the other is a dead end!" cried Lilith.

Sydney did as he was told and soon enough they found themselves airborne on the descent to Moonlight beach. He compensated for the hard landing and anticipated the next turn. Sydney pulled the emergency brake and turned to the right, putting the car into a slide. The morning dew helped the feat. The car was at the beginning of Encinitas Blvd. Again, Sydney floored the accelerator to its maximum. The automatic gear shift made the acceleration un-symbiotic but functional. Half way through the ascend from Moonlight beach to I-5 viaduct, Sydney realized that Judy was not alone. He gathered that the brand new rental mustang carried Judy as a driver and the shotgun seat was held by his best assumption, the same killer that had left him hanging out on the ledge in Coconut Grove, Florida. Sydney took the 300ZX on a second 90 degree slide to climb the ramp to the Freeway.

"Where did you learn to drive like that?" Lilith inquired.

In a British accent he responded, "At the services of your Royal Majesty under training for the Royal Intelligence in 1939 and thanks to you, now I remember it!"

As soon as he finished the climb to the interstate, Sydney slammed the car into reverse and hid the car in the emergency lane waiting for the mustang to merge onto the freeway. They both heard the screeching tires of the mustang approaching. Sydney turned off his headlights and gave chase to the red car. The Mustang's passenger had half of his body nestled out the window holding on to a submachine gun with both hands. Sydney gained on Judy's blind spot, the gunner facilitated by blocking her passenger's rearview mirror. Sydney's car noise alerted the Russian and he turned to look and found Sydney behind him. Instead of turning his body, he switched hands holding the gun to shoot it backwards.

"Duck now!" he said to Lilith and violently turned the wheel.

Sydney slammed his Nissan's fender forcefully against the Ford's right rear fender, nudging the killers out of control. Immediately, Sydney slowed down his car and watched the show. The Mustang hit the left guardrail and Newton's first law of motion[i] took effect. The sudden stop of the front left tire became a pivot for the rest of the car to continue its constant velocity. The Mustang became airborne dazzling the early morning drivers with a horizontal pirouette.

Anticipating Lilith's next question Sydney said, "This I learned watching a cop-show on cable last week. It's called the PIT Maneuver."

The last attempt by the gunner pierced the Nissan's right headlight upwards at the three inch spread all the way to the top of

---

[i] Principia Mathematica, circa 1687 § Objects at rest tend to stay at rest and objects in motion tend to stay in motion unless an external force is applied to it.

the windshield. The mustang finally landed upside down in the middle of the median, mile 44 on I-5 just half way to La Costa exit. Sydney pulled the car off next to La Costa exit ramp.

He checked on Lilith. "Do you have any bullet holes?"

"I don't, but Priscilla must have at least a dozen."

"Who is Priscilla?"

"My baby, look at the odometer this is the original 50 thousand miles, I bought her new and until today she'd never had a scratch."

Sydney got out of the car and scanned the situation half a mile away and already noticed the southbound traffic slowing down. The San Diego morning's work force had something to describe at the water cooler, he thought to himself. He squeezed the one dial feature of his cell phone and heard a voice on the other end.

"Sarturo here, what's up?"

"Hey Rick, it's Sydney I just survived a house explosion and a car chase. I have a license plate for you, California K2L93W. It would save us a lot of time if you gave the Encinitas Police and Fire Department an idea of what is going on."

"I'll see what I can do. A good friend of mine works for San Diego. We first met at the academy a dozen years ago, Roger Thompson."

"Is he FBI?"

"Yep, tell the local officers that you cannot answer any questions. Where is the house that got blown?"

"The house used to be at 4th Street West between D and E Streets, but most of it went down the cliff at the beach."

"Did you lose the person chasing you?"

"Actually, there were two. The Russian, I recognized from the Coconut Grove stake out killings and his female companion, is probably the lady known as Cler, the 97 year old librarian."

"I just got the results about the car," said Sarturo. "I ran it on the computer. It was rented from the airport to Robert Orman."

"Gosh!" screamed Sydney.

"What happened! Do you know this name?"

"No, I'm about half a mile away. I was looking at the mustang flipped over the median and the car just exploded."

"Do you think anyone was killed?"

"I didn't see anyone getting out of the car, but some of the rubbernecks that stepped out of their cars to get up close got hurt by the blast."

Lilith saw the fireball from her rearview mirror and stepped out of the car. She walked to the rear of the car where Sydney was and said, "Oh my God! Can't we go and help them?"

Sydney said, "First, you count the bullet holes Pricilla took for you, and if we go there they will still have a couple more shots waiting for us."

"Who are you talking to?" asked Sarturo. Over the phone and faintly Sydney heard, "Joshua call San Diego, get Roger and brief them."

"Next to me is Lilith Mary Black, her house was just blown and her car sprayed with bullets."

"Sydney, I have two questions for you. The first is, why do you think it took so little time for the killers to catch up with you?" Sarturo asked.

"Sure," said Sydney, "There's only one thing that's not a lie about my assailant. She is not 97, her name isn't Cler, but she is a librarian."

"I don't get it."

"A Vatican librarian once said to me, *Qui imperium scientia, imperium mundus*, who controls the knowledge controls the world. She must be more than a reference librarian, she must have access to your database, my credit card purchases and airline passenger lists. So before I landed in San Diego she already knew that I was coming. What was your next question."

"Sydney, don't be offended, I am trained to notice these things. There's something different about you. You sound mature or more confident, like you've aged a couple of decades since I talked to you last what happened?"

"You are right. I did a lot of maturing in the last few days. I guess that happens to everyone whose gluteus maximus is being peppered with bullets."

"Take care Tobias. Keep me posted."

Sydney flipped the mobile phone closed, looked to the side, and said, "Scrambled eggs, toast and coffee?"

"Sure."

They circumvented the local mess on the freeway south by taking the coastal road, 101. In Leucadia, they stopped at the first restaurant on the right and sat indoors.

"*Qui imperium scientia imperium mundus.*" It was the first thing Lilith said when the young waitress left the table with their order. "I like Latin, who said that to you?"

"The same person who just blew up your house. The first time I heard it was in the year 1071 maybe 1072... After being in a dungeon for years hearing torture and being tortured near the Vatican grounds, the years begin to melt into each other. Father Nicholas Valerius, the one we left toasting right now on the freeway."

"I'm sorry I asked."

"No, it's okay. I think we all should elect a motto for our lives. Mine is *Character est Fatum.*"

"Character is fate or destiny?"

"Your Latin is not bad. Do you have a motto?"

Lilith waited for the coffee to be poured and said, "Fulfill your purpose in life. But I don't know how to say it in Latin."

"It's a beautiful one, you could say it like this, *Presto vestrum propositum in vitae.*"

"Thanks, I'll probably engrave it on my bracelet, but tell me more about your motto and what is behind, *qui imperium scientia imperium mundus.*"

"Since I am an astrologer, I must educate my clients and friends that their behavior will dictate their destiny. In every consultation I explain the reason it is called the Zodiac. It's because everyone behaves or tends to behave like animals. So astrology is not a religion but a guide to teach people not to behave like animals, but like human beings. A frightened dog or a scorpion would bite back but a human's challenge is to offer the other cheek."

"I didn't see you offering the other cheek back in the house." said Lilith.

Sydney contested, "A true Christian would, but in a way I didn't draw from anger or fear like a dog. I drew inspiration from years of training under the code of Shaolin that says, anger is not a weapon but a weakness."

"Touché!"

Lilith was about to ask a question but she noticed that an Encinitas cop entered the coffee shop. Officer Thomas Swank turned, looked at her and waved. He ordered the coffee at the counter to go and turned to meet her.

He nodded at Sydney, a contraction of tipping the hat, and started to talk to Lilith. "I needed some coffee after what I heard on the radio."

"It's already on the news?" asked Lilith.

"I don't know. I heard on the radio dispatch, I'm about to start my shift…"

She interrupted, "Sydney this is Tom Swank. Our kids went to school together."

"Pleasure, Sydney," They shook hands. "So it's true that your house was blown away?"

"Unfortunately it is. Sydney was there."

"I saw Priscilla sprayed with bullets when I walked in."

"I didn't know Priscilla was famous," said Sydney.

"Our kids, Stephanie and Paul, borrowed the car once without me knowing it. So Tom tracked the car down to find our kids in it."

"Lilith do you mind telling me what is going on?" the policeman picked up a chair from the next table, flipped it backwards, and sat resting his arms on the back rest.

"Sydney came for a consultation. Someone is trying to kill him, and then someone broke into the house. Sydney fought him off; we left the house immediately because Sydney had sensed that there was something wrong. We left a few seconds before the explosion. So as we left they were standing outside and started to shoot at us…"

Sydney interrupted, "Then we got on I-5 north as soon as we could, and finally, they lost control of their car and flipped on the median. We pulled off and two or three minutes later the car exploded. We figured that the people who were trying to kill us are dead so we stopped for coffee."

"I heard that on the radio too," said the officer. "I probably need to take some statements from you both."

"Officer Swank, do you know Roger Thompson, from the local office of the FBI?" asked Sydney.

"No I don't think so."

"Actually, that's how they operate. The FBI knows more about you than we know about them. By this time your local office must have had some phone calls from Miami, New York and the FBI's local office. They probably want to turn I-5 into a federal crime scene."

From the corner of his eyes officer Swank saw that his order was ready. "Okay, we don't get too much excitement in this town, but now we have a plate full. Let me nurse my coffee in the car and talk to dispatch... Excuse me."

Before he left, Sydney said, "We are not going anywhere until we have our green eggs and ham. We figure it's going to be a long day with paper work and picking up the pieces."

After Swank left, Lilith said, "You were about to start explaining the quote, "*Qui imperium scientia imperium mundus,* tell me more."

Sydney stared at his cup and started "Now, I had a lot of time to think about Nicholas' motto, who controls knowledge controls the world. Unfortunately, it's one of the few things that organized religions have in common. It's actually an unspoken code. Conditioning of the masses starts at the tender age of five or less, then the myths that defy science, mathematics, and logic, live and continue to live unquestioned for centuries."

"Like what?" she sipped her coffee.

"Male superiority, virgin birth, creationism, the chosen people, 72 virgins, dogma... For example, if anyone read on the *National Geographic* that an anthropologist had found a tribe in the Amazon jungle that's never met a Caucasian and they believe that their god created them out of the mud and their women out of their bones, then anyone would conclude that they are a primitive bunch. However, we got the same indoctrination at the age of five; that's why it is not challenged for centuries. Who controls knowledge controls the world. Bigotry and racism are just as strong mores to break because they are learned at the same age."

"Who does it serve the creation of all these myths, as you say?" asked Lilith.

"The parents learn to control their children with spanking or fear, the same way the masses are ruled by either force or fear. Fear of invasion by another country or fear of God. Very early in our history the clergy learned that by controlling knowledge they can not only control the masses but kings and queens as well. For instance, Constantine, the ruler of the Roman Empire, knew that the amount of Christians grew to such an overwhelming number that in order to avert a revolution, he made Christianity the official religion of the Romans; soon after he'd declared an edict that started the persecution of Jews. So, who was the true ruler of the Roman Empire, Flavius Valerius Constantinus or the Christian Church?" and Sydney continued. "The latest thing that Nicholas did was to start a campaign of propaganda in Gemany. To propagate his anti-Semitic and xenophobic ideas, in which foreigners bring disgrace and chaos to their country. They are the superior race blessed by God. Soon after, Hitler started burning all the books that did not agree with their agenda. Back then, in England, I knew that it was Nicholas again starting his anti-Semitic war."

"Are you here to stop him?"

"No, but he knows that as long as I keep coming back I will not let him advance. I can't take credit alone for stopping him during World War II, but he knew that I was profiling his moves to the Royal Intelligence."

"So now that you have met Nicholas, what is going to happen?"

"I know for sure that whenever he is around, people will die. If he is not dead right now, people are going to die. Nicholas never took the front stage, but his hands were there during the Crusades, World War II; if there are mass killing of Jews and libraries burning then Nicholas is behind everything."

"Huh…" She pondered.

Thomas Swank, came in for a refill at the counter and moved to Sydney and Lilith's table. "I've got some good news and better news. I don't have to do a ton of paper work. The feds just picked up your case. Now I just heard on the radio, the sucker that was shooting at you got spliced in two. When the car landed on the median, half of his body landed on the emergency lane and half was cooked in the car." Swank noticed that the breakfast order was arriving and he made space for the endeavor. "They asked me if I could offer some protection until they have an agent to accompany you. So I'll be waiting outside and I'll take you back to your... Well to where your house used to be."

"Sure," said Lilith.

The officer asked, "My I have your car keys?"

"Sure, why?"

"I called the tow-truck; your car is also part of the crime scene. The Feds probably, want to get the slugs buried in your car panels."

The keys were on top of the table. Sydney handed them over.

"We don't have a car now," lamented Lilith.

As Swank left, Sydney said, "The rental must still be parked nearby."

Lilith smiled.

XIV
Capitulus Quattourdecim

**Encinitas, California,
Three Days Later**

eventy two hours later, Sydney returned to the lobby of the Pacific Waters Hotel in Encinitas. The back of the lobby as well as the room balconies allowed a pristine view of the ocean.

"Hello, any messages?" Sydney approached the receptionist.

"Just a moment sir, there is a fax for you."

"Thank you," Sydney took the manila envelope and assessed the content as he took the elevator. Exiting the elevator he flipped his cell phone open and called Sarturo. "Rick, I got the picture of Robert Orman and his file."

"So what do you think?" asked Sarturo.

"I never met the guy." Sydney pondered for two seconds, then asked, "Do you have make up software?"

"Only the best, why?"

"Could you remove this guy's beard, give him light eyes and a short female hair cut?"

"I'll send you another fax later."

"Sure." Sydney flipped the phone off and knocked on the bedroom door S-T [... -] in Morse Code announcing his arrival. They organized the deed for safety. Her Morse code knock was L [.-..]. After his arrival was announced, he inserted the hotel's card key. He found Lilith on the phone, television on mute. The room was organized and clean. Some of her totem masks were already back on the walls.

"What you are saying is ridiculous. Why would I blow up my own house then spray my own car with bullets and cause a car chase disaster on the freeway?" she was silent for a few seconds. "Having the gift of premonition is one thing, insurance fraud is another. Mr. Stuart, I'm going to give you a little insight into my world. If you dare to do a paternity test to your son, you will discover that he has more in common with one of your friends than with you. Then call me back and tell me how suspicious you continue to be and how I was able to set you up as well." She hung up the phone and smiled at Sydney.

"I never thought you could be capable of insurance fraud." Sydney rested his belongings on the dresser. "The police already cleared you, why the hold up?"

"The insurance company finds it suspicious that all of my furniture and belongings have been in storage for the last 3 months. The furniture and things that blew up with the house were rented. They are also suspicious that I took extra coverage two months ago."

Sydney responded laughing. "If they only knew what you are capable of, they would hire you immediately to screen out people with bad luck and bad karma. They would reap a fortune."

"You are wrong. I wouldn't be the best benefit for them, you would."

"How do you figure that?"

"I can only look at a certain number of files a day, you on the other hand; could set up a computer program and they could screen millions of files on the same day. They could anticipate astrological influences."

"Oh, I see! They could deny coverage for someone who has tendencies to be robbed, Neptune in the Fourth House. Diabetes, Venus in the Sixth House or racketeering, Saturn in the Twelfth House."

"You got the idea!" she started a conspiracy smile leading to sarcasm.

"Don't you think they've already tried to explore that option?"

"I wouldn't be surprised," she replied.

"I get in trouble for saying this from time to time, but I love the fact that astrology is not mainstream and not an organized religion; there are planetary influences but there is still a chance for free will."

"You get in trouble?"

"Sure. Sometimes I get a chart of someone who should have a lot of trouble but his or her life is fine or vice-versa. It could be dirty data[i] but I like to think it's free will. So I go on TV and say that astrology should be used as a guide and not a law. Later in the same week the letters start arriving from astrological associations, magazine editors, etcetera saying that I am dismantling years of work that they've had to make astrology acceptable and credible."

Lilith questioned, "Is this still your opinion after making *the link*?"

"It's obvious if astrology didn't work there wouldn't be a *link*. Luckily Luke and I shared this... sorry Horace. We shared this opinion long, long ago even before we'd made our first link.

---

[i] Dirty Data is the incomplete natal data information to cast a Natal Astrological Reading.

While he and I taught astrology, we also taught the importance of free will. Actually, this is the main reason that Christianity has had a beef against us. On one hand they like the fact that Immanuel was announced and greeted by three astrologers, renamed as three wise men, but on the other it clashes with determinism, free will and divine intervention. How could astrology predict something that has not been decided yet? I guess the preachers and Popes did not want to share the spiritual world with us, astrologers or anyone, else even with their females. There have been anthropological and geological records about astrology for the last 12,000 to 40,000 years, but for the last 5,000 years of written history, all religions have like to call themselves God's favorite, but I call it monopoly on God.

"Ka-Ching! Ka-Ching!" Sydney rubbed his thumb onto his index finger to pretend he was counting money. "They all say things like: we are the chosen people, there's no god but God, and I am the life and the way. I have no doubt that if Jesus, Moses, Mohammed, and Buddha met, they would get along instead of converting each other."

"You forgot John Lennon and Krishna," she interrupted with a smile.

"I didn't know John Lennon had a church?"

Joking, Lilith made a peace sign with both hands and began to wave as if she was in a chant trance during rock concert. "If you were around in the seventies you would have been one of us, brother," she spoke slowly and smiled.

"Sure, thanks. Like I was saying, I think that if they all met, including John, they would not argue about religion but instead join in prayer or meditation and treasure each other's companies. However, the plight of the followers is another story. They neglect the mercifulness of their prophets and stage wars. I don't want astrology to become one of them."

"Do you think it would?" asked Lilith.

"Of course," Sydney paced the room. "Every organized religion has blood on their hands. In ancient Greek history, people that worshiped Mars or Aries would stage a killing against the temple of Apollo. Even the Mormons[i] killed settlers crossing the Utah territory. Name a religion old enough and I'll name you a war."

"I get your point," said Lilith, "But if you and Horace felt like that why have you been chasing Jesus all these centuries."

"When you see the message being changed through the years the way that Luke and I have witnessed, you begin to wonder why. Why was a message so pure changed to something so extreme? The message used to be, if you are not free from sins you'll have to be born again or reincarnate. The message since then has been changed to, I was a sinner but now I am born again."

"Why was the message changed?"

"Monopoly! Of course, do you think the illiterate peasants and nobles alike would buy indulgences[ii] from the Church if they knew that they wouldn't go to heaven and would have to reincarnate?"

"Indulgences?"

"A person could buy a prayer at the Church after confession to liberate them from their sins. When the Medici Cousins became Popes, they cranked up the printing even more. It became so much that a humble priest in Germany began to make noise. They would not listen to Martin Luther, so he broke away from the Roman Church. So the Lutherans came to be."

"Sit, you are making me nervous pacing up and down."

---

[i] The Mountain Meadows massacre occurred on Friday, September 11, 1857 in Mountain Meadows, Utah, about 120 unarmed men, women and older children were killed. A Mormon militia killed an entire wagon train known as the Baker/Fancher Party, traveling from Arkansas to California.

[ii] The Catholic Church sold *indulgences* which are the pardon of sins; it was usually a scroll containing prayers. This practice grew exponentially during the years of Popes Leo X and Clement VII, the Medici cousins. The selling of indulgences led young Catholic priest Martin Luther to shape the Protestant Reformation in 1517.

Sydney sat on the edge of the other double bed and continued, "There is more, Jesus' symbol was the fish. Many of his disciples were fishermen and He was also entering the era of Pisces. But as soon as the Church grew bigger and started to dictate rules for the Roman Empire, they began to persecute the Jews. An act of propaganda was to change the symbol of the Church from Pisces to the cross."

"Propaganda? How can the cross be propaganda?"

"It's difficult to explain when you weren't there, so let's try this way. Imagine one thousand years from now the whole solar system is populated. By then, an electrician named Bob becomes famous for speaking at the union meetings and later becomes a celebrity on all media across the solar system. Bob preaches against inequality roaming in the solar system, how the rich are exploiting the workers on Mars. The Christians by then, do not marry outside of their faith. They are convinced that they are God's favorite. If you are not born a Christian, you cannot be one. Although Bob was born a Christian, he is not preaching the same way the main Church has been teaching. Bob is saying how the Church Institution and the Government became one huge theocracy and how basic spiritual values have not being followed. Everything spiritual has a price."

She interrupted, "I like this… I'm following you, Bob is the new Jesus and the Christians and the government are like the Romans and Jews having Herod as a king."

"You are getting ahead of me, but I'll get there. Now the government incarcerates Bob at the secret request of the clergy. Continuing to preach what Bob did will be considered subversive, and also treason. The Bobians watch Bob being tried for treason and fried on the electric chair. When the followers of Bob, the Bobians, will have their secret meetings, and they will use a symbol to recognize themselves. The symbol is two parallel lightnings similar to the icon of the sign of Aquarius. The first reason is because some of the disciples are electricians as well and the second, it is the age of Aquarius. Aquarius is the sign that represents equality and friendship and will be right in line with what Bob preached.

"Then, three hundred years later, the Christians continue not marrying outside of their faith. They are now the minority. However, the Bobians have multiplied and become a vast number, the Bobians are now the main religion in 3300 A.D. or C.E.[i] The President of the coalition of planets meets with the Bobian Coalition in order to be re-elected, and he is also converted to being a Bobian.

"Since the Bobians have the ear and influence of the administration, they begin to persecute and antagonize the Christians to convert them to Bobianism. As an act of propaganda, the Bobians hard liners change the symbol from the two lightnings in parallel to the electric chair. Then the electric chair starts to appear on top of their steeples, and Bobians also start to hang little electric chairs around their necks as a sign of instigating guilt to Christians. Three hundred years earlier they would have been taken to jail for wearing an electric chair around their necks but now they are the ruling majority, they don't have to fear prosecution. What is sad in this story is that Jesus never spoke about the cross and Bob never spoke about the electric chair. They both had the philosophy of offering the other cheek and not making a big deal about it. However, the followers have an ax to grind. This is how propaganda works."

"Wow! That was powerful. I'll never look at the cross the same way again. In fact, I feel more inclined to wear an electric chair for all the innocent people who died in the name of racism

---

[i] A.D. is short for *Anno Domini* or Year of the Lord (Jesus) name imposed due to Vatican's world dominance for many centuries. Today C.E. (Common Era) is used by all other religions that don't employ Jesus as their prophet. So they can still feel that the current Gregorian calendar is inclusive of all faiths.

and from unprivileged backgrounds," said Lilith touching her necklace.

There was a knock at the door. Sydney looked through the peephole, he saw the receptionist and opened the door.

"Mr. Tobias, I had to come upstairs and you got another fax, so I brought it here for you," the young clerk hesitated.

"Is everything okay?" Sydney asked.

"I don't want to get in trouble for asking you this. My mom is a big fan of yours. Since her birthday is coming and I got a copy of your book. My question would be, if you don't mind signing it?"

"Not at all, do you have the book with you?"

Book autographed and door closed behind him, Sydney turned to the room and took the fax out of the folder to find the latest edition of Nicholas as Judy who he'd met and fought three days earlier. The cell phone rang and the caller identification showed Sarturo.

"Hey Rick, I've already got the fax."

"Then?"

"Then it's her, the mastermind. What is her name?"

"Her name is Judy Orman, clean sheet, twin sister of Robert Orman."

"I don't think he is alive," said Sydney.

"We never found his body in the car fire. He might be at large."

"No, I think he was killed as a child and Judy has been impersonating him."

"How do you know that?" asked Sarturo.

"She told me," Sydney had to think of something fast. Explaining two thousand·years of the *link* would take a long time and incredulity. "She believes that Horace killed her brother and she is trying to avenge his death."

"Well, she really holds a grudge. A lot more innocent people have been caught in the crossfire." Sarturo's detective mind never took a break and he asked, "Why would your father kill her brother?"

"Dad never mentioned it, and Judy left in haste just before the house blew up. I am giving you all the information that it is available to me. I wish I had more," he had to conceal the truth.

"Thanks. My work as a detective is to play these four dimensional puzzles."

"She must have meant this brother, unless she has another one."

"I guess we'll have to bring her in and play twenty questions with her."

"Rick, if she is alive it's going to be hard to squeeze a drop of information from her."

"Thanks for the heads-up. See you."

"Take care." He flipped the phone closed and turned to Lilith. "Where are we?"

"Planet Earth, let's grab something to eat."

"You know the town, where do you want to go?"

"There is a nice place by the water just about entering Solana Beach."

"I'm game. I just don't want to miss the federal agent."

"You could have him meet us at the restaurant. He should call you anyway before he arrives."

"Sure, let's go."

The room telephone rang and Lilith picked up the phone and said, "Send him upstairs." She hung up. "The F.B.I. agent is here."

In about a minute, two clean cut agents, one was wearing a tie and no coat and the second wearing a suit, came into the room. The one with no coat was holding a large envelope.

The special agent extended his hand to Sydney while the second was two paces behind. "I'm special agent Jordan and this is special agent Crawford. For your safety as well as the lady's, we need five to ten minutes alone."

"Lilith, do you mind?"

She interrupted, "I was on the way out anyway. I'll wait in the lobby."

Both agents were silent and waited for the door to shut. Mr. Jordan began. "Mr. Tobias," he pulled a sealed folder out of the large envelope and handed the empty envelope to silent partner, Crawford. "We work with the witness protection program. You are a rare exception that Mr. Thompson is making for Mr. Sarturo…"

"I appreciate that," said Sydney.

"We are not allowed to see the documents inside the folder although we know what they are," he handed Sydney the folder.

Sydney used a knife to cut the seal around the folder, and once inside he found a Florida driver's license and two major credit cards. All three documents had the name of Ned Toby Syais. The Florida documents displayed Sydney's latest photo on file; however, the address and birthday were unknown to him.

Officer Jordan continued, "There must be a driver's license in your hands and two major credit cards. Each one of the credit cards has one dollar credit on it. You can go to any cashing store that allows money transfers to bank accounts and increase your credit card limit. They will work like a debit card. The routing numbers and accounts are on the back of the card, hidden within the 1-800 numbers. The first corresponds to the bank routing number and the second corresponds to the account number. You also have a sheet enclosed elaborating what I am saying. Use these cards and documents sparingly. They are just for car rentals, airplane tickets and hotel rooms where they don't take cash. Do not use them to leave the country. Keep your real documents and credit cards in a safe and secure place, just in case you get pulled over by an officer or have an accident. Needless to say, avoid TV and Radio appearances. My supervisor, Mr. Thompson sends his regards." Mr. Jordan extended his hand and his shadow, Mr. Crawford remained on guard. "I'll take that." He waited for Sydney to hand him the discarded folder.

Sydney watched the agents leave the room and closed the door behind them. He placed the documents into his wallet, then read the page with the instructions, tore it in tiny little pieces, cupped them in his hand and flushed them down the toilet.

XV
Capitulus Quindecim

"*I* don't believe this!" the middle aged man at the Dallas Airport Terminal said to a stranger in the waiting area at Gate-23 after folding his magazine. "My name is Earl, what is your name?" Earl spoke with a southern drawl.

"You can call me Ned," said Sydney, "Some article on that magazine must have startled you." Sydney folded his laptop computer.

Earl continued, "Something sure did! I picked up this old magazine at my uncle's waiting room. I was visiting him in Wichita Falls. He is a dentist. I was browsing through it and I saw an article on cloning cows. I thought, I can read this on the plane. I worked with cattle for a while in my youth." He hesitated how to put the emphasis on the story he was about to tell. "I'm reading the article half way through it… They inserted; remember this is an old magazine. Well they inserted the new DNA in this cow's extracted ovule or egg. Now, to get the egg to start dividing to become a blastocyst and continue to grow into an embryo all that the lab scientist has to do is to zap it with an electrical charge. I thought that they had to use a zygote, but not at all, all they need is a double-A battery or less."

"Why does that bother you so much, Earl?"

"I used to work with cattle before college but now I am a marriage counselor and I see a lot of unhappy ladies out there."

"I still don't see the connection."

"Pretty soon, they are not going to subject or bother entertaining a husband if they have an option to germinate themselves. It will be the end of mankind or actually male-kind."

"Don't worry about that, they have had the option of germinating themselves for years and marriage is still here."

"Like what? Not the way they show in this magazine."

"They have had sperm banks for years, and that was not the end of marriage."

Earl protested. "But the sperm bank has the DNA of an unknown person and with this other type of fecundation a woman could make a copy of herself as a daughter or a copy of her favorite movie star, and with this form of process the result would be identical."

"Earl, if you treat your woman right and not the Texan way, you will have nothing to worry about." Sydney saw that Earl was pensive and continued. "We have similar professions, I am a psychologist. I am presuming that all your life you have been exposed only to the Judeo-Christian culture and religion."

"Yes, go on."

"Well, the Judeo/Christian archetypes indoctrinate that women are inferior to men. In fact, in most major religions God has a penis and God is a reverent male and never a female. The few religions that had equality in gender in their archetypes were the Egyptian Religion and part of the European Pagan, but now they are all extinct. As we go deeper into the Age of Aquarius, things are going to become more balanced. Now, God could have made us multiply as hermaphrodites or by mitosis; however, without being a couple we don't learn about love."

Sydney stopped and let the airport's noise fill the silence while Earl assimilated his thoughts.

Earl continued, "I was worried about the end of my gender and you've concluded that the lowest denominator that is going to stop my fear is love?"

Sydney added, "Usually, it is said that money is the lowest denominator, but I think money is the replacement of a deeper need. When people don't have love they seek it in other ways. Although, from time to time people use love as a commodity as well, but I can only speak for myself, and to me, it is the meaning of life."

"So you think you can teach me the meaning of life?"

"I can't teach you the meaning of life, I can only tell you what the meaning of life is to me."

"I'm listening, and we have more time before we board. If it doesn't hold water, I'll tell you."

"Earl, thanks for the candor. To me, it starts like this; a soul comes to this material realm to learn about love. The first love a baby learns is very egocentric because of self preservation, I'm not going to include family and paternal love, because it's not every child that has this privilege. So now we fast forward fifteen years and young Johnny's hormones start to kick in and Johnny as a soul is beginning to learn and experience love for the first time outside his egocentric circle. Now, the lessons of love are interesting; a person cannot move onto the next step without learning the previous one. Generalizing of course, a person is unlikely to fall in love with Johnny if he does not have self esteem. Johnny starts dating and he makes many mistakes until he learns enough to find his partner for life. This partner starts as a total stranger that soon is going to become a family to him."

Earl began to make notes on the back of the magazine. "I'm listening. Keep going."

"If anyone offends his wife it's like offending him, so now his ego encompasses both. Out of this comes Johnny junior. His wife would not let the circle grow if Johnny did not respect her." Sydney anticipated the question and said, "Idealistically speaking, of course." He saw Earl put his index finger and pen back on the back of the magazine. "So now Johnny's family circle has grown from one to three, four or more kids. Johnny will feel responsible when his kids start to date. He will feel that their mates should also have love or self esteem. So the meaning of life to me is love. Love, because it's the lowest denominator in Johnny's life. He started to learn from his love of self preservation to an altruistic step by encompassing his family. His sons, daughters and in-laws were nothing but unknown spirits at one point; now they are a part of his ego." Sydney paused for a second. "But this is the meaning of life for the average person; there are saints among us that don't need to wait to have blood ties in order to experience love. They are volunteers that have altruistic love from the start without expecting anything back. For instance, Mother Theresa was pure love; she didn't preach, she became love. The more love we feel the closer we are to heaven."

"So where are you? Are you closer to Johnny or Mother Theresa?"

"Well, I would love to know how to love like Mother Theresa, but in the meantime I think my love is more like Hugh Heffner's. Well… It's a start." They both laughed.

"It's the first time I hear the founder of Playboy Magazine and Mother Theresa mentioned in the same sentence… Ned, I'll tell you what… I'll consider it. In fact, you took away my earlier fear." He threw the magazine towards Sydney. "Check out the article in case you decide to go into cow cloning." Earl winked.

Sydney took the magazine and browsed through it. On the cover, mostly red, there was a hopeful and long abandoned Soviet Space Rocket. Sydney heard his flight number being called; however, very few people responded. On that Wednesday afternoon there were not a lot of passengers heading to Jackson-MS.

New York, New York

It was another beautiful, busy, polluted morning in New York City. When it came to business, it was still the capital of the world. Looking from a satellite angle it could be best described as a hive with rational bees driven by ambition, debts, duty and conditional routines, instead of hunger and instinct. The only thing that the metaphorical bees shared with their literal counterpart was the drive for self preservation. Looking just like other bees in the hive, two Caucasians entered the hotel lobby wearing suits. The taller carried two briefcases and the second, average height, pulled out a business card from his wallet and gave it to the receptionist with his left hand.

"Hello Mr. Orman and welcome to the Imperial Request Hotel." She went into a multitasking mode, talking, typing and supervising the floor. "I see that you've booked the suite that has a conference room." She typed a little more and produced two key cards. "Your room number 1010 is written on the envelope."

Silent until now, Robert Orman took the cards and said, "We are going to have some training with local representatives, and I would appreciate if you could bring coffee, tea and munchies for ten associates. The training might run for a while longer and I don't want anyone to go hungry and lose their concentration."

Orman noticed that the receptionist was paying attention, and she began typing. "Thank you very much."

"Certainly sir, I just sent the order and we can have an Imperial continental buffet for ten, ready in 30 minutes or sooner."

"Just add the charge to my card on file. Thanks again."

One hour later two businessmen arrived, followed by another two, ten minutes later. They all arrived in the bedroom. They were met by the tall, head shaved bodyguard and asked to wait. In the meantime they began helping themselves to the buffet and refreshments laid out for them.

Fifteen minutes later the bodyguard's cell phone rang and he directed the four guests to advance to the next room. When the four entered the room, they were met by the Caucasian that they knew as Riald Aly standing behind a table.

Two brief cases were on the table. Four chairs were placed at equal distance from each other. In a distinguished Saudi Arabian accent the host said, "*Assalamu 'Alaykum*[i] and the conversation continued in Arabic. Robert Orman attempted to salute with his right arm but a cast a sling prevented him from properly placing his hand over his heart, then mouth and finally his forehead.

However, this effort was enough for his guests and they said, "And Peace be upon you as well." The words were followed by the hand salute and partial prostration to show respect.

"Please forgive me for not greeting you closer, I had an accident with my arm." Robert Orman showed a little bit more of his cast covering his right hand. "Also I am overcoming a little bit of cold... Please sit," and they all did.

There was a little bit of silence before they commenced.

"Here we are my brothers, we finally meet in person. Here we are united in our fight against the infidels... Before I continue,

---

[i] Peace be upon you.

I want to know that every single one of you has been funded as well as our martyrs."

The first one on the left spoke, "Thank you very much for your generosity, honorable Riald, it is much appreciated. May *The God*[i] reward you tenfold."

"Honorable *habibi*[ii], today for and as always for security..." Robert Orman used his arms to indicate the possibility of bugs or surveillance equipment in the room. "We are all going to address each other as *habibi*."

They all looked around the room to see if they could spot the devices, but they never left their chairs.

The host continued, "We all have no doubts why we are here. We are in our continued struggle to push the infidels out of our holy lands. The oil is not the best gift *The God* has given to us. Our martyrs are the best gift. One day we may run out of oil but we will never run out of martyrs."

The first on the right spoke, "Well said *habibi*, our martyrs are our best commodity, best arsenal and best silent warriors. They can inflict the terror of one army. How can we help today to continue pushing the infidels and the sons of Isaac[iii] out of our holy lands?"

"If I could execute part of this task on my own I wouldn't have to bother you and risk exposure, but before I tell you of the task at hand, I must educate you all about the importance of this mission." Robert Orman sipped his tea. "I know the efforts of our

---

[i] Allāh is derived from a contraction of the Arabic words *al* the and *ilāh* deity thus meaning The God.

[ii] Habibi is the Arabic that literally means "my beloved", it's commonly used as in darling, honey, dear, or friend.

[iii] Both Muslim and Jews have Abraham as their ancestor. Abraham's wife Sarah couldn't bear a son for him, thus their slave Hagar bore Abraham his first son, Ishmael. Later Sarah bore Abraham a second son, Isaac. At Sarah's insistence, Abraham banished his first born and his slave into the desert. It has been historically accepted that Muslims are sons of Ishmael and Jews are sons of Isaac. To validate Sarah's deed, Jews to this day, only recognize a person as a Jew if the person's mother was born from a Jewish lineage.

brothers from *The Base*[i] are already in progress. We shall not disturb them. What I have in mind is going to cause a much greater destruction. While our brothers at *The Base* are creating a token attack against the symbol of the financial institution, our attack is going to destroy the whole financial set up and the government as well."

The guests looked at each other and they began to murmur to themselves and to each other, trying to guess what could be stronger than the attack already underway.

"Brothers, I ran into this source of information after I learned from a report of what happened in Brazil in September of 1987. It was in the city of Goiânia near the Brazilian capital. Some scavengers dismantled a metal canister. The canister happened to be from an old radiotherapy machine used in a cancer clinic. Those infidels pried the canister open and were happy to find a pretty glowing blue powder. The whole town was eventually exposed to 1400 curies[ii] of Cesium-137. A six year old girl died on the same day from radiation complications and 244 people were contaminated, 54 of them seriously. This was the biggest radioactive disaster since Chernobyl, and people don't speak of it." Robert noticed that the second guest to the right was eager to ask a question. "*Habibi* and brothers, allow me to do the presentation. I feel confident that I will cover most of your doubts. Please keep your questions to the end.

"So as I was saying, many houses in Goiânia had to be bulldozed, and all of the contents discarded and buried in concrete and later covered with a layer of dirt. Thirty four thousand people were screened with a Geiger counter. Cesium-137 has a half-life[iii] of 30 years. This means that unlike the attack that *The Base* is

---

[i] Al-Qaeda, transliterated means "the base" or "the foundation."

[ii] The curie is a unit of radioactivity, defined as: 1 Curie = 3.7 times 10^{10} decays per second.

[iii] The half-life is the interval a radioactive substance reaches half of its original decay rate.

setting up, that is going to show our wrath and terror, our attack is going to cause permanent damage.

"Brazil was not prepared to contain or handle what had been an accident. If an accident was so costly, imagine a deliberate attack. It could cause permanent damage to this economy.

"I have harvested throughout the last three years 20 canisters of Cesium-137. I also have studied the wind pattern for the distribution, and I have selected the ten best locations in New York and Washington to broadcast it."

Robert Orman took four sheets from his folder and said to the two seated at the center, "Please, I need you to switch seats. I need you to be seated New York, Washington, New York, Washington." Orman observed them switch seats and he explained his request. "We need to keep our task private from each other because if one of the cells gets caught, it will not interfere with the work of the other. The more secretive we are, the more effective we become.

"Before I hand out the task and location to broadcast the radiation, I need to know if you all can provide us with ten martyrs. Five for New York and five for D.C."

Robert Orman noticed that he had the agreement of all of them. He got the first two sheets and gave them to the first and the third from his right, and the second set to the second and fourth. "The locations pointed out on this list provide necessary privacy and elevation for the radioactive particles to float farther. The more elevated the distribution, the farther the airborne particle will spread."

The guests looked at each other's faces showing a smile of triumph and encouragement, but they didn't utter a word.

Orman, the host asked, "Are we ready for a demonstration?"

"Sure *habibi* we are," said the first on the right.

Orman with both of hands, the right hand immobilized yet with partial movement just offered support. He didn't want to offend his guests by only using his left hand. The first brief case was opened, and nestled in cutout foam was a Geiger counter. The device had a box shape and a handle right on the top, the same classic look of the charcoal clothes pressing iron. Besides looking new and yellow it had a digital dial. The side of the device had a grid for the speaker. Robert turned the device on. A red LED[i] indicator turned on. Then Robert moved the Geiger reader next to the other brief case. Robert Orman rested the Geiger counter on the table and opened the locks with his left hand.

Robert said, "Dear *habibi,* would you help me lift this case and open it? It's a little heavier than usual because it has lead plates on the inside walls."

The case once opened, the Geiger began to measure the Rehms about one bit per second. Inside the case there was a canister that resembled a metal thermo-bottle. It had a shiny body and a cap. Robert moved the Geiger closer and the Rehms began to sound like the static noise of an AM Radio out of reach of the broadcast.

After two seconds Robert said, "That's enough, please close the case. We have been bombarded with the equivalent of ten X-ray doses already."

The case was closed; the Geiger turned off and nestled back in the case.

"It cost me a lot of money to harvest this from junkyards, school technicians, weapon dealers and the Russian Mafia. What I brought with me today is five percent of the arsenal."

"May *The God* pay you tenfold *habibi*," said the second to his left.

---

[i] LED Light Emitting Diode, usually used in equipments to indicate function or on/off.

The host continued, "I am not looking for payment, I am already re-paying…" The smile was faint but it was on Orman's lips. "Like I've said before, our brothers at *The Base* may paralyze and demoralize this country for a while and Washington for a day or two. We can make the combined of twenty to thirty million people homeless. Hysteria, panic, even a revolution may begin. This will paralyze the Jewish banks. The Europeans and Asians might not sit around until Wall Street is back in action. They might drop the dollar and start to use Europe as a financial base. If America runs out of money to finance the Zionists, then we can free Palestine and the Holy land to our brothers. The half-life of Cesium-137 is thirty years; it will take them at least ten years to clean up, both New York and Washington. The city will not collect taxes because there will be no one living here."

"Habibi!" almost in unison the guests had a question for Riald, but only the elder in the second chair spoke. *"Habibi,* we have our lives, businesses and property in our towns, what should we do?"

"We are talking about our war and our *struggle*[i] against the infidels and you bring profit to the table?" he noticed that no one answered. "But I understand that you have your families to feed and honor… My suggestion is that you have a couple of months to sell your property and move your businesses. However, if any of this and the real reason for your move gets revealed, I will personally erase the heirs attached to your names. Your family names will never be spoken again, understood?"

The elder again spoke to Orman, *"The God* is my witness and you have my word and secrecy." The remaining three acknowledged the same pledge.

---

[i] *Jihad,* from the Arabic "to put forth utmost effort, or to struggle," which is supposed to connote an inward spiritual struggle, unfortunately connotation is lost to denotation and thus an excuse for war. For instance, Saint Augustine spoke of his *jihad* or spiritual struggle in his many autobiographical books called *Confessions.*

"I have to keep my harvest," Robert pointed to the radioactive case, "in a very secure place. The American secret service has scanners in all tunnels coming to the Island of Manhattan. I brought this harvest by private boat. After all the members from *The Base* are successful with their attacks, five martyrs will meet me in Manhattan to disperse the contents in the air. Then I will travel to Washington by the afternoon so we can disperse in D. C. as well."

The second to the left asked, "*Habibi*, why do they have to be martyrs? Can't they survive after dispensing the Cesium?"

"All of the martyrs will have to die after their distribution. The reason is that each of them will be near the substance, unprotected from 20 to 40 minutes and in two to three days they will be diagnosed with severe radiation poisoning. Therefore, you will also arrange for their accidental death, by mugging, car wreck or permanent disappearance. Believe me, their organs will stop functioning and they will be in agonizing pain, coughing up blood and not able to hold anything in their stomachs.

"They'll have to be killed in a way that causes the coroner not to order an autopsy; if they do perform an autopsy, the secret service will track them to us. So the best solution is total and permanent eradication of the cell. I'll leave it up to you... You have experience in these matters."

Happy with the response the same guest said, "It makes sense; my martyrs are ready for the sacrifice and to meet their brothers in paradise."

"Well spoken *habibi,* and so are mine." said the other.

"Brothers," spoke Orman, "Our wrath will be much greater than our brothers' from *The Base*. Rest assured that our participation will be seen in much higher regard."

After they all had left the room, Robert Orman removed his disguise, Judy was aware that as a woman she wouldn't have had the respect or credibility to set up her agenda. She had to impersonate her late brother.

Jackson, Mississippi

The flight to Jackson was uneventful, and the airport's car rental had just rented a car to Mr. Ned Toby Syais. Sydney took his inconspicuous silver sedan on Interstate 20 eastbound to Meridian. He turned the radio on and left it on the AM dial. The announcer was talking about basketball from the previous night, so he hit the seek/scan bottom to find something more appealing or educational, or even the news. Soon enough, he realized why these lands were known as the Bible-Belt. The money changers that Jesus had fought not to commercialize God were no longer at the entrance of Synagogues, but they were upgraded to a more septic method. They were comfortably nestled in the radio booth with telemarketers standing nearby, waiting for a call on a 1-800 telephone number. Marketing was definitely a strong force in the world. In the name of Jesus, billions of dollars are raised. However, love alone will not make the phone ring. Fear is a much stronger inducer to activate the 1-800 phone lines. The fear of the devil is always placed on strangers. The Jesus whom Elijah had met, had the looks closer to a Persian or a Middle Easterner, but every photo he had found of Jesus, had the appearance of an Anglo-Saxon. This was not the first time he remembered confronting this deceit. The Italian rendition of Jesus when it was fresh by the hands of Michelangelo and Leonardo da Vinci had given him the same antipathy, since the looks of Jesus is an act of propaganda. Why wouldn't the American version of Jesus look American? Would a foreign looking Jesus take away the national or regional pride? Would a Jewish looking Jesus take away the propaganda that most Christians have been projecting against the Jews for the last two millenniums? Sydney was cooking all these thoughts in his head while he kept searching for a voice of equanimity on the radio; however, he found none. There was only fear and loathing in the name of Jesus for only $19.95 plus shipping and handling, call fast while supplies last. These thoughts took him back to the last time he was with Lucia, except that in this lifetime she still wanted to be called Lilith.

San Diego reminded Sydney of the soothing temperature of Italy during Spring. The sky was so deep and bright blue, it only needed the rocky landscape to take him back to the Greek city of Mikonos. He set his drive on mental cruise control so once again he could, in his mind, treasure the view of the restaurant overlooking the water, and graced by the company of Lilith.

"This place is beautiful and bright." said Sydney.

"I come here at least once a week. They cater to a vegetarian and organic menu."

"Excellent!" Sydney remained silent scanning his surroundings.

"So where do you go next, now that you know your mission?"

"The first thing that I need to mention is my gratitude for keeping *the Link* alive and my regret for getting you involved in this wrath."

"I was only fulfilling my purpose, *presto vestrum propositum in vitae.* Don't worry. I saw it coming—if you don't believe me, ask the insurance adjustors."

They both laughed and sipped their beverages.

"Where do I go next?" Sydney asked himself. "Continue with my calculations and try to track Jesus? Nowadays he must go by another name and I doubt that he is wearing long hair and robes."

"One can never tell…"

"You are right, we will see… The region that Luke and I narrowed down last time together was back in 1950. He was to be born in the year of 1991 in Mississippi."

"Why didn't Horace make the intervention then?" she smiled, "Did he bring gold and myrrh?"

"I'm glad to see that you are such a comedienne in this incarnation."

"Of course, I'm a double Sagittarian, I can't help it!"

"Luke and I agreed that it would be very difficult to narrow down to one or three families. The global population today is pretty much five and a half billion more than it was two thousand years ago. We thought that it would be best when He could speak for Himself and talk to us. Meeting Him as a baby would only attract Nicholas to spoil the event that we had been planning for so long."

"Ironic, the Bible-Belt is waiting for Jesus and He may already be there. I thought *The Rapture* would come first."

Sydney explained, "Now you touched on the subject that I have to talk to Him about, I have always imagined that *The Rapture* was an inner struggle like the Muslim Jihad. Well, Jesus had left a message of love and detachment from anger but not too long after his death and until now, it has been mostly a message of fear of God and fear of the devil; God is watching you and the devil is watching you. In most sermons the same amount of time is spent talking about the devil as talking about God. If anthropologists were to study these sermons 10,000 years from now, they would conclude that the Christians are not monotheist but they hold a duotheistic view.

"The Christians have observed good and evil in the world and they've found the gods to represent them spiritually, a dualistic approach. The good god is worshiped with love and the bad god is worshiped with fear and loathing. They would conclude that duotheism, otherwise the good god would not allow the bad god to exist. The good god has infinite power but not infinite enough to destroy the bad god."

"Hum, I'd never looked at it that way, but when you mention it, it's true. They do give the devil equal time. In fact, that's all I hear when I have soul savers knocking on my door."

Sydney concluded, "So you see? I need to speak with Him and ask, why has the message changed so much?" he paused for a second. "Why don't you want to come Lilith?"

"It's tempting but no. What would be the point of looking for the Big JC if He is already inside my heart? Whenever I want to meet Jesus, Buddha or Krishna, I don't have to travel far but only twelve inches from my head." She pointed her index finger to her heart.

"You are a much better person than I am," said Sydney.

"Let's not argue about that, you win!" she started to laugh.

They both laughed again and Sydney's mind found itself reading a passing sign, 56 miles to travel to Meridian, MS.

XVI
Capitulus Sedecim

Miami, Florida

he elevator door opened inside the Federal Building in Miami. Two agents stepped out, one had a folder. Rick Sarturo was then handed the folder and they continued to walk towards the conference room.

"Dave, is this folder complete with all the info that we have available on Judy Orman?"

"Yes sir, down to the credit card purchases for the last two years." Dave opened the door of the conference room for his superior. They took the seats at the corner of the large table so it would be easier for both of them to read the same file. "Agent Sarturo, let me turn the pages and give you a summary of her life."

"Go ahead." Sarturo dropped the folder and saw Dave starting the presentation.

"Sir, by now I know her better than I know some of my relatives. Judy Orman, Jewish family born in Alberta, Canada. Father had a law degree but worked as a banker and the mother was a homemaker. At her age of nine the family moved to Montrose, New York in the Catskill area.

"A year later at the age of ten, her twin brother Robert Orman was kidnapped. It was assumed by the local police that he'd been killed; at least it was what the police report said. His body was never found."

"If he was kidnapped, was there a demand for ransom or exchange?"

"The school secretary along with Judy reported that a 35 to 42 year old man had taken him from school. The boy was never seen again. The whole town was sad because according to school records, the boy was a genius.

"Moving along; there was nothing exceptional about her academic achievements except for when she got to the university level. She speaks seven languages that we know of, some of her classmates reported that there was no language that she could not understand. She never dated anyone during high-school or at the university."

"Not even girls?"

"No sir, we didn't find anyone."

"Hum?"

"But that's not the interesting part." He saw Sarturo's puzzled expression. "She got three PhD's in two years."

"Is that possible?"

"She paid for all the required courses and *clep* all of the courses."

"What is that?"

"She would pay for the courses, then never attend classes but she would show up for the tests and ace them. One time she challenged her history teacher; he lost and she got an 'A' without showing up for the entire semester. The few times her classmates saw her they had a nickname for her, Robot Orman, but they would say robot-or-man. The epithet questioned whether she was a robot or a man, as in human.

"A lot of companies were seeking her for employment. Even our *compadres* at the CIA tried to recruit her for intelligence, language and code breaking."

"What about her family?"

"Actually, I was debating which info was the most interesting, the schooling or this. Both of her parents were killed in a fire a few days before her eighteenth birthday.

"She inherited a million and a half, which she turned into a half a billion dollars according to her last year's tax return using the stock market."

"So the broad is rich, single and does not work?"

"No sir, she does, at least she did. After leaving school she worked at the Library of Congress for seven years, then she left for Europe to work as a librarian at the Vatican as well."

"So far I have one big question. A Jewish girl with three PhD's and language skills working at the Vatican Library, who made a killing on the stock market, who may or may not try to kill another astrologer, who is known for giving stock market tips to Paul Stein, another billionaire. What's wrong with this picture?" Sarturo drifted on a puzzle looking at the paper in front of him.

"Sir if I may?" Dave waited for acknowledgement. "I think it will be a mistake to call her for interrogation about the killings of two months ago. I think we need to keep her under surveillance and catch her in the act. By calling her in, it's just going to make it more difficult for us to keep an eye on her."

Sarturo contemplated the suggestion but it was too late. The telephone buzzed.

"Agent Sarturo, your two o'clock is here," said the voice from the device.

"Please send them in." He depressed the button and directed to Dave. "We are the anti-Houdinis. We are about to let our magician know that we are sick of her tricks and wait to see if she can make a mistake."

There was a knock on the door and an agent opened it for the two guests.

"Welcome," said Sarturo professionally. "I appreciate you both taking the time to see us."

Instead of offering a handshake, the esquire offered his business card and a challenge. "My name is Jerry Rosemblaum and before we start, I would like to know if my client Ms. Judy Orman is being charged with anything?"

"No Mr. Rosemblaum, today's visit is totally voluntary."

The middle aged man going sixty said to his client, "This is just a harassment tactic and it's my advice that we should leave."

"It's okay Jerry; let's see if they offer us coffee." She sat down and saw Jerry follow.

They both sat across from the table. Sarturo signaled to Dave.

"What would you like?" asked Dave, upset that once again he was turning into a waiter.

"Right now I am fine. However, if this takes more than twenty minutes, then I will love to have one of the cappuccinos they sell at the concession down in the lobby."

Mr. Rosemblaum started, "Why are we here?"

"I was getting to that," said Sarturo, "Today we would like to clear out some of our misinformation… You see? We don't have anything against Ms. Orman, but we have on record that her twin brother died at the age of ten and suddenly his name and social security resurfaced in San Diego a couple of months ago in conjunction with an explosion."

She whispered in her lawyer's ear and he did the same to her. "This is the first time I've heard Robert's name since I was ten. I saw a man come to school. I thought that he was our new driver, to take him back home early. However, Bobby never arrived home. If he is indeed alive he is due half of my inheritance."

"So you don't have or never had or don't know any clues about Robert Orman?"

"I think that was what my client just said."

Judy saw her inquisitor waiting for an answer and said, "Yes."

"So you have?" asked Sarturo watching the lawyer to see if he was going for the block.

"Mr. Sarturo, I have a doctorate in languages and it is not customary for me to answer a question like this in the negative. When you play back the tape you will hear that your question was; *So you don't have or never had or don't know any clues about Robert Orman?* And my answer to that would be; Yes, I never did... Please ask me your questions in the affirmative to make things clear."

Sarturo took a second to let the implosion of anger subside and not show; then started the second question. "Have you ever contributed money to a Neo-Nazi group in the United States, Spain or Gemany?"

The lawyer got up, "This is an insult! My client is from a Jewish family and I knew her father in college."

Sarturo noticed that not only Rosemblaum was surprised but Dave as well; with the new revelations about a person Dave thought he knew. He also noticed that no emotion was coming from Ms. Orman. "Mr. Rosemblaum please sit, I am doing my job. Did you know that your client converted to Catholicism at the age of fifteen and her father was going to disinherit her?"

Ms. Orman replied, "Impressive, I never thought the FBI would have a file on me; however," she continued, "my parents were non-practicing Jews and they held no judgment when I became interested in another faith. Now, in regard to the Nazi contribution the answer is no."

"Ms. Orman, you hold 55% of the stock in a Spanish internet/telecom company and we were able to track the funds to it."

"We had problems with one director a couple of years ago, and he has been replaced, moreover I've been no longer a majority share holder since last year."

"Do you know Sydney Tobias?"

"Who doesn't? He is the astrologer that comes on TV sometimes during *The Margaret's Show*. I browsed his first book, but I didn't find it interesting." She turned to her lawyer and said, "Do you think you can treat me to a cappuccino downstairs? The questions are no longer about me."

They all stood up and Mr. Rosemblaum said, "If you have any more questions or comments please call my office."

Both Dave and Sarturo cordially acknowledged in silence as they left the room.

After the door was shut behind them Dave pointed, "I didn't find this Nazi or Spanish connection."

"And you won't. I have a friend from the Bronx that now is CIA. They are also tailing her. This same Spanish company continues to make contributions to Hezbollah and Al Qaeda."

"I've heard of Hezbollah, but who is Al Qaeda?"

"A group of extremists that branched out of the Mohajadins and the Taliban that fought the Soviets out of Afganistan."

"No wonder I've never heard of them."

Meridian, Mississippi

"Excuse me…" Sydney asked the reference librarian. "Is it okay if I leave the mess on that table? I just need to grab a bite and I'll be right back." Sydney's southern drawl made him sound indigenous.

"No problem," the male clerk answered. "Just hand me the box of microfilms. I won't put it away, I'll keep it right here behind my desk for safety."

Sydney did what he was told and went to his table next to the microfilm projector, brought the selection back. "Do you need anything from the diner across the street?"

"No, I'm good, but thank you for asking."

Sydney sat down with the neighborhood's newspaper. It was refreshing for him to notice that on his third day, the waitress already treated him like a regular. From afar he waved his hand in greeting, and then signaled her with a number four.

Beatrice Preston understood that a grilled tuna sandwich was to be ordered, and that the ice tea and salad were part of the routine as well.

Sydney had already memorized all the newspaper clippings and pictures of the diner hanging on the walls. He noticed the timeline by the shoddy old plaster work that was done, probably by the owner and not by a professional. He opened his town tattler press to wait for his meal, and to entertain himself. Sydney noticed a man in his forties taking an interest in him. Sydney began to feel a little tense because that same gentleman commenced to walk toward him.

"Excuse me, are you a salesperson too?"

Before Sydney could answer Beatrice placed the salad and the ice tea on the table, "Here we go. I see that you've met Gerard… Ned, Gerard… Gerard, Ned." She left.

"Thank you Beebee." Sydney also thanked Beatrice for something she wouldn't be aware of, by presenting Gerard, Sydney realized that he was not one of Nicholas' lieutenants. "I was never asked that before. What gave you this impression?"

"I'm a traveling salesman, car parts. East Mississippi is my territory. I reckon that I must have seen you at least, in three different towns."

"You are correct, I've been traveling around, I am doing a book research. I've been scavenging old archives at the local libraries."

"Now I know why I ran into you." Gerard continued, "I upload my sales order using the internet from the libraries."

"Your food hasn't arrived yet. Why don't you have a seat?"

Gerard took the seat, "Book research? What kind?"

"Local folklore, but mainly looking for children around nine to eleven with special talents, or events with special circumstances."

"Special talents? Like juggling or something?"

"No not quite. Something more subtle — every town has some special circumstance that they can't explain or something that would be rare or misunderstood."

"Oh... I see..." He was pensive for a little bit and said, "I guess this could qualify."

"Let us hear it, everything helps."

"Although I work in Mississippi now, I am actually from Demopolis, Alabama, not far from the west border with Mississippi. It's a small town, off I-20 interstate; the usual suspects milling around, the name of the town on the water tower, you get the picture.

"Next door to us there was a black family. One of them was Joyce Johnson, who even babysat me when I was young. I lost touch with them when I went to college, but then as I was away in college this thing happened to Jojo.

191

"Jojo was our nickname for Mrs. Johnson, who was always volunteering at the Baptist Church. She continued to baby-sit for other families and she was always busy, there was always something to do.

"So one day she saw that a storm was coming. She went to the church to close the upper windows. But for her to close the upper windows she had to use a long metal rod. When she still had one window to go, a lightning bolt found a shorter path; it went through the steeple, then the window hardware, the long rod, Jojo's body and finally, a wet floor. The lightning bolt threw her backwards and luckily they found her still alive but on the ground, with burns and unconscious."

Sydney was eating and listening. "If you were in college who told you this story?"

"My younger sister had heard everything and told me, but the entire town knew Jojo and everyone had a version... But that's not the interesting part. She was in a coma at the hospital for about two months. She recovered and started to talk again. However, while at the hospital they did some more tests and discovered that she was pregnant. She told my sister that she had never been with a man. She pleaded with all of her family that it couldn't be possible but no one believed her. Some thought that she had been taken advantage of during her coma.

"But by the time her son, Charlie started to go to school the kids began to harass and to mock him and her. They were saying things like, 'In case the power goes out, could I use Charlie as a generator?' or 'Hey kid, tell your father Thor, that we need rain again.'"

"People can be mean," said Sydney.

"Kendrick Johnson, a pastor and a second cousin of Jojo, was looking after Jojo's mother. When the old lady died, he took Jojo and Charlie to another town where people didn't know of the incident."

"Where do they live now?"

"The last I heard they moved to either Eutaw or Akron."

"How old is the kid now?"

"He must be between eight or ten."

"I told you this story because only my sister and Jojo believe that she was never with a man. I don't partake with this opinion, but I'm passing on this information as I got it."

Sydney calculated for a few seconds and said, "Lunch is on me. I am looking for stories like that."

"Don't I know you from somewhere?" asked Gerard.

"I've been told several times that I look like a celebrity on TV."

"No that can't be, I don't watch it, but you look familiar."

Sydney started remembering some imagery from post WWII. There, right there, he saw Gerard's face and he said, "Maybe we met in a past life?"

"Whatever you say, I'm cheap, I don't argue with a person buying me lunch," he chuckled.

After lunch, as soon as he left the restaurant crossing the street to the library, Tobias dialed Rick Sarturo.

"Sarturo here."

"This is Ned, remember me? We met in another life?"

"Hey Syd, good to hear from you, unfortunately I don't have anything new, unless you do."

"Nope, I've been chasing my tail doing some research but it would have been faster if I had my leather bound book you found under the safe. I lost it in Coconut Grove. Actually, the contracted assassin took it from me."

"Sydney, you've been no more than four months down there and you've already picked up a Southern drawl."

"*Ain't that somethin'?*" Sydney emphasized.

Sarturo chuckled, "I'm sorry about that. Does the book have a relevance to this person chasing you?"

193

Sydney replied, "No, not really, but it would have been a good thing to fine tune my calculations."

"I have some good news for you. Before giving the original back to you, I made copies of all of the pages. I can send them to you."

I'm in Meridian, Mississippi. Could you overnight it to the Hotel Meridian Fest?"

After Sarturo wrote down the address he said, "I've got it."

"Rick, I appreciate it." Sydney hung up and noticed Gerard waving good bye from the restaurant. That brought him back to the last time Gerard had waved goodbye in Lisbon, Portugal in 1947. After two years together, they went their separate ways except that then, Gerard's name was Wilhelm. Sydney went back to his table at the library but continued to reminisce on their past lives together.

XVII
Capitulus Septemdecim

**Soviet Occupied Germany,
1947 C.E.**

*err* Nielsen! Wait up," screamed Wilhelm to Peter Nielsen. They were catching a train in Soviet Occupied Berlin. In a few hours they would be in Chemnitz.

"Where do we get off?"

"This train makes several stops in Leipzig where we switch locomotives. *Comprenez-vous ?*"

"*Oui monsieur, je comprends… Herr* Nielsen, please no French lessons today."

They walked into the car and sat opposite each other. Each pair of chairs sat four. Peter and Wilhelm were joined by a stranger.

Twenty minutes after the train moved, the man who sat holding on to decorum of better days spoke, "*Hallo, mein name ist* Karl Krupke. I hope you enjoy the city of Chemnitz and Rabenstein, my neighborhood."

Wilhelm responded, "Well thank you, but what makes you think it is our first time in town, *Herr* Krupke?"

"First, you are both well dressed, fresh fabric. Germany for now lacks a lot of goods, especially fabric, since the cease fire two years ago. Secondly, I know every face from my town and the faces of their families and neither of you resemble anyone I know."

Wilhelm remained silent but Peter spoke, "*Ich bin* Peter Nielsen *und er ist* Wilhelm. *Herr* Krupke, thank you for your welcome. You have a keen eye for observation."

"*Es ist mein vergnügen, Herr* Nielsen, my pleasure indeed. The observation is the latent instinct that one acquires during war for basic survival."

"So if you allow my observations…" Peter waited for Karl's consent and he began. "You are a believer of Madame Blavatsky and her Teachings and Theosophical Society. You were also a member of the National Socialist, the Nazis, when they were still called the German Workers' Party. You've either sold or recently lost your wedding band. So how is a Nazi like you getting along these days?"

"Please, keep your voice down. You are right about everything except for one. I didn't sell my ring. It was taken from me at a Soviet check point."

"I'm sorry about that, I thought the war was over," said Wilhelm with ambivalence and a mix of contempt and sympathy.

"It will take some time for all wounds to heal," said Peter.

Karl Krupke replied, "But how did you know about my membership in the Theosophical Society and that I was also an ex-party member?" the last words he said softly, just above the railroad noises.

"You carry a posture and demeanor of the proud. The allies may take away your weapons but the pride still remains in your posture. The hint that you are a Nazi was when you used the word ceased. Most people, the non-Nazis, call it surrender. I could also tell that your hand is not comfortable with the absence of the ring. You keep touching the finger where your wedding band used to be."

Wilhelm asked, "*Herr* Nielsen, who is *Frau* Blavatsky?"

"She was a psychic, her name was Helena Petrovna Blavatsky, born in Russia. She immigrated to the United States and there she created the Theosophical Society. It was a mixture of New Age, Christianity, Paganism and the Occult."

"Why would a Nazi like her teachings?"

He looked at Karl and continued, "Because, *Frau* Blavatsky wrote a book called *The Secret Doctrine,* in which she described seven stages that the human race ought to advance to by suppressing the inferior ones. She had followers in Germany like Guido Von List[i]. He used Madame Blavatsky's theosophy and gave birth to Ariosophy, the philosophy of White Supremacy. These are all very familiar arguments to *Herr* Krukpe."

Looking from one side to another Krupke responded, "I don't think we should continue this conversation."

Peter replied, "Oh no, I think we should, when we arrive in Chemnitz we are going to stop somewhere without many prying ears so near us and have a little chat."

They all arrived in Chemnitz. Instructions were given to the porter to take their bags to the hotel. They followed Krupke to a secluded tavern. On a Tuesday afternoon there was no one at the place except for the owner, reading a hand me down newspaper and listening to the radio by the counter. The room was not properly lit, the windows were scarce and the lights were off to conserve energy. They picked the outermost table in the room. The owner managed to bring three mugs of beer.

---

[i] Born as Guido Karl Anton List, (1848 - 1919), author of *Secret of the Runes*, he was fiercely influenced by Madame Blavatsky's thoughts, List merged his own racism into Germanic mysticism during late XIX and early XX century.

Krupke took the first drink and said, "We used to have the best beer in all of Germany. Now we get this thing from Russia, and I bet this is horse's urine mixed with alcohol."

Peter puts down his mug, "I've tasted horse's urine and it wasn't this bad."

For the first time they all laughed and smiled, it was a good thing to break the tension. Finally, they all had one point that they could all agree upon.

Krupke asked, "So are you going to coerce and interrogate me? Offer me to the Soviets as a token?"

Peter continued, "No *Herr* Krupke, we don't partake in such crude methods. They don't elicit good results."

"Who are *we*, the French, Americans, English or the Jews?"

"None of the ones mentioned. *We* are here and *we* are your new friends, who will remain anonymous. With each piece of information we receive from you, we... Actually, I will give you ten American dollars."

Karl Krupke protested, "I'm not going to sell anyone!" he muted his exclamation.

"Of course not, this money is not to buy anything; it is to pay for your time as a consultant, if you will."

They were silent for a while and after they sipped their beers, Peter began. "We are trying to connect or to get some information that may lead us to Gustav Markus Dornberger. He must be in his mid sixties."

"I've never heard of that name." Then Krupke noticed that Peter moved his mug just slightly to reveal a folded ten dollar bill under it. "But perhaps we may be talking about Father Dornberger." Karl saw Peter push the mug across the table and bring it back, exposing the note next to him. "When Father Gröber died in an air raid in Berlin, Father Dornberger was brought to replace him. Although his sermon was in German, he'd only celebrate the masses in Latin. Some of us appreciated, some didn't;

however, one thing was interesting, he would make statements that would inspire and incite nationalism." Karl was interrupted by what could be magic. He was already seeing another note appear beneath Peter's mug, but instead of questioning the trick, he continued his testimony. "Many of the things that Father Dornberger preached sounded like articles from Lanz Von Liebenfels[i] that I used to read in my copies of Ostara Magazine[ii]. Father Dornberger would call us *gottmenschen*, god-men and that we were here for a mission. The mission was to make this planet a paradise again by eliminating the impure or Jesus' killers. He used to end his sermon with this phrase, *Er, wier Kenntnis kontrolliert, kontrolliert die Welt, He who controls knowledge, controls the world. We are Germans and we have the knowledge on our side.* It was always a variation of this."

Peter slid his mug again, revealing the new note, before he brought the mug to his lips he asked, "Where is he?"

Karl took the note and said, "After every able teenager and adult man enlisted in the army, he moved to another parish; I heard that the same happened in Rabenstein. I have a cousin Frida, she may know more than I; she used to be a nun for the same parish. I'll take you both to see her tomorrow."

"*Vielen Dank Herr* Krupke, thank you very much."

Next day in the afternoon they met Frida Krupke, a lady in her forties who carried herself as though, every step and every

---

[i] Adolf Josef Lanz (a.k.a. Jörg Lanz) 1874 – 1954, he was the founder of *Ostara*. As a former monk he pushed for anti-Semitic theories and the revival of the (new)Templers; calling them *gottmenschen* or god-men and the Holy Grail as a metaphor for Aryan blood purity.

[ii] *Ostara, Briefbücherei der Blonden und Mannesrechtler* was the full title of the racist publication (1905 – 1917). It was founded by Lanz Liebenfels and quoted by Hitler in *Mein Kampf.*

breath was a bad memory. A veil covered her platinum blond hair and her clothes had several patches. Unlike her cousin, she didn't carry pride on her shoulders but remorse, guilt and the whole weight of the war.

"*Willkommen Herr* Nielsen and Wilhelm. I wish I had something to offer you to drink, but it is difficult to be a good host nowadays."

"Please don't worry about that, we don't want to take much of your time," said Peter.

"How can I help you? My cousin Karl said that you are kind strangers."

"We are looking for Father Gustav Markus Dornberger," Peter delivered without ceremonies.

"You are good men, why do you seek the devil?"

"We have a score to set with him."

"As you can tell, my cousin and I hold very different opinions of the war. He is one of the few who still thinks that the Nazis were justified, he bought the whole propaganda.

"Father Dornberger," she continued, "is one of the main reasons why I left the order. I couldn't bear being a part of an institution holding hands with Hitler," she was looking at the ceiling, no place in particular. "The first time I met Father Dornberger was in 1933, Cardinal Faulhaber[i] introduced him to the congregation. He said that he had come from the high ranks of the Vatican. He was also very good friends with Cardinal Eugenio Pacelli." *Frau* Krupke noticed the look of loss in the face of Wilhelm and said, "Eugenio Pacelli is the real name of our current Pope Pius XII."

"Sister Frida, may I address you this way?" asked Peter.

---

[i] Cardinal Michael von Faulhaber (1869 – 1952) was main liaison between the Vatican and the Nazi Party. Later 1951 he ordained Joseph Alois Ratzinger as a priest who became Pope Benedict XVI. *Herr* Ratzinger's choice of papal name was a subtle homage to the Nazi-liaison and progenitor because Cardinal von Faulhaber was appointed cardinal by Pope Benedictus XV.

"Sure, I continue my vows to Christ but no longer to the Vatican."

"Tell us more about Father Dornberger, all information is important, something may lead us to him."

"People think that I left the order because I couldn't take the discipline... What I couldn't take was the silence. Unlike many, I had higher education so I ended up working in the offices for a long time. When the government started passing the anti-Semitic laws, they needed our records to see who was either a Jew or a Christian German."

"How come?" asked Wilhelm.

"The government only started to keep track of the births in 1874. As I was saying, a couple of years after I had joined the convent I was transferred to Berlin. I had to evaluate papers and names to see if the person applying to be a government servant was either an Aryan or a reject. I am sorry to use this word, but it was what was written on the form sent to me.

"So I started to do some digging in the papers on my own, and did you know that our dear *führer* Adolf Hitler was a Jew himself, or at least not a pure German? This was the highest recorded kept secret at that time.

"Theresia Pfeisinger and Johannes Schicklgruber gave birth to Maria Anna Schicklgruber. Later, Maria Anna worked as a maid and as a cook in Graz for a Jewish family, the Frankenbergers. During that time, she gave birth to Alois. She didn't want to register the father, so her son was recorded as Alois Schicklgruber, illegitimate. I also found out that the Frankenberger family had a nineteen year old son at the time, and they continued to pay her allowances for her child even after she was no longer working for them. When Alois was five, his mother finally married Johan George Hiedler. The story goes that Alois wanted his stepfather's inheritance and wanted to use his name. Instead of spelling his name correctly, he gave the clerk the name the way he thought it was spelled, thus the name Hitler commenced. We treated this knowledge very secretly because to be a German, and especially a German official, one's ancestry needed validation."

"Sister Frida, we are not interested in Hitler, we want to know about Father Dornberger," Peter addressed gently.

"You will see why I told you this story. This story, I would never tell Karl, he wouldn't believe me anyway. Now, if you are looking for Dornberger it's because he doesn't want to be found, and if he doesn't want to be found it's because his wrath is finally catching up to him. To gather all of these facts, I discovered I had to rely on more than one source, and during my investigation Father Dornberger came across it. He took all of my information and went a step further. He met the Frankenbergers, took pictures of them and found out that Alois, Hitler's father and *Herr* Frankenberger, Hitler's possible grandfather, were a duplicated painting of each other. All documents, photos, and receipts were taken to a safe place. Later I heard that after the first bomb was dropped over the Vatican, the *führer's* ancestry was going to be exposed. It was sad for me to think that the Vicar of Christ and company would consider blackmail to protect themselves, as well as working as an instrument of the Gestapo."

"We know that Father Dornberger's hatred of Jews is intense. Why is it that he did not expose Hitler?"

"I thought about it… The conclusion that I came to was that Hitler was doing Father Dornberger's deed better than he could have done it himself. Eradicating Jews and the anti-Semitic laws as well as neighbors telling on each other had a name. Father Dornberger and Cardinal Faulhaber called it *Volksgemeinschaft,*[i]

---

[i] Joseph Goebbels was appointed as Minister of Propaganda and *Volksgemeinschaft* was an attempt to enforce a national determination and a single collective mind. It was important to sell the Aryan ideology especially to the very young (a.k.a. Hitler's Youth). This indoctrination was another attempt of the Nazis to copy the Catholic Church seeing their tremendous success in creating a single collective mind through Dogmatic Catechism to the young.

the Community Spirit." She felt a lump in her throat and stopped to wipe her eyes.

They all heard a truck pull up at the sidewalk. A few seconds later a Soviet soldier knocked on the door, then allowed himself in without waiting for a reply. Sister Frida froze at this situation.

Peter stood up and said, *"Доброе утро, спасибо."* He continued in Russian, "Please, place the boxes along the wall."

One soldier waited in the truck and two soldiers unloaded eight boxes in the kitchen next to where they were seated. Peter escorted them back to the door and gave each of them some money. Then he returned to the kitchen. The print on the boxes was in Cyrillic markings. Neither Wilhelm nor Frida understood what they could have been.

"What are these?" asked Sister Frida pointing to the boxes.

"Let us not talk about them now. In time I'll explain."

Apprehensively she said, "All right."

"Sister Frida, what is your best assessment of where or with whom Father Dornberger could be now?"

"Did you look for him at the Vatican?"

"We already did, we also have agents working in Italy. Italy is clean, he is not there."

"He could be anywhere or dead, let me see..." She placed her left hand over her face and looked at the ceiling, as if she was trying to read a name. "Oh, the only person that comes to mind is Father Diefenbaker in Düsseldorf."

"Do you think he is giving him shelter?"

"No! No God no! Father Heinrich Diefenbaker could be the only one who might know his whereabouts. We had a talk years ago, I wonder how he is doing these days."

"What do you mean by that?"

"He was just as disillusioned with the Church as I was. Go and ask at the Holy Mary parish and you will find him."

"Both Will and I would like to thank you for the time you've taken to see us."

"Before you go... What are these boxes?"

"They are some provisions to make it through the winter."

"I can't accept this, this is too much."

"Sister Frida, you have a big heart. I never said that you can't share with anyone."

In silence she clasped her hands in prayer, looked at the sky and them cupped them over her heart. She looked at Peter, "May the Lord be with you. *Auf Wiedersehen.*"

It took the better part of a week to cross the Soviet held Germany and its blockades. They finally arrived in Düsseldorf, a city they'd visited before in search of Nicholas, Father Dornberger, but the name of Father Diefenbaker had not manifested back then. The next day, they arrived at Holy Mary Congregation and asked for Father Diefenbaker. At the door, they were kept waiting and the cleric returned with a phone number and a downtown address. Twenty minutes later, they walked into a book store. The entrance was constricted by walls of books on both sides. Normally, this wouldn't be the case but Peter came to the conclusion that the store was also lodging books from some destroyed buildings. As they advanced through the corridor they noticed that all the walls were covered with books, luckily these volumes had escaped Nicholas and Hitler's Book Burning Propaganda. Finally, Peter and Wilhelm approached the clerk who was placing a stack of books on the counter.

"We are looking for Father Heinrich Diefenbaker," said Wilhelm.

"Father is no longer his title. Now he is Professor Diefenbaker. He is in the back. There is a class in progress, but if you don't interrupt the class or the professor you are welcome to sit in. He doesn't have more than thirty minutes to go."

"What is the class about?"

"What else? Hitler! The man has a Ph.D. in Hitler... I am tired of hearing his name but not everyone else is. People keep coming to listen to his classes." The clerk noticed that the newcomers just exchanged glances. "This group today is interested in learning how Hitler could seduce the whole country."

"We either wait here for thirty minutes or we may learn something new about the former-*füehrer,*" said Wilhelm towards Nielsen.

Peter Nielsen said, "Then, please excuse us," they walked through another corridor.

Farther ahead they heard the dissertation in progress. They came to a room that was well lit by the sun and found three empty chairs. They became part of the crescent moon formation around the host and the blackboard.

Professor Diefenbaker noticed the newcomers but continued his speech. He placed a piece of chalk carefully at the bottom groove of the board, turned to the class, and said, "Some of you know that I used to be a priest for the local diocese. A war changes a man in many ways, my faith in Christ has not changed but my faith in the Institution has. I was asked to do things that if I did, I couldn't call myself a Christian in good conscience. Since I had been a history professor at the seminary, I resumed my teaching career.

"Very well... The Christian faith, now with many denominations, started with a compilation of beliefs, cultures and rites. Although Jesus has enough spiritual substance to stand on His own, after Jesus died, how could the followers call Him the Messiah without a connection to Adam and Eve or Genesis? Back

205

then, when they started to preach, Christians found out soon enough that He had to be more than just a young carpenter roaming around Judea telling people to forgive each other. Thus, they borrowed a birth certificate from the Jews to validate their claim. The Nazis as well, soon enough came to the same conclusion. To validate their existence they needed a birth certificate," he turned to each single member of his audience and posed a question. "Why would the Nazis bother validating their genesis or looking for a birth certificate?" the old man waited for a response.

As the professor started to scan the room for a response, Peter took it upon himself to do the same. Nielsen counted sixteen heads including himself and almost at the end of his count he recognized a face; the face of a young man. It took him just a second to realize that that person was a colleague of young Horace at Bentley Park, most likely a secret agent currently undercover... Unless he had become a reporter, but Nielsen found that very unlikely. *What was his name? Erick Hatcher, yes...* Nielsen was about to bring his eyes back to the professor when Erick made a very subtle hello. *I was right, Hatcher must be still in the British Intelligence; otherwise, there was no need to suppress the acknowledgement.*

Nobody dared to opinionate a response, thus the professor continued, "The reason why the Nazis wanted a Genesis or a birth certificate was because they wanted to be more than a political party. They wanted messiahship." He picked up a chalk and wrote three items on the blackboard and annunciated each syllable as it became visible. "Plutocrats, Theocrats and Democrats." He turned to his audience and pointing back to the board he said, "Anywhere in the world, any time in history, one of these groups is always ruling. Usually, one group needs the support of the other. This is when a little bit of brain washing is required and comes in handy.

"The Nazis were or still are, in hiding for now, a fascist group or plutocrats. They had the support of their industries and bankers. But how do you get the support of the people?" asked the professor. "By creating an alliance with the Theocrats; the Christians, the Nazis would become bigger. However, they didn't want to be subordinate to the Vatican or the Lutherans, so they created their own brand of Messiah. Hitler as the new Christ... The savior of the Aryan race and the world.

"To substantiate their beliefs, the Nazis created the Ancestral Research Unit[i]. They even invited me, but I could smell the propaganda from far away. They were not interested in the truth, only in their own conclusions.

"In the beginning, just like Christianity before the First Council of Nicaea,[ii] the Christians did not have their doctrine in one bible. The Nazis went through the same steps, compiling their beliefs and rule of conduct."

Peter noticed that a gentleman on his right raised his arm for a question. Peter deduced that he must have been a reporter or a historian.

"No need to get up... What is your question?"

As he took his seat he asked, "Professor, you keep making comparisons between the Nazis and Christianity. Why is that? Were the Nazis and the Church connected?"

"Not an institutional connection, just similarities in the steps of its genesis. The Nazis had to find a way to grow strong and fast in the minds of the Germans. Therefore, since the people were already familiar with Jesus, the Nazis found a way to paint Hitler in Christian colors, if we may say that.

"Today Christianity is an old institution, but they picked what was popular in peoples' minds and they made the old

---

[i] Founded in 1935 and incorporated into the SS Gestapo in '39 it was called the *Nazi Deutsches Ahnenerbe – Studiengesellschaft für Geistesurgeschichte*. The Ancestry Division looked for occult connections to the past to corroborate their beliefs that Nordics must have ruled the world.

[ii] The First Council of Nicaea, requested by Constantine I in 325 A.D., became the first worldly conference of the Christian Church to consolidate disagreements. It was attended by 300 priests and bishops.

knowledge part of the Christian tradition, like the Solstice Tree Celebration from the Nordics, the Christmas tree today. The concept of heaven and hell is also very Christian today; however, it is a copy of the Greek Mythos, where Zeus or Jupiter was replaced by a monotheistic God and the lesser gods assembly was substituted by angels and saints. Another one is the act of communion. Ancient tribes, especially cannibals, would eat their elders upon their death to assimilate their wisdom and spirit. Today this tradition has been sanitized. It is called Christ Communion, where Christians eat the body of Christ and drink His blood in the symbolic form of wafer and wine, to embody His spirit unto themselves. This borrowing and taking from different cultures have made the story of Adam and Eve just as much a Christian tradition as a Jewish one.

"In the same way, the Nazis did not pull the idea of the Aryan race[i] out of a hat. Aryan is of course, a Sanskrit name just as much as the Swastika[ii] is borrowed from the Hindu culture. The idea of a superior Aryan race was being developed in Germany and Austria for a long time. There was a publication named Ostara that kept these sentiments alive. Heinrich Himmler[iii], Rudolph Hess[iv], Hitler and many others grew up reading these publications. So by the time they took power, these beliefs were the foundation of their philosophy. They had to exercise these beliefs…"

An interruption came from the left of the professor, "That's not right!"

"What is not right young man, the facts or the moral aspects of it?"

---

[i] Aryan comes from the Sanskrit meaning noble or exalted.

[ii] Another symbol taken by Hitler from the Hindu tradition; however, the Nazi's used the mirror image or reverse direction. In the East symbolizes prosperity and in the West is a symbol for racism.

[iii] Heinrich Luitpold Himmler (1900-1945) Commander of the SS or *Schutzstaffel*. Himmler was the leading organizer of the Holocaust during WWII.

[iv] Walter Richard Rudolf Hess (1894-1987) Hitler's deputy.

"Of course it is the moral aspect," said the reporter, his age to be in the mid-twenties, he was young and eager.

"Listen up everyone! Today we are not here to discuss the moral aspect of the Nazis or any group. If you get me started on the moral grounds, we are not going to have enough time. Morality is what has made me turn the white collar in. When you see your cardinal giving you orders to make copies of a list of baptismal certificates so that the Nazis may validate their purity, filter and dismiss people working for their government, you come to the conclusion that that is immoral. I thought that by being transferred to Rome and the Vatican for a while I would find a moral institution. Later the Nazis sent a lieutenant, Herbert Kappler[i] to round up all the Jews to transfer them to the killing camps. See? The Nazi rationale was to keep the objective of the camps hidden. To everyone else, it looked like the Jews were being sent to a reservation vacation camp, where they would be concentrated. The Nazis called it concentration camps to have a more neutral and moral tone, but they were actually killing camps.

"I begged my superiors but I was told that the Pope was more concerned about saving the art work of the Vatican and buildings than using his political power and weight to stop the genocide in progress. Pope Pious XII[ii] paid more attention to the Vatican librarian's pleas than to a school of his cardinals and bishops that were trying to save lives. I think the Sistine Chapel is beautiful but not worth the lives of 1026 Jewish mothers, fathers and children."

Wilhelm nudged Peter Nielsen upon hearing the reference to the Vatican's librarian; Father Dornberger. Peter kept his eyes on the speaker, showed no emotion, and made a small gesture to his assistant for him to abate his excitement.

---

[i] Herbert Kappler was posted in Rome in 1939 he was a SS-*Obersturmbannführer* Officer.

[ii] Pope Pius XII (1876-1958), named Eugenio Maria Giuseppe Giovanni Pacelli reigned as pope from 1939 to 1958.

Professor Diefenbaker continued, "Actually 1023—only three returned from the concentration camps..." He removed his handkerchief from his left pocket and his spectacles from his face, dried his eyes and continued. "So let us keep the emotional and moral aspects away from the facts.

"The facts are that the Nazis were able to recruit many more and have them fight with more disposition, because they were able to turn Hitler into the savior and messiah of the Aryan cause. They were so in love with their own propaganda that even they started to believe it. The case in point is: Rudolph Hess parachuted into Scotland[i] because he was sure that he could convince their Aryan cousins; the Anglos, that the Nazis had a spiritual calling..."

"Was Hess able to have his audience with Churchill?" the first reporter asked.

"Nope," replied the professor, "they locked him up for the remainder of the war. Even Hitler severed association with him."

"What had possessed him to take such an action, to parachute into the United Kingdom?" another question came.

"It's because the House of Windsor in England, the nobles and their families are actually of German descendants. During World War I, the Windsors changed their name from Sachsen-Coburg und Gotha[ii], to the name of one of their Castles that they owned, so Rudolph Hess thought that the Anglos would make a good ally for their cause."

Erick dared to ask a question. "Sir, could you give us more information about the dealings with the Vatican?"

---

[i] Helped by the astrologers Karl Ernst Krafft and Ernst Schulter-Strathaus a date was picked for the flight to Britain May 10, 1941, this would provide the most positive outcome for Hess to gain the British alliance for the Nazis. Hitler was not informed of such attempt and denounced Hess as insane.

[ii] Saxe-Coburg and Gotha was changed to the House of Windsor in 1917 upon the will of King George V.

"Okay! Let me stop you right there. I know that some of you are not who you claim to be. I know that some of you are gathering intelligence and still hunting down Nazis. Some of you could also be gathering information for the tribunals at The Hague. So let me ask you this, even if I deliver the Vatican or Eugenio Pacelli on a silver platter, what can you do with it? The Vatican will deny everything I say. This is not a fight worth fighting. The war is over."

"Even on moral grounds?" Erick asked.

"The war is over. As a matter of fact, I think we've had enough for the day. I prepared this class so we could see the steps of how political force can use religious patterns to exert influence over the population so we won't go through the same process again.

"In summation, every nation that wants to start a war will go through these three stages; first, start by demonizing the opponent and telling how this demon is about to destroy their country and their way of life. Second, make a point that the war is a cause on behalf of God and, the third is to keep the propaganda alive as much as possible and to control all of the information and access to it. The Nazis had complete control over the news in their conquered empire."

The professor thanked everyone for coming, Peter and Wilhelm remained seated until the others were gone. Their host turned to them, they got up.

"Don't get up, I want to sit down." He approached, dragged a chair and said, "I'm Professor Heinrich Diefenbaker. What can I help you with?"

Peter extended his right hand and Wilhelm soon followed with a handshake. "I'm Peter Nielsen, I hope my German fluency is good enough."

"Don't be modest, I thought you were German."

211

"Let me get to the point. We... I am searching for one character, probably the same one that you mentioned in class today; Father Dornberger, the Vatican Librarian."

"What are you... British Intelligence?" asked the professor.

Nielsen replied, "Very good, I'm impressed, but my search for Father Dornberger... We have an old score to settle."

Professor Diefenbaker said, "Father Dornberger was right! I can't believe it! I finally meet you! Now, may I validate your identity?"

"I can show you my passport." said Peter.

"No, that won't be necessary; I was told to validate your identity by giving you a message in Latin. Are you fluent in Latin as well?"

"A little bit, yes."

"Don't be modest, you either are or you are not."

Peter said, "Quis est suus nuntius, dico nuntius, comodo?" he asked for the message in Latin.

Professor Diefenbaker proceeded in Latin, at which point all was lost to Wilhelm. "If you find me, I shall find you. I found you in Constantinople and I shall find you again. The cat-mouse game should stop."

"Good, thank you... Is there anything else?" asked Peter.

Heinrich Diefenbaker smiled, "No this is all."

Wilhelm asked, "Professor Diefenbaker, what made you smile?

"Did I smile?" he answered with another smile. "I guess old age negates us some privacy through our facial muscles. I am sorry that I showed my emotions, but the truth is: I just now finished paying my debt to whom spared my life, Father Dornberger."

"Do you care to elaborate?" asked Peter Nielsen.

Professor Diefenbaker continued, "Sure, why not? I've held onto this message for the last four years... When I was transferred to Rome, the Nazi lieutenant arrived six months later. I knew that there was going to be trouble again. The Italian army was disbanded and at some point, people took it upon themselves to fight the Nazi army. They killed thirty Nazi soldiers. The order came from Berlin that per each Nazi soldier it would cost 50 Italian lives. We were able to convince Pious XII to intercede, he asked for leniency and the sentence was reduced to ten Italians per Nazi soldier. However, soon after that the Nazis discovered that I had fifteen Jews hiding in the chambers of my home in Rome. I was to become one of the three hundred to be executed."

Wilhelm said, "*Herr* Professor, you are German. Would they still kill you?"

"Dead people don't talk, especially in photographs. I was going to be just another body on the pile of three hundred. However, that was when I was approached by Father Dornberger, who asked if I would be willing to carry a message with me. He would find a way to spare my life; I also would have to leave the Church. I'd have to deliver a message to a person who would be looking for him. He would be about the same age as Markus and he would be proficient in Latin." He bowed his head, brought it back up. "*Herr* Nielsen, may I ask you a question?"

"Certainly."

"I understood the message but there's a problem. When he spoke of Constantinople[i], I had a feeling that you both were there or had met there."

"And?"

"You see? Constantinople has been called Istanbul since the mid fifteen century. I can't help but notice that there is a great time lapse."

Wilhelm was struggling to follow the conversation, but he did not interrupt.

---

[i] Constantinople fell to the Ottoman Empire in 1453 and renamed Istanbul.

Nielsen took time to think and lied, "Father Dornberger is very traditional; he probably thinks that the Middle East is still under the Vatican's domain. But don't worry about that.

"Professor Diefenbaker," continued Nielsen, "I don't know what kind of picture he painted of me. Usually, when I seek him he leaves a trail of assassins to meet me."

"Father Dornberger has told me enough to paint you as the second coming of the devil, but four years is enough time to discover that behind that soft voice, he has a wicked mind that would make Niccolo Machiavelli[i] green with envy."

"Do you know his whereabouts?"

"I wish I could help you, but as the Allies were advancing he might have done what a lot of German defectors did five years earlier, moved to South America."

"Thank you, *Herr* Professor."

"*Herr* Nielsen, if you find him, do tell him that may the Lord have mercy on him. He's tested my Christianity and I've failed, because I wouldn't have mercy on him..."

They left the bookstore and found a place to eat. During the course of the meal Nielsen asked Wilhelm, "How are your Spanish and Portuguese?"

"I don't know enough to order food for us, I would have to resort to sign language."

Peter asked, "Don't you want to come along?"

---

[i] Niccolò di Bernado dei Machiavelli (1469 – 1527) *IL Principe* or *The Prince* was published after his death. It's a political guide of how to attain and retain power detached of morals and ethics. Eventually the adjective Machiavellian became attached to people who conspires through unscrupulous deception, or dishonesty.

"Since I am a Sagittarius and love to travel, it is a very tempting offer to turn down. You've been very generous by paying for all of the meals in the last two years; however, I think if I tag along I would only be slowing you down."

"Is that how you feel?"

Wilhelm continued, "I have enough savings now to open a small shop."

"You said shop. What kind of shop?"

"Germany needs rebuilding, probably hardware and locksmith. My parents used to have one and I ran it for a while. I could, probably let the family run it and continue to cast astrological charts on the side."

Peter ascended his cup of wine, "May you and your shop prosper and rebuild *Deutschland*."

Wilhelm raised his cup, "Thanks for the two years, and may you find your nemesis soon."

Wilhelm joined Peter on his last European trip. They traveled all the way to Western Europe and finally arrived in Lisbon, Portugal. Peter to catch a cruise boat bound for Buenos Aires, Argentina with a two-day stop in Rio de Janeiro, Brazil.

At the hotel in Lisbon, there was a telegram waiting for Peter. The message read, "Counterfeiter captured Sorrento [period] Father Dornberger now Gustavo Petrini Sarno [period] Signed E.H. from PCO [period]."

𓊪𓁶𓏛𓈗𓅆 𓇳𓂻𓎛𓍯𓏲𓄿𓆓𓂝𓐝 𓂋𓈖𓉐𓂻 𓄿𓃀𓌳𓂋𓏱

𓈗 𓃒𓄿𓂝𓈗

XVIII
Capitulus Octodecim

Atlantic Ocean,
On Route to Brazil
1947 C.E.

First day at sea, Peter was finally alone again. Although it was called a cruise ship, The Oliveira, of Portuguese registry, it was always crossing the seas at top speed. It had the usual crew and passenger load; however, it was primarily financed by the cargo and the economy class at the lower decks. Typical of the passenger ship during this time, it had white as the primary color, accented with blue and black and most of the wood at deck hand rails was very light.

Peter Nielsen, clearly in his late fifties, had time to reflect on the two years of hunting since he'd been buried during an air raid in London. Although he had foreseen traveling overseas in his astrological calculations, he could not give himself the luxury of a mistake. Wherever Nicholas was, the infamous Father Gustav Markus Dornberger or now Gustavo Sarno, a new storm was

216

brewing. He wondered, *could I accept the truce offered by Nicholas? Could I afford to accept this truce? The answer is, of course not.* Even if his personal persecution ceased, Nicholas would continue to rage his anti-Semitic war.

Peter Nielsen had to work with the only clues that he had. He didn't know where Nicholas could be, he only knew where he was not... Europe. No stone was left unturned in the old continent. Luckily, *Herr* Heinrich Diefenbaker had provided him with the first sign of life of his nemesis. Elijah and Nicholas had not met in this lifetime, they only knew of each other as Peter and Markus. Peter had calculated that he was due to come back during the time of war. The Nazi campaign illustrated the very steps that Nicholas has always taken. The only difference this time was the use of technology to proliferate the mass propaganda at an even higher rate.

During the time that Peter had spent in London, casting charts of the rich, noble, famous, and consulting with businessmen, he was approached by the British secret intelligence for the profiling of certain characters. Upon the capture of certain individuals, his services would give him access to people of greater influence in the political arena. During his service with the Secret Intelligence Service, S.I.S. he was also educated into reading fragments of information or using partial information to ascertain the missing portion. That, greatly enhanced his profiling abilities. So, for the years before and during the war, the spy network offered him a detective's insight, how to work only with the clues available.

Was there something available in the message that was passed by Herr Diefenbaker? Nielsen wrote the lines on a sheet of paper, cut them apart and assembled them together again. *Si vos reperio mihi, Ego reperio vos... Ego reperio vos Constantinopolis, quod Ego reperio vos iterum. Cattus-muris venatus quod desino.* He scanned the words over and over again, like a rejected lover obsessed with a picture of his beloved. "There must be a clue!" he exclaimed to himself. He checked the hall to apologize and found out that he was still alone. He went back to his thinking mode, *What clue should this be? Erick Hatcher, according to his telegram, knows about my search and must be working for the British P.C.O., Passport Control Office and probably the S.I.S as well. So what is the clue?* He pondered.

For the next two days the Latin words began to sound like a Hindu mantra, "*Si vos reperio mihi...*" Luckily, the serenity of the horizon and the constant picture provided the equanimity and focus that he needed.

One evening after dinner he walked to the deck and saw a young couple arguing in Portuguese. She was fair and gorgeous and he appeared to be a few years older but no more than twenty five years old. They were both seated in the deck's chairs enjoying the cool breeze and the stars.

"… So how do you expect to be a Hollywood actress if you don't want to learn English?" the young man asked her in Portuguese.

"I'll be an actress of a silent movie then." She pouted her lips and gesticulated a dramatic scene, with her right wrist on her forehead and a surprised look on her face.

"They are called talkies now, you will have to talk."

"Why couldn't English have the melodic sound of Italian or Latin? Oh Latin, so traditional yet colorful?"

That conversation distracted Nielsen for the moment yet her words came back, "*...O Latin, bem tradicional e mesmo assim muito colorido.*" Nielsen repeated the Portuguese words in his mind. It silenced his previous obsession with *Herr* Diefenbaker's mantra beating on his head for the last two days. "…so traditional yet colorful?" then he recalled the lie he told *Herr* Diefenbaker. There was a hint of truth in the lie he told. *Father Dornberger is very traditional; he probably thinks that the Middle East is still* *under the Vatican's domain.* A few seconds later an eureka moment startled the only sound of the night, the wakes created by the ship's movement. Peter Nielsen exclaimed, "Yes of course, Latin!" the clue was in the language and not in the contents of the message. Another thought came back to him, *he only celebrated the masses in Latin,* according to the testimonial of Karl in East Germany. *"Sic, verus, verus[i]!"* Peter exclaimed again. He looked around to see if he had startled anyone but discovered that the Brazilian couple was gone, including all the signs of life on the deck. He realized that he must have been leaning on the rail for a few hours analyzing his clues.

The next morning, satisfied with his code breaking and progress, it was time to proceed with the next phase of his trip. His endeavors were much easier with the help of a secretary or traveling companion. Since his mission was unofficial to the British intelligence, and also a private matter to him, the human and financial resources of the spy network were not available to him. Because of the fact that he was financing his own manhunt, he was a little surprised with the telegram from the P.C.O. Perhaps the secret enterprise of Father Dornberger, his contemptuous nemesis Nicholas, had aroused the S.I.S. or the War Trials in progress. Whichever was the case, he had to find a replacement for Wilhelm. The thought of bringing young Horace emerged; however, as they'd learned before, the chance of both dying would completely sever *the link.*

Peter began his recruitment. Instead of fraternizing with the upper class, he decided to dine and get to know the passengers and crew in the lower cabins. By the time the ship was docking at the Brazilian capital, Rio de Janeiro, The Oliveira was going to

---

[i] Yes, true indeed!

continue one crew short. A *Carioca*[i] gentleman, a Rio native called Reynaldo Gaspar, left his duties as a steward and joined Nielsen. They took one day to rest their sea legs, and for Reynaldo to visit his family. They were taking a flight to Buenos Aires the next day. That would still place them four days ahead of The Oliveira docking at the proximity of the Tango and Bolero nights.

State of Paraná, Brazil
1949 C.E.

"Pedro," called Reynaldo, "I've been checking on our calendar."

Peter Nielsen had adopted the Spanish and Portuguese version of his name since the second day on board The Oliveira, "So what have you found out?"

Reynaldo replied, "In exactly two months, it is going to be two years since we took the airfare to Buenos Aires."

"I had no idea, time really flies…" said Nielsen behind the steering wheel of an imported 1939 Ford sedan, while negotiating the holes of dirt roads driving through the state of Paraná, Brazil. "Were you keeping a traveling log of our manhunt?"

"Actually I was, our average visit per town or village while in the south of Argentina was four days. Then in the North of Argentina it was three days." Reynaldo fought to accommodate his notebook on his lap while the Ford was behaving more like a bucking bronco. He sat on the front passenger seat and he took his

---

[i] *Cari* (white) - *Oca* (house) literally means House of Caucasians, *Cariocas* was the name given by the annihilated *Tupi* tribes to the Portuguese settlers in the State of Rio de Janeiro. To this day, it is the nickname given to the people born in Rio.

eyes off the book, and commented, "I thank God that we traveled north because Winter was coming."

"All *Cariocas* hate Winter," Peter made a statement.

"Especially this one." Reynaldo pointed to his chest. "So Pedro, I have some numbers for you."

"Go ahead, let me hear them."

"At our present average, it is going to take three years to cover Brazil."

"How did you come to this conclusion?"

"Okay, this is what we have done, south of Argentina took us six months."

"We didn't have a car."

"Right, after we got that old dump truck we covered north of Argentina in three months, and Uruguay the next three months. Then the old Chevy finally broke down in Porto Alegre, so we got this nice ride. She is a decade old but she doesn't mind taking the road."

"Okay."

"So continuing... We are crisscrossing Brazil northbound. We did the state of Rio Grande do Sul in about four months. Then Santa Catarina State in three months and we crossed to the state of *Paraná* last month."

"Are you sure?" asked Nielsen, "Three years?"

"Pedro, what you Europeans forget to take into account is the size of Brazil. You can put the whole of Europe and also part of Russia in it. Here is another perspective. Brazil was just about the same size as the continental United States or the 48 States."

"Thanks for the lesson, professor Gaspar."

"Also, as we get closer to São Paulo and Rio, the cities are going to be more populated. Then, north of Belo Horizonte the density will go down again... I was thinking..."

After one minute of silence, driving Peter asked, "You were thinking about what?"

"Oh, sorry... I was thinking, if I had to hide like Father Dornberger, I think I would rather hide in a big town instead of a small one. I could keep my identity a secret much longer. But in a small town everyone would know me."

"You have a point. You could keep your anonymity much longer; nevertheless, you wouldn't have any control over who would recognize you in a crowd. However, in a small town you can see who comes and goes and you wouldn't have to be looking over your shoulder."

"I had not thought of this angle."

Peter continued, "I know how this guy operates. He works in the shadows, otherwise I would have covered Rio and São Paulo first."

"I see."

"We will be in Curitiba in two hours. Do you mind driving after lunch?"

"Not at all, sure."

At the edge of town they found a convenient stop. There was a mechanic shop, a gas station, a restaurant and a fruit stand, all next to each other. The soft breeze carried the incensed air from the restaurant; it was the seductive smell of steak and onions on the grill.

The place was small, it was impossible not to be within in the earshot of the next table. Peter and Reynaldo came into to the restaurant. They saw a couple with an eleven year old being served a meal. They skipped a table to have and to give privacy.

"Mother, may I have some bread please?" said the boy in Portuguese.

"Isaias, ask for it in Latin. Let's hear it again?" the mother spoke in Latin.

"Come on mom! Enough with the lessons."

She continued in Latin, "How can you expect to learn if you don't practice?"

Peter Nielsen noticed that the father at the table was too busy with his steak so Nielsen said in Latin, "Your mother is right, only through practice will you attain perfection."

The boy was startled and so was the father.

The mother turned to Peter and said in Latin, "Thank you."

The father expedited his chewing but spoke even before his bite was quite swallowed, "Are you priests?"

"Nope," said Reynaldo with a chuckle.

"How come you know Latin?"

"We are…"

Peter interrupted his assistant, "I used to live in Europe for a while."

"You spoke well. I learned it in the seminary." He took another bite. "Sit next to us. You haven't ordered yet."

Peter got up to move to the closer table and Reynaldo followed. "So you mentioned that you learned Latin in a seminary?"

"Yes I did, but this was twelve years ago. Sister Luiza," He used his fork to point to his wife, "Looked too good as a nun."

"I see," said Peter.

"You know what they say… You can kiss a nun once, you can kiss a nun twice but you cannot get into the habit."

They all laughed, except for the boy. Luiza kept smiling while looking down at her plate.

"What does that mean?" asked the boy. "You keep saying this joke but I don't get it."

Luiza spoke to him. "Eat now, I'll tell you later."

"My name is Pedro and this is my assistant Reynaldo."

"My pleasure, I'm Paulo, Luiza my wife and this is our son Julio Isaias."

Peter and Reynaldo ordered, and the food came really fast. Half way through the meal, the chatting started again.

Luiza said, "It's so refreshing to know that Latin is not a one hundred percent dead language. In fact, you are the second person that we've met who knows Latin."

"Yes, but he was not as nice as you. He was correcting my Latin all the time," said Paulo.

"Did you catch his name?"

"His name was Father Augusto."

"Was he a priest?" Peter asked Luiza.

"Wow, now I'm not sure."

"Could his name be Gustavo instead?"

"Nope," responded Paulo. "His name was Augusto. I am sure because my uncle is named Augusto as well. So when he said his name I couldn't forget it... Much less his arrogance."

Luiza interceded, "Come on honey, he is just another perfectionist like you." She turned to Peter and said, "He told us that he also knew Aramaic and Coptic."

Peter fought his internal jubilation, *Nicholas must have changed his alias once more from Gustavo to Augusto*, this was not the time to explode, instead he asked, "Where did you meet him?"

"We met him at *Foz do Iguaçu*. We went there for a vacation, and he told us that he teaches there."

"Why did you call him a Father?"

"You know, the soft talk. He reminded me of a priest."

Peter whispered to Reynaldo and gave him an order. He left and came back to the table a few minutes later.

Paulo signaled to the waiter, "The bill please."

The waiter approached the table and said, "It's all taken care of, there's no bill."

"You mean, the meal was on the house?"

"No these gentlemen have already paid for it."

"I don't know what to say. Pedro and Reynaldo, thank you very much. May God repay you."

"He just did," Peter Nielsen spoke while getting up.

Before Paulo and family left the table the kind strangers had left in haste. No dessert and no *cafezinho* as an after taste.

They were all packed and ready to take the road. The '39 Ford was gassed up with all its fluids checked.

Reynaldo primed the accelerator four times and turned the key. "Next stop, downtown Curitiba."

"Nope, turn the car around. We are going to *Foz do Iguaçu.*"

"But we were there two weeks ago!" regardless of the complaint, the car was already turned and set toward the direction of Iguassu Falls.

"That much I remember, but I don't remember running into Father Augusto."

"What makes you so sure that he could be Father Dornberger?"

"There is only a hand full in the world that can teach Coptic and Aramaic."

"What is Coptic?"

"It's an Egyptian language."

"But I thought that the people over there spoke Arabic."

"Now they do, Arabic and French. But it is Egypt's ancient language."

Reynaldo continued, "Pedro, during lunch I noticed something."

"Go ahead," said Peter.

"During lunch and also throughout the trip everyone notices that I am *Carioca* because of my pronunciation."

"Yes, indeed! You draw and husk your S's and R's a lot. People at the coast of Santa Catarina do also but not as much as you *Cariocas*."

"I know all of that, but here is the thing, when I first met you I didn't think you were English. I thought that you were from Lisbon. It was just by handling your documentation that I found out. Now you've been in Brazil no more than ten months and nobody can tell where you are from. It's as though you have spoken Portuguese your whole life. When we were in Argentina, on the second month your Castilian accent was gone too. I could hear the difference."

"Thank you."

"You're welcome, but how do you do it?"

"I think it's a defense mechanism. If you sound like the people around you, they are less likely to suspect you and to harm you. I have been traveling for a long time. Now I know how to adapt really fast."

"I don't know... I've never seen this before. It's like you have supernatural powers."

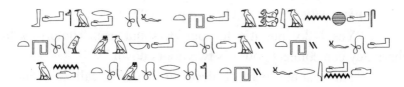

XIX
Capitulus Novendecim

*a*fter being lost for one hour, they finally arrived. It was nine at night when they entered the city of *Foz do Iguaçu*. There was not too much commotion in the city after nine. The hotel doors were closed but after the second knock the owner opened up. He was a character to Peter—it was like looking at a large and bulky Bavarian.

"Where are your suitcases?" the owner asked as he moved to the counter.

"They are in the trunk, but we can unload them tomorrow."

"Nonsense." He punched the bell three times. "My kid can get it for you and take it to your room."

Peter saw his muscular kid show up, he was much his father's younger clone. "Here is their car key. Take the suitcases to room twenty."

"We need two single rooms."

"No problem." He turned, "Werner, put the cases at the corridor between twenty and twenty two." He turned to Reynaldo, "How many nights?"

"Go ahead mark us down for three."

227

Peter asked, "Do you have a phone?"

"Yes I do, but it's for our personal use. Tomorrow the pharmacy can connect you. It's two doors down."

"This cannot wait. I need to make a call to London, probably fifteen minutes. It's an emergency. Tell me your price." Peter was quoted a cost and saw Reynaldo rolling his eyes in dismay. "No problem, we will come back in fifteen minutes with the phone number."

"If you have the number now, I'll pass it to the operator. She will call us back when the call goes through. We called Portugal last week and she called us back forty minutes later. It will take a while to get a good phone connection."

"Sure, I'll get the number and I'll be back soon."

It took a whole hour before the knock on the door.

"Come fast!" said Werner, "The guy on the phone does not speak Portuguese, my sister is holding on to him."

"Graeme Carlton! This is Peter Nielsen."

"Speak up! There is a lot of noise on the line... Peter is that you?"

"Yes Graeme, it's me. I need local police support."

"Finally kid! Good to hear! Where are you?"

"I'm in Brazil next to the border of Argentina and within minutes of Paraguay as well!"

"I've been waiting for this phone call for the last year! Give me a minute! I have a phone number to give to you! It's in the library I'll be right back!"

"I'll wait!" Peter motioned to Reynaldo to arrange for a pen and paper.

"I'm back! Peter, are you there?"

"Yes, go ahead!"

"I got this name and number from the ambassador of Brazil here in London! You have to call General Timóteo Vasconcelos at the *Polícia Federal* in Rio, the capital! He will get you local support. Tell him it's about Operation Jericho! I also have another agen…" The line suddenly dropped.

Peter kept calling. "Hello Carlton, hello…"

"*A linha caiu.*" The line has dropped said the operator, she continued in Portuguese. "Would you like me to try to reconnect?"

"No, I already woke him up at three in the morning. Could you call the *Polícia Federal* in Rio de Janeiro tomorrow morning a little after nine?"

The operator responded, "Would you like me to get General Vasconcelos for you?"

So she was monitoring, thought Peter. He was alarmed. He had thought that his only audience was Reynaldo, Werner, Patricia and Haroldo, the hotel owner. "Yes, that would be excellent."

"I won't be here, but I'll leave a note for the morning's operator." A noise in the background and a muffled, *I know! Leave me alone.*

Peter had just realized how transparent a small town can be, the audience was growing.

Peter was too excited to have a full night of sleep. The roosters, canaries and parrots of the nearby forest began to honor the new dawn. The room became unbearable when the fresh scent of coffee percolated through the cracks of the wood paneling walls.

As Peter was dressing, he said in a normal voice at the direction of the wall. "Good Morning Reynaldo, I'm going to have breakfast. Please, bring the car keys. I want to go for a recon drive before nine."

"How did you know I'm awake?"

"The walls are very thin and you stopped snoring."

"That darn rooster… I'll be right there."

Peter enjoyed the architecture of the building. Although there was no snow in the region, the high vaulted ceiling and roof impersonated the Bavarian look. The hotel's restaurant was adjacent to the main building with its entrance from another street. For this reason the doors were open to the public. The smell of coffee was rich. Peter gave up on his English incarnation and tradition. It was easier to adapt to local customs than to carry bags of Earl Gray tea around the world. Besides, fresh baked palm sized French bread, corn cakes, fresh butter and locally grown coffee beans were not a difficult compromise. Each table had a small combination of the items, except for coffee. Peter saw Werner eating with his head down.

"*Bom dia* Werner."

There was no answer. *Perhaps the kid is not a morning person* thought Peter. Shortly after, Werner abruptly left the restaurant. Peter continued his routine while waiting for his assistant. Suddenly, the two double wooden doors that provided most of the illumination to the alcove was blocked by the passage of six well built locals. The seventh stood outside the door.

"*Bom dia, tudo bem?*" Peter was surprised, for the second time there was still no reply. It looked like the beginning of a rough day, no one responded to his good morning greetings.

The group flanked at a V formation, blocking the view of the restaurant from the sidewalk.

"Get up and come with us!" demanded the leader of the formation.

Peter stood up and said, "I don't think so."

"We were hoping you would say that." In a rich hick draw he said, "Zé Carlos, close the door!"

Zé Carlos, the youngest of them, did what he was told and stood guard outside of the restaurant.

"This is not a fair fight," said Peter. "Six of you young men versus a man old enough to be your father?"

The leader advanced with a club and as he charged to strike he said, "You speak of fair, say that to all the Jews and others that you killed, you Nazi!"

Peter moved away from the arch of the club in motion during the last possible moment. The assailant lost balance by not finding a place to strike. Peter got his left arm locked against the striker's neck and with his right arm he held the club as well. His keen sense told him that another blow was coming soon from the second in command. Peter used the first man as a shield as he turned, then saw the machete traverse the guy's back and come a few millimeters from his own belly. Still startled by his own action the machete holder did not see his friend's club descending on his left temporal lobe powered by Peter's motion, which also knocked him out. Two bodies on the ground did not stop the third to charge with another machete using a classic fencing attack stance. Peter waited to move out of the way at the last possible moment and used the club again in his hand to deliver a blow to the side of this third attacker. As the body of the third was falling down, Peter rose to the table escaping the three others that came to follow. Peter hastily leaped to the other side. All three had also their machetes drawn.

Peter shouted, "Wait! Please wait. I'm not the Nazi. I'm a Nazi hunter. Let me call the police and explain. I have a picture in my pocket. I can explain everything!"

The new leader responded, "Today we are the police, we have been waiting for you since last year. Father Augusto told us about you. Let us kill you first, and then we'll talk."

The new leader of the now smaller platoon charged with a machete from the top. Peter grabbed a burning log from the concrete wood burning stove behind him. Before the machete could come down, he poked the attacker in the belly. The assailant uttered a cry, saw his shirt on fire and backed away.

Two other machetes were now closing in on Peter from the side. Again, he used the log but this time as a shield. The first attacker's weapon became stuck on the log. Peter pulled him forward as he did not let go of the handle. Simultaneously, the blade of the last assailant struck the man on the shoulder. Then, Peter used the butt of his log to deliver a final blow under the chin of the last one standing.

"That's enough, turn around! I don't shoot men in the back!" shouted a voice across the room.

There, standing right in front of him, Peter saw the man with the burnt shirt.

"No need to raise your arms... Any last words?" said the gunman.

"Yes, I want you to remember the first time you were hit in the head."

"What are you talking about? I was never h..."

From behind the gunman Reynaldo used the bottom of a cast iron skillet to interrupt the phrase of the gunman. Next, Peter and Reynaldo walked over the front door.

Peter placed his index finger onto his lips to motion his silence, "Zé Carlos come in." He imitated the very first assailant's voice.

Young Zé Carlos came in. He was not expecting to see all of his buddies on the ground. The whole fight had not taken more than two minutes, three at the most. Reynaldo immobilized the youth as he came in.

"Wow! What happened?" Zé Carlos saw all of his friends down, then he noticed a barrel of a revolver next to his nose.

Peter asked, "Who do you think we are?"

"You are Nazis hunting the people that escaped the concentration camps. You are coming after Father Augusto," said Zé Carlos.

"You are wrong," challenged Peter. "Your bunch is no cops. Who the hell are you?"

"Father Augusto took care of us. Now he has asked us to protect him."

"Listen to me. If I were a Nazi we wouldn't be having this conversation," said Peter. "The person who you are protecting; Father Augusto, his real name is Gustav Markus Dornberger. He helped to kill millions. We have been looking for him since the end of the war. It has been four years... Pay attention, go to the other room, call the hospital. All of your *compadres* were playing with knives and they hurt themselves. Some may need urgent attention. Do you understand?"

Zé Carlos nodded his head in agreement hearing the wailing and groans from the floor.

Peter Inquired, "Is Father Augusto near?"

"We left him at the end of the street this morning before we got here."

"Go call the hospital, get help." Peter signaled to Reynaldo to release Zé Carlos. "Bring the car around; let's go after the so called Father Augusto."

Peter walked outside and there was not much life on the streets, it was very early in the morning. He saw the pharmacy sign above the door. He hastened to it and pounded hard.

A couple came to the window and the man said, "You're going to have to wait. We open in one hour."

"It's not me. There was a knife fight at the restaurant, there are six men bleeding."

"I'm coming down, she is a nurse!" they disappeared from the window sill.

Peter turned and at the far end of the cobblestone street he recognized Haroldo, the hotel owner, talking to another man. This was a great distance, a hundred yards, perhaps more, yet his countenance was familiar. *Oh life, there's no memento stronger than love and hatred.* Now that he had his nemesis in sight he did not want to move. When Haroldo was talking, the second man started to walk, then Peter recognized Nicholas now portrayed as Father Augusto. The scene was familiar to Peter Nielsen, he'd seen it not in past reincarnation but on a Western Silent movie with fast guns drawn, except that they had no hats and they were out of range for a street duel. At the same time, in his peripheral vision Peter saw the couple from the pharmacy passing him by and advancing slowly towards him he noticed the milkman on the horse carriage. "Come on! Where is that car?" Peter muttered to himself, while waiting for Reynaldo.

As the couple entered the restaurant, Reynaldo came out running and said almost out of breath, "Someone has cut all of the spark plug cables."

"Reynaldo, pay attention, this town is not safe. Dornberger has had about four to six years to spread his propaganda or his version of the history here. Try to call the *Policia Federal* but not from here. I think the operator is an informant for him as well. Try to get the cops from a nearby town, or find someone to talk to the cops of this town. I think if we get to them directly we will get beaten and arrested."

"When I make contact where should I send them to?"

"Reynaldo, now things are beginning to make sense to me. We would have saved more than a year's worth of quest if we had just stuck to searching the towns near the borders: where he could jump to another country in twenty minutes or less. And that's exactly where he is going next if I don't catch him first." Suddenly, Peter's jaw dropped, he saw the hotel owner hand Dornberger a horse. "By Zeus, I can't believe this!"

"What happened?" Reynaldo exclaimed.

"I have to deal with this now, I can't let him escape again and you have to run and get help."

Peter swiftly approached the milkman. José Inácio was just finishing pouring milk into his client's carafe and placing it back on the top of a column at the entrance's gate.

"How much milk do you have left?"

"I'm almost at the end of my run. I should still have twenty liters."

"Would fifty *contos de réis* buy it?"

"Fifty *contos* would buy a hundred liters!"

Peter threw a fifty *real* note to him. José Inácio saw the money land by his feet, and he quickly picked it up.

"Unfortunately, I am commandeering your wagon on behalf of the *Polícia Federal*."

"I don't believe it; I want to see some credentials!"

"It's right here!" Peter jumped onto the cart seat, took the reins and pulled the recently acquired gun out of his pocket.

It had been a long time since José had seen a gun. He stepped back, stood on the sidewalk holding the fifty in one hand and an empty one liter tin can in the other. "Please don't hurt Michelangelo. He is all I have."

Peter vigorously drove the chariot up the hill. The street had a smooth incline; however, it was not the speed that he needed to pursue Markus. Next, he opened the valve of the one hundred liter cylinder and allowed the precious lactose juice to pour onto the cobblestone. He was hoping that this would lighten the load; but it did not. He studied the harness and stopped the cart. He noticed that the milkman was coming as fast as his 68 year-old legs allowed him. Before José Inácio could finish one block, Peter released the straps and the chariot's weight flipped it back like a rickshaw without a driver.

As Peter ripped off the side blindfolds he spoke to the horse. "Dear Michelangelo we meet again, time flies, uh? What, 400 years? Well it's been almost five hundred since I rode bare back, I hope you don't mind." He grabbed the horse by the back of its mane. Michelangelo pounced forward taking Peter into a leap and onto its back.

Peter was much happier with the increased speed and so was Michelangelo. It had been years since he went for a fast gallop. As soon as he reached the dirt road, Peter took the renaissance named horse for a run at full throttle.

Shortly, no more than two minutes, Peter arrived at the end of the street and had to make a decision. As he got to the fork on the road he had to decide. To the right was Paraguay and the crossing to the *Puerto Flor de Lis*[i] and to the left was Argentina and the crossing to the city of *Puerto Aguire*[ii].

A thought occurred to Peter. He was standing at the crossroads of three nations and three towns, *There must be more than one Nazi hiding here, the perfect place for someone having to escape.* The thought had crossed his mind but it was too obvious. He thought Nicholas would not take such chances, but he did. "How come I didn't see him last month?" he asked Michelangelo. "Huh?" then he answered on behalf of the horse. "He must have been hopping into countries for a long time anticipating that a day like today would come." He continued his monologue to his only listener. "When I was here last month he was either in Argentina or Paraguay."

Nielsen stooped to the side of the road and studied the ground for tracks. To the right, Paraguay, there was a fresh track, single horse but no dusty horizon. On the left, there were only traffic prints of horses and chariots rolling to town. As he looked towards the end of the road it was loaded with haze and dust. Peter decided to take the right to Paraguay and followed the horse's track for two minutes. Suddenly, Peter noticed the tracks took a left turn to the sidewalk's wide dirt gutter. "There you are

---

[i] *Puerto Flor de Lis* was renamed *Puerto Presidente Stroessner,* and later renamed *Ciudade del Este* in 1989.

[ii] *Puerto Aguirre* was renamed *Puerto Iguazú* by Evita Peron in 1951.

Nicholas, trying to throw me off the track again!" exclaimed Peter, doubtful that the horse understood English. Peter then turned Michelangelo around and took the road to Puerto Aguirre, Argentina. After a few minutes on the road, Nielsen saw some fresh tracks left by Markus; he pressed on. Peter again took his horse to its top speed. Ten minutes into his ride he saw an exit to the right. It was the crossing point to Argentina. The boat would ferry passengers and with limited cargo. Peter noticed the border guard housing, a covered stage area and a boat speeding away toward Argentina with half of its crossing completed. He looked at the boat in the distance, tried to recognize anyone on board, his best count was around five heads.

Scanning the area, Peter realized, there were no other boats in sight, not even a canoe. His hopes of continuing a pursuit were abruptly stopped. A small group of newcomers was waiting for transportation to the city. Peter dismounted hastily, tied Michelangelo to the post as fast as he could and ran to the edge of the dock.

"Peter Nielsen! By Jove! Is that you?"

Peter turned around, to his surprise it was Erick Hatcher, now with a full grown beard. "Erick what a pleasant surprise! It is not 9:00 AM yet and today has been one disaster after another." Peter turned his head and said disappointedly, "Markus is escaping to Argentina on that boat."

"Nielsen, I am happy to say that you are wrong. I just came from that boat."

"You didn't see him leave? How can you be so sure?"

"I have twenty faces very well memorized and I would even recognize their relatives... Markus was definitely not there."

"If he didn't come this way, he is already crossing to Paraguay."

"Relax, I have two agents there at *Puerto Flor de Lis* crossing to Paraguay."

"Americans?"

"No, they are from the Yard. In this matter, we cannot work with the Yankees anymore."

"How come?"

"You may have been out of circulation; their O.S.S.[i] is about to be detached from the Army and be an independent agency called C.I.A., and the O.S.S. provided passage to Nazi criminals, through an underground corridor called The Rat Line[ii], an alliance with the Vatican."

"Bastards! Why?"

"They want to start a war with the Soviets. They will make any deal to get intelligence on the Reds. So they traded battle information for underground safe passage. Most of the papers were processed by the Vatican, and the Church also gave the fugitives some bountiful cash from the devoted parishioners for their trip. I know that you are only after Markus; however, I have also been able to trace to this area, Josef Mengele[iii], Adolf Eichmann[iv], and Walther Rauff[v]. Juan Peron in Argentina is helping with the cover up, a sympathizer of the Nazi cause. Beware of the alliances thou makest, today thy foe, tomorrow thy friend."

"Geoffrey Chaucer?"

"Thank you, but no… Erick Hatcher," Erick smiled with pride.

"I'm sorry Erick, I'm still shocked about this disclosure of American underground involvement… Gosh these Yankees!"

---

[i] OSS Office of Strategic Services was attached to the armed forces during WWII, by presidential Act it was restructured as CIA or Central Intelligence Agency.

[ii] Ratlines were escape routes used by Nazis fleeing Europe to Argentina, Canada, Chile, the Middle East and Paraguay. The details of Vatican involvement is related in the book *Unholy Trinity* by Mark Aarons and John Loftus.

[iii] Josef Mengele (1911—1979) Died in Brazil by accidental drowning, his identity was confirmed by DNA test.

[iv] Otto Adolf Eichmann (1906 – 1962) Captured in Argentina, executed by hanging.

[v] Walther Rauff (1906 – 1984) Escaped to Chile, his extradition to Germany in 1962 was denied.

"Don't be, there are many sympathizers on the American side as well. If it was up to Charles Lindenburg, and that early American ambassador to England, Joseph Patrick Kennedy, Heinrich Himmler would be marching into Piccadilly Circus."

"Is the Yard going public with this information, about the Rat Line?"

"No, we don't spit on the plate that we ate from! The Union Jack might even have to join the Yankees in a war against the Soviets."

"Erick, when this thing is over we'll have to sit down, have tea and talk about *auld lang syne*[i] but until then, I've got to get going."

"Not yet. Let me tell you why am I here… Yesternight I got a call from Graeme Carlton. I didn't speak with him but Harry did. He is still back there in Puerto Aguirre and this is what he told me. Your voice cut out and he heard three other voices on the phone. Two men and one woman arguing in Portuguese, they were arguing on the line for twenty seconds. Since this normally does not happen and he doesn't understand the language, he thought that you were in trouble. Carlton had me cross here to try to meet up with you."

"It is good to know that I'm not alone here." Peter noticed an officer from the border guard passing by, he switched to Portuguese and said, "Good Morning, my friend I need your help. Do you know this area well?"

"Good Morning. Yes, I was born here, what's the trouble?"

"If the police were after you and you had to escape from Brazil, what would you do?"

"If crossing the check points were out of the question… Then I would try hopping onto the islands at the waterfalls… Some daredevils tie ropes trying to cross over the top of the Iguassu

---

[i] Auld Lang Syne (or Old Long Since) it's an old Scottish expression for good old days.

239

Falls[i]. When the current is not strong, during a drought, it is possible to cross."

"Do you have a phone here?"

"Yes we do. Come to the cabin."

"We need to call General Vasconcellos in Rio..."

Peter left instructions of Operation Jericho with both Erick and Manolo Rossi, the border guard at the crossing, and kept them posted about Reynaldo. During the briefing, Manolo reacted in a shocked manner.

"Oh Jesus! No, that's too much... So you are telling me that Father Augusto is actually a Nazi German? I saw his papers so many times. It couldn't have been a forgery, I can tell the difference..."

"It's no forgery. The documents were made by real institutions, they were given new identities. Several government institutions and even the Vatican are involved."

"How am I going to explain this to my wife? This so called Markus has been teaching Italian to both of my kids." He bowed his head in discontent.

Erick said in Spanish, "Manolo, don't be hard on yourself."

Peter continued in Portuguese, "It took us many years to get to this point." Peter was tense, he had to go. "Manolo, may I use your horse? I think Michelangelo has passed his stallion prime."

"You've got Michelangelo? My horse is his son... José Inacio the milkman, sold its young colt to us."

"I'm afraid to ask, does your horse have a name?"

"Raphael."

"I thought it would be Leonardo."

"No, Leonardo is his older son."

---

[i] *Foz do Iguaçu* (or Iguassu Falls *en.* means *i*-water and *guassu*-big from the *Tupi* language) consists of 270 falls spreading 1.7 mile, roughly 3 times bigger than Niagara Falls.

"I have to go and catch up with Markus." Peter left in the south direction heading to the falls.

"Why don't you wait? The Jeep should be here in fifteen minutes," said Manolo.

"It might be fifteen minutes too late." Peter started to mount the horse; he heard the phone ring in the background but kept moving. As Peter was galloping away, he thought he heard Erick screaming. He couldn't make out the words.

XX
Capitulus Viginti

eter admired the rich tapestry of the region. The vegetation was green and dense. The road was dark, a carpet of red dirt and some erosion on the nearby hills revealed the same scarlet red. Peter felt the moisture generated by the waterfall caressing his face. The road was moist, thus it kicked up no dust. Slowly the trees were closing in, at a certain point Peter was in the dark. The canopy formed by the trees was dense. He saw the entrance to the park approaching; one side of the gate was closed and there was an abandoned chair. He realized that the guard was temporarily gone, so Peter sped through the gate. As the road made the first turn he heard the whistle of the guard signaling him back, but he disregarded it. Nielsen was unsure if he was on the right track or going to the right place. It was a long road ahead, a dense canopy and a variety of exotic birds marking their territory or exalting their romantic bonds. The road in the park appeared long; however, Peter's doubts were erased when he saw a truck returning from the end of the park. As Peter continued to gallop, a familiar sound came to mind, the sea. *This should be impossible*; he thought, *I am in the middle of the continent, at least a thousand miles from the oceans in each direction, yet I hear the sea.* As he persisted, the sounds became a strong roar reminiscent of waves crashing onto the shore. It even muffled the sound of the 1937 Ford dump truck going in the opposite direction. There was a clearance ahead, the dense foliage and the road came to an end. Peter Nielsen dismounted Raphael. On his right was the constant droning roar of the Iguassu river, the view still hidden by the brush. Ahead he saw a single horse tied up, still no sign of Markus. On his left a building was being erected, perhaps a hotel. Instead of embracing the Deco movement of the times, the builders optioned to a Spanish/Portuguese colonial motif.

No tourists had yet arrived at the park. Peter was taken by surprise when he noticed that nine of the nine workers had stopped their duties to stare at him. He continued his advance on foot with caution. Fifteen more from the other side, of the construction site joined the group. The head count now was twenty five humans and one horse and Markus remained elusive.

Peter tied the horse to the sidewalk rail to his right. "Good morning, is one of you the foreman here?"

The only one wearing a straw hat responded, "Why don't you get back on your horse and get out of here for your own good?"

"My name is Pedro Nielsen, I am here on behalf of the Nuremberg Tribunal and the *Polícia Federal* do Brazil, to apprehend Gustav Markus Dornberger, the man you know as Father Augusto."

"Father Augusto is not here. He but long ago he said that you were due to come. That you are a Nazi and are hunting him because he helped a lot of Jews escape the concentration camps."

"What else was he going to say? That he is the Nazi and needs help to escape to Argentina?"

Some in the group started to talk among themselves.

Peter started again, "You said that he is not here although his horse is. So let me look for him, if I don't find him I'm on my way. I don't want any trouble."

"There's not going to be any trouble," said the foreman. As he spoke, he turned to his side and said, "Bahiano, beat this Nazi up. It's time to see if you really know to fight Capoeira or just know how to dance it."

Unlike the rest of the group; two had a darker skinned complexion, Peter recognized them to be from the north east estate province of Brazil, Bahia. As one advanced, the other brought up a long bow, at its bottom there was a bowl or chamber. Peter realized it was a musical instrument.

It was a percussion single string instrument which used for timing when the strung line was struck by a bamboo baton. Only later, Peter found out that the bow with a bowl used onomatopoeia for its description, thus the name became *berimbal*. The instrument was used for melody and timing, mostly during Capoeira fights.

A guy in the crowd screamed, "João! Kick his ass!"

As João advanced, he took off his shoes and his white shirt. Only wearing loose slacks João, instead of attacking, decided to move like a drunken man as part of his tactic. To Peter, it looked like as if João was cornering or trying to chase a chicken.

The *berimbal* player intensified the rhythm and João started to show off his Capoeira moves. Peter marveled at the acrobatics displayed in front of him. João appeared to defy gravity, balancing his body either on one hand or on a lightning sweep move. That brought back a memory to Peter when he learned *The Drunken Master Style* while fighting Kung Fu in Macau[i].

---

[i] Portugal made its presence permanent in Macau as trader, later in 1999 it reverted to Chinese control.

After forty seconds of display, Peter was ambivalent towards João's intentions, whether this was an exercise as a distraction or intimidation.

The same heckler in the group yelled, "That's enough João, finish with the old man!"

João entered the Capoeira routine called *Queda de Rins*. Peter noticed that with every move João came in closer. João aimed to tumble Peter to the floor with a speedy sweep of his legs. Nielsen back flipped his own body and landed into the attack-defense Kung Fu stand, body sideways with left foot and left arm forward and right knee slightly bent. João took this opportunity to dive into an *Aú* sequence closer to the ground but aiming to strike his opponent on the rear of his left shoulder. As João stood on one arm, Peter avoided the shoulder hit by diving into a spin. He started the dragon tail spin or leg sweep, he hoped to knock João to the ground.

The audience saw violence and speed, but most of all they saw excellence and beauty. Although Mars or Aries rules wars and fighting in Western Astrology, the martial arts of the East are ruled by Venus. The choreography and beauty brought the crowd to exclaim cheers.

João saw the leg sweep approaching, and he switched hands to bypass the strike and he did; nevertheless, something else struck João, his anger. *How could a person twice my age still be standing?* Pondered João, yet he decided he would resort to use his heavy arsenal. As Peter was emerging from the floor João jumped into the *Martelo Rotado*. Peter was surprised that the Brazilian had a very similar move to the Kung Fu's air twist, as he was struck in the chest and fell backwards.

The crowd cheered, they finally had their first strike. As Nielsen fell backwards, he used the inertia to leap forward into his *Monkey Forward Spring*. As anger always takes away the best tool of a fighter, Joao was not aware of his missed opportunity. Angry to see that after his best move his opponent was back on his feet in a fraction of a second, Joao swung his right arm at lightning speed to slap Peter in the face. Next, Peter saw an opportunity and he seized it. Joao's right arm came closer, Peter grabbed and twisted João's arms which locked the assailant's frame. Nielsen followed the move with a right hand punch under João's chin.

João's cortex and top cerebral hemisphere tried to regain consciousness, but just like a shaken gelatin it would take a while to find its natural state of rest. Peter grabbed João's arms with both hands, twisted his body under them, and threw João's anesthetized frame over his shoulder.

Only after João had landed on the dirt like a sack of potatoes, did Peter release his arm. "João, just lay there quietly, the blood will rush back to your head."

Joao muttered softly, "All right, I will."

The group was shocked, the *berimbal* stopped droning. Peter saw 23 disappointed faces while he regained his composure. However, he became aware of something else, the face of Nicholas behind an entry way incarnated this time as Father Dornberger.

Peter exclaimed, "Listen up! Before any of you try something else…" He moved his hand slowly to his vest pocket. "I have here with me, in my breast pocket a picture of the man you know as Father Augusto standing next to Hitler. Besides, if I were really a Nazi, would I have the help of the local authorities? Some of you may also recognize that this horse belongs to Manolo and the horse's gear belongs to the Border Patrol. They are also on their way. Just wait another twenty minutes, everyone will be here."

The foreman spoke, "Bring Augusto here, we're all going to wait."

Before anyone had a chance to move, Markus came out running from behind the group aiming his Lugar P08 and blaring four shots in Nielsen's direction. Peter rolled onto the ground as he heard the shots being fired. He gripped his gun nestled in his pocket as he finished his rolls. Markus had escaped towards the waterfall. Peter followed in pursuit; none of the working crew was in sight anymore. Shortly, Peter found a long catwalk hugging the side of a cliff. It was a marvelous sight to contemplate but the wrong time to enjoy it. Peter took chase on this walkway shortly after he had seen Markus straight ahead. Suddenly, Markus stopped and took aim at his pursuer. Nielsen's abrupt stop didn't take into account the slippery path, a coat of mildew formed due to the constant moisture. As he fell down, the handrail knocked his gun over the cliff. The gun fall was not a detail missed by Markus, who started to run backwards to castigate his target without a doubt. Peter escaped to his left; he pierced through the brush and shortly found himself into the dark forest again. Soon after, he heard Markus' question.

Screaming to overcome the roar of the falls Markus said, "So Elijah, you didn't take my offer?" Markus was looking for a target for his gun.

"The last time I took your offer I was tortured for years under the Vatican's dungeons!"

"We had to, for the good cause of the Church! Torture? We were not Barbarians. Besides, we had a protocol. If we didn't draw any blood, it could not be considered as torture!"

"You and your Church are just a bunch of hypocrites! You and your lieutenants popped every single one of my joints out of their sockets! It was a sacrifice even to breathe!"

"Don't worry about the pains of your past. Just worry that in your next life you won't make your *Link*. Bye, bye to Elijah and Luke… Elijah, I must confess that for the last 1700 years you have been nothing but a pain." As he talked; Markus swept his arm from side to side under the dense canopy peering from the back of his gun.

Peter responded, "Why do you want to kill all the Jews?"

"I don't want to kill anyone! I just want to end their history. Does anyone miss the religions that don't exist anymore?" he paused for a response, but nothing came, "You never understood me Elijah! It's not that I don't like the ideas of the Jews, what I don't like is the idea that the Christians ever had to exist. Here is my point of view; I may be more Jewish than the rest of them because I am one of the few that have recognized the true Immanuel according to the passages of the Torah or in Isaiah 7:14 or 8:8."

Peter saw Markus coming closer from behind the logs and brushes and said, "Did you awaken anyone from the Nazi Party? Like Hitler or Himmler?"

Markus finally felt the direction of Nielsen's voice. "That would have been a mistake, the minute that they found out that they'd been Jews many times in their past lifetimes, they would not pursue my anti-Semitic cause."

"Nicholas, one more thing… Tell me, how do you awaken yourself without any help, even bypassing so much karma? You should be in hell by now."

Markus moved the gun in the direction of the question and said. "I burned that answer along with the techniques of the best way to *link* when I burned Alexandria's Library. But since I am going to sever your link in a few decades, I'll give you a hint. The answer is in the book of Genesis." Markus heard police sirens blaring in the distance. Suddenly, he recognized Peter's dark brown coat and white shirt sticking out at a distance. He unloaded the remaining shots by holding the trigger down. The semi-automatic pistol responded as designed. Markus was sure of his shot, but he did not have the luxury to check on his quarry. He hastened in the direction of the falls.

Markus ran down until the end of the walkway. The suspended walkway worked as a bridge to a third of the way that he had to cross. After he gained some ground and made across some of the island, he looked back to find the deck populated by uniformed men and the construction's working crew. Markus couldn't hear the shots being fired, but he heard the high pitch of the bullets passing by near his ears.

Lying in the mud wearing only black pants, black socks and shoes, Peter Nielsen saw his coat and shirt being sprayed with nine millimeter bullets. He continued to lie down to see if Markus would come any closer. At that point the element of surprise was his only weapon. He was amazed by the fact that two minutes had gone by uneventfully. Then, he peeked ahead and realized he was alone. He got up and dressed his shirt and coat on his wet back and resumed his chase.

Peter arrived at the watch deck and found it fully engaged with people and heard bullets being shot. He advanced and at the end found Erick Hatcher to be the gunman. Hatcher was wearing a light blue short sleeved shirt; Peter finally noticed a long string of numbers tattooed into the arm of the shooter.

"I got him!" Hatcher exclaimed. "Take this lead, it's for my time in Auschwitz!"

Peter saw Markus' body tumble and surrender to the current of the waterfall. Erick was still holding his Enfield revolver upward and Peter read the time on his wrist watch.

Peter felt Reynaldo tap on his shoulder and he turned. "Reynaldo, write this on your pad, it's important for my calculations, Gustav Markus Dornberg, time of death, July 16th, 1949 at 9:56, Saturday morning Iguassu Falls, Brazil.

꠸ ꠸꠸ ꠸꠸꠸ ꠸꠸꠸꠸꠸ ꠸꠸ ꠸꠸꠸
꠸꠸꠸꠸꠸꠸꠸꠸꠸꠸꠸꠸꠸꠸꠸꠸꠸꠸꠸꠸
꠸꠸꠸꠸꠸꠸

XXI
Capitulus Viginti Unus

Meridian, Mississippi

*T*wenty four hours later, Sydney was holding on to the copy of his calculation book. He was expecting it to be a facsimile in black and white, but was happily surprised to realize it was actually a photographic and bound copy of his ephemeris book. The photos of each page were 8 ½" by 11" making it twice as big as the original. Even subtle stains on the pages were visible. Sydney used his laptop and began his plotting. Today what took the longest was to enter the data, and no longer the mathematical analysis and corrections that he'd had to make for the last centuries. Some of the dates were older than the Gregorian calendar but the computer compensated for it very well. At his first calculations Jesus was due to return circa 1991, Mississippi. After entering all that data again and recalculating, he found Demopolis, Alabama to be slightly off center in a 30 mile radius. Sydney thought, *Why couldn't the coming of an Avatar be as easy to spot as any Nativity decoration suggested?* But this time, just like the original two millennia ago, only the well trained astrologer could find Immanuel.

Wise men? Three kings? Oh Nicholas you've had so much time for creative editing and re-editing since then. If you'd had any idea what Guttenberg was creating with the printing press you would have burned him too. The Church no longer had a monopoly on books, no longer a monopoly on information, just like an old cephalopod the empire was losing its grip. The Christian theocracy, after many centuries of causing encephalopathies in the human consciousness such as keeping the Earth flat, lost its cartel. Nowadays, the *cephalopod* can only control the most fanatic and the simple minded. It was the most complex and scientific minds of five thousand years ago that wrote the Torah. *Would they have had it written it in the same manner if they had had the benefit of the scientific understanding of today? Why is the cephalopod insisting that evolution is a theory, and the dinosaurs are a myth, and where does life end and begin?* The answer is, and Elijah remembered seeing it many times, when the law is changed it is because the *cephalopod* has been able to regain control of the society and this control is gained by controlling information. Just as Sydney was riding back to the hotel, a Bible Belt broadcaster was telling tales about Mary the mother of Christ. But he never called her Jewish, he would only refer to her as a Palestinian girl. Such negligence to accuracy would be offensive to both Jews and Palestinians even today. There was no point in calling the radio station to point out the correction. The agenda had been set long ago, the plan to de-Jewishize Christ.

Does the memorization of the airplane manual and being able to quote pages and paragraphs make one an expert in aerodynamics? Does the memorization of an edited, re-edited, and translated Bible make one a holy person? Hitler had a version of Christianity, the KKK had another and so many other denominations had a de-Jewishized version of Christ. The Pictures of Christ are always more likely to resemble an Anglo Saxon like Erick The Viking than Golda Meir, Sigmund Freud or those with a string of numbers tattooed on their bodies by the holocaust; Sydney evaluated all of these concepts.

It was morning. For his last meal Sydney Tobias stopped by the same restaurant. He had his last Meridian brewed cup of coffee and uniquely spiced bowl of grits. He saw all the regular folks with regular lives and for a while it was nice to pretend that he too, had regular problems. But for a change of pace Sydney had just discovered that he had a regular problem, indeed his rental sedan wouldn't start. It was more than a battery problem, the tow truck driver's speedy diagnosis pointed to the alternator. The sporty sedan was replaced by a minivan. Sydney liked the additional anonymity it provided. The passing of the border to Alabama was faster than he thought; in fact, distracted by all the bells and whistles of his new vehicle Sydney overshot his targeted exit. He got off the first available exit, then instead of heading back on highway I-20, he decided to short cut by using the farm roads or local access roads. Shortly, Sydney found himself on Road 7 South. Concentrating on road signs Sydney was oblivious to the noise on the radio; since exiting the main road he had lost the radio signal. The white or static noise filled the mini-van, mimicking the sound of a distant waterfall.

Sydney saw, at his left, two busses parked on the roadside. The first had a banner, "SPECIAL" and the second displayed the name "BROOKLYN."

"Brooklyn," repeated Sydney; shortly after that, he negotiated a U-turn and approached the rear of the second bus as the front bus was leaving. Sydney was trying to recall the words from Lilith. He pulled the minivan up about twenty feet behind the bus still parked. He saw only the bus driver, and a family of Negroes. A middle aged couple and a child were all sitting on top of their suitcases. The exact words from Lilith still escaped him,

Sydney saw the odometer of his van bring a familiar year to mind, 1562.

The static noise on the radio persisted and gave Sydney the impression that he was hearing the sound of a water fountain. He stood looking at his dashboard but nowhere in particular. Lost in thought he went back to the year 1562 in the city Salon de Provence, France, when his name was Pasquale Greco.

Salon de Provence, France
1562 C.E.

Two men approached a third who was enjoying his afternoon tea overlooking the green view of Salon de Provence from the upper deck of the hotel.

"Excuse-moi," said the hotel manager. *"Pardon,* for the interruption of your afternoon tea. This is Monsieur Jean-Aimé de Chavigny. He insisted on meeting you."

As Pasquale Greco stood up he said, "Monsieur Renault, it is no interruption at all. In fact, tea has a sweeter taste in good company." Pasquale turned to his visitor, "Would Monsieur Chavigny join me for an afternoon tea?"

"Certainly."

"I shall return with more provisions," said the manager Monsieur Renault as he left.

The bare handshake had not returned to fashion, as most of Europe was still under the shock of the plague. So the court bow was the understood greeting as long as one of the parties had gloves on. Since Chavigny was still wearing his traveling garb, they chose that expression of reverence.

After they exchanged pleasantries about the weather and the view Monsieur Chavigny started, "News travels fast, especially in a small town. Rumor has it that thou art an astrologer."

"It all depends where the rumor comes from? My income comes from entertainment as a story teller, as a musician or as a music teacher."

Monsieur Chavigny contested, "This is a very expensive hostel[i] for a teacher or a musician."

"Then I shall find the nearest piano to defend my reputation."

"That shan't be necessary. The news of your arrival and expertise came from Monsieur de Florenville."

"I see…" said Pasquale, "That's comforting."

"Actually, it is a little more than a rumor, it is an endorsement." Monsieur Chavigny paused so that the waiter could set the utensils, serve the tea and leave. "However… Salon de Provence is not big enough to host two famous oracles, much less three. I have been studying astrology and divination with Monsieur Nostradamus since I resigned my post as mayor ten years ago."

"Monsieur Chavigny, do not concern yourself with competition because I am a transient and before long, I shall be nothing but a distant memory… If you don't mind me prying… How do you like having Monsieur Nostradamus as a teacher?"

"The first two years were such a struggle for me. He was very taciturn with dramatic outbursts. How can you learn from a teacher who speaks so scarcely?"

Monsieur Greco replied, "More than ever, we live in times where our words should be guarded from strangers and the listening behind walls."

"Verily, Monsieur Greco, verily. In fact, years and years ago there was a cast done of the Virgin Mary and Monsieur

Nostradamus voiced his opinion. He said that the statue was the work of the devil. By the time this anecdote reached the office of the Cardinal, he was brought to trial in Toulouse for heresy. Luckily, he had friends in high places and he was allowed to explain himself."

Greco commented, "I saw a few inquisitions; the accused is never given a chance to respond, since the words coming from his mouth are already seen as the opinion of someone possessed by demons."

"He was able to explain that the Virgin Mary should not be cast by just anyone, but only by a highly acclaimed artisan. Devilishness was the craftsmanship and not the icon of Our Lady."

Monsieur Pasquale Greco asked, "Who started this inquisition, the artisan?"

"No, it was the Bishop of Lyon. I heard that he was a Vatican librarian for many years and now he is in charge of imposing conversions and the persecution of Jews. His name is Bishop Octavius Montaigne. The Church has been enforcing this for centuries. Even Nostradamus' grandfather was forced to convert from Judaism to Catholicism. His previous family name before Notredame was Gassonet. Today Bishop Montaigne has become the Vatican's new policy enforcer."

Monsieur Greco said, "I am very familiar with this bishop. I avoid his shadow at all cost."

"Last year Monsieur Michel de Nostradamus was imprisoned for two months for the publication of his Almanac. Later, he confided in me that he needed to travel for so many years to avoid a Saturnian influence from his charts. Since he has not isolated himself anymore with trips, Saturn has found a way to exercise its pressure on him."

---

[i] Traveling Lodges became known as hostel by the XIII century, and as hotel since the XVII century.

Monsieur Greco said, "I am also aware of the influence of planet Khronos, when I cast my charts, it becomes my star trek to avoid Saturn's wrath."

"Monsieur Greco, it is rare to find someone that can understand our jargon. Speaking of that, how come you don't have an accent? From your name and looks I ascertain that you are Italian."

"Genovese to be more precise, Monsieur Chavigny; however, I feel as though I've been speaking French for the last 600 years." Pasquale joined Jean-Aimé in laughter.

"But if you are not here to forecast charts; what brings you to Provence?"

"I have made some calculations, and it would be wise to have a second opinion and your professor embodies the secrecy that I demand."

"When would you like to meet him?"

"Dear Jean-Aimé, yesterday is already too late; however, I am at his mercy. The first opportunity that Monsieur should have available would be the best. Please also inquire as to the fee for his service."

"I shall talk to him. Go ahead and come one hour after sunset, by this time all six of his kids will be asleep. He does most of his esoteric work at night when silence is an abundant commodity."

Assisted by the hostel's servant, Pasquale Greco walked the narrow streets of tiny cobblestones in Salon de Provence. Every new city was a mazing journey, but soon enough he found the townhouse. All of the windows were already closed and silence reigned.

Before the hostel's servant could knock on the main door, Nostradamus himself opened it. He stooped towards the teenager, whispered in his ears and gave him a note and a large coin. The servant left in a dash.

Nostradamus was wearing a long dark blue velvet robe. Instead of his four pointed hat, he wore a sleeping cap that draped down to his shoulders and covered part of his long beard. He scanned the short view of the street for prying eyes. Holding a Malacca cane with a silver handle, he motioned to Pasquale to enter.

Nostradamus sealed the door, brought his finger to his lips, gesturing silence. "Follow us."

Pasquale saw a female holding a candelabra; it was the only lighting provided in the house. Greco couldn't tell whether she was the maid or his wife. The path of the stairway felt endless because they were climbing it very slowly. They finally arrived at Nostradamus' work studio and office already illuminated by a fixed lamp. They sat for a while in the stillness. Greco realized the oracle was having another vision, so he waited.

Nostradamus began, "I've been expecting you for the last five years. No need to tell me your name and your cause. I know who you are."

Greco spoke, "So allow me to ask you the question of all ages. Who am I?"

Nostradamus paused, "For lack of a better description, I'll explain it this way; you are one of the quartet here on this planet who makes my predictions more difficult."

"What kind of quartet?"

"I call your quartet *The Interferers*, because all four of you get in the way of the natural path of history."

"I had no idea our actions would cause interference, I have been living a life with no involvement. Also, I had no idea we were four."

257

"You interfere because you bypass the laws of heaven, hell and purgatory to return to earth, your path is beyond the knowledge of the scriptures."

Greco defended himself, "What you call interference is only an act of self preservation on my behalf, and one of us always returns to end the plight of the Jews."

"I know…" said Nostradamus, "One of you always returns as a *Saturnian* embracing the plight of the *Papists*, and another as a *Papist* defending the unfortunate circumstances of the *Saturnians*."

"Monsieur, I am not familiar with your terminology," stated Pasquale.

"I refer to the Catholics as *Papists* because they elect a pope. I call the Jews *Saturnians* because they worship the day of Saturn or Sabbath. Consequently, many of them fall under the influence of this planet."

"What do you mean?"

"They isolate themselves by marriage and commerce, follow austere behavior and are frequently tormented. We both know that Saturn rules isolation, orthodox and strict behavior, as well as teaches through suffering and pain."

Greco waited for a second to assimilate the comment and said, "I seek answers to a couple of questions and have even brought some charts with me."

Nostradamus saw Greco pull papers out of his coat and said, "We don't need to look at charts anymore."

"How come?" Pasquale contested.

"After many years of research I've come to the conclusion that there are three levels of consciousness; the elementary, the celestial and the intellectual. Astrology transmits the divine to the mundane. However, I've learned to go straight to the source where time has no bounds, everything that was, is and shall be, is stored in the archive of eternity. I just need to take time to concentrate on my meditation. This is how I've been able to read the future."

"So may I ask you the questions, then?"

"I already have your answers in this envelope, they are in one quatrain."

"First Monsieur Michel, I have not asked the questions, and secondly, I've read your quatrains and they are too obscure. Why is that?"

"You have been thinking about seeing me for a long time and I have been hearing your thoughts. I need to tell you a story that should explain my obscured sonnets."

Nostradamus commenced, "A king went to an oracle and he was told that he was due to die from an object falling on top of his head. Therefore, the king decided never to live under his palace or a building. He spent the remainder of his life living in a tent next to his palace. One fine day an eagle was carrying a turtle to its nest. However, the bird lost its grip and dropped the reptile, which from a distant altitude, was able to strike the king in the head and kill him. The question is… Who killed the king? His fate, the eagle or the oracle?

"My quatrains are obscure and there is a reason for that. I have many detractors nowadays and I shall have them in the future, as well; however, if I make the predictions too easy to decipher, there shall be many people changing their lives for no consequence. My goal is to describe and not to interfere like you do. I am always confronted with challenges about revealing my predictions because an innocent person may even be killed.

"Since you've already met Monsieur Florenville," continued Nostradamus, "You know this story. As we walked through his gardens, we came to two piglets, a black and a white one. He asked me which one we were going to eat and I said, the wolf shall eat the white one and we shall eat the black one. So to challenge my prediction he ordered the cook to prepare the white one. During dinner, he asked me again which one we were eating and again I said, the black one. He called the cook to tell us which one we were eating. The cook explained that while the meat was roasting, the tamed pet wolf had eaten the white one. He had no choice but to prepare the black one. Next day Monsieur de Florenville asked me, if he had not challenged my prediction, would the wolf have still assaulted the roast? Then I said to him… This is a question that he would have to ask the wolf.

"So this is the reason, if I were to spell out everything that it's going to happen on the Vatican's grounds, even four hundred years from now, they would accuse me of heresy today."

"I completely understand," said Pasquale. "I've been walking a very thin line and guarding my words for the last fifteen centuries."

Nostradamus demanded, "Tell me about your life and your experiences and I'll tell you without codes what you are yet to see, under the condition that you can't write or speak about it until they come to pass."

They exchanged their opinions; Pasquale narrated the highlights of his existence since he had met Anaxagoras as Elijah. Nostradamus told of situations yet to come. He spoke of armies underwater, people on the moon, carriages without horses or drivers.

Later that evening Pasquale asked, "May I read what's in the envelope now?

"You should read it when you see one man defeat many in front of a mountain with twin peaks."

Pasquale pocketed the envelope. "Monsieur Chavigny described you as a taciturn and reserved person; however, I find you to be loquacious."

"The reason why I can talk freely with you, is because after we separate today, you shall never meet me again or return to France until after my death."

"I have learned enough tonight not to challenge you."

"You are very wise Elijah," said Nostradamus, "Had you decided to challenge me in the near future it would have been too late. A small battalion is due to arrive tomorrow, they shall say that they have orders to escort you to Toulouse for your inquiry; however, en route they shall make you dig your own grave and bury you."

"Monsieur, can't you get in trouble for talking to me?"

"I shan't, because we never met," continued Nostradamus, "Is the other interferer alive and hunting you now?"

"Yes," said Pasquale, "he is the bishop of Lyon, Otavius Montaigne."

There was a soft knock on the door. They both got up. Pasquale was removing some crowns to pay Nostradamus for the consultation, but he was interrupted.

"Don't bother, I have had your consul as well, I don't think I had been so well entertained in my entire life; besides, you shall need all the money you possess. You shall embark on a long journey ahead."

Very slowly they descended to the street level, as they hugged, Nostradamus whispered into Pasquale's ears, "Once you arrive at the coast, take the first boat out and when you arrive there, take the first one out as well. Octavius has spies in Europe, use an alias from now on."

Pasquale departed, and was surprised to see that the same hostel's servant was waiting for him.

"Monsieur, I have packed your bags and they are waiting for you with the carriage."

"Shall I trust that everything is there?"

"Most certainly Monsieur. Monsieur Nostradamus saved my father and sister during the plague and we, the Beltrans, don't take our debts nonchalantly."

When they arrived at a secluded part of town, young Beltran lifted the hay from the back of the open carriage to expose his traveling bags underneath. Next, he pulled a robe out and said, "Wear this over your garments and be sure to use the hood as well."

Pasquale soon resembled a Franciscan monk; he noticed the driver did as well. They took to the road immediately. It was sunrise when Pasquale saw a group of soldiers advancing in the direction of Salon de Provence. It was comforting to know that once again he had escaped the grips of Nicholas, known in this life time as Bishop Otavius.

The first boat left for Lisbon, and then the first from Lisbon left for the Easter Indies, specifically to a Portuguese trading post called Macau. After a couple of months at sea, two major storms, and several port stops, the Port of Macau was finally on the horizon.

As the galleon approached the landing, Pasquale noticed that there was a man fighting seven others on the dock. The sailors on the vessel started to cheer. Very soon the fight was over and the lonely warrior had triumphed.

"I want to fight like that!" said Pasquale to no one in particular.

A Portuguese sailor next to him said, "That was a demonstration, I was here before, they call it Kung Fu."

"Thank you." Pasquale rolled his eyes to find that in the background rested a mountain with two peaks. He ran to his bunker inside the ship to retrieve the envelope. When he first broke the seal he read the words, "Welcome to the Orient." Then Greco pulled open the folded page to expose this obscured quatrain.

"On the birthday of New Amsterdam all sirens shall sing,
The Hearted shall start new enterprise
The Terrible shall stop departed with the King.
No time for tears, story must…"

The end of the quatrain was illegible, and then Pasquale realized the ingenuity of Nostradamus. If he had opened the envelope on the same day, he would have found blank a page. The seer, also knowledgeable in chemistry, had written the quatrain with lactose based ink, which only reacts with heat. Time and heat made the page reveal the quatrain only partially. He brought the letter to the upper deck and let the page enjoy the intense sunrays of the tropic of Cancer. Suddenly, all of the letters of the quatrain intensified, and Pasquale was able to read the last line, *No time for tears, story must be notified.* At the very end of the page a new phrase was revealing itself. *It was a pleasure to meet thee, Elijah.* Signed *M.N.*

XXII
Capitulus Viginti Duo

Thirty Miles South of Tuscaloosa, Alabama

Sydney was startled by a sharp, loud tapping at his car window; he turned his head to discover a large middle aged black man, using a coin to thump on the window pane. Sydney rolled the glass down.

"Are you okay?" asked the black man.

"Sure, sometimes I lose myself into thoughts," responded Sydney.

"I first tried to get your attention by knocking, but you did not notice me. Then I got this quarter to wake you up. We saw you park about fifteen minutes ago. I thought it was to help us but then you didn't move, so I came over here to see if you were okay."

Sydney responded, "You are right, do you need a ride to the next town?"

"Yes, we could use some help."

"Let me roll the van a little closer and I'll catch up with you." Sydney saw the gentleman talking to his family and shortly he joined the conversation in progress. "So are you folks ready? We could get going."

"I think we are almost, but we should introduce ourselves first. I'm Reverend Kendrick Johnson, this is my wife Joyce and our son Charlie."

"My name is…" Sydney pondered whether to use his alias but decided not to. "Sydney. I will help you get your suitcases into the back of the van and then we can be on our way."

As Rev. Johnson was carrying the luggage, he said, "This morning our choir left for Brooklyn on two busses, then our bus broke down. The company sent a replacement; however, there were three fewer seats."

"Two fewer seats," said Mrs. Johnson.

"Jojo is right, but by law every passenger has to have a seat. Two of us would have to stand. So we decided that the kids in the choir should go ahead and we would find a way to catch up."

"What was the problem with the bus?"

"The driver suspected that it was something electrical, the second bus arrived with a technician but he couldn't fix it."

"Don't feel bad, I had to change my car this morning too." Sydney nestled the last bag in the back of the van. "Is that all?" he shut it down.

"I think so," said Mrs. Johnson, "This small one, I'll bring with me."

"So I guess… All aboard." Sydney slid open the side rear panel and the front passenger door. When all the three passengers were buckled in place, he turned the key in the ignition and said. "Where do we go from here?"

"I guess to get to another bus from here it's either Meridian or Tuscaloosa, so we should head north east, on the I-20 east."

Soon they were on the interstate, Tuscaloosa was approaching according to the road signs.

"Sydney," spoke the reverend, "This is very kind of you. Let me at least treat you to breakfast. Pull over at the next stop."

"That won't be necessary Reverend. I ate less than an hour ago."

"We have been up since 4:30 this morning, and I think I could use another cup of coffee and a restroom stop if that is agreeable to you."

Shortly thereafter, they were all seated and relaxed at the next restaurant. Rev. Johnson started to chat.

"So Sydney, where is your home?"

"It used to be Miami."

"So what are you doing in this area?" the Rev. Johnson continued the interview.

"I am conducting research for a while and maintaining a low profile."

"What kind of research?" inquired the reverend.

"I hope I won't offend anyone Reverend, but my research is based on astrology."

"Well, that doesn't mean that you don't believe in Jesus!"

"Of course not, astrologers find a strong spiritual bond with religion; however, for centuries the only purpose people have taken from astrology is prediction. And this is the main aspect of the clashes between organized religion and astrology, everyone has a different opinion about determinism and free will."

"I'm not going to focus on that, I've already formed an opinion about you. Of the two hundred cars that passed us by today, you were the only person who placed our needs above yours. You are nothing but a Good Samaritan that stopped on the road to help a family in need."

"The word Samaritan brings back very old memories. It's good to be mentioned as such."

"But what kind of research brings an astrologer to Alabama?"

"To put it into simple jargon, I am engaged in a type of talent search. I'm looking for a youngster about Charlie's age with special talents."

Rev. Johnson said, "I don't know what you mean by special, but if eccentric classifies as such, you have to go no further than Charlie here. Isn't that right, Charlie?"

"I don't know what normal should be." Charlie tucked his head under his mother's arm hoping to hide.

The reverend with a deep base chuckle continued, "Oh, he he he. Charlie doesn't like to toot his own horn. So let me tell you. First, Charlie never cried, he was able to talk before he could walk, not the goo-goo stuff but complete sentences. Such as, *I'm hungry now. Where is mother? Can we go outside?* and so on. Also, there have been many cases of people that held Charlie as a baby and their diseases magically went away, so we had to hide him for a while."

"That's impressive! Is there more?" asked Sydney.

Rev Johnson, "Yep, animals are perfectly silent when Charlie is around. Isn't that right, sister Jojo?"

Mrs. Johnson replied, "Yes it's true. Another interesting thing is that I was struck by lightning a little before I was pregnant with Charlie, but by the time Charlie was born, all the burn marks on my arms had fallen off as if they were scabs. They all vanished. Look!" She extended her arms.

"Actually, I've heard your story before, I met Gerard in Meridian, and he told me that you used to baby-sit him and his sister in Demopolis."

"Oh boy… Small towns, our lives are so transparent!" She moved her head in disbelief. "Is he well?"

"I believe so; he works as a distributor of car parts in the area." Sydney changed the subject, "But what is taking you all to Brooklyn?"

"My cousin is a minister there and we host each other once a year with a very Southern Baptist Festival of Music and Tolerance, but there is also good food and games."

"That sounds delightful," commented Sydney.

Charlie joined the conversation again. "Lots of singing, clapping and cheering in the name of God."

"I could use some excitement; could I join you?" Sydney thought it was a good idea to investigate Charlie. "I can enjoy the festival and have a chance to get to know Charlie."

"I don't know." Charlie went back to his refuge, under his mother's arm.

"What's the problem, Charlie?" asked Reverend Johnson.

"What if I'm not the person you are looking for, I will feel bad that I made you drive for a long time."

Sydney said to Charlie, "Don't worry about that. It comes with my job..." He turned to Rev. Johnson, "If we take turns driving, we can be in the Big Apple by morning."

"That would be great, let me call my cousin." The pastor was getting up to look for a pay phone. "So he can be ready for us."

"No need to get up. Just enter the number and press the green button." Sydney handed him his cellular phone.

After traveling over many bridges, under many viaducts, negotiating many turns, two meals and one sunset, the chat inside the van dwindled to a monotonous silence. Rev. Johnson was stretched out on the back seat, his cavernous snoring blended with the sound of the engine which led Charlie to the same unconscious path. Charlie slept on the middle seat, a folded coat nestled his head sideways.

Mrs. Johnson, on the front passenger's seat, read that the exit to Gettysburg was approaching. To break the silence she asked, "Aren't you afraid that you could be doing a whole lot of driving for nothing?"

"A person will never reach a destination by taking the road of regrets."

"So do you think Charlie could be that special talent you are looking for?"

"Yes I do. Don't you think that he is special?" he asked.

"Are you asking a mother if her son is special? There can be only one answer. Do you want the long version or the short one?"

"We still have six hundred miles to travel, so take your time."

"These are the best and also the most complicated years of my life. Everyone who doesn't know me thinks that I am Charlie's grandmother instead of his mother. Pregnant at 49, and I am 61 now with an eleven year old son…

"Ever since I remember myself as a child, I've always wanted to be a nun. I know we don't have a sisterhood like the Catholics, but the idea of life in a convent, isolated, praying, was my only wish. When I was to enter high school I was ready to start my chosen path, but this coincided with Hurricane Flossy in 1956. We had a lot of damage; a couple of months later my father died and my mother became ill. So I had to go to work and take care of my brothers. I've raised my brothers and hundreds more as a maid and nanny since then. I never dated men and the dream of being a nun was long gone.

"I came to one conclusion, I could either isolate myself in a convent and serve Jesus or live my life seeing Jesus inside everyone I met and served. It worked. I was always working, volunteering, I don't think I would have worked as much had I become a nun. So four decades flew by, my brothers were raised and so were their kids and I thought that any day now it would be my time to go.

"One day I was coming back from my work at the hospital and I saw a storm brewing. Since I had the keys to the Church with me, I decided to close its windows. The handle I held became a lightning rod, the floor was already partially wet.

"I was told that I was thrown fifteen feet and that I had second degree burns. I was in a coma for four months. It must have been a deep coma because it only felt like I was gone for 20 minutes. When I recovered, I asked the doctors what were they feeding me. Then they asked why, and I said, because it feels like my stomach is moving. When they told me that I was pregnant, I was in a state of shock."

Sydney asked, "May I ask you a question?" Sydney saw that she nodded, "Do you remember anything about or during your coma?"

"Not at first, but later it came back to me. I went through this tunnel, except that the tunnel was not dark, it was very white and bright, but at the end of it, it was even brighter. It was such a beautiful place. I didn't remember anyone's name but they all looked familiar to me. The morning when Charlie was born, I dreamt that I was back there in that bright place, except that Charlie was already ten years old; holding my hand he looked up and said, *I'm glad you chose to be my mother.* Then I heard someone shout, *Charlie, look!*

"It wasn't easy... I don't remember ever being with a man and then, all of a sudden, I was due to become a mother. If it wasn't for my faith and prayers I would have gone crazy; there were so many rumors. I heard that I was violated when I was in coma. All of this sounds crazy, doesn't it?"

"Actually, it's not totally impossible." Sydney pulled an old magazine from the pocket of his laptop case and said, "Open on the folded page and read the article."

While Sydney drove, Mrs. Johnson turned on her dome side light. She put on her reading glasses and for the next twenty minutes she read in silence. "I worked and volunteered at the hospital for many years. I remember seeing two young doctors arguing about this type of cloning, which is a problem in my case." She saw the puzzled look on Sydney's face, "In my case it wouldn't work, this type of cloning can only produce female offspring, since this type of insemination doesn't have XY chromosomes."

Sydney contested, "By showing the article I'm not justifying your case, but just showing that your situation is not infinitely remote."

"I appreciate the effort." She clicked the dome light off, "I'm at peace with it now, I have chosen to see it as a private miracle."

"Speaking of miracles, is everything that the Reverend said about Charlie true?"

Mrs. Johnson, waited to check on the other passengers, the snoring continued and Charlie had not moved, "He might have stretched the truth a little but only because he loves Charlie."

"Stretched? Like how?"

"Charlie never cried, it's true, but he complained by making a loud hum when he wanted attention."

"What about his early talking?"

"There were several situations where people swore that they were alone with Charlie and they heard things in a baby's voice. The first one was my friend Shirley. She is a nurse at the hospital. When she was taking care of Charlie on the day he was born, after bathing him and preparing him for the incubator she heard, *I have returned to this dimension.* She told me in secrecy. One time Charlie was babbling with me in the supermarket, and this Indian lady dressed in a sari asked me how my baby knew the Holy Scriptures in Sanskrit. She bowed to Charlie with her head to the floor and left. Another time a Hassidic Jew asked me how my baby could recite the Psalms in Hebrew. But this time the stranger wasn't so nice, he wanted to tape and record Charlie. I stopped taking Charlie out with me for a while, and I also told him not to speak anything Mom couldn't understand and later I taught him some spirituals, he hummed them."

"How about the healing stories?"

"My friends and people claimed that by holding Charlie they would heal themselves, but I think that it was just a coincidence, because if Charlie could heal others, why wouldn't he heal himself?"

"What do you mean?"

"Remember the part that Pastor Johnson said that Charlie could speak long before he could walk? It was because Charlie was born with both ankles twisted inwards. We had to let him grow for a while before the operation. I also forgot to mention the epileptic seizures."

"I see… So as far as you know Rev. Johnson is not the father?"

"Our union brought benefits for all of us. Both Charlie and I were covered under his insurance. The marriage also stopped all rumors that Mighty Thor is the real father, and finally all the rumors about Rev. Johnson's preference stopped." She noticed that Sydney seemed pensive. "You see, I'm sharing my entire story because I'm afraid you may be wasting your time. I think you are looking for a family with a lot more virtue than us."

A few seconds later Sydney asked, "How many of you are under the sign of Aquarius?"

"We all are, in fact our birthdays are close to each other… What made you guess that?"

"Archetypes… Uranus, the Aquarian ruler, is also the ruler of lightning, charities, unorthodox love, and in Medical Astrology, he rules seizures and ankles."

"So this means that you may still be interested in Charlie?"

"Mrs. Johnson, you have nothing to fear. If Charlie is the person I am looking for, only you and Charlie will know. I'm not going to announce it to anyone and nobody is going to be taking him to a lab for study... I was invited to a Baptist Festival and I am looking forward to it."

Twenty minutes later, the snoring stopped. Sydney Tobias and Mrs. Johnson looked at each other and smiled.

After uttering, stretching, and waking up sounds Rev. Johnson asked," Where are we?"

"We are about four hours from the Tappenzee Bridge into Manhattan."

"Fantastic! Praise the Lord! Sydney, if you pull into the next rest stop we could shake our legs a little and I could take the van for the rest of the way."

Sydney said, "Are you familiar with New York?"

"Sure, I preached there for years... A lot of hungry souls there, y'know?"

Thirty minutes later, Sydney found himself looking at the stars. His head was propped up by his folded jacket and the last seat in the van allowed him a partial view of the night sky. The pound cake and warm milk were working their magic as sleeping aid. None of the stops and commotion woke Charlie.

Sydney began to analyze what constellation he could be looking at. However, the road turned and headlight flashes offered constant distraction; and soon enough Sydney drifted off to sleep.

Lying on his back, Sydney realized that once again he was Elijah, the constellations were much easier to spot. Elijah had company and was camped on a dark stretch of road outside of Heliopolis en route to Alexandria, two thousand years earlier.

"Professor, are you awake?"

"Yes Luke, what troubles you?"

"I am worried, I thought I would miss my village life, my family, especially now that my uncle is gone, but instead, I think I would have missed my life on the road more, had I decided to stay."

Elijah responded, "Dear Luke, just like me you have now become a certified wanderer, just like the planets in the sky."

After a few seconds Luke got up, looked at the horizon and said, "Professor! Get up! What do you think that is?" Luke pointed to a valley and an expansive area to look at and he repeated, "Right there on the horizon!"

Old Elijah pulled himself up and scanned the horizon. "I just see some lights. You have better eyes. What do you see?"

"To me it looks like an entourage, the biggest I've ever seen! It cannot be an army; they would not announce themselves with lights. I don't know why these people would choose to travel at night."

𓂻𓂋𓏤𓄿𓀭𓂽 𓂧𓆓 𓃀𓀭𓂋𓏤 �◯𓉐\\
𓈖𓇳𓉐𓆓𓂋◯

XXIII
Capitulus Viginti Tres

Brooklyn, New York

S ydney woke up, he told himself this was certainly a dream, he didn't recall ever seeing such a massive entourage or procession. After him snoozing for a while, the van finally pulled into the parking lot of the Church in Brooklyn. He saw one bus parked, the second hadn't arrived yet. There were a lot of surprised faces and cheers when Rev. Kendrick stepped out of the minivan. They were expecting him to be arriving on the second bus. Twenty minutes later, the second bus pulled in, the new arrivals descended and began to cheer.

One lady in the crowd yelled, "We prayed for you to get here soon, we must have prayed too hard—you got here before us!"

"Your prayers sent this good Samaritan to us." Rev. Johnson pointed to Sydney, "He gave us a ride all the way here." Rev. Johnson waited for everyone to get off the bus and said,

"Listen up! The hotel is across the street and Lillian is in charge. Only ten in a group and one group at a time! Not like the last time! Okay?" Rev. Johnson turned to Sydney and said, "Come with us; we are staying here at the guest house."

There was a lot of comradeship and cheerful greetings. Charlie was soon lost among his peers and friends. Sydney was assigned a room in the large complex adjacent to the Church. Soon he found himself in bed trying to catch up with a not well slept night. The shades were drawn, and the New York City's background hum provided a seductive lullaby.

Heliopolis, Egypt, 2000 years earlier

Once again Sydney found himself in a familiar place, back in his recent dream.

"Professor! Wake up! Get up! They are much closer now," said Luke.

When Elijah got up, the entourage had become the biggest procession he could have ever seen or dreamt of. He could see adorned elephants, monks, dancers, people from other regions dressed in garments he'd never witnessed before. The procession line continued to the original horizon point and looked liked there was more to come from beyond.

As the next adorned elephant passed, Elijah shouted at its rider, "Where are all of you going?"

He turned and answered. "We have come to see the king!"

"Which king?"

"The King of the Universe!" shouted the elephant's rider. His elephant joined in the response and started to shout and the loud noise continued. Soon, Sydney realized that the dream was over and the elephant's trumpeting was actually a truck's loud fog horn, announcing the commencement of the afternoon grid lock in Manhattan. Since he had seclusion and peace in his accommodations, Sydney powered up his laptop and went over his calculations once again. An hour and a half later he landed upon the same conclusion, which took him to Demopolis. *Could I have been on the right track? Could I have been wasting my time?* Mrs. Johnson gave him some very important yet conflicting information. Elijah recalled near misses of trying to find Immanuel for the last two millennia, but it doesn't matter how good his technique may be or had become to find Him, if He doesn't want to be found.

Brooklyn, New York

Sydney left his room and when he approached the parking lot of the Church, he found a very different scene. Gone were the busses and also his minivan. He found instead, a fair was being assembled. A roll of tents followed the contour of the lot in the shape of a horseshoe and another roll was at the center. From a satellite angle it looked like the tips of a trident. He contemplated giving his friends in New York a call, but if he did his anonymity would be long gone. What he did instead, was to join the volunteers and become one as well. He was surprised to find a couple of Hare-Krishnas also working on the endeavor; the Krishnas were not dressed in their traditional robes but wearing slacks and T-shirts. Later, he found out that many of the tents were from different denominations, and religions as well. They only had two items in common, God and Brooklyn. Sydney found himself unloading trucks and setting up displays, since none of his traveling companions were in sight, he continued to make himself useful, and the twilight turned into night very fast.

New York, Next Morning

"Welcome!" there was a microphone feedback that grew and died, Reverend Marshall spoke off the mike, "Ready now?" from the stage he continued to his audience, "Welcome to our tenth *Festival of Love Thy Neighbor!"* the tall and slender Rev. Marshall waited for the cheers and applause to diminish, "If this is your first time here, then I want to wish you a very, very, very, very special welcome! Twenty years ago our neighborhood was not as safe and we didn't have a place of our own to gather and pray but thanks to our neighbors, the Yoga Meditation Center, the Hare-Krishnas, and the United Church, we then began having a place to meet. Later it was our great pleasure to be able to return the favor when their temples were under renovation or had a roof leak, you name it. Rev. Marshall paced the stage with his robe. "Ten years ago we began our Christian duty of honoring our neighbors, so for the next two days you are going to enjoy the best choir of my native Alabama. Here is my dear cousin, Rev. Kendrick Johnson." Some applause started, "Brother Kendrick, please stand up and take a bow!" after watching Kendrick take his seat Rev. Marshall continued. "This is a festival of my favorite things, God, food and love." He heard sporadic shouts of Amen came from the multitude. "So today no one is here for conversion or proselytizing, we are here only to rejoice. We have prepared and selected some hymns and songs that celebrate our faith. We all are going to take turns on stage, today and tomorrow. You are most welcome to stay and enjoy the songs and the unique selection of ethnic foods that we have set up outside." He changed to a serious tone, "Folks, I just want you to keep your drinking and eating outside, inside we are already nourished by the word of the Lord... As I was saying before, I hope you enjoy the eclectic selection of music and food. The meals cover the gambit from jambalaya to grits to Indian pakoras, from chai teas to yogurt as well as good old American ice-cream." Rev. Marshall studied the reaction of one member of his audience, "When my sister Theresa heard the word *pakoras*, she started to smile like a kid in a candy store. I think she got addicted to them, did you?" he saw her and her friends' vivacious laughter and dismissals. "Yeah, she couldn't wait to eat some!" he paused. "I know you!" he redirected his attention to the whole audience. "If any of you don't know the lyrics get a hold of the magazine in the pocket in front of you, it's our program for the next two days.

"Now without further delay," Rev. Marshall saw one of the members of the choir break the formation, and becoming the conductor. "Please join and welcome my brothers from my favorite Baptist Church in Alabama."

The conductor waited for the applause and cheers to lessen and he started a forty minutes medley of hymns and spirituals, led by *When The Saints Go Marching In.*

After the hymns, a new group took over, taking center stage. There were six in all. The guitarist brought along a chair in front of the microphone stand. One sat cross-legged on the floor and allocated his double end drum in front of his legs. The remaining four paired up into two mikes, two females and two males.

"Hello everyone, my name is Roy. I'm from the Meditation Center two doors down, and I want to thank all of you for being my good neighbors. I want also to give special thanks to Rev. Marshall for all the kindness over all these years, from time to time we borrow a cup of sugar from each other. Many times he's been kind enough to let us use this parking lot... Now, I don't want you to be fooled by my Indian garbs, I was born in Mississippi." The speaker accented his Southern drawl. "Yes I am, and my faith has led me all over the world and back to my roots..." He used the Southern preaching tone, "Last year I went back home to see my folks, driving from New York to Jackson, Mississippi along the local roads. While driving, I heard a lot of faith music on the local radio, but to me they all sounded exclusive..." Roy switched back to his normal tone, "So when I knew today was coming up I prepared a very inclusive song. It's on page eleven, it is called, *Carrying an Ego*. I imagined, what would happen if Jesus, Buddha, Krishna and Mohamed were together having tea? I hope you enjoy and join us."

Sydney turned his booklet to the page mentioned and he found, *Carrying an Ego*, not only the lyrics but also the chord progression in front of it.

CARRYING AN EGO

G	C	If everyone was like Jesus
Am	G	Then everyone would be free
G	C	But everyone is carrying an ego
Am	G	Then everyone is like me.
G	Em	If everyone was like Jesus
Am	Em	What would be the need for locks?
Am	Em	What would be the need for prisons?
Am	D	What would be the need for laws?
G	C	If everyone was like Buddha
Am	G	Then everyone would be free
G	C	But everyone is carrying an ego
Am	G	Then everyone is like me.

G	Em	If everyone was like Buddha
Am	Em	What would be the need for keys?
Am	Em	What would be the need for guns?
Am	D	What would be the need for armies?
G	C	If everyone was like Mohamed
Am	G	Then everyone would be free
G	C	But everyone is carrying an ego
Am	G	Then everyone is like me.
G	Em	If everyone was like Mohamed
Am	Em	What would be the need for rules?
Am	Em	What would be the need for games?
Am	D	What would be the need for duels?
G	C	If everyone was like Krishna
Am	G	Then everyone would be free
G	C	But everyone is carrying an ego
Am	G	Then everyone is like me.
G	Em	If everyone was like Krishna
Am	Em	What would be the need for property?
Am	Em	What would be the need for markets?
Am	D	What would be the need for profit?
G	C	If everyone was like Them
Am	G	Then everyone would be free
G	C	But everyone is carrying an ego
Am	G	Then everyone is like me.
G	C	Jesus, Mohamed
Am	G	Buddha and Krishna
G	C (3X)	Are getting along in heaven
Am	G	So then we should try

After the applause and cheers Roy continued, "I want to tell you the story of this next song on the next page, *What If Your Name Were John?*

"Years ago, I was having breakfast with a friend and the war in Bosnia-Croatia-Serbia was being shown on TV. Then, my friend made a racist comment about another friend of mine named John. When I heard that, it was like a dagger through my heart. What was also very sad to realize was that a war on TV which I thought was so far away, was actually right there with me at my breakfast table." He started the song.

Sydney turned to the page to find the song, except that this time he only saw the lyrics and no chord progression.

WHAT IF YOUR NAME WERE JOHN?

What if your name were John or other than John?
What if your name were Mary or other than Mary?
Would you feel the same way you do?
Would you sacrifice a thing or two?
What if your name were John or other than John?

What if your eyes were blue or other than blue?
What if your hair were black or other than black?
Would you change the color to disguise,
Feelings or likes you may carry inside?
What if your hair were black or other than black?

What if your name for God was other than God?
What if my name for God was other than God?
Would you hurt me just to prove you're right?
Would you kill my kind for holy rights?
What if my name for God was other than God?
What if your skin were gray or other than gray?

What if my skin were green or other than green?
Would I be a threat to all your kind?
Would we find peace in being color blind?
What if your skin were gray or other than gray?

What if a high-rise were home or other than home?
What if the streets were home or other than home?
Would you feel the need to Balkanize?
Would your notions get to galvanize?
What if the streets were home or other than home?

What if your eyes were blue?
What if your skin were gray?
What if we had no God to pray to today?
What if the streets were home?
What if your lies were true to me?
And happy times too blue to see?
Would you still be a friend to me?
What if your name were John...or other than John?

Sydney read the lyrics but as the music played he started to scan the room for his hosts. Sydney left the space at his pew and ventured out, where many now were enjoying the delicatessens provided by the many tents. Sydney walked the loop, recognized many faces from the previous day but still no sign of Charlie or Jojo.

𓏤𓂋𓈖𓅱𓃀 𓂻𓏏𓅱 𓂝𓊪𓏏 𓃀𓆑𓃀𓈖

𓊪𓂻 𓏤𓂋𓈖 𓃀𓂺 𓏺𓂝𓏥 𓆓𓃀𓏏𓆤 𓂝𓆑 𓆑𓂝𓏏

𓂝𓊪𓏏 𓆑𓂝𓊪𓏏 𓊖𓊪𓏏

XXIV
Capitulus Viginti Quattuor

S ydney explored the compound for a short while and found it deserted. The only other place left to search was the hotel across the street. Sydney advanced towards the entrance of the parking lot to see the hotel across the street; however, the view was partially blocked by the end of a park dividing the automobile traffic. Standing on the edge of the sidewalk was a man with hefty build; he had a shaved hair cut, just like the ones used by the Skinheads. The manner of the individual reminded Sydney of the Imperial Roman Guard. At his discretion, Sydney searched his two millennia of memories to see if he indeed had met the fellow. The recognition came to him very suddenly and accompanied by a squirt of adrenaline. The reincarnated and disguised guard was the person that he recalled from the time and last days of the Library of Alexandria. He'd made a note then, never to forget that face. He was the one who'd dragged and killed Hypatia, the philosopher and head librarian of Alexandria. Hypatia, daughter of Theon of Alexandria, was the only person who could have present a threat to the Church, by holding evidence to disprove the conclusions of the First Council of Niceae. She had to be dealt with, and the man standing across the street did the Church's dirty work in the name of the redrafted and newly franchised Jesus. *What is his purpose, standing on the edge of the sidewalk?* Immediately Sydney question was answered, a motorcycle rear rider passed the skinhead a metal cylinder. He turned around and took the vessel to a woman sitting on a bench. Sydney thought, *No! That cannot be possible*! Judy Orman, herself, was about to take the object from her subordinate. There was a car exhaust pipe that backfired nearby, that distraction made the pass a fumble and the cylinder dropped and bounced on the ground. As Jojo and Charlie were walking by, the tube found its final resting place next to the foot of the child. The boy picked it up and handed it back without ceremony, just a smile. Defending Charlie at that moment would only spike curiosity in Judy Orman and the revelation of Sydney's true identity. The best thing to do was to be out of the field of vision, be cautious, and hope that Judy and the Skinhead would find their separate ways soon. Sydney's concentration and attention to the situation made everything play in his mind like a slow motion event. Judy reciprocated the smile, took the aluminum cylinder and thanked the boy. As Jojo and Charlie crossed the street, Judy and her henchman were gone.

Sydney picked up his cell phone, "Sarturo?"

"Yes… Sydney? Where are you?"

"I'm in the Big Apple, and I am sorry to disturb your Saturday, but I just saw an old ghost!"

"Tell me more!"

"Judy Orman and her new assistant made a pickup in Brooklyn."

"How did you come to see this?"

"Dumb luck, I guess…"

"I have two guys on her tail; they probably lost her and are still parked in front of her apartment."

"She is not your average librarian. Tell them."

"I know, I know… Did you see the transfer, what was it?"

"The way that the thing bounced on the ground it was very light. I think it was a tube with a message."

"Why do you sound so sure?"

"Because if the contents were delicate it would have come in a padded case."

"I see… Sydney, please stay out of sight, if you are recognized you will only alert her, and people around you will die again."

"I'll try to stay out of trouble, I promise."

The first day of the festival came to a conclusion; it was a success, but now were just closed tents resting for the night. Sydney was sitting on a bench near the compound. The droning sound of New York's traffic was his only company. Everyone must have gone to rest their voices and their stomachs. Sydney rested his elbows on his knees and looked at the ground.

"Sydney… Are you sad?" a young voice spoke and stood in front of him.

Sydney rose to see who'd called for him, "Hey Charlie, no not really."

"So how come you are looking into nothing and hanging by yourself?"

"I am just thinking about the decisions that I've made in the past few days."

"Do you regret coming with us?" asked Charlie.

"No, nothing like that. I have been worried about my goals, I have an invincible enemy and a very difficult quest, and have traveled for a long, long time."

"I know Elijah… I know."

Sydney could not believe his ears, "Rabbi Jesus is that you?" Sydney began to get off his chair to show Charlie reverence with a bow; however, Charlie stopped his actions with a gesture.

Charlie explained, "Rabbi Jesus is an old edition, let us not revisit it, but I am the one that you have been seeking for a long time. Please keep my identity a secret as I will yours, and I will lead you to the end of your quest."

Sydney tried to speak but a sudden lump in this throat choked his words. "Master, why the secrecy? I've seen most of your teachings being altered and changed, I was looking for your permission to show the corrections. I buried some of the scripts 1900 years ago in Egypt and some before the fire in Alexandria."

"Dear Elijah, let the scripts stay where they are. Haven't you seen enough wars between religions for the last two thousand years?

"I have returned and preached my philosophy on many occasions, and each time people are more interested in the literal interpretation than the essence of my message. If I announce myself, I cannot bear the new devotees of Charlie fighting the Christians, or Muslims and so forth."

"But Master, why couldn't you now make the quintessence of your teachings clearer, so we could stop these wars and monopolies on God?"

"Elijah, verily, verily, dear Elijah, you know that I've spoke in many parables so listen to another one. A father taught his son to read and to discriminate the good in life. One day this father set his son free to face the world. The father wished no longer to make the decisions for his son but to rejoice in the glory and pride of his son's triumph. This Master wants also to be proud of the people that truly understand his teachings."

Sydney nodded in agreement and saw that his tears had fallen and wet the patio ground.

Charlie continued, "Elijah, with one move of my finger I could stop all the wars, cure all the diseases, control the earthquakes and all weather patterns. However, by doing so I would also bring an end to all the drives and forces that lead all our brothers and sisters to find God on their own, through the joy of discovering cures for ailments, finding an end to hunger and attaining world peace.

"Elijah, more than anybody, you understand that nobody dies. The forgetfulness of reincarnation is bestowed on most and the remembrance of it is granted to a worthy few. Without this forgetfulness, this merciful path granted by God, we could not achieve a new beginning and a better outcome. Brothers and sisters return with a blank slate or in today's jargon, with a blank hard drive and a better version of their operating system. They will be forming new friends who used to be enemies, fighting for new opportunities and conquering old obstacles. They will also come back to harvest the fruits of their good karma from past lives.

"Elijah, you have been looking for me for the last two thousand years in your charts and everywhere around the world, but you've forgotten to look for me in one direction, towards your heart." Charlie reached to Sydney's chest.

Sydney felt the touch just upon his heart's chakra and he felt a rush of euphoria take over his whole being. If love and electricity could mix and touch every cell of his body, it would still not do justice in describing the sublime emotion that he was feeling. "Dear Master, what ecstasy! Please spread this message about so people can experience their heart vibrating in Your glory!"

"Elijah, you are my witness that very little has changed in the last two thousand years. A new religion will not bring the wars to an end. You may speak of our meeting after I leave, only with the condition that no new religion is formed."

Sydney said, "But Master, people are always hungry to believe in something. If I tell this story, people will still want to form a church."

"Then you should make it a work of fiction; change my name, my location. Inspiration will come to you. Show that the *Link* was your mission to witness that too much blood has been shed and that we all should get along."

"Master Charlie, I don't have the power to enlighten people like that. In the last two thousand years I haven't seen anyone succeed in making people look into the essence. Even Saint Augustine had violent opposition from the narrow minded, the literals, and the Donatists. I am sure a new Donatus Magnus[i] is going to come after me." Sydney paused, "Master, why did we wait so long to have this conversation?"

"Dear Elijah, two thousand years is not even a blink of an eye where eternity dwells. This time is an incentive for you to understand that emotionally, we have not evolved. We can soar to the moon but we are still unable to offer the other cheek. If you don't take this mission upon yourself, there will be two thousand years upon two thousand years upon two thousand years with the same result as of the last two millennia."

"Master why…"

Charlie interrupted, "We might not be alone for long. You should remember to honor my secrecy and also refer to me as an eleven year old, and I will treat you like an adult," Charlie winked, "Sydney…" which he said with emphasis.

---

[i] Donatus Magnus (331 – 355 estimated dates) was the leader of the Donatists, an extremist literal group and an Early Christian sect in North Africa.

Sydney laughed and said, "Okay, Charlie... Oh please forgive me, this is very difficult." He paused to catch his breath and asked, "So, why are you here this time? I don't think you came only to reveal yourself to me."

"Elijah, it's not only some of the living who do not believe in God, also many don't believe that they have died because for many, it has been a traumatic passage. I have been returning many times and more frequently than you and Luke, I come incognito to this dimension to guide my brothers back to their spiritual path, either to their new lives here on earth or back to heaven when they cannot find their own way.

"I have returned this time to rescue my brothers wandering on this planet as ghosts since the Croatian and Serbian war of '94 and '98, lost souls[i] still lost from the Soviet occupation in Afghanistan, as well as from the killings in Africa, and all other countries.

"This includes all the people killed in the Gulf War, Iraqis as well as Americans, and recurring conflict in the Middle East between Palestinians and Jews. From all religions everywhere, from all accidents, victims and foes, they are coming with Me. They are all waiting for my guidance, to continue their journey back to their individual holy quest."

"Master, so when are you leaving?"

"Elijah, why spoil the surprise? Don't waste time casting your charts, trying to discover when I will be leaving. The right time has been decided and with each second we are closer to it. Years from now when my words are just echoes in your mind, I want you to remember that I am no more important to God than

---

[i] Not only some of the living has problem accepting reality being alive; many spirits have problem with the reality of being in another dimension. The spiritual dimension is not constrained by linear time; spirits in shock can be lost in one terrifying moment reliving it in a perpetual trauma or roaming a region in a continuous loop.

you are, and the day that you can break the mirror of the ego, everything will be revealed to you."

Reverend Johnson shouted from a distance, "There you are!" he walked to find Sydney and Charlie talking. "What are you both talking about?"

"Daddy, we were talking about our long trip."

Sydney understood the code, *I could not have put it better myself.*

"Let us all get some sleep," said the reverend, "We will need all of our energies for tomorrow's activities."

As they all walked back to their quarters, Sydney remembered his preoccupation of having Nicholas or Judy nearby. He wanted to ask a question but decided to wait until next time alone with Charlie. He thought, *Dear Lilith, thank you for the Brooklyn tip.*

𓉱𓄿𓄿𓃁〰〰𓊪𓏲 〰〰𓏲𓇋𓏤 𓃭 〰〰𓏤 𓋴𓆑𓏤𓂻𓏤𓏨𓆄〰〰
𓃭𓏤 𓄿𓃭𓏤𓊪 𓂻𓏲 〰〰𓏲𓇋𓏤 𓃭 〰〰𓏤 𓏤𓈖𓊡𓏤𓆄〰〰

XXV
Capitulus Viginti Quinque

*T*he Choir was finishing a selection of spirituals. However, this time Rev. Kendrick Johnson was the one getting ready to take the microphone.

"Thank you very much!" Rev. Johnson joined the applause in progress. "I also want to thank my first cousin by blood and my dear brother before God, Rev. Marshall for once again making us feel at home... We have some delightful rumors to spread. This may be our last time with the Festival at this location. We have more denominations and sects that want to join us next year and we will need a larger lot for more tents." He paused as the applause subsided, and moved over to allow more people to join the stage. The single Christian Choir moved to the left. The Hare-Krishnas and the non-uniformed group took place on the right. Roy and his gang from the previous day took center stage in the same fashion. A group of kids lined up below the stage, Charlie was at the center facing the whole temple and the main aisle.

Rev. Johnson continued, "We are going to close our music selection today, and this festival with a requested favorite, *When It Is My Time To Go*. So once more, let me thank you for coming, God bless you, bless me, everyone who has come, and all those who couldn't come. Hallelujah!"

The drumming started a very euphonic beat and the guitar followed for a couple of measures.

The Christian side chanted, *"Moses, Abraham, Jesus, Ave!"*

The Eastern flank replied, *"Shiva, Krishna, Buddha, Hari!"*

The calling and response continued for a while and Roy sang above the chant:

> *"Whoever is your prophet…*
> *I want you to know*
> *Just take me by the hand*
> *When it is my time to go!"*

Sydney heard the packed church join the singing in progress, which for the last three years had become the festival's favorite. However, Sydney soon realized that there was something different in the room. He sat in the third pew by the center aisle and had a clear view of the whole stage. As the song continued, he couldn't believe his own vision; floating down from the ceiling celestial beings were forming flanks behind and above the existing choir. Shortly, there was no space left, the celestial beings filled the wall and its windows, and the entire area was covered by souls. He saw Mrs. Johnson ahead scanning the same images and drying her eyes. As Roy was about to start another verse, Sydney heard the loudest and yet harmonious thunder break the front door. He looked towards the back and found a procession advancing towards the stage, but when he turned to the stage concerned about Charlie and others, he only saw Charlie. The musicians and celestial singers were replaced by another cosmic infinity. Sydney could see the whole universe behind Charlie, from planets to galaxies and little Charlie still concentrated on his singing, dancing and clapping. The scenery continued to morph and change, illuminated beings were emanating from Charlie's presence. There was something different about Charlie as well... He appeared to radiate a luminous yet deep azure. Sydney realized that he was witnessing the true image of the Self as an Omnipresent Being. The Hindus had a name for that type of manifestation, Vishwarupa[i] or Totality of Lord Vishnu. Sydney experienced a profound sense of reverence when he realized the privilege that was bestowed upon him. He concluded that two thousand years of traveling had all been worthwhile for that opportunity. He recognized the procession as the one that he had dreamt of two dreams ago. He muttered to himself "Oh Dear Luke, I wish that you could have been here with me to witness this..."

The pageant was comprised of people walking, Sufis dancing, beautifully adorned elephants and horses. People and animals were draped in gold attire, monks from Christian, Franciscan, Tibetan, and Hindu denominations as well as American Native Shamans paraded in harmony. There was no separation of groups, they all marched together. Physically or materialistically speaking, Charlie was just a few paces from Sydney. The entourage advanced to a distant horizon, yet it appeared faraway as they approached Charlie. They would prostrate and disappear before entering Charlie's heart and becoming one with him. Sydney no longer heard Roy's song or the choir, instead there was a melody in which all the notes and octaves blended in harmoniously. Time, sound, and distance were all fusing into an unbelievable supernatural sight or better yet, the illusion of time, sound and space was being unmasked by the

---

[i] *Vishwarupa* or *Viswaroopa* is represented in many ancient paintings as described in the Epic of *The Mahabharata*. The total manifestation or Universal image of God can be viewed at once.

incredible glory of the Vishwarupa. Sydney heard his name Elijah being called; he looked in all directions and only discovered the Church members singing as if in very slow motion unaware of the glory before them.

"Elijah! Elijah, look up! Over here on top!"

Since the first impressions are indelible in the soul, Sydney could not visualize his late father Horace, he could only see his original friend Luke of two thousand years ago. He saw Luke waving from inside of an adorned canopy mounted on an elephant.

"Luke!" Sydney hesitated because he was afraid that everyone would hear him, but then he realized that everyone would be hearing the sounds of their own voices. "I'm so glad you are here! This is a joyous moment!"

"An angel named Lilith put a good word in for me, I have the best seat in the house! Would you thank her on my behalf?"

"I sure will."

Luke waved good bye, turned forward and joined the prayer in progress. Sydney saw his old friend vanish just after he bowed to Charlie.

All concepts of divinity were represented in the illustrious convoy, from Christian saints, to deities Sydney had never heard of, that was all suspended in time; they all moved towards their Master's heart. Closing the procession was a deity with the most terrifying face, she resembled the looks of Medusa, yet she had many arms and weapons. The multiple limbs were swaying as she was riding an enormous tiger[i], she was the destroyer of the world and the dissolution and destruction of time itself. Sydney had heard of her, she was known as the mighty Kali Durga.

Very soon the temple was gaining its original appearance, the universal vision was disappearing and being replaced by the

---

[i] Kali Durga is also depicted riding a lion or a corpse of a demon. Whichever depiction is chosen the manifestation of Kali is to remind us of the terrible yet candid conclusion that everything in this universe is temporal.

current illusion of time and space. The song was coming to a conclusion as well.

From across the aisle in the middle of the congregation a heavy set lady started to shout, "My sweet Jesus! My sweet Jesus! My sweet Jesus!" as she moved through the pew.

Charlie made eye contact with Sydney to intercept her in order to keep his anonymity secure, Sydney understood and proceeded. As she came out to the aisle, Sydney in an instant had her in his arms and embraced her. The whole church assumed that they were witnessing an act of redemption and so they cheered.

Sydney softly spoke, "He is not Jesus, His name is Charlie."

She backed off, looked him straight in the eyes and said, "Don't you come telling this old black woman she is not seeing Jesus, when she is seeing Jesus!"

Sydney whispered to her, "Sister, He needs your help. Charlie needs you to keep his identity a secret, and I'll do what I can to arrange for you to see or meet with Him." Sydney walked holding and supporting her to a bench outside of the temple.

"I know this is the happiest day of my life, not only did I see Jesus, but I saw a beautiful black Jesus." She paused to breathe and cry; when she recovered she asked, "Why was that man on the elephant talking to you?"

Sydney realized that she'd seen the Vishwarupa as well, he asked, "Sister, what is your name?"

"Emma Jefferson."

"Sister Emma, only the ones with pure hearts were able to experience Charlie today in His divine glory. That's why we need to be grateful and honor His request for secrecy."

"Are you one of his angels?" she asked as she took the empty bench.

Sydney took a seat next to her and said, "No I'm not, just someone who looked for Charlie as long as you have... Just a second…" he requested, Sydney concentrated on her face and Mrs. Jefferson began to morph into another black lady, then for the next five faces she appeared as a fair Caucasian lady, into different races and skin tones until Sydney finally recognized her. She was now a Jewish lady whom he had met in Egypt long ago. She used to be his landlady in Alexandria and he said, "Your name used to be Elisheva when we met long ago."

"When your name was Elijah?"

"Precisely, how did you know?"

"That was the name I heard the man on the elephant calling you."

Sydney smiled, "Sister Emma, I know you mean well but please don't make a scene, Charlie is counting on you." Sydney had noticed that people were leaving the temple and populating the tent area and Jojo was bringing Charlie with her to meet them.

"Is he coming?"

Before Sydney had a chance to answer, Charlie arrived. Sydney got up and stood across with Mrs. Johnson.

"Oh blessed be the Child! Dear Lord, what should I call you?"

"Call me Charlie. This is my mother Joyce Johnson."

Mrs. Jefferson said, "Mrs. Johnson, blessed also be your name. May your son give this old mother a hug?"

Mrs. Johnson released Charlie's hand and Charlie advanced with His arms open wide. Mrs. Jefferson held onto him for a good minute as she wept. Sydney could feel that her chakras[i] were opening with a sublime energy just as he'd had the day before.

Mrs. Jefferson released Charlie, dried her eyes and said, "Charlie, today is a very special day for me for two reasons, I'm

---

[i] Chakras are psychic centers of our spiritual body that work in symmetry with our physical body. For example; when we experience fear or anger *Manipura* or solar plexus, the chakra responds with indigestion or adrenal secretion. When love is experienced the *Anahata* or heart chakra vibrates intensively.

immensely grateful for having seen You, and today my son Clarence would have turned 46 years old. He was executed by the state when he was 34. I always felt that he was innocent but he hung around people that were up to no good and he was framed."

"Sister Emma, I bring you a message from Clarence and he said, '*Mother, please forgive the people that killed me by mistake, my karma was to die this way because I'd also committed the same mistake once long ago.*' He also thanks you for all your prayers and he comes to visit you as much as he can."

"Oh! I knew my Clarence was innocent. Charlie, thank you for healing this aching heart after all these years." she dried her eyes. "Do you see him?"

"Sister Emma, brother Clarence helps everyone who has been wrongfully killed. He is one of my most dedicated guides at work."

A couple approached the bench and the lady asked, "Momma… Is everything okay? Why are you crying?"

Mrs. Jefferson replied, "Child, today your mother is crying because she is happy." She turned back to her guests and said, "Charlie, Mrs. Johnson and Sydney thank you for the gift of your company." Mrs. Jefferson left with her daughter and son-in-law.

Manhattan, New York,
Two days later

It was a sparkling blue Tuesday morning in the city, the choir had left on Monday afternoon. After all of the tents were dismantled and the parish was completely cleaned, Sydney accompanied Rev. Johnson, his wife and Charlie to the Lower District of Manhattan.

The family and Sydney entered the building's lobby and they were soon spotted by their friend Vince. He was a security guard, he waved at them from a distance, left his post and walked towards them.

"I'm glad you were all able to make it... Come with me." said Vince.

They all followed him and Rev. Johnson started, "Vince, thank you for taking us in."

"No problem... This is one of the few perks of my job." As they entered the elevator, he continued, "That was a great festival, I'm glad I was able to make it this year... They sounded like angels, this time."

Rev. Johnson replied, "They sure did."

Sydney, Charlie and Jojo exchanged smiles because of the comment.

"I'm happy that you are all bundled up because it gets cold up there," said Vince.

After a couple of elevators, doors, and stair cases, they were all exposed to the deep blue sky and the expansive view of New York City. In a distance, Vince waved to another guard who was already accompanying either a tourist or a photographer.

Charlie sprinted around the observation deck and returned running. "Dad, dad, could we take some pictures?"

"We don't have a camera, Charlie," said the reverend.

Vince interjected, "Our souvenir store is still closed but you can get one across the street. When you come back just have them page me on the radio and I'll let you back in."

"Okay, wait here, I'll be right back."

"Sydney, please go with him," requested Charlie.

Sydney left without a second thought. He caught up with Rev. Johnson, and passed by the photographer; she had long black hair, a baseball cap and sun glasses. Reverend Johnson and Sydney arrived in the lobby then proceeded across the street looking for a shop. They entered what appeared to be a souvenir shop and convenience store.

Rev. Johnson scanned the narrow aisles then asked, "Do you carry disposable cameras?"

The clerk at the counter answered, "Unfortunately, I ran out of them yesterday but if you go downstairs to the underground plaza," the clerk pointed out the windowpane behind him. "See right there? That's the underground concourse, and I'm sure you will find a camera there."

Sydney turned to look in the same direction but he was distracted by a framed poster of Manhattan that hung directly right above the windowpane. The poster depicted the tip of Manhattan in its natural historical state, consisting only of green pastures and a fort. The name under it read, New Amsterdam.

Rev. Johnson noticed that Sydney was intrigued and said, "Sydney stay here, I'll be right back."

Mesmerized by the poster Sydney answered catatonically, "All right, I'll wait."

The clerk noticing his customer captivated by the poster, pulled a fresh one from the bin and trying to push a sale he said, "I'm no scholar but this is a very special day. Henry Hudson at the service of the Dutch discovered this parcel of land where we are standing today, September, 11 1609."

Sydney immediately remembered, the memorized words of the quatrain given to him by Nostradamus and muttered to himself once again.

> *"On the birthday of New Amsterdam all sirens shall sing,*
> *The Hearted shall start new enterprise*
> *The Terrible shall stop departed with the king.*
> *No time for tears, story must be notified."*

Sydney looked through the window and saw Rev. Johnson entering the underground concourse and disappearing down into the plaza. Suddenly, a familiar face reappeared. Sydney was disturbed; the same Skinhead that had worked for Judy on Saturday was now standing on the edge of the sidewalk, once again scanning the traffic. Out of the blue, Sydney realized that that was not the only menacing encounter of the day; the long haired photographer on the observation deck was Judy Orman.

With the conversation on the phone already in progress Judy blasted abruptly, "Are you sure? The day of the strike is today? And here I am taking some photos!" she paused, "*Shukran habibi, ma'assalama*[i]." She thanked the caller and said good bye. As she folded the phone and hastened her departure, she noticed that a young black boy approached her.

"Judas my friend!" said Charlie.

"Excuse me, my name is Judy. Wait a second… I know you, I saw you at a Brooklyn park, Saturday."

"Judas my friend, son of Simon, born in Kerioth versed in the scriptures and languages."

"No." Hesitantly, "You must have me confused." She started to walk away.

Charlie spoke again, "Judas who has been called Nicholas for the last thousand years? How could I be wrong?"

Judy returned, approached Charlie, fell to her knees, dropped the camera case and said, "Rabbi… Is that really you, in flesh and bones again? I've always doubted that Elijah and Luke

---

[i] Thank you my friend, peace be with you.

could have been right, even though I used their tools." Judy dried her eyes.

"Why have you forsaken my teachings? Sacrificing others in the name of my Glory is no sacrifice. The only sacrifice I ever asked from you was to sacrifice your ego, by offering your other cheek."

Judy recovered from her tears and said, "Master, we must leave immediately, this place is doomed. You are back and you must reveal yourself and your teachings again."

"Dear Judas, I am not going anywhere. Humanity needs a new religion as much as it needs a new weapon of war."

Charlie saw Judy begin to weep profusely, then stated, "Today it is an important day just like in Judea twenty centuries ago. Today the paths to God shall be reopened to the unguided souls[i]."

Judy started to ramble in a soliloquy, "Master, I did what I was told, I surrendered you. I even took your command, *that thou doest, do quickly[ii]*... The Jewish council had promised that they wanted to debate you and interview you. I set the meeting up as I was told that they wouldn't hurt you... That they wouldn't... Hurt you... I took the money as the Roman law required. None of our brethren believed me! That this was the plan."

"Judas, I had brought a message of detachment and forgiveness, and I had to live it. I could have walked away before the Roman soldiers arrived, couldn't I? But it was my way to live my teaching... My message of surrendering came to replace the eye for an eye understanding. A tooth for a tooth is Divine Justice that should be enforced by Divine Forces; mankind should only learn to live like I did by offering the other cheek. After two thousand years you should know that no one reaches God by

---

[i] Ghosts or spirits who are still in shock with their own reality.
[ii] John 13:27

forced conversions… The essence has always been the same in all religions but the collective ego of the masses wants to enforce only their points of view and versions."

"Rabbi! We must leave immediately!"

"My friend you are free to go, but I would rather have you come with me and help our brothers." Charlie touched Judy's heart and she felt a charge of energy spread through her being. When she raised her eyes to look at Charlie, she witnessed a prodigious congregation of souls surrounding the deck area, coming through the floor and through the sky. Soldiers in many different uniforms began to populate the area. "Master what is to become of me?"

"It has taken two thousand years for you to learn one lesson, now it is time for you to learn a more sublime one."

The two security guards were standing off at a distance and discussing work. Mrs. Joyce Johnson found it interesting, yet not unusual, that a full grown woman was on her knees prostrating by her son.

Sydney dropped the poster on the counter and quickly left the store. He paced himself to find a space in the traffic and charged across the street. He continued at top speed to tumble the massive body of the Skinhead. His victim never saw it coming, fell to the ground and hit his head on the sidewalk.

The two seconds that he took to recover was enough time for Sydney to disarm him, Sydney had a grip on his collar and a knee on his chest, "What is she doing here?" he shouted.

"Look man! I don't even know her name, I only know that the chick pays well." He moved his hands about and said, "Hey! you took my gun?"

"I'm asking the questions. What is she doing here?"

"Man… The woman left with a camera and told me to stand by the limo, which is going to arrive at any…"

The loudest jet roar was heard overhead and a deafening explosion followed suit. American Airlines' Flight 11 just hit the North Tower of the World Trade Center.

"Holy Moses!" said the man pinned on the ground. Shortly after, a piece of the fuselage missed them by a couple of feet.

"The bitch pays me well but not enough for this! I'm out of here." He felt Sydney's release. "Can I have my gun back?"

Sydney got up, dropped the magazine of the semi-automatic and tucked it into his pocket. Next, he recoiled the top assembly to spit the bullet out the chamber, caught it in the air and handed the gun to the man.

"I want my bullets too."

"Tell the cops or sue me!" Sydney started to run toward the lobby and found a stampede of panic stricken people exiting the building. A stranger, a middle aged Caucasian man grabbed him by the arm and said, "Elijah, don't go in there!" he released Sydney and ran away. Another stranger, an Asian man was next to stop Sydney's progress and said, "Remember, your mission is not in the building!" he just as urgently went away. As Sydney came closer to the door, a woman blocked him and asked, "Who is going to take my father back to Alabama?"

Sydney reconstructed the messages from the three strangers and realized that Charlie was speaking through them. He went back to the entrance of the Plaza Concourse under the World Trade Center Complex, to wait for Rev. Johnson. Sydney, in his own thoughts had lost track of time and without a warning it came to him.

In the midst of the rapidly emerging chaotic scene, the quatrain written centuries of years ago, was materializing before his eyes. There he was on the birthday of New Amsterdam, witnessing the deafening sirens of ambulances and fire trucks.

Sydney had lastly solved the encoded quatrain; the one he'd always seen as terrible, Nicholas was finally leaving with the king of kings, the king this time incarnated as Charlie. To conclude the prophecy, he had to share this knowledge with the world in the form of a novel, to avoid confrontations and to imply that *The Link* never existed.

When Rev. Johnson came out of the ramp running with the cameras in his hands, he saw Sydney contemplatively gazing at the ground.

He was about to ask, "Sydney what is going…" His phrase was interrupted by another suicidal explosion overhead.

Mrs. Johnson approached her son. She saw the woman in tears kneeling next to him and asked him, "Is she going to be alright?"

Charlie answered, "We all are!" Charlie felt his mother taking him by the hand, he looked up and said, "I'm glad you chose to be my mother…"

Vince screamed at his colleague next to him, "Charlie, look!"

Charles, the second security guard, turned around to see a commercial jetliner hit the North Tower. They both ran to the edge to see more of the details and were terrified by an awesome sight. They were distracted by the explosion, for a full three minutes forgetful of their guests. They were both called by radio and asked to return to the lobby.

"Vince!" asked Charles, "Where are your people?"

"I don't know. I don't see your photographer here either. I think they might have left. Charlie, let's get out of here!" The two security guards, Vince and Charles, left the observation deck, unaware of the illusion of invisibility created by the little boy known as Charlie Johnson.

"Sister Mary and brother Judas, I am so happy to have your company once again." Charlie waved his hand and made possible for both to view all the souls coming and populating the area. "Very soon we shall depart the boundary of time and space."

Epilogus

Alexandria, Egypt,
Year 36 C.E.

It is always said that people recall their lives, moments before their death, Judy found out to be true. After she felt the quake and thunder beneath her feet, Judy Orman knew that her fate was sealed, and the canisters of Cesium would never be delivered. She went back in time, not too early to recall her life as Judas with Jesus, but later when she had assumed the identity of Theophilus and heard for the first time the names of Luke and Elijah…

There is no greater pain than to be separated from one's beloved, the second biggest is to be exiled by friends, family and country. That was the fifth year of exile and pain for Judas as calling himself Theophilus, and the fifth year for his new identity in Alexandria, Egypt. Since all of the people of Judea had given testimony of his death by suicide, even if he wanted to say that he was Judas[i] no one would have believed him. Life was very simple

[i] One may call psychic intuition or forensic history montage, but it was always suspicious to the author of *The Link* that Judas was reported with a convenient expeditious suicide shortly after the crucifixion of Jesus. The forbearers of Christianity crafted a story of suicide in order to create a

for Theophilus, he worked at the Alexandria's port as a translator or as a language teacher for hire. Just as long as he had enough money to drown his sorrows and memories with wine or other fermented beverages.

That morning was no different than any other where he woke up on the street under somebody's window. He could have used one carafe of wine to stop his hands from shaking but he had no energy to get up. So there he remained. From under the window and through a hole in the wall lower to the ground, he could hear the conversation of two astrologers in a language of his past, Hebrew. He heard two voices, one sounded much older than the other.

The younger voice said, "Professor Elijah, I have just completed the calculations again."

The elder voice responded, "Very well, let me see that." A few seconds later the voice continued, "Do you think this is possible? This calculation shows that Jesus could be back in 300 years or less."

The younger voice said, "I have also recalculated our reincarnations, and it looks very likely that you will be fifteen years older than Jesus when He returns."

"Let me see that page." The elder asked...

During that pause the weak and forgotten man on the ground thought, *Jesus! Return! Reincarnation! Astrological calculations! Could this be possible?* He had to hear more.

The elder voice continued, "We both shall see it, if it comes to be when you *link* me for the first time thirty years from now. You shall be five years younger than me today."

---

franchise of guilt or *Mea Culpa*. The author was raised Catholic but always suspected that the story of Judas' suicide is a farce. B.Sandy was validated in April of 2006 when National Geographic Society made available to the public the existence of *The Gospel of Judas*. Judas did not commit suicide and lived long enough after Jesus' death to write and relate his own account. The first draft of *The Link* was copyrighted in January 22nd of 2002, four years before the publication of the Judas' codex.

From that day on, the drinking places and wine merchants stopped seeing the wanderer that they knew as Theophilus.

Bartering with a few items, he approached their landlady. The man called Theophilus now had complete access to all of Elijah and Luke's books, the very notes which he would duplicate whenever the astrologers were traveling abroad.

At the end of ten years, Theophilus had become as knowledgeable as the best astrologers in the region, and now he had better tools as well. What he came to discover was that his *Link's* process was even superior to Luke and Elijah's *Link*. Judas couldn't rely on anyone; no one would re-awaken the most infamous betrayer. Not even he would like to re-awaken himself to the fact and relive all the pain and agony he'd witnessed his best friend go through. To offer the other cheek was a lesson that had not been repeated enough to him, it was more like a concept, but an eye for an eye was more than a law, it was a tradition that the Hebrews had chosen to live by. *So be it!* He reasoned to himself, *if this was the tradition the Jews would live by, then it would also be the tradition that they would die for.*

What was once the pain of separation and the loneliness of isolation, had become rage and revenge. His quarrel was not with the other disciples that depicted him in a bad light. He was going after bigger enemies. Although all the disciples had turned against him, they were not the ones that caused him the pain but the mighty Jewish tradition, the tradition that wouldn't recognize its own prophet.

If it was the Jewish tradition that could not accept the coming of Immanuel and killed Jesus, then it was now in his power to destroy that tradition. He had discovered that power is in knowledge and who controls the source of knowledge can also control the source of power. As the ancient Roman elite used to say, and he muttered to himself for the first time, *"Qui imperium scientia, imperium mundus."*

New York, New York,
September 11th, 2001

Judy Orman returned to the present, she recounted the twenty times that she'd re-awakened to her past. The unbearable pain that a ten-year-old would endure when reawakening, the pain of discovering that once again she had been the betrayed betrayer for the last two thousand years. How unsavory it was to discover that tarnished past. Each re-*link* brought back the pain and refueled her rage and commitment.

That was the past as Judas and later as Nicholas; Judy Orman was now in the present. *The present is forgiveness. The present is surrendering to higher a justice,* she thought. The best hope she ever had was to hold hands with her beloved friend once more. Mrs. Johnson, Charlie and Judy Orman created a circle by holding hands, and around them Judy noticed another circle of souls and another circle after that and another and so on... She glanced in the distance to find that millions of souls were holding hands, and reason wouldn't allow them all to stand together at that one spot; however, logic did not feed the hungry multitude either with a few fish and some slices of bread. At that point there were no sounds, no thumping of helicopters overhead, no traffic noise of ambulances or fire trucks emanating from below.

Silence, pure silence, the kind of silence found in meditation caves allowing one to hear his own heart beating the mantra, Om.... Om... Om... Om...

Charlie broke the silence, "*Pater Nosterⁱ...*"

Millions of voices joined in unison, "*qui es in caelis, sanctificetur nomen tuum. Adveniat regnum tuum. Fiat voluntas tua, sicut in caelo et in terra. Panem nostrum quotidianum da nobis hodie, et dimitte nobis debita nostra sicut et nos dimittimus*

ⁱ Our Father Prayer in Latin.

310

debitoribus nostris. Et ne nos inducas in tentationem, sed libera nos a malo. Amen." Later as a unified voice all the souls kept on chanting. "*Kyrie eleison* [i] *... Kyrie eleison... Kyrie eleison...*"

From a distance below her feet, Judy recognized the World Trade Center where she'd once stood, going down. Not much later, everything turned white around her and Earth was just a remote memory.

Encinitas, California, Four Years Later

A few years later, Sydney stood in a room with an expansive breath of the sunset from his coastal view. Lilith's house was at last rebuilt, freshly painted and redecorated.

She walked into the den area where Sydney had his studio. "Look what I finally got in the mail today." She pointed to her collar.

Sydney glanced at her, "I see... It's hard to understand whether you are in favor of the death penalty or against it. Who would, in their right mind, wear a tiny silver electric chair around their neck?"

"No you fool, stop joking around..." Lilith chuckled, "I was impressed by your analogy about Future Bob having his message being misunderstood. So I am wearing Sparky around my neck for all the innocent people killed. I have no doubt if Jesus spoke again against the status quo today, He would be framed, and this time not hung on the cross but fried with 100,000 Volts."

"Well, it will certainly be a conversation starter."

"It's almost show time, are you coming?" Lilith asked.

---

[i] "Lord have mercy" in Greek.

"Get the bubbly started, I'll be right there," said Sydney.

Sydney saw Lilith leave the room. He took a good look at the photographed file of his notes, recovered to him by Rick Sarturo. He spent a few minutes looking at it. There, in the last pages, were the time and coordinates to locate friend Luke or more recently as his father Horace again in his new skin. Sydney looked at the distant orange aura and highlights of the horizon, those very lights flooded his office quarters. He looked at his astrological notes once again and said, "Luke old friend, our mission is over, a new mission has begun." Sydney pulled the pages out of the folder bindings and placed them into a device. "I made you a promise at the hospital to find you, but I must have faith and leave you in the care of holy hands, character is destiny. I'll sure miss you Luke, and I wish you a happy birthday a few years from now!" he dried a tear with his left hand and pressed the paper shredder's button with his right. The pages turned into dust.

As he stood up from the chair, Sydney saw Lilith on the veranda inviting him to enjoy the sunset with the champagne flutes filled. He made a sudden move and left the room. Sydney's sudden movement created a vacuum that made the first page of a freshly printed stack of paper, land on the table top.

The page read, "*The Link*, a novel by Sydney Tobias."

The second page of the stack began, "I have been given a mission. This is the last chapter or perhaps the first, depending on how you accept my story or my history. Today my name is Chris Hall—it hasn't always been my name. I can start my story from anywhere, from any point in the past. But for you to understand the consequences of my actions, I'd better begin at the end of innocence, my innocence. It seemed too much to handle all at once, but I had no choice. Life as I know it began to change. I am not going to describe my physical appearance here, I want you to see this through my own eyes, I want you to feel what I felt; from now on you are Chris Hall.

"Listen. Listen very carefully because perhaps we have met—then you may see or find yourself here with me, and if we have met this is our story. To me, the paradigm shift began with my last time in the Hamptons—the last time I thought my life was normal. For many years I had a very wealthy client there. He wanted to employ me full time, as a consultant, because a position as an astrologer in a Fortune 100 company would be suspicious. In spite of his persistent and varied requests, politely, I declined. I continued providing my insight to his path, always ending the sessions with the most important phrase to myself, and my teacher: *Character est Fatum...*"

The End.

Post Script

*O*riginally, my intention was for the hero to meet a saint during the wars on the Balkans, in the Yugoslavian region, to show that ethnic killing, racism and religious differences have been a bad disease to humankind and throughout our global history. In fact, I was very depressed during the days of the first conflict in the Balkans as well as the second during the late XX Century. While I sketched this novel, I had not yet written the part where the hero and the saint were to meet; the messiah incognito, until after the actual attack on September 11th, 2001. Therefore, I decided to turn this novel into a message of hope to all the people who perished in recent and not so recent wars and attacks in the name of God, monopoly and bigotry.

Although I cannot prove that Jesus or *his enlightened likeness* reincarnates incognito, many times throughout our history whenever injustice prevails, I cannot disprove that Jesus or an enlightened being does not come here either. Even if we could all agree on one religion and one God, the rest of the Universe and all the other galaxies might have different names or templates for God. So let us keep an open mind and respect each other's differences on this planet as an exercise of friendship, so that when we finally meet other beings from other galaxies, we will not spread our religious doctrines and consequently our *pathological holy wars* throughout the universe. May you find and experience Jesus or the Messiah of your liking in your own way... May God have mercy on us all... May we not turn our understanding of God into a reflection of our collective ego and therefore into an excuse for new wars and territorial disputes and may we all live in peace.

Hieroglyphic Alphabet

This alphabet is an approximate guide to the phonics of the hieroglyphic alphabet. The group of letters [K, Q, C], [U, W, O], [I, Y, E], [F, V] and finally [S, Z, soft C] are interchangeable within their groups in reality. For the purpose of decoding the hieroglyphic messages in this book they will only represent their assigned values.

A =   J =   S =

B =   K =   T =

C =   L =   U =

D =   M =   V =

E =   N =   W =

F =   O =   X =

G =   P =   Y =

H =   Q =   Z =

I =   R =

Meus profundus gratia

*O*nce in a while we run into a saint, many times we don't recognize him or her. We still need to grow and learn how to identify this person. In my case it was my late astrology teacher Horacio Valsecia, he was the first person who would predict my life as a writer while I was hitting my head against the wall trying to be a rock-star. The core of all of his lessons, whether they were lessons about prosperity, astrology, tarot, or many other mystical teachings was that our conduct foretells our fate. He never allowed us, his students, to speak ill of anyone including ourselves. He would stop us in mid sentence and show us how our negativities or our negative words were a self fulfilling prophecy and how they were holding us back. Horacio Valcesia left us too soon; the angels coveted him from us. I feel that we as spirits take turns being each other's teacher. So dear Horacio thank you very much for the privilege of your company, I look forward to meeting you again in your next *Link*.

Also, my deepest gratitude I want to offer to everyone who helped me during the course of this book, and to all those who purchased the first edition, thank you for your patience with the typo, and thank you for the kind feedback. Special thanks to Jerry B. Grayson, Maureen Mohan, Dirk Thomas, Amber Rossiter, Deo MacEna, Shelly Cochran, Dean Austin, Anna M. Chapman, Kimberly Caasi, Jeff Thomas, Mark Tyler, Debbie Montgomery, Lynn Weaver, Melissa Alvizures, Lauren M. Adams, Nick Mora, Emily B. and Franz F. Zapata for making *The Link*'s first edition possible, and again for Deo MacEna, Dirk Thomas, and G. Thompson, for being a sounding board and inspiring me to continue with the second edition.

ⲕ Bibliography

The purpose of the bibliography is to be a source of continuous exploration on the topics of the book as well as validations to the arguments and situations encountered in *The Link*.

Aarons and Loftus, *UNHOLY TRINITY: The Vatican, The Nazis, & The Swiss Banks* 1991-1998, St. Martin's Press ISBN 031218199X

Burt, *ARCHETYPES OF THE ZODIAC* 1999,
Llewellyn Publications ISBN 0-87542-088-5

Campbell, *THE HERO WITH A THOUSAND FACES.*
1972, Princeton University Press ISBN 0691017840

Campbell, Moyers, *THE POWER OF MYTH.*
1992 Penguin – ISBN 0942110927

Cayce, *REINCARNATION AND KARMA.* 2006 Are PR - ISBN 0876045247

Cheetam, *THE MAN WHO SAW TOMORROW: The Prophecies of Nostradamus.*
1981, Berkley Books ISBN 0-425-08757-3

Fergunson, and Poter, *FOUR FACES OF NUCLEAR TERRORISM*,
2005, Routledge ISBN 0415952441

Hamilton, *MYTHOLOGY* 1998, Little, Brown and Company ISBN 0316341517

Heindel and Heindel, *THE MESSAGE OF THE STARS* (Original pub. 1922) 1973 Rosicruciam Fellowship ISBN 076612682X

John, Luke, Mark, Matthew and Peter, *THE HOLY BIBLE* 1611, King James

Kasser, Meyer and Wurst, *THE GOSPEL OF JUDAS*,
2006, National Geographic Society ISBN 1426200420

Subramaniam, *SHRIMAD BHAGAVATAM*. 1987, Bharatiya Vidya Bhavan, Bombay - 400 007

Subramaniam, *MAHABHARATA*, 1988, Bharatiya Vidya Bhavan,
Bombay - 400 007

Sri Yukteswar, *THE HOLY SCIENCE.* 1990 Self Realization Fellowship
ISBN 087612-051-6

Dr. Etcetera Media, LLC

Quick order form
(Please check website for products and prices)

☏ Telephone/Fax orders call: **1-800-247-6553**

Email orders: **thelink@bsandy.com**
www.bsandy.com *for products and prices*

✉ Postal Orders: Dr. Etcetera Media, P.O.Box 80164 Las Vegas, NV 89180

☐ Please include me on an emailing list for new books or upcoming events.

Name: _____

Address: _____

City: _____ State: __ __ Zip: _____

Telephone: (___) _____
Email address: _____ @ _____

✈ Shipping by air:

Domestic Shipping: U$4.55 for the first "The Link" book and first music CD "Hello," U$2.00 for any additional book.

International shipping: U$9.00 for the first "The Link" book and first music CD "Hello," U$5.00 for any additional book.

Payment : ☐ Check ☐ *Paypal®* ☐ Money Order

☐ Please autograph "The Link" copy with: Best wishes to _____
(Please Print Name Clearly)

☐ Please autograph "The Link" copy with:
Dear _____ you and I will stop bigotry in this world (and date)
(Please Print Name Clearly)

☐ Please autograph my CD "Hello" copy with: Best wishes to _____
(Please Print Name Clearly)

www.LOTTOAPPmovie.com

Action Packed Romantic Comedy

B.Sandy 310-463-5446